TROUBADOURS
AND SPACE PRINCESSES

Other Works by Jaleta Clegg

Dark Dancer

Autumn Visions (collection)

Brain Candy (collection)

Llama Tell You a Story . . . (collection)

Soul Windows (with Frances Pauli)

Waiting for Elephants (collection)

ALTAIRAN EMPIRE SERIES

Nexus Point

Priestess of the Eggstone

Poisoned Pawn

Kumadai Run

Cold Revenge

Jericho Falling

Obsidian Tears

Chain of Secrets

An Indecent Proposal

Phoenix in Flames

Redemption

AS EDITOR

Wandering Weeds: Tales of Rabid Vegetation (with Frances Pauli)

Other Works Edited by Joe Monson

ANTHOLOGIES

A Universe of Stories
The Horror at Pooh Corner

COLLECTIONS

Thin Air: The Cosmic Crime Fiction of Gustavo Bondoni

LEGACY OF THE CORRIDOR PUBLICATION SERIES
The Florilegium of Madness (D. J. Butler)[*]
Dragon Soup for the Soul (Emily Martha Sorensen)
Down the Arches of the Years (Lee Allred)
Sharks in an Inland Sea (Lehua Parker)
The Bacillus of Beauty (Harriet Stark)
In the Haunting Darkness (Michael R. Collings)
Interplanetary Edition and Other Tales of Tomorrow (Emily Martha Sorensen)
All the Monoliths in the Universe (Michael C. Goodwin)
Waiting for Elephants (Jaleta Clegg)

[*]Co-edited with Callie Butler

EDITED BY
JALETA CLEGG AND JOE MONSON

HEMELEIN PUBLICATIONS

Troubadours and Space Princesses
LTUE Benefit Anthologies, volume 6

Cover artist: Bradley Williams, bradleywilliamsart.net
Cover art, *The Proposal,* copyright © 2024 Bradley Williams. Used by permission of the artist.

Ornamental break artist: Kevin Wasden, kevinwasden.com
Ornamental break art, *Troubadours and Space Princesses,* copyright © 2024 Kevin Wasden. Used by permission of the artist.

The Hemelein shield and stars H logo and "It's worth your time" slogan are trademarks of Hemelein Publications LLC.

Edited by Jaleta Clegg and Joe Monson
Cover Designer: Joe Monson
Interior layout and design: Joe Monson

Managing Editor: Joe Monson
Publisher: Heather B. Monson

Published by Hemelein Publications, LLC., hemelein.com

First Hemelein printing, February 2024
10 9 8 7 6 5 4 3 2 1

ISBNs:
978-1-64278-041-3 (trade paperback)
978-1-64278-042-0 (ebook)

Library of Congress Control Number : 2023939842

To David Farland.

You have been,
and will continue to be,
an inspiration to thousands.
Thank you for sharing so much with us.

Contents

Path of the Hero

Joe Monson

Over the years, there have been many well-known and very well established authors, artists, and editors who have been guests at *Life, the Universe, & Everything*.

Orson Scott Card, Elizabeth Boyer, Frederik Pohl, Alan Dean Foster, Madeleine L'Engle, Stephen R. Donaldson, Jack Williamson, Julius Schwartz, Algis Budrys, Tim Powers, Ray Bradbury, Michael Whelan, and the list goes on and on. So many extremely talented individuals who took the time to share their knowledge and experiences with the budding writers, artists, and editors who attend LTUE each year. There are few other small conventions that can boast the lineup that's come through Provo. Even with all of that talent, one person has been a bigger influence than just about anyone else: Dave Wolverton, perhaps best known under his pseudonym, David Farland.

I first met Dave back in the early 1990s. He was one of the founding people who got LTUE and *The Leading Edge* off the ground, and he continued to help them through the years in all sorts of ways. He worked with administration at Brigham Young University multiple times when departments wanted to cut funding. He talked up both the symposium and TLE in professional circles, allowing both to gain access to many people they wouldn't have been able to work with otherwise.

He won the Writers of the Future contest in 1987 with his novella "On My Way to Paradise". Two years later, he put out a novel based on that winning story, and his second novel, *Serpent Catch*, was coming out in

May 1991. I was one of a few lucky people who received a proof copy of the cover (his publisher had sent him several). Despite being relatively new on the publishing scene, Dave was already helping others along the same path.

He went on to publish over 30 novels, over 60 works of short fiction, and countless essays in the speculative fiction field. Through all of that, he was always taking time to answer questions, offer encouragement, and teach others wanting to pursue success in their writing. When I started a science fiction club at UVSC, he accepted an invitation to come and talk about his experiences and to offer tips for those of us interested in getting into the field, and our club was tiny. That didn't matter to Dave.

He was coordinating judge for the Writers of the Future Contest for many years. He left a lasting imprint on the speculative fiction community, helping future highly successful authors such as Brandon Sanderson, Stephenie Meyer, Brandon Mull, Eric Flint, Jessica Day George, James Dashner, and too many others to name here.

In more recent years, he ran a number of different very effective workshops that helped many nascent authors hone their skills and discover others they didn't know they had. He helped found the Superstars Writing with Kevin J. Anderson, Rebecca Moesta, Eric Flint, James A. Owen, and Brandon Sanderson. And most recently, he founded Apex Writers, an ongoing project to help writers improve their craft and help each other. He spent his entire career helping and building up others.

From my perspective, he's been as huge an influence on the speculative fiction field as other more well known names such as Isaac Asimov, Ursula K. Le Guin, Ray Bradbury, J.R.R. Tolkien, Anne McCaffrey, Roger Zelazny, Robert Silverberg, and more, though perhaps in less visible ways. Most of Dave's influence, I believe, can be found behind the scenes: one-on-one, spending time with writers out of the spotlight. He's given boosts to so many of us, lifting our spirits, helping us coax out our ideas, helping us learn to flesh out and expand our stories, and smiling his quiet smile as he watched us grow, improve, and succeed.

For those who never got to meet him, you missed out. For those of us who did, his sudden passing in January 2022 was a devastating blow to the writing community. His legacy of helping others lives on, however, through all of us whose lives he touched. If he had a positive impact on you, take some time to remember how he helped you, and then pay it forward. Even if you can only encourage someone in their efforts, every little bit helps, and you, too, can make a difference.

This anthology, *Troubadours and Space Princesses*, was created to honor him, his life, and his impact on our local and worldwide speculative fiction creator community. These sixteen stories are stories we think Dave would have loved (especially the one Dave wrote!), and we hope you enjoy each of them. Jaleta and I had fun (and more than a little stress) picking them out of a very solid field of submissions.

There are some established short fiction authors, as well as brand new authors. A couple of these are even the first stories the authors have had accepted for publication! We are so excited for you to read them.

I'm sure Dave's watching us, tipping his signature cap to us each time we help each other improve. So sit back in a comfy chair and escape into these interesting and wonderful worlds. Then consider how you can help and encourage the creatives around you. And then do it.

This is the way.

Joe Monson
January 2024

Luck, Life, Light,
and Other Frivolous Pursuits

Jenny Perry Carr

Princess Lanta narrowed her eyes as the rose gold-plated droid took a knee in the throne room of clan Arcod on planet Karn. Its hip joint squeaked as it kneeled.

An ancient herald shuffled forward before the court. He rang a copper bell that echoed in the cavernous marble room, the air laced with a spicy resinous incense.

"Designate Trate, artificially intelligent android, representing Prince Reglan of planet Parthine of clan Siculus, seeks audience with Princess Lanta."

Lanta flicked her chestnut hair over her shoulder, sending it cascading down her iridescent gown. She grew tired of the incessant suitors, desperate to win her hand. But today was different. Not another ugly, old, or unintelligent royal paraded in front of her, begging for her interest. No, this was a robot, sent on behalf of Prince Reglan. A robot. The Prince couldn't spare the time to present himself? Interesting. She had to hear this.

The droid bowed to the new king, her grandiose brother Iasus. Lanta hated the pomp and ceremony of royal life, which Iasus wholly embraced. He pressured her incessantly to marry, but she refused every offer thus far, still heartbroken from the loss of their father only weeks before. Only a shadow of the man with the same icy blue eyes, Iasus could never fill the throne like the King. He didn't know her like her father, who would never accept one of these buffoons as her mate.

Iasus waved an invitation. "State your business."

The robot rose with a clumsy creak, straightening its articulated joints. "I have traveled from across the galaxy, between star systems, through the folds of space, past nebulae and—"

"Yes, yes, understood. What is it that you want with my sister?"

"I have a song to deliver."

A song? Most definitely more creative than other suitors, or suitor stand-ins as it were.

Iasus rolled his hand, signaling the droid to get on with it.

The robot lifted its chin. A low baritone note rumbled from within its frame. It slid to a higher key, an octave above. It repeated this low-high intro, like the call of a blowing horn from a great tufanelo, the massive hooved mammals of the Karnean grasslands.

Ahhh, ooooo. Ahhh, ooooo. Ahhh, ooooo.

The throne room, usually chirping with gossip, hushed. Attention turned to the metallic troubadour. Its voice rang clear, like a bird song, with a trill of notes at the end of each phrase.

A distant land, a faithful prince,
Sent his man far to convince,
The lovely Lanta, pure and true,
He offers his hand across stars for you.

Its song continued for numerous rhyming stanzas, weaving a yarn about the history of clan Siculus and the beauty of Parthine. It boasted of the bravery and might of Prince Reglan.

And with this song to you addressed,
He prays your answer will be yes.

Lanta pursed her lips, dimples bore deep into her cheeks. "Ohh-hhkay." Just another proposal from a self-indulgent prince. One who didn't even bother to show up.

"Interesting proposition," Iasus said. "Clan Siculus is quite renowned."

She rolled her eyes. "You expect me to consider this? Hardly." Lanta wanted to marry but would only consider the right offer, from the right man. But time was getting the best of her. Should she give this offer some consideration?

The droid cleared its throat, or the robot equivalent, perfectly mimicking human behavior. "If I may be so bold, your majesty. May I speak?"

Iasus turned to the android, an eyebrow raised. "Yes?"

"A deal has already been struck, sire."

"What?" Lanta lurched forward in her seat, her stomach turning.

"The King, former King that is, traveled to Parthine earlier this year. Prince Reglan invited him to ask for your hand in marriage, and the King accepted."

She shrunk back into her chair. "That can't be possible."

Iasus drew Lanta close and shrugged. "Maybe you should hear this Reglan out, especially if father approved. I do recall he spent some time on Parthine."

"No. Father would have never forced me into marriage." Lanta shook free of Iasus' grasp, emphasizing each syllable. "No. No. No."

Iasus lounged on the throne, stroking his new beard, not yet fully filled in.

He stiffened, his voice booming across the throne room.

"We accept the proposal."

Lanta gasped.

Stars streaked past the view port of the space cruiser. The only sound came from the hum of the ion engines that gave the cabin a faint smell of ozone. Lanta had never been off-planet before. While her world centered around the palace, she longed to explore the vivid and mysterious worlds she'd only read about on her holopad. Though here she was, being shuttled from one palace to another.

But she had no plans of going along with Reglan's proposal. Instead, she intended to march up to him and give him a piece of her mind. How one simply does not order a wife. *She* would choose her mate.

"So, what kind of name is Trate, anyway? Unusual for a droid, no?"

"Quite unusual, mum."

"Trate. Sounds like traitor."

"You are not wrong. May I speak frankly?" The flexible rose-colored metal mesh of the droid's face parroted her inquisitive expression.

Lanta nodded.

"When I came into service in the house of Siculus, young Prince Reglan was far from happy to have me as his personal attendant, assigned by his father. Reglan said he couldn't trust a droid, that one day I would betray him like a traitor. Instead of using my true designation, C9-814, he started calling me Trate, and it stuck."

Her reaction hinted at a laugh. "Amusing. Why send you? Why didn't he ask me himself?" She rested her head on her crossed arms on the ledge of the viewing window, already longing for home.

"He is currently preoccupied."

Lanta bolted upright. Perhaps he believed his status higher than hers. The nerve. "Preoccupied? Not even showing up himself. Thinks he can just demand a wife?"

"Well, yes, mum."

She chuffed. The thought of being fetched like merchandise sent hot lava through her veins. Lanta clenched her jaw.

"Why didn't father tell me about this deal? We'd never kept secrets from each other before."

"If I may, perhaps he wanted you to make the decision for yourself."

She leaned in. Her father had been known to set up situations that required her to problem solve her way out. Like taking her into their hedge maze when she was just six years. He left her in the middle and told her to figure the way out, which she did in record time.

The droid punched commands into the ship's console. "Or maybe he was nudging you toward marriage. You are twenty-nine cycles now and not getting any younger."

Lanta whirled to face the robot, eyes stirring with fire enough to melt it. "Excuse me? That's rude." Though he wasn't wrong.

"Apologies, mum." Trate shrugged. "I thought we were speaking frankly."

"Well, yes. I wouldn't want you to sugar-coat it. So, tell me about the Prince. He's getting older as well, and never married, in his thirty-odd years, correct?"

"Yes, that is correct."

Lanta leaned back in her chair and smirked. "Getting desperate, is he?"

"On the contrary, mum. He's never sought a wife until now."

She frowned. "Miserable sod, is he? Unattractive? Didn't think anyone would say yes?"

"Oh no, mum. A woman should be so honored to take his hand in marriage."

Lanta snorted a hrmph.

"He is quite a beast," the robot said.

Her eyebrows raised. "Oh?"

"Yes, on the battlefield. He is highly decorated."

She turned away, back to the port window. "I see."

"You were hoping I said 'in the bedroom?'"

Lanta gasped. "Excuse me? I said nothing of the sort."

"Apologies, mum. My sensors detected arousal."

She blushed. "Stop doing that."

"It's my programming—"

"Just stop!" She crossed her arms over her chest. "Let me understand this. He wants me to travel to Parthine to meet him?"

"My instructions were to fetch you and your belongings and convey you to Parthine for relocation."

"Confident, isn't he?"

"Quite, mum."

"Of course he is. I may be willing to travel to Parthine, but only on my terms. This is a trip, a courtship, a meeting. Then we'll see what happens. I make no promises." She would be on the first ship back to Karn.

"Understood, mum."

"My father must have had a good reason to agree to this, so I will honor his memory and see it through. How long is our journey to Parthine?"

"We are not traveling directly to Parthine, mum."

"What?"

"First, we must complete several tasks and gather certain items for Prince Reglan."

Her jaw dropped, mouth agape. "He's sending me on errands? This is what he expects of a wife? An errand girl? Are you kidding me?

"I am kidding you not, mum."

She sighed. "What does he want me to get?"

Lanta's eyes scanned a rocky ridge up from the valley floor, littered with black and grey stones that had tumbled down the hills. She held her hands over her brow to block the glare from the morning suns over Drich.

"What am I looking for?"

"Our destination lies there." Trate pointed above the ridge.

She craned her neck up to near vertical to take in the entire mountain as black as night.

Her eyes widened. "There?"

"Yes, mum." Trate hummed a single note, then sang a song. The dark and brooding melody matched the landscape.

The highest peak, with the blackest stone,
Holds a secret where luck is grown.
Over the valley, Mount Rano towers,
There we must collect the clionon flower.

"A flower? Like these?" She motioned to the field of delicate lavender flowers that surrounded them, smelling of honey.

"Yes, these are clionon flowers, but we must fetch one from the highest peak."

Lanta held up the fabric of her full dress. "How am I supposed to climb up there in this?"

"Take it off. I assume you have knickers on underneath."

Lanta gasped. "Have you not heard of modesty? I can't take my dress off in front of you."

"Remember, mum, I am an android and lack the ability to blush."

"Okay, but only if you don't save any images to your storage banks."

"I cannot make that promise. I am programmed to accompany you and record the journey."

She eyed the mountain, then the heavy folds of material cinched around her. "Whatever." Lanta stripped off the garment, her thin white chemise and bloomers fluttered in the cool breeze. Chill bumps dotted her skin.

Up the hill Lanta climbed. At first the path was smooth and even, then transformed into crumbly dirt that slipped beneath footfalls. They climbed for several hours, the morning suns rose high in the sky and beat down on their backs, burning her tender fair skin pink. They rounded a bend in the path and dirt became shale that broke away with each step.

Lanta trudged forward, her feet coming out from under her, stumbling backward. Trate caught her and steadied her balance.

"Careful now. The path becomes steep from here."

"It hasn't been already?" She wiped sweat from her forehead with the back of her arm. "How much further?"

"By my calculations, we should reach the peak by nightfall."

"Nightfall? You have got to be kidding me."

"I am kidding—"

"I know, I know. You aren't kidding."

Lanta took a deep breath and pushed forward up the mountain. Soon her upright gait became a crawl on all fours, her fingers desperate for a stable hold. She gripped a rock a foot overhead and strained to pull herself up. The stone quivered in her grasp, threatening to fall away from the wall.

"Don't you dare," she muttered under her breath.

She pressed her lips together and forced herself forward.

The handhold made good on its promise and slipped away from the mountain, taking Lanta with it down the rock face. She slid on her belly, down the slope, knocking Trate from his feet. The two tumbled backward down the stony path, rocks crashing around them, until they skidded to a stop in the dirt below, like one of the chunks of shale spat out from the mountain. Sharp rock had cut Lanta's hands and knees. Mud smeared the front of her chemise. She must have looked a fright. While battered and bruised, she was alive and the droid intact.

Trate extended a hand and helped her stand. "Shale we try again, mum?" It winked.

Lanta blinked. "A joke? Now?" She planted her hands on her hips. "Not a chance. There is no way we're going to make it to the top of this mountain. We aren't outfitted for this kind of climb. Nor skilled. I know when to call it quits."

Lanta marched down the trail toward the valley.

"But mum? The flower?"

She stopped, stooped to reach a grassy patch on the pathway, and plucked a clionon flower from a lavender swath.

Lanta shook the flower above her head without looking back at Trate. "This will do."

"Very well, mum. Whatever you say."

Long life is promised, it is vowed,
For a silent seeker on the plains of Shroud,
Find a feather, fine and slim,
But beware of the flittergrimm.

"A FEATHER? SEEMS EASY ENOUGH." LANTA TROMPED THROUGH THE meadow on the rolling hills of Tarcan-5. Colorful wildflowers painted the field as far as she could see. The wind strummed the golden plain like a stringed instrument, waving with each gust like a whisper.

"We must take care not to disturb the flittergrimm." Trate tread through the dry grass, his hip squeaking with each step.

"You're not helping us with that creaky hip of yours. You're a droid. Why don't you have it repaired?"

"Reglan told me not to fix it. He thinks it gives me character."

She chuckled. "Oh, does he?" Most interesting. "What's a flittergrimm anyway?"

"They are purported to be tiny dangerous creatures that can swarm if provoked."

"Let's not provoke them then. Where can we find these feathers?"

"They are said to be littered along the ground within these fields."

"Easy." She scanned the fertile soil for any sign of feathers. Is that a leaf or a feather? She crouched to inspect the find. It was a petal of a dried flower. Not a feather.

The grass rustled up ahead, like the rattle of seed pods clattering against each other.

She stood and froze. "What's that?"

The rattle turned into a faint buzzing sound.

"I'm detecting low decibel frequencies and minute heat signatures to the northeast."

Lanta whispered, "I think we need to be quiet." She pressed a finger to her lips, then turned back to the field ahead.

She took one step forward and a burst of air exploded up from the surrounding grassland. A creature swooped in front of her face, like a miniature, blue-skinned humanoid, mere inches tall, with clear wings like a dragonfly. It lurched toward her, its sharp black teeth bared in a snarl, like a mouthful of obsidian needles.

Lanta screamed and ducked.

A black mass erupted from the tall grass, streaking into the sky with a whoosh.

"Run," she shouted.

The swarm of flittergrimm pursued them. The strokes of their wings like the buzzing from hundreds of beehives.

Trate shouted something to her, but she couldn't hear him over the din.

Grass slapped against her tender face, stinging, still burned from their mountain trek. The dark cloud of beating wings blocked out the sun, shrouding them in shadow.

Lanta ran until it felt like her legs would give out. Trate surpassed her, squeaking as he pumped his limbs. She couldn't keep this pace up for long, her speed faltering. The muscles in her calves seized. They would get her if she didn't go on.

As her momentum slowed, she feared they were goners, but the flittergrimm never caught up with them. Did they tire as well? Were they keeping their distance, waiting for the right moment to attack when they were most vulnerable?

Lanta jogged, her breath heaving. Still, the flittergrimm pursued but didn't attack.

What if they weren't actually chasing them? What if they were only following?

There was only one way to find out.

Lanta stopped.

The swarm surrounded her.

Trate whirled around, several paces away. Too far for him to do anything if she was wrong.

The hum of their wings enveloped her.

She took a step to the left. The swarm shifted left. She stepped to the right. They flittered right. She crept forward through the swarm, extending her arms out. The creatures brushed against her skin, their wings tickling like tiny strokes from a paintbrush.

They didn't attack. A female flittergrimm alighted on her arm, her wings drooping down as she came to rest. She grinned at Lanta, lips pressed together, hiding her teeth. Another landed on her hand, then another, and another, until dozens perched upon her hands, arms, and even atop her head.

They cooed a lullaby of words she couldn't understand into her ears, sweet soft voices like the peeps of baby animals.

Those that buzzed around her plucked flowers of crimson, gold, and ivory from the field and placed them in her hair.

These creatures meant her no harm. They were curious and playing, mimicking their movements. While the sound had startled them and evoked the reaction for which they're known, they posed no real danger. In fact, they were gentle creatures.

As she examined the beauty of the flittergrimm, she spotted a feather on the ground. Lanta pointed at it.

A trio of creatures swooped down and collected the feather, laying it across their three sets of arms, presenting it to her like a gift.

Lanta accepted the tiny, clear feather that sparkled in the sunlight.

As the cruiser roared through the atmosphere on entry to Ceto, Trate broke into a melodious song as he piloted the craft through the raging winds.

Under the ground, in the caves of Astriant,
'Neath clear waters, a gem most radiant.
Tho wary the adventurer of the terok bite,
It hunts its prey in the dark of night.

Trate settled the craft onto rocky ground above the evergreen tree line. A rush of air released from the compressors as the engines shut down.

"Caves? This prince of yours better be worth it. He's really putting me through the ringer, isn't he?"

"I do not believe his intention is to ring you." Trate engaged the airlock, and the door slid open with a hiss.

Lanta followed him out of the craft, shaking her head as she traipsed down the ramp. "How far do we have to hike this time?"

Trate pointed to a dark opening in the rocks ahead. "We have arrived."

"Easy enough. And what am I looking for? Some gemstone?"

"Luxenite, to be precise, mum. It only grows in this star system, on this single planet."

Lanta rushed forward, reaching the cave entrance first. She braced against the wind, which carried the scent of the pine forest.

"Proceed with caution, mum. According to my estimate, the sun will set in ten minutes. I have been cautioned not to enter the caves at night."

"Why not?"

"The terok hunts these caves and is active after dark."

"Then let's get going." Lanta stooped to enter.

"Are you certain?"

"It's our last stop, right? Let's get this over with. I'm tired and don't want to spend the night on this planet. Let's go."

Darkness obscured the low, but wide, passageway, even as the last light slipped from the sky at their backs. She crouched to navigate the icicle-like stalactites that hung from the ceiling of the musty cave, the sound of dripping water echoing across the stone. Up ahead, a dim circle of light appeared, ever brighter, as they descended. The passage opened to an enormous domed cavern, tall enough to hold full-grown trees. A pool of water at their feet filled half the cavern and glowed blue-green, illuminating the whole cave. The intensity made Lanta squint.

Below the surface, the glitter of gems speckled the bottom.

"Where is the light coming from?" Lanta bent to inspect the shiny stones from the water's edge.

"From the gems. They give off a radiance that can be seen for miles."

Lanta perched on a boulder overhanging the pool. "What? The stones create this light?"

Trate squeaked as he approached. "A rare phenomenon creates the gems here in these caves. A combination of the minerals that drip into the pools from the rocks, the blend of elements present in the water, and a secretion from the carnivorous terok that inhabits these caves."

She dragged her hand through the water. "What are these teroks anyway?"

A deafening screech roared from the cave opening.

"I believe *that* is a terok."

Lanta scrambled off the rock and scanned the cave. The passageway where they had entered appeared to be the only way in or out.

"Let's get out of here." She tugged Trate forward.

As Lanta turned toward the passage, a giant bird crawled down the opening, its talons gouging into the rock, rubble tumbling into the cavern. She recoiled behind Trate.

The terok squeezed through the passage, into the open cavern, unfurling its two sets of charcoal-colored wings, its wingspan over twenty-five feet across. A hoarse scream came from its razor-sharp double beak, one inside the other, each as wide as Lanta's head and as long as her legs. Its outer beak, ringed with tooth-like extensions, snapped at them as it advanced. Its soulless black eyes reflected the aquamarine pool.

Lanta dashed deeper into the cavern with Trate. She imagined the terok capturing and holding its prey with its toothy beak, then tearing apart its victim's flesh with the inner beak. She didn't want to be its prey.

The terok pursued them, each hop toward the pair shook the ground.

She crashed against the back of the cave.

Trapped.

The bird's claws dug into the rock, splashing them into the water as it sought its next meal.

No way to escape.

Lanta peered into the shimmering water.

"Can you swim?" she shouted over the cries of the terok.

Lanta took a deep breath and dove into the frigid waters. Trate splashed in behind her, presumably watertight. She kicked toward the bottom.

The terok's screech warbled through the water. Its talons grasped for them on the surface, creating turbulence.

She descended deeper into the glowing water and plucked a gem from the bottom. Lanta propelled herself toward the cave opening. If they could get past the creature and make a run for the door, they might make it. She stroked her arms and kicked through the water, her lungs burning.

Lanta reached the edge of the pool and hoisted herself up onto the bank, clambering to her feet, darting for the passageway. Trate squeaked behind her.

The terok stormed toward them, stalactites crashing down, piercing the ground, as it flapped its winged in fury.

The bird's screech rumbled in her chest as it closed in.

She dodged a falling stalactite and rushed into the passageway, clawing at the rocks to climb the incline.

Lanta burst into the night air, and they sprinted for the space cruiser. Trate sped ahead, already initiating the pre-launch sequence remotely. The robot reached the cruiser first.

The terok shot from the cave entrance into the sky, soaring high above, screaming as it circled them.

The engines glowed beneath the belly of the craft, and Trate disappeared into the vehicle. The ramp lifted from the ground, retracting into the ship.

Trate was leaving without her, living up to his name. The traitor. Lanta pushed herself, her muscle screaming, struggling to get to the cruiser. Blood pulsed past her eardrums

The droid appeared. It clung to a support beam, dangling off the ramp, holding its arm out to her. "Take my hand."

The terok swooped down from the sky, blasting her with a gust of air. Lanta dodged its attack, its wing grazing her as she neared the ship.

She extended her arm, straining to reach the droid, fingertips mere inches from the robot. They made contact, and Trate yanked her onboard with ease. They rolled off the ramp into the ship as the door thudded into place, the airlock hissing behind them.

Lanta flopped into her seat, gulping air as the craft's engines roared beneath them, vibrating the cabin.

"That was interesting." Trate said.

Lanta huffed. "Interesting? You've got to be kidding me?" She waved a hand. "I know. Never mind."

The cruiser jolted hard to starboard, nearly tipping the craft on its side. The terok screamed outside the vessel, clawing at the ship.

"Let's go."

"Affirmative, mum."

The cruiser lifted off the surface. The terok bashed its head against the cockpit, rocking the ship. Trate plotted a course and engaged hyperspeed, blasting them into the sky. The terok's screech faded into the distance.

Lanta collapsed against the chair, breathless, the glowing gem perched on her lap.

LANTA THRUST OPEN THE HEAVY CEILING-HIGH ROSEWOOD DOORS WITH A loud creak that spun all heads in her direction. She stormed into the throne room unannounced.

Trate hurried behind, hip squealing with the droid's rapid steps.

She refused an offer to freshen up before meeting the Prince. Lanta didn't care what he thought of her at this point. She blew a stray hair out of her eyes, her cheeks flushed. He needed to hear her now.

The guards sprang forward, long pikes clanging together, crisscrossing, and blocking her path. Trate waved a hand to call them off, and they returned to their stations.

"How dare you!"

The Prince reclined on the throne, his fingers steepled in front of him. "And I am delighted to make your acquaintance as well, Princess Lanta. Lovely as ever." His eyes traveled up and down her silhouette.

She glanced at her filthy garment, once a prized gown, now torn, muddied, and frayed. Lanta straightened the waist of her frock, growing ever more self-conscious of the state she found herself in as she presented herself before the court of clan Siculus. She smoothed her frizzed hair, pulled out a twig, and hid it behind her back.

"With what you put me through, should you be so surprised? You nearly got me killed. You put me in danger, in harm's way."

"I disagree, my lady. You put yourself at risk by agreeing to attempt the tasks. I never forced you."

She huffed. He wasn't wrong. "Why send the robot? Why didn't you come to ask for my hand yourself?" She awaited his response, to hear his explanation on why he was *so* preoccupied. What could be so important that he couldn't make the trip?

"My father is dying, and even now resting upon his deathbed. I am the sole heir to the crown and therefore could not leave the planet."

"Oh." She twisted the little twig between her fingers, eyes fixed on the black and white tiled floor. A good excuse indeed. Maybe she shouldn't have been so quick to judge. Or not. Her eyes narrowed, and she planted her hands on her hips. Her icy gaze shifted to the Prince.

"Why these tasks? Why send me on this frivolous journey for random items? Some kind of test?"

The Prince sauntered down the steps from the throne platform and circled her as he spoke. "I assure you, this was no test, nor was the journey frivolous or the items random. My father's dying wish is for me to take a wife. But not just any woman will do. No. He bid me marry a woman that challenged me as my mother had challenged him."

"I see." She fidgeted with the twig, studying her hands. Dirt caked the undersides of her nails, and a bloodied scratch traversed the back of her hand. She clutched them to conceal the grime.

He towered over her, at least two heads above, with a chiseled jawline and rakish good looks. His thick brunette hair matched his full beard, which gave him distinction. Far from the old and ugly lot that pursued her before.

Reglan took her hands in his, pulling the twig from her fingers. "Who was I to send for you without trying to get you to know me first?" His deep sapphire eyes stared into hers, the color complimenting her own clear-blue eyes.

She nodded.

"I wanted you to experience treasured times from my life and see the type of person I am before you met me. This journey, these tasks, were the only way I could see doing so without leaving my father's side."

Reglan stepped over to a table covered in red velvet where Trate had laid out the items collected during the journey. He picked up the flower and strode toward her. Perhaps these were gifts intended for her. An interesting courtship indeed.

He passed Lanta and crossed the room to a long table set with refreshments for the court. Bowls of fruit piled high perfumed the air with exotic scents of faraway lands. Decanters of wine, displayed in order from lightest to darkest vintages, presented a rainbow of decadence.

Reglan held the lavender flower in front of him and crushed it in his fist.

Lanta gasped. How rude. Not gifts. He taunted her. Was he testing her patience?

He opened the lid of a fine pot and let the crumbled petals fall inside. He poured steaming water from a metal pitcher into the pot.

She furrowed her brow.

"My mother died when I was very young, but she told me the story about the clionon flower, and how it is said to bring luck to those who drank tea made from its petals. Most sought the flowers from the highest peak, thinking they were the best, but she said she preferred the petals from the valley that grew in the shadow of the mountain. They didn't have the scorched taste of the blistering suns."

He poured the tea into a cup and brought it over. He presented it to her, and she accepted, taking a sip, the warm liquid covering her tongue, floral and sweet with no sugar.

"I wanted you to walk in my mother's steps. To take the journey she had taken many times to gather the clionon. And to taste her prized tea and gain its luck for a happy future."

Reglan took back the cup and sat it on the side table, going again to the items she had collected. Reglan plucked the tiny feather from the velvet and held it up for all to see.

"You journeyed into the fields of the flittergrimm, feared by many, misunderstood. It takes a gentle heart to see that they too were gentle, if treated with kindness. My father once fought a battle on that planet, where the plains were in danger of being destroyed. He brokered a truce, not to his advantage, which moved the fighting away from the innocent creatures, sparing their home and their lives. Like my father, you used your mind and your heart to see beyond what others could see. The truth. This feather will be sewn into your robes, said to bring long life to those who wear it, so that you can cherish many more years sharing the generosity of your gentle heart."

A lump formed in Lanta's throat. She swallowed hard. The Prince was far from what she had expected.

He fetched the glowing gem from the table.

"The luxenite gemstone is intended for your wedding ring. I wanted you to see the brilliance of the caves of Astriant that so enchanted me years ago. The luxenite will light your path forward, never allowing you to be in the dark again. And Trate tells me you were brave enough to face the terok. Even I didn't have the courage to enter the caves at night." He smiled, his white toothy grin warm and inviting. "You are something else.

"Only a woman able to complete these challenges could win my heart. A woman with courage, determination, intelligence, and a gentle soul. One who could match my spirit and rule Parthine with me as an equal."

Lanta bowed her head and blushed. How truly wrong she was about the Prince.

Reglan lifted her chin with his muscular hand. "You have been quiet. What do you think of my proposal? Do you still wish to return to your home on planet Karn?"

She touched his hand. "If you would allow it, maybe I'd like to stay a bit longer. See what happens."

Reglan beamed.

Lanta's crooked smile accentuated her dimples.

Trate squeaked as the droid positioned itself before the court in the throne room of clan Siculus. The faces had changed over the millennia, but always he returned to his favorite song, to share the history of his beloved benefactor. The rosy metallic troubadroid finished its song.

Strike the bells and sing the chorus,
Hark, good news for clan Siculus before us.
Summer, fall, winter, then spring is springing,
And thus ends the story of the beginning,
Promises, vows, a ring, and a paired clan,
The union of Queen Lanta and King Reglan.
They ruled fair and just, lucky with cheer,
And reigned long into their twilight years.
Their family, always surrounded in light,
No love like their o'er the galaxy in sight.

Bards of a Feather

Henry Herz

Pride and gluttony caused my expulsion from Faerie, despite being a Princess of the White Wood, but that is a tale for another time. Keeping my translucent wings hidden in the mortal realm quickly grew tiresome. I walked the Earth alone, posing as Evangeline the minstrel-mage. I traversed rarely trodden trails to astound audiences and, more to the point, to collect their coins with my spellbinding music, storytelling, and spell casting.

A chill wind blew, stinging my ears (glamoured to look human) and tingling my fingers. I pulled my multicolored mantle tighter about my shoulders and tucked-in wings. Onward I trudged, following the lowering sun westward.

I topped a gentle rise and spied a distant but welcome sight—a small town, its far edge nestled against a dark green wood. Wisps of smoke from hearth fires beckoned. *Ah, a chance to warm my chilly hands, rest my weary feet, and fill my empty belly*, I thought. *I could really go for a curd-smothered beef round between trenchers with a side of fried fingerling potatoes. But there's got to be a catchier name for that . . .*

Encouraged by the prospect of sleeping on a bed rather than al fresco on unyielding earth, I marched without pause, reaching the hamlet before sunset. The peasants seemed pleasant enough and I obtained without difficulty directions to the only inn. I strolled toward the central square, navigating narrow alleys lined by the wattle and daub buildings common to this province.

But I soon discovered this was like no other town I'd ever before beheld, for the villagers wore blue bretona birds on their heads like living hats! Being winged myself, birds held a special place in my heart.

The birds sang sweet songs. The villagers primped and played with their precious pets.

How odd! This place is for the birds. Hunger outweighed my curiosity, so I held in abeyance my questions about their feathered fedoras until I reached the thatch-roofed inn on the square. There I discovered that the innkeeper wore more than one hat, as they say, also serving as the mayor. I spent the last of my well-earned coins to secure dinner and a modest room for the night.

"I'll have a curd-smothered beef round with fried fingerlings," I told the barkeep.

"A number seven!" he called to the kitchen. "Would you like an ale with that?"

I SIGHED CONTENTEDLY AFTER FILLING MY BELLY. *TOMORROW, I'LL NEED TO fill my purse.* I yawned, eschewing the rustic evening entertainment scheduled for the common room, and climbed the rough-hewn wooden steps to my room. Miffed by the absence of a mint on my pillow, but exhausted by the day's exertions, I blew out the sputtering candle and sprawled on the straw-filled mattress.

I DREAMT OF TRAVELING IN STYLE AND COMFORT VIA FOUR HORSEPOWER luxury chariot. Intermittent slurping sounds woke me. I opened an eye. Beams of moonlight peeked through the curtains, softly illuminating the room. Spying nothing amiss and too tired to spare the noises any further thought, I fell back asleep.

I rose in the morn, refreshed though still sore from days of hiking. I longed for a chicken coop of fried eggs, a pigpen's worth of bacon, and a hot spring of coffee. But my empty purse dictated a different plan.

Tightening my belt, I resolved to remedy the situation by finding a suitable spot on the square to play for passersby and pass the hat, as it were. *These rustic folk are probably starved for good music. Ugh, I've got to stop thinking about food.*

I stepped outside and breathed the fresh morning air. But villagers scrambled helter-skelter in alarm like pheasants fleeing a flushing spaniel. For an overnight onslaught of scaly vermin now disrupted the harmony of the pastoral village. *Who will toss me a coin now?* I wondered. *I'll have to don my thinking cap.*

"Pestiferous niblings dug up my flowers," complained one villager, pointing.

"You don't say?" I replied, having previously encountered such rodents of unusual shape in my travels.

"They snuck into cupboards and ate our berry scones," cried another.

"Is that a fact?" I responded. *That explains why they smelt of elderberries.* My stomach growled, but my brow smoothed as a pecuniary opportunity percolated in my mind. *Percolated? Stop thinking about breakfast!*

"They gnaw my toys, and snurfle while I sleep," wailed a small boy.

Hence the strange sounds last night. I nodded with empathy. Yet of all the niblings' offenses, the villagers deemed most egregious the torment of their bretona birds. For the tree-climbing niblings gave the birds no respite, chasing them from roosting spot to roosting spot, whether for play or as prey I could not say.

As the tally of complaints multiplied, the mayor strode into the square, huffing and puffing, shouting and pouting, but in no way improving the situation for his folk. He frequently fiddled with a large, lavishly plumed bretona bird perched atop his head. I've traveled enough to know a nincompoop when I suffer the misfortune of meeting one.

The grievances grew, and when he could countenance no more, the mayor stamped his feet. "Mifflestones! This will not do."

Incompetent and irritable. I mentally doubled my de-infestation fee. "I am Evangeline the minstrel-mage. I can help," I said to the mayor, throwing my hat into the ring, so to speak. I bowed my head with more manners than were due the backwater bumpkin.

The mayor did not reply. Instead, he ordered the villagers to build cages, weave nets, and set traps.

The indignities I endure to earn a meal. He lacks the courtesy to reply, the wits to solve the problem, and the humility to seek aid. He should hang up his hat as mayor. Biding my time, I made myself comfortable as a spectator. *This will be entertaining.*

The milking of animals, the planting of crops, and other daily routines ceased. But all to no avail. The pestiferous niblings dodged and evaded. The cages, nets, and traps remained empty. Shoulders slumped as the villagers resumed their regular duties.

The mayor's face reddened.

I stood. "I am Evangeline the minstrel-mage. I can help. Ridding towns of their troubles is old hat for me," I said, pointing at a nibling preparing to nibble on a dozing dog's tail.

The mayor glared, but approached nonetheless. "What will my townsfolk think of me if I let a stranger solve our problems?" he replied rhetorically in a whisper, tilting his head toward the square.

I smiled, saying nothing. *That you are not a prideful fool. Instead, you make clear that you possess the wits of a donkey's back end, but with less aesthetic appeal. I* sighed. *Oh, the insults I ignore to earn a meal. He won't be able to pull a solution out of his hat. Sooner or later he will bow to the inevitable and hire me.* I mentally tripled my de-infestation fee.

After a pause, the mayor's face lit with an idea, possibly a rare experience for him. "Let us loose our woolyfloof herd to chase off the pestiferous niblings!" he cried.

At the drop of a hat, the dutiful villagers again ceased the milking of animals, the planting of crops, and other daily routines. They drove the woolyfloofs from their split-rail pens.

But the pestiferous niblings, while small in stature, possessed the tenacity of terriers. They bared their fangs, swiped with their claws, and snurfled most defiantly.

The larger but timid woolyfloofs bleated and fled pell-mell. Or was it helter-skelter? Higgledy-piggledy? I can never keep those straight.

The niblings resumed their depredations, while hapless villagers scrambled to recover their errant livestock. "Wobius!" they cried. "When shall we be free of the pestiferous niblings?"

Third time's the charm. "Shall I rid you of these rodents?" I hailed the mayor, spreading my arms.

Emotions played out on his face like a stage performance. Eventually, he grinned, which I found strangely disconcerting. "Very well. Name your price, minstrel."

"I shall wipe out your pests in exchange for . . . *cue dramatic music . . .* your bretona birds," I said, pointing at the one perched on his head. *My fame would soar as the only minstrel this side of the Great River with a personal gaggle of bretona birds. Or was it a convocation? Parliament? Regardless, in a pinch they could serve as lunch. There I go again, thinking about food.*

The mayor's eyes bulged, his fists trembled, and his face reddened further, if that were possible. With a visible effort of will, he gradually regained his composure. "A moment," he sputtered, storming to the center of the square.

Townsfolk crowded round the mayor. They argued in heated whispers, casting glances at me. A lengthy debate ended with the mayor having the last word, a polysyllabic one at that, incrementally raising my estimate of his intelligence.

He approached me and doffed the bird from his head, cradling it with affection. "We cannot abide the pestiferous niblings. But bretona birds are cherished pets, dear to us as children. Will you accept a hogshead of pike as payment?" he asked, hat in hand, you might say. "Our pickled pike are the pride of the province!" he proclaimed.

I tilted my head but did not reply. That was far too low a price to dignify with a response, and in any event, fish, like this fool before me, tend to stink after a couple of days.

The mayor furrowed his brow. "How about a mule and cartload of woolyfloof milk, butter, and cheese? Is that not a valley of plenty for a humble bard?"

"Hmmf," I grunted, scowling. *A better offer, but still too stingy.*

The mayor glanced back at the villagers, stared at his feet, and finally sighed in defeat. "Five splendificant rubies, the size of which are seldom seen?" he offered, touching the leather pouch at his belt.

The villagers gasped.

Now that's a horse of a different color. "Agreed. I shall face the mighty horde," I declared, making the task sound far more daunting than it actually was. "Clear the square," I shouted to the townsfolk with a grand sweep of my arm. The cut of my cloak rendered such gestures très dramatic.

The villagers' faces brightened at the prospect of the niblings' imminent removal. They hastened to comply. Many held their breath. A hush fell.

I strode to the center of the square and drew my sorciful flute with all the theatrics I could muster. I traced an orniculous symbol in the air. That would not aid my casting, but wizardry is 50% showmanship. I raised the instrument to my lips and played a dulcet canticle, followed by Bourée. The latter is not part of the spell, but the melody is always a crowd-pleaser.

At once, the niblings desisted their digging, forsook their foraging, and stopped their snurfling. Instead, they swarmed about me, drawn to the sweet sounds like hummingbirds to honeysuckle.

The villagers' eyes widened, their mouths agape.

I led the bespelled beasts out of the village, through shadowy woods to a distant glade. There they stayed.

I hummed a tune for my own amusement as I skipped back to the village, savoring the prospect of a lavish luncheon for their savior. The anticipation of a full belly raised my spirits considerably. But it turns out one should never count their birds before they hatch. *Hmm. That's a catchy saying . . .*

"Huzzah! Hurray!" cheered the villagers. "Hats off to Evangeline!" They leaped and wept. They danced and pranced. They wirbilated in harmony with their beloved birds.

"The niblings shall vex you no more," I declared. *Cue dramatic music.* "Now, fulfill your oath."

"What now?" the small boy whispered to the mayor, unaware of my keen hearing. "You knew we had no rubies."

The mayor turned to me. "Well, I um . . . misspoke. Alas, we have no gems," he said, holding up empty palms.

"Yet you kept that under your hat," I growled. *He suffers from pride* and *greed.* The irony was not lost on me.

"How about ten woolyfloofs?" asked the mayor, pointing at a pen.

"That was not our accord," I declared, putting my hands on my hips. "Beware. I will brook no betrayal. I wield great power."

"No one threatens me," growled the mayor, clenching his fists. "Certainly not a white-haired mottle-mantled piper. The pestiferous niblings are gone. You may have woolyfloofs or nothing." He turned and marched off.

He defrauds and derides me? I'm a friend of humanity, but even I have my limits. My face flushed.

The faithless villagers retreated from my baleful glare.

I would have swept out my flaming sword of fire and separated his duplicitous head from his shoulders, but that sort of thing is frowned upon by humans as too wrathful. Nor does it tend to encourage attendance at my musical recitals . . . except by the teenagers, that is.

Again I drew my sorciful flute. I tapped a tree trunk two times and trilled a 'taliatory tune. The bretona birds flocked to me. Again I trod toward the tenebrous trees.

The villagers gasped. "Wobius! What have we done?" they cried at the sight of their poultry in motion. They wailed and flailed to no avail. For they would never again behold their beloved birds.

Far from the village, but no longer alone, I composed a new tune and sang with my flock. Or convocation? Parliament? In any event, it began thusly:

"If you fail to play it straight, you'll no longer wirbilate.

So, pay the angel, heed your words, and you won't lose your cherished birds."

I Am Gorbunk, Hear Me Braawr

Scott M. Sands

The blonde hotshot poised with his foot atop a felled space pirate? That's not me. The infamous smuggler beside him—not me either. And the princess? Just no. But the imposing, white-furred behemoth, out of frame in this metaphorical picture of galactic heroism, whose language no one understands?

That's me, Gorbunk the Tob.

I stomp up to them, along the third-deck hallway on the enemy starship. I crouch so my head doesn't scrape the ceiling, but I'm used to that. Even here, in space. The air is filled with a sizzled-hair scent from discharged plasma fire. Artificial lighting flickers off hotshot Binky's expensive jacket ahead.

I hold my breath to listen for movement or noises from hidden pirates. I hear none. Behind Binky and Princess Elara, stacked crates and webbing signify a cargo hold. Clue, the smuggler, seems calm. She owns the *Hyperlane* and I'm her co-pilot. She's amazing at everything, with the exception of translating for me. She sucks at that. But her long, dark hair and light-hearted tone inspire me. Of all sentients I've met, I like Clue the best.

Binky still has his KL2 plasma pistol angled down at a pirate—the one *I* disarmed and winded. The look on the hotshot's face says it all: he thinks this thug beneath his boot will help him find Faranon Var, recover the stolen starzium and gain the galaxy's unending thanks. He's probably right about that last part—galactic gals go for the well-dressed, robust type.

I give the hallway another check. When I look back, Binky's smiling at Elara. I mean *really* smiling. He's staring at her blue eyes—and a dozen other places—entranced by the young lady's beauty. The pirate notices, too. His hand sneaks to his weapon holster.

I want to shout out, save Binky's life. I know what everyone will hear when I talk; gibberish. It's sad and annoying at the same time that no one understands me. I speak, anyway.

"Braaaaawr!"

The three heroes stare in my direction a second before the pirate's hand flings to his side. The motion startles Binky, who flinches and ducks his head, giving a short squeal to accompany the movement. In his shock, he discharges his KL2.

Just like that, our best lead to finding the stolen starzium is dead.

"Braaawr-aawr!" *You idiot!*

"What did he say?" Princess Elara says, brushing her hands against her slimming tan jacket. She looks at Clue.

Clue pauses. Her eyes study the smoking hole in the pirate's chest. "I think he said the pirate was going for a weapon." She eyes Binky. "You saved us."

Binky did not save us. Binky couldn't save hot air from falling. He's the biggest coward I've ever seen. A terrible wuss, and an even bigger pretender, posing every ten seconds. My vocal chords don't resonate like most species, so I can't pronounce his real name, Pell. In my native tongue, he's Binky.

Princess Elara strides over next to Binky and places her delicate hand on his arm. *She*, on the other hand, is the most graceful female I know. Flowing, caramel hair, a round face and skin that makes you want to caress it, just to test whether it's softer than silk. Damn sexy, if you go for the furless type.

"Gorbunk, you're lucky your distraction didn't cost someone their life," says Clue. She pats Binky's back. "If it wasn't for our friend's lightning reactions, things might have gone differently."

I can only gape at Clue. An amazing smuggler. I've flown with her for eight years. She thinks she can speak my language. She has no idea. None. If she wasn't crafty and fun, I would never have stayed with her. She's 'Storm' to others. I usually call her Clue, to remind myself she has none.

I shouldn't blame her, though. Nobody else understands my species. Not since the minstrel incident. Everyone thinks that lunatic's translation through song is accurate Tobspeak, Clue among them. My fur-tips knot just thinking about it. I tolerate this job's risks for the credits, and, more importantly, the chance at fame that might help undo the past, bring the true voice of my species to light.

While the other three heroes celebrate that no one is hurt, I lean down near them to search the dead pirate's pockets. My thick, white fur touches against his scrappy shirt and pants. I manage to keep away from the scorching hole Binky made. After several minutes, I'm satisfied. The pockets are empty.

As I go to stand, a slow-rising arm pulls out from behind a crate up ahead. It's holding a KL2 pistol, pointed in our direction. Without thinking, I grab Princess Elara and pull her down, kicking at Binky's knee to make him tumble.

A shot rings out through the hallway. The next fraction of a second feels like every other moment in my life. Something's happening, but I'm not a part of it. Heat burns suddenly in my shoulder and I grasp it with my paw.

Clue whips out the pistol from her waist holster and launches a blast down the hallway. It strikes the exposed arm attached to the weapon. The injured pirate falls from behind cover, clutching his wound. Clue's a great shot.

The pain intensifies in my shoulder. It's really burning. "Braaawr-aaawr!"

Clue, eyes fixed down the hallway, translates. "He says to check that pirate ahead. He feels fine."

"Braaawr!"

"Yep, he's good."

There I am again in excruciating pain, shot and bleeding all over my beautiful white coat, with people *right* there, able to care for me. But no. They don't understand. Someday I'm going to flip over that.

In agony, I spot a squad of red and brown uniforms running up the hall from the way we've come. They're a Jointar squad, like us, from the princess' homeworld. Eight troopers to reinforce us. Took their time. I'm half flopped on my back, overtop a dead pirate in the hallway between a large, stinking waste tube and a few damaged wall shards. Two troopers stay to help. A minstrel in a green hat with a black feather accompanies them. What on earth is he doing here? The remaining troopers press forward up the hallway to where Binky, Clue and Princess Elara interrogate the second pirate. I already hear something about Faranon Var, the dreaded galactic warlord we're here for. Who knows, maybe we'll catch a break as to his whereabouts so we can stop him before he attacks any more planetary hub stations or steals more precious starzium.

Starzium. I've only held a handful of the self-heating mineral before. A biological wonder. A renewable heat source that works anywhere, it keeps many sectors with harsher climates from freezing. Heat has many applications, though. Goodness only knows what Var plans to do with it.

Two troopers help me to my feet. My hero friends return.

"Faranon Var's headed to the Balimi Sector," Binky says with a grin. Then he's walking back toward our transport, a step behind Elara. His eyes are still glued to her. The contingent of Jointar troopers trails in their wake, congratulating the heroes. Even the wounded pirate cuffed in their midst seems pleased.

The galaxy just isn't fair.

Beside me, the minstrel hops from one foot to another in some pathetic attempt at dance. He waves an ovular, stringed buitar afore his chest and jerks out three woeful chords repeatedly as he sings.

"Blaring and brightly the starzium shines
A galaxy's thanks for the heat it does bring
Wicked, old pirates may shout 'it be mine!'
Heroes, brave heroes, will dull their fell sting

Mightiest lionheart, Pell stands above—"

Thud. I slam the large waste tube down over the minstrel's head, cutting him off mid-song and knocking his buitar from his hands. I can't help it. I can't stand those guys. I *must* get my species properly translated, so I can quit dreading them. Though my shoulder kills, I manage to drag the well-tubed musician to the nearest open door. I shove him inside and close it.

Sweet relief.

Clue shuffles back. I thought she'd gone with the others. She points at the door. The minstrel's instrument spins at my feet. "What's that about?"

I don't answer. I just head for our ship and Clue follows. I'm sure someone there will tell us where Faranon Var is headed so we can catch him and get that starzium back.

WHEN THE *HYPERLANE* DESCENDS THROUGH BALIMI'S UPPER ATMOSPHERE and the scope of the vastly tropical planet comes into view, I'm not the only one on the starship to gasp. Golden sand stretches for miles against turquoise oceans, shimmering amid Bharm City's morning light. Now Tobs as a rule don't love sand—too easily stuck in your fur. Yet the place's charm has even me wanting to lose a few days relaxing my sore shoulder.

A shame we'd come to a tropical paradise to hunt a galactic warlord.

"We're touching down," Clue says from the *Hyperlane's* cockpit.

When the starship's engines shut off, Clue and I amble to the guest quarters to retrieve Binky and the princess. Binky's frustrated brow demonstrates his opinion on having his 'princess chat time' interrupted. Elara gets up and makes for the loading ramp. Binky follows.

A Balimian official with a bald head and wide orange glasses meets us at Landing Platform Seventeen. High thatch walls surround the area in an attempt to block out ruthless sand. Golden specks invade my fur, anyway. Dumb walls. The official extends a hand to Clue and Binky, then shakes my right paw—an unfortunate lapse in cultures. Paws hold your weapon. With them occupied, you're vulnerable. Only intimate friends or mates touch Tob paws.

"Braaaawr," I say, spreading bulky arms.

The official tries to maintain his smile, but cannot quite shroud his fear. He shuffles back.

"Oh," Clue says, "Gorbunk displays great emotion toward you. He really likes you. You should feel privileged."

If he does it again, he may feel knocked out.

The official, pleased to keep things moving, ushers us along. Two waitresses bring trays with light, fruity liquids and drape coral necklaces over us as we walk. I take a long sip; it's smooth and apple flavored—with bite. Balimian cocktails live up to their reputation. We reach our destination at a hut village that overlooks the serene waters.

"You believe that villainous scum Var will come to our peaceful planet?" the official says.

Princess Elara replies. "Obviously. We acquired the information from one of his goons. He's coming for your starzium. Soon." Balimi has particularly large deposits of the mineral for such a small planet.

"Where do you keep your biggest mined reserves?" Binky asks, gazing into the distant ocean like some mystic being.

The official glances away briefly before replying. "Oh, we don't mine the resource much. We rarely need to. It warms our beautiful beaches naturally. It brings us many tourists. Now, while you await Faranon Var, please enjoy our hospitality." He indicates four reclining wicker chairs.

"Braaawr-aawrr," I say. Mood turns my fur dark. We didn't come here to sunbathe.

After five hours lazing in the chairs, I'm starting to melt beneath my thick fur. Clue looks content. She'd live out the rest of her life here—a smuggler at heart. Binky is happy as he's seated near Princess Elara, who has stripped down to modest bathing wear. The fool human male can't stop drooling. Only Elara appears troubled.

I look at her. "Braawr-aawr?"

"What?"

Clue 'translates'. "He says 'this is the life.'"

No, halfwit. We've waited too long. One of these days . . .

As the red sun begins its long descent behind the ocean, the official from this morning heads over. "Ah, esteemed guests. We've been tracking all ships entering the system, as per your request. Nothing matching your description for Cauldonian vessels has approached our humble planet."

"Sure about that?" Princess Elara says.

"Of course."

He's still nervous. It's more than just my presence—the man is hiding something. He scratches his bald head.

"Braawr-aawr-aaaawr?" I ask. I need the truth on the planet's starzium.

"He says 'do the cocktails come in strawberry?'"

"Why, we have—"

"Braawr!"

My sudden outburst throws him off. I stand and move closer.

Elara stands, too. "Look, your planet's lovely and all, but Var won't be coming for sand. I'll ask again: does anyone mine your starzium?"

The official shuffles, about to reply. I place huge paws on my hips, glare down into his face.

"Well, ah yes. I suppose our leaders might maintain a small stockpile. For emergencies."

That would have been worth mentioning before. I adjust my stance and start my paws close together then further apart, questioning the stockpile's size. The official looks at Clue for translation.

"He's dancing to display thanks for your hospitality. Tobs have surprisingly good rhythm."

Right then, I want to squeeze the wicker recliners into tiny pieces and toss them over the ocean. No one should have to put up with this. Maybe it's hopeless. I'll never be heard.

Elara perceives the same thing I did. "How large is this stockpile, exactly? Tell me now."

She really is bold, this one.

"Oh, just modest really."

"How large?"

The official squirms. "About forty-six thousand pounds."

"Forty-six thousand! That's a fortune! Var is sure to go for that. Any fool would."

"Fortunately, the location is a planetary secret."

The official lied to us. I turn my back on him and wait. "Braaawr-aawr-awr-ar."

"Not sure what corn and diamonds have to do with anything, Gorbunk," Clue says.

Oh, that makes my blood boil.

Princess Elara grabs her drink, Binky quick to indulge her with a Balimian robe. She ignores it. "We are here on Jointar's behalf to capture and detain a galactic fugitive," she says to the official. "So get us the coordinates for that stockpile, or I'll revoke Balimi's tourism privileges." She storms off in a huff.

Smooth-skinned and fire-tongued, our princess. Odd for royalty. Her ability to get to the point adds to her natural seduction.

Back at our starship, we cram into the cockpit. The smell of fruity cocktails on our breaths permeates the air. I power up the systems needed to get us moving and Clue takes the yoke. The engine's pulsing thrum responds through the hull and vibrates my arms. We lift off.

The coordinates for this secret starzium stash arrive swiftly to the *Hyperlane's* dataports. It's a vault, a solidified dune a few klicks from Bharma. Shouldn't take long to reach, but I've no idea what we'll find when we get there.

An hour in the cockpit chills the skin beneath my fur after so long on the beach. The sun has almost vanished when we approach a grand dune. Red starship lights hover and it's as I feared; Faranon Var's ship, *Duress*, is here. It's already pulling away. While we sipped cocktails, Var plundered the planet's most valuable resource. He might get away with the starzium, he might not. Hard to tell at this distance.

I think up an idea. If I don't try it, our target might escape—so too any chance for my fame and reward. Goodbye decent Tobspeak translation. If I do try my plan and it doesn't pan out how I think it will, our target may still escape and *I'll* be blamed. Fun choices.

"Braaaawr," I say, adjusting dials. I need to convert every ounce of power into the forward thrusters and primary mounted cannons. Feels desperate. I guess it is. But I don't want Var escaping.

Several warning alarms beep, and Binky, bless him, asks questions. "What are you doing? You're draining our shields!"

I'd be more concerned about the life support backup I just pulled, Binky. I'm glad he doesn't know, and I can't communicate it to him even if I wanted to.

"Gorbunk, what *are* you doing?" Clue asks.

I point ahead at the red lights in the distance, fumes from *Duress'* rear engines. Our villain, in the act. As I continue my work, the gap between our vessels closes.

We're going to get him before he hurts anyone else. I can do this.

We race forward. We gain ground. We almost reach the starship. My vision is so locked on our prize, I miss the exotic Balimi birds flocking cross-path to us.

Too late. Several crash into our hull. By freak chance, one hits our navigations antennae. Next thing I know, we're heading full speed in other directions. Up, down, sideways. The safe thing to do is quickly power down thrusters and land. Somewhere behind us, the ship's drive whines.

"Well, that's just great. We'll never catch Faranon now." Binky's words are directed at me. "It was a sure thing and you blew it."

Shut it, Binky. We'd have never caught him, anyway.

I watch in horror as our quarry's red lights flare and *Duress* vanishes into space. We've lost him. Our spotlights illuminate the open vault door as we pull in closer. I don't need to set foot inside to know the starzium is gone, and so is Faranon Var.

Along with any hope to complete our mission.

THE PRINCESS FUMES. BALIMI IS A POLITICAL NIGHTMARE. IT ONLY TOOK A day for news-holos to report that a huge starzium storehouse had been robbed from the planet the night before—under the noses of a Jointar taskforce, who relaxed on the beach. It doesn't look good. I never did get my strawberry cocktail.

"I can't believe it. What will we do now?" Binky says. He's pacing. Behind him, Elara is too furious to talk. "We had Var in our sights." He points at me. "You sabotaged our mission!"

I want to explain my reasons for adjusting power dispersion. How can I? Instead, I rise from my chair and let out a low, guttural rumble. He sees the challenge in my eyes and backs down. I knew he would. Coward. I wish there's another way to explain, though.

If only you understood.

Clue joins the conversation. "I know Var got away, but Gorbunk is a darn good navigator. If he changes anything on my ship, I trust him. We lost this round, is all."

Thanks, Clue. Always looking out for me. It's why I like her the best.

"Great," Binky says. "Where does that leave us?"

I don't honestly know. I stay silent.

A buzzer bleeps on Princess Elara's communicator. She reads the message, gasps. Her eyes begin to water like Balimi's oceans.

"What is it?" Binky asks.

She ushers him over. Clue and I follow, trying to peer at the *Hyper-lane's* small screen she's plugged her comm into. I'm not ready for what comes up. None of us are.

A red, hot wasteland. Embers still smolder, flames still burn. I can tell from the visuals on screen the area used to have buildings. Little remains now.

"It's Eminon Prime. Reports say minimal casualties. But the infrastructure . . ."

I shudder before I speak. "Braawr-aawr-aawr."

Clue translates. "He can't believe it."

"Braaawr-aawr."

"So terrible."

"Braawr."

"Like gravy."

Binky blinks twice. "What?"

Clue shrugs. Any attempt to correct her seems heartless, given the destructive images on the screen.

In the background of the final picture, a large starship with Cauldonian markings hovers over an area. A devastating blue-white heat beam flashes out from the ship's bowel and burns up what's left beneath.

How could they construct a weapon with such heat? One obvious answer.

At least now we know what Faranon Var wants the starzium for.

A silence falls upon the group for Eminon Prime's tragic loss. Elara manages to look as striking as ever, despite her sobbing. "It's over," she says. "Did you see that ship? If it can obliterate Eminon Prime's defenses, no vessel in the fleet can match it."

"I'll think of something," Binky says, trying to look determined and failing.

I want to throw him out the airlock. Maybe I don't need to yet.

"Braaaawr-aawr?"

The princess and Binky look at Clue, awaiting translation.

"He wants to clarify about blue planets with fields."

My white hackles raise. Two *planets in the* Shield.

Two planets make up the Shield, the inner galactic sector's unofficial protectorate worlds. I'm pretty sure I remember Eminon Prime being one of them. I need to know the other. But Clue is my only translator. I try basic words.

Okay. Shield. "Brawr."

"Peeled!"

"*Braaaawr.*"

"Seal!"

Brawr, darn it.

"A peeled seal!"

They're not getting it. This goes on for ten minutes. To try a different tack, I spend a further ten attempting to act out my intentions, with no better results. Time for something more direct.

I rip a thick metal panel off the wall, much to Clue's immediate disgust, and shove it against Binky. While he's still holding it, I withdraw my KL2—that I'm pretty sure is set to stun—and fire at the panel. Binky shrieks.

The shot ricochets off. I march over to Binky, who's crouching like the galaxy's biggest wuss behind the panel, and yank it back from his hands. He seems happy to be rid of it. I point at the panel. Point, point, point, point, point. Then at Binky. Back to the panel.

"Shield," Clue realizes. "You could have just said that, big G. We need to shield ourselves now, with a ship like *Duress* running around."

I slap my forehead with my big, furry paw and cover my eyes. *Maker's fur, she still doesn't get it.*

Princess Elara ruminates. Tears momentarily ceased, she gazes back at the screen's images. Her blue eyes light up as she stands and our gazes follow her intriguing movement, even mine. Elara's something else.

"Never mind a shield for us," she says. "Eminon Prime is one of two shield planets for the inner sector. Laying them both to waste would send a message to the whole galaxy. The other shield half, Getis, could be Faranon's next target."

Everybody nods like it's some great revelation because *she* said it. Never mind that I've been trying to say the same thing for the last twenty minutes.

"Is this junk pile good to fly?" Elara asks.

"Sure is. Gorbunk fixed navigations this morning."

"Then get us moving."

I sigh. At least we're following my plan, even if someone else 'thought it up'. I can worry about explaining it later.

We have a galactic warlord to catch.

OUR SHIP BURSTS FROM HYPER TRAVEL AND INTO SPACE'S DARK FOLDS above Getis. We're alone, except for a small, local security craft. Our ship's comm rings as Getis security hails us. They're explaining how unwanted our presence in the system is, when *Duress* jumps in from nowhere and a blue-white heat beam erupts from its bowel. The Getis craft explodes.

Poor troopers.

"Hang on!" Clue says.

The *Hyperlane* rolls to avoid the next beam. The princess yells. Binky's hysterical. Clue and I keep our heads.

Faranon Var's starship is huge, as though it could sweep in and swallow ours whole. Fearing it may try, I watch through the canopy. Another shot from Var clears our starboard by mere meters. Then another. A direct hit and we're fried. We won't last much longer.

I notice the barrel at the base of Faranon Var's ship glows exponentially brighter before each shot. I study it closely—there. A tiny, red spec indicates it's ready to fire. If we time our run, we should be able to get safely underneath *Duress*. If . . . if . . .

If I try the same trick that failed last time.

There's no way the others will go for it. I'm not a hundred percent sure *I* go for it. It's stupid to repeat proven failure, isn't it? Nobody does that. Maybe that will make it work?

I try to explain. "Braaaawr-aawr, braawr-a-aawr."

"You want to find your men? Sky a hen? Die in ten?"

"He's not very optimistic," the princess says.

Listen! I need to try again.

"Braawr-a-aawr."

"Fly a pen?"

I give up. Nobody gets a word I say and it kills me. No matter how badly some ferret massacred his musical rendition of Tobspeak, the fact remains: nobody in the galaxy understands me because nobody cares enough to try. That stings like blazing shots passing through my body, and not for the first time I wonder if I'm going to do something rash. Blow it. We're out of time. I start bashing commands into the ship's controls.

"He's doing it again!" Binky cries.

Clue starts on me. "Gorbunk, this isn't the best time to—"

I whack a heavy fist down on my chair's side.

"Okay, do your thing."

Binky would stop me if he could. He can't. I stare at the point beneath Faranon Var's ship and wait for the tiny glow to indicate he's powering his main weapon. When I see it, I drop the *Hyperlane's* nose and speed ahead. We're good; the heat beam passes well above us. I race us toward *Duress* and picture us making it. The weapon's glow starts again, sooner than expected. I try to drop us again, but don't quite dodge the beam's extremity. It obliterates our rear hull. Our engines die, shields blink off and we drift below Var's larger vessel, dead in the proverbial water.

"We're going to die! We're going to die!" Binky yells.

He may be right.

I feel a tractor beam rock us as it grabs our ship and pulls us toward Faranon's. We wanted to get to him, right? Looks like we still will. The circumstances around our arrival will just be slightly different.

Who am I kidding? We're dead.

A cutting sound resonates at our ship's boarding ramp.

A rat runs across the holding cells' top bar on Faranon Var's *Duress*. The rodent squeaks and I wonder how it got there. I remember with some distinction how *I* arrived, past the big heat gun and the legion of armed pirates, through a short corridor with a terribly low ceiling, into the rough hands of two servant masters with plasma whips and into the metal cage. My friends lay unconscious beside me.

A hideous moofer waves a stunner at me from outside the cell. He's wearing some ridiculous attempt at a cape; a burnt orange rag with fist-sized, metal chunks sewn onto the bottom. Looks about as comfortable as fish boots. "Oy. Get up," he says. "Boss wants to see you. All of you."

"Braaawr-aawr." *We're tired.*

"I know."

What! He understands?

The pirate wraps his arm across his great belly and laughs. "Gotcha! No one gets your babble, you furry oaf. Ah, ha, ha. Now get up."

My paws fill with fury. I struggle not to leap at my captor and pull his toenails off. I shake Clue, then Princess Elara. Both wake. Elara stretches her leg out as she sits, sliding her hands slowly from inner thigh to shin. She even wakes up sexy.

I go to nudge Binky. His eyes open before I do. He sits up.

"Alright, let's go," the pirate says.

We're marched in cuffs down several corridors into a wide galley, where pirates litter tables spread about. They cheer as we're led in. Plasma rifles are waved and fists pump the air. Into their sweaty, ale-drenched midst we march. A man with spiky, dark-brown hair and cunning hazel eyes sits on a makeshift throne against the wall. His scraggly body struggles to fill his blue shirt and beige jacket.

"Welcome, welcome. I am Faranon Var. You've no doubt heard of me. You must belong to Jointar's squads, eh? Nipping at my heels? Well, we're not all short-sighted like your masters. I'll prove it." He taps a button on a wrist device. "Light 'em up, boys."

We watch on a screen as another Getis security ship flies into our proximity. The starzium heat weapon opens fire. Faranon Var simply laughs. "Another pompous scum destroyed," he says. "All thanks to my starzium."

"No!" Elara cries.

I can tell Binky wants to say something but he's quivering in his boots. Wuss. Elara jumps in again. "Starzium isn't meant for this. It saves planets."

"You mean the way your precious starzium could have saved *my* planet? But no one would share it with us, would they? Cauldon's people freeze while the rest of the galaxy warms their toes in comfort. We'll show them how useful starzium can be. Now that we've gathered it in the lower hangar—"

Wait, is he telling us where his stash is?

"—we use its own heat to charge our weapon. First Eminon Prime, now Getis. Next we'll hit Forgas, Duptune and Hillion until we've taken out enough planets to move against the galactic core, then—"

He's giving us their whole plan. What kind of idiot villain does that?

"We'll be unstoppable," Faranon Var finishes.

I'm dumbstruck. The fool told us exactly how to beat him. We just need to get free, move the starzium in the lower hangar and his starship will lose its primary weapon. Getis security can handle things from there. I figure a distraction will help get us started.

"Braawr-aawr-aawr," I begin.

Var frowns at me. "What did that thing say?"

I touch my chest and extend my cuffed paws toward him. *We could be friends.* "Braawr-aawr, braaawr."

The galactic warlord looks at Clue, points at me with one brow raised.

Clue offers a translation. "You should try flying pens. Sorry, he's been stuck on the idea lately."

Come on, Clue. This is important. Blood pumps through my muscles like fire. I've just about had it up to my big, furry ears with these people.

Var spits while laughing and slaps his leg. Elara shouts some bold threat she has zero ability to back up. When we need a hero most, Binky shakes like a meteor entering atmosphere. Clue, perhaps my only real friend, still can't understand a word I say.

I need to tell the others to break for the lower hangar. "Braaaaaawr."

No response, save for boisterous jibes from the pirate crew. I clench my jaw, tighten my fists. Everything starts turning red. Red walls. Red galactic warlord. Red fingers in the crowd pointing at me. Red, red, red. Pent-up rage from a thousand misunderstood conversations threatens to explode.

Faranon mocks me with talking gestures from his hands. "Silence, Tob. We all loathe your beastly sound. So annoying, on and on and on."

I'm ready to snap. "Braaaaaawr!"

"Are you even speaking? It's just sounds, grinding away at our ears. You're worse than a bad minstrel."

The room bursts into hysterics. My eyes flare.

That. Is. It.

I flex my wrist cuffs. They break like candy. With a bloodthirsty roar, I yank the moofer's cape free and start swinging. Three pirates slam into the left bulkhead. I bat away half a dozen more. I'm careful not to kill anyone, but they sure get my meaning.

Two blasts zip past me. I toss the cape. My left arm takes a hit, but in my fury, I ignore it. Downed pirates provide a plasma rifle for each paw and I unleash hell.

As more and more enemies are incapacitated, I spin and find myself facing my old squad. Clue and Elara are smiling. Binky's in awe. They've done nothing to help. Nothing to understand. I realize with clarity that if I don't need them now, at the most important time . . .

. . . I don't need them at all. My thoughts jump to what I *do* need. If not to communicate— that nova's blown—then what? To captain a ship? To see the galaxy? What do I even *want*?

I know one poshyr pie I'd like a slice of. She's staring right at me. It's a new world with new possibilities. I take down the remaining pirates, save for Faranon Var, and march over to Elara.

Chucking down the stolen weapon in my left paw, I wrap my bulky arm around her and pull her close. She's shocked for a moment. But she sinks into my fur, sees the strength in my gaze. Finally, she relaxes into me.

That's right, babe. Soft as butter.

Binky opens his mouth to protest. I stuff my weapon paw across his face and shove him six feet back. Clue observes me with passive interest.

Hugging Elara to my side, I stroll to Var's throne. The villain squirms but my carnage has tied his tongue. I flick my plasma rifle setting to stun, point it at his chest and fire.

He'll feel that when he wakes up.

My enemies are beaten. Elara, Clue and Binky probably think it's over. But I didn't take down some thirty guys for nothing. There's starzium on this ship—enough to buy myself a planet or two and get away from all this. Maybe even a decent translator. Maybe not. In any case, if I'm making the rules now, I might as well be rich.

I pull Elara along with me toward the lower hangar. My imagination was right; her soft skin feels like heaven against me. Maybe I'll convince her to grow her own fur. Clue and Binky go to follow us through a doorway. I turn. My growl is for them both, my message clear.

Not this time.

More pirates will be onboard. I'll overpower them too, but first things first. The starzium is in the lower hangar so I need to head there. I don't know the exact route, but trial and error win out; I arrive with Elara and K.O. the few pirates guarding the area.

The hangar is large enough for the *Hyperlane* to fit twice. There are containers piled in a heap and several doors. A camera marks the west wall. The temperature in the room is like the hot springs on my home-world. The reason lies near the center; starzium glows red through a massive containment box rigged with wires and charges. Heat. Power. Credits. All mine.

Faranon Var's personal, dual-winged shuttle is tucked into a bay. It will do nicely for my escape. Sizing up the cargo hold's shape, I judge it to fit most of the starzium, if not the entire hoard. A nearby hydraulic lifter will help me make short work of loading it.

I place Elara back from the starzium cache and head for the lifter when a monitor beeps on the side wall. I'm hardly interested, but I check it out. Three ships have entered Getis' orbit. Var's pirate vessels. I wonder if they realize *Duress* is in disarray.

The image flashes to a pirate lord. I don't recognize him, but he fits the bill for Faranon's minions, though he carries a kindness in his face unusual to most. He asks how the fight against Getis progresses, then queries when their people might have access to the starzium. In the background, a little Cauldonian girl shivers beneath a worn blanket.

I don't answer, just stare at the girl. She reminds me why Jointar hired us in the first place. So many planets depend on starzium. So many people. My heartrate drops. Hadn't Faranon Var mentioned his home planet's suffering? Cauldon is an ice world, if memory serves. Part of me wonders—what if Var didn't start out wanting to hurt anyone? What if he just wanted the starzium to keep his people warm, like this little girl? He wouldn't be alone. It hurts me to think we might be similar, but I know what's worse than being thought poorly of. I despise it each and every day.

Being misunderstood.

With sadness and shame, I gaze upon the starzium that could buy all my wildest dreams. Or it could help endless people across dozens of star systems to survive. Can't it do both? My throat clogs. I may be frustrated, and angry enough to injure a few pirates. But I'm not ready to leave a galaxy out in the cold.

Air rushes in and announces two interior doors opening. I spin to face them. To my immediate left, not far from Elara, a strange figure in a green beret with black feather and two pirates at his back. He's brandishing a buitar in one hand, KL2 pistol in the other. He looks familiar. Wicked fire burns in his eyes.

That hat. I've seen him before. A waste tube comes to mind.

Binky rushes through the other door, unarmed.

As it seems to be the day for revelations, another strikes me. Whether pirates, Tob fools like me or infuriating musicians, the next villain will always rise. And win—unless forces rally to meet them. Forces united under a hero, with a face for the galaxy to believe in, to inspire hope. Stereotypes being what they are, the galaxy isn't ready to rally behind a Tob, like me. The best chance at ongoing peace and security is a hero with a more familiar face.

Shoot. I know a candidate. The idea makes me gag.

The minstrel breaks my concentration with a ditty. He's way off pitch.

"A tube overhead could not keep me well bound
A pitiful hero thought victory won
This musical champion in hell's circle found
The will to grow devastating as the sun

"So oh, fear the morning! You helpless, unlearned
The heat song is coming, and with it shall bring
Destruction and end thus to all you have gathered
As Minstrel of Cauldon 'comes galaxy's king!"

Knowing I could crush this musician-come-pirate with one paw, another fiend would soon replace him. Starzium's faintest touch heats my back, and I see my beautiful princess almost close enough to touch. My eyes note the camera again on the west wall and realize that everything is being recorded. I charge.

When I near the minstrel, I pretend to overbalance, sliding across the floor to bump into his feet. A necessary move, the embarrassment is still unbearable. The green-hatted musician laughs a ghastly laugh and plucks a few out of tune notes on his buitar's strings.

I could stop him. I could save myself. I don't. My heart is for my people, who yearn to be heard. But deep inside my warm, furry chest, I know the galaxy is much bigger than my species alone, and right now it needs a hero. I cringe for what comes next.

Binky rescues me.

With lanky valiance, Binky's pristine, beige jacket flaps as he leaps from the pirates' blind spot. He bumps the closest one, manages to steal a weapon. A few awkward shots from close range later, and it looks like he'll mess this up. I pretend to squirm backward in fear and knock the minstrel off balance for him. Binky finishes up, then deals with the two pirates. The camera will have captured it all.

Princess Elara rushes over and pulls Binky's lips to hers. They kiss long and hard, the starzium pile in the background. Just like that, my fame, my princess and my credits disappear. I moan quietly for all Tobkind, but this is for the best. Many star systems will be safer now. The galaxy's hero is forged.

CLUE AND ME LEAN AGAINST A HALLWAY ABOARD THE *DURESS*, WATCHING holo reporters swarm like freezing rodents seeking heat. Pulled from camera footage, the recording with Binky's rescue plays on a huge screen in the background. He stands at the center of focus, prouder than ever, wearing a stoic gaze and clutching a Jointar plasma rifle. The perfect picture for trooper recruitment posters. A hero is needed and he actually looks the part.

I'll bet he's forgotten to put the safety on that rifle, though.

Princess Elara loops her arm through Binky's, symbolizing Jointar's support. Faranon Var is beside them in cuffs. The message is loud and clear: victory belongs to the good guys.

Clue bumps my hip, getting my attention. "I almost wonder if you didn't have a firm hand in the way things turned out. You wiped out half *Duress'* crew. That could have been you up there in the spotlight."

I shrug. It's true.

She smiles. "You might be the most misunderstood person in the galaxy, Gorbunk. I thought *I* knew you, at least. I'm starting to think I don't yet. You deserve more credit than you've been given." Clue punches my arm in friendship, avoiding my paw. "I'm sorry I can't understand you. I'll work on that."

My chest warms at her sentiment. Clue smiles again and I return it. She may not be able to interpret my words, but I sense she *knows* now. That tiny change makes my white fur bristle with glee. She's not clueless, after all. Maybe I'll use her proper name. Later.

"Braaaaawr?"

Clue laughs. "I have no idea what you said, furball."

I laugh, too.

We both stare one last time at the commotion. With Faranon Var in custody, our contract is done. We're free to roam the galaxy again as we please.

"You know," Clue says, "I wonder where we should head, now that Getis security have the pirates under control and Balimi have their forty-three thousand pounds of starzium back."

Forty-three? But I thought . . .

Clue tilts her head up at me, grins slyly.

Yes. I've always liked Clue the best.

Troubles with Troubadours

TALES OF MYRICK THE (NOT SO) MAGNIFICENT

Berin L Stephens

Would you believe I once performed on stage with the greatest troubadour group of all time, the Tumbling Rocks? No, really. I even played "I Cannot Achieve Fulfillment" with them. Oh, you still don't believe me? Well, this is the true and honest story.

I HAD RETURNED TO CASTLE FRINGOL TO EVALUATE MY LIFE. EVEN though I was still a teenager, I'd recently reached full wizard status according to the Wizard High Council. This was mainly because I possessed magic socks. I had also received some intensive spell casting training from a lizard wizard. Still, the thought that I had so much power at my disposal, and could do so much damage with it, scared me. I'd seen what magic could do to some people. It often brought out the worst, or the most evil, aspects of their personality. I didn't want that to happen to me. At the same time, being a wizard could be a lucrative career, if only I knew how to make money at it.

At least, for the time being, I had a room at Castle Fringol where I could stay and mull things over. Thanks to my friendship with Princess Frederica, she allowed me to stay in the castle itself and I no longer slept in that smelly messengers' barracks with a bunch of teenage boys. Unfortunately, my former messenger companion, Nutboy, stayed in the castle with me. Even though he was still a messenger, he didn't like to stay in the barracks with the others anymore, either. And it meant that I couldn't escape from his snoring every night.

It was a cold, winter morning when I sat in our room studying one of my spellbooks. I had the fireplace cranked up to ten logs when Nutboy burst into the room. "Myrick, you won't believe what I heard!"

I grunted. The little guy could get so excited about the most trivial things. "What?" I didn't look away from my book.

"The Tumbling Rocks are coming! Here! To Castle Fringol."

I slammed my book closed and spun around to stare at him. "Shut the front portcullis! You're not lying to me, are you?"

"No, honest, I heard Sergeant Uchdehn talking about it. They will be here in one week."

My skepticism kicked back in. "Yeah, right. You know you can't believe anything Bumstabber says." That was my name for Sergeant Uchdehn because of how he liked to use his spear on me.

"Yeah, but I also overheard Princess Frederica talking to some of her servants about building a stage for their concert. It's true!"

My skepticism faded. The Tumbling Rocks . . . coming to Fringolia? They usually stuck to the bigger cities and kingdoms. Why in the world would they come here? Well, it didn't matter. This could be the chance I'd been waiting for.

I tossed the spellbook onto my desk, bolted up, and clapped. "That's it!"

Nutboy jumped and took a step back. "What?"

"My new career. Instead of messing around with all this dangerous magic, I'm going to join the Tumbling Rocks."

Nutboy stared at me with wide eyes for several seconds before he burst out laughing. "You? Join the Tumbling Rocks?" That sent him into another fit of laughter.

I put my hands on my hips. "I'm serious. I can do it."

"But you don't even know how to play an instrument. What are you going to do for them, carry their instruments from town to town?"

"No, I'm going to become a musician and join their group. How hard can it be?"

"Pretty hard, actually," Nutboy said, sobering up. "You have to do things like, you know, practice."

"Practice is for peasants. I'm a wizard. I'm sure there's a spell in one of my spellbooks that will turn me into a musician."

Nutboy raised an eyebrow. "Oh? I'll bet you three coppers there isn't."

We shook hands, "I'll take that bet."

Needless to say, I lost three coppers. Not even the evil necromancer Arnabet's spellbook had anything close.

I couldn't sleep that night, though, thinking of how great it would be to tour with the Tumbling Rocks. There would be *lots* of girls, of course. Oh, and the excitement of performing on stage. And screaming girl fans. I'd get to see all Twelve Kingdoms. And there would be *so* many girls.

The next morning, I went on a search throughout the castle for a musical instrument. I found a storeroom that contained some instruments left there several decades before. I wanted to play lead lute but unfortunately, the only lute they had didn't have any strings. The drum head on the drum was cracked and unusable, too. None of the shawms had any reeds. And someone had taken all the post horns and turned them into spittoons. The only thing I found that could still make music was a recorder. I snatched it up and returned to my room to prove how easy it would be to learn.

A couple of hours later, someone pounded on my door as if the castle were on fire. I put the recorder down on my bed and opened the door. Princess Frederica stood on the other side. She wore her everyday leather armor instead of her full set of plate mail and her hand rested on the mace hanging from her belt. I'll just say, it's nice to have the brawny princess around during a fight. "Is everything okay in here, Myrick?"

"Yeah. Why?"

"Well, there have been some strange noises heard in this part of the castle. We didn't know if it was a ghost wailing in anguish or a troglyn giving birth. The sounds seemed to be coming from your room." She looked past me, searching.

"I have no idea what could be making a noise that horrible."

"Are you performing some kind of summoning spell?" She tilted her head. "You're not bringing the dead back to life, are you?"

"No, no. Nothing like that. I was just here practicing recorder."

She raised a brow. "Recorder? But you're one of the most powerful wizards around. Don't you have, you know, wizard things to do?"

"Let's just say I'm open to other career options." I sighed. I guess I needed to confess to her my dream. My goal. "I want to audition to join the Tumbling Rocks while they're here."

She cleared her throat, covered her mouth, and looked down for a few seconds as if something were funny. She cleared her throat again and looked up at me. "I'm afraid to tell you this, but it doesn't look like they'll be able to come."

"What? Why? I heard they were coming."

"They were, but there have been some problems in Duragath and no one can get through. Rumor has it that there is a giant spider infestation in the Moragan Mountains."

My face probably looked horrified. The only thing worse than giant spiders were evil necromancers who desired to turn everyone into zombies. Barely. Which is why it surprised the cabbage out of me when I said, "What if someone went over and cleared out the spiders?"

Frederica scrunched her lips to one side and shook her head. "Then maybe they could get through. But who would do such a courageous act? Nonac is still up in Airamic getting things ready for our wedding."

I bravely announced in a small, squeaky voice, "Me." See how stupid it is to be a wizard? You commit yourself to dangerous causes.

Frederica nodded. "I knew you were brave. Then I shall come as well. I'll gather as many volunteer soldiers as I can find and we'll leave in the morning."

"That's wonderful." My stomach felt like it contained a hatching dragon egg.

She turned around and left.

I closed the door and leaned my head against it. "What have I just gotten myself into?" At the same time, if I cleared the road for the Tumbling Rocks, they might feel so grateful that they just let me join the group without an audition.

The next morning, our troop had gathered. It was me, Princess Frederica, and Nutboy. Apparently, all of the soldiers she'd asked had other more pressing matters of business. And the only reason Nutboy joined us was that I *sort of* accidentally left out the part about the giant spiders. For extra protection, Frederica gave me a short sword and a jacket of leather armor. I also carried my pack and a new, smaller spellbook containing some of my favorite spells. My pack also carried premixed components for each of those spells. Chuggit, my lizard wizard friend, had taught me a spell for infusing components into mundane items that would be easier to carry, but I hadn't gotten around to doing that yet. The spell required a lot of magic to perform so I'd been putting it off.

Oh, and, of course, I brought my trusty recorder along. I figured it wouldn't hurt to practice for my audition while we traveled. You can never have too much music while on the road.

Frederica wore her chainmail, had her mace strapped to her hip, a bow and arrows, and several spears. Also, one of the nice things about having a warrior princess as a friend is she could get us horses.

As we rode out the main gate, someone shouted from behind us. "Oi, you can't be goin' out without an escort, my princess."

We turned around and saw none other than my favorite guard of all time, Bumstabber.

"I'll be fine, Uchdehn," the princess said. "Myrick is with me."

Bumstabber gave me one of his loving sneers. "That runt can't protect you from a falling leaf." He pointed at Nutboy, "And li'l Brutus is even more useless."

"We'll be fine, sergeant. I'm well-armed and Myrick is a powerful wizard."

Bumstabber snickered. "Like I believe that pile of garbage. Just hold up and I'll join ya." He turned around and trotted to the stables.

I groaned. The last thing I wanted was to have Bumstabber around. Of course, with luck, maybe he'd get eaten by a spider. Just kidding!

Sort of.

Once his gear was loaded on a horse, we started our journey.

It felt strange seeing the countryside from the back of a horse. Not only did my magic socks grant me the ability to use magic, but they also allowed me to run great distances without growing tired. Maybe riding a horse wasn't as fast, but it was nice to be able to relax while we traveled.

After we'd been on the road for an hour, I pulled out my recorder and started playing. Bumstabber, who'd taken the lead, spun his head around and grabbed his spear. When he saw me, he cast an affectionate glare at me. "I thought a slime beetle swarm was attackin'. Stop making that awful racket."

I tootled a few notes at him in defiance. I then continued wiggling my fingers over the various holes without much effect.

"Here, let me show you," Frederica said. She took the recorder from me and showed me how the fingers were supposed to go on the instrument. "You need to make sure to use your left thumb to cover this hole in back, otherwise the pitch won't change much." She handed it back to me.

I tried to imitate what she had done but it took several tries before she nodded and said, "Yeah, that's it."

"I didn't know you played recorder," I said.

She shrugged. "It was a part of my princess training, back when my father wanted me to wear dresses to attract the attention of any eligible royal young men who happened by. I kind of enjoyed music, but weapons training was my preferred pastime."

As we continued riding, Frederica coached me more on how to play the instrument. I'm not sure whose glares were more vicious, Bumstabber's or Nutboy's. By sunset, I could play three songs.

When we gathered around the fire that night, I dazzled Nutboy and Bumstabber with one of my new songs. Once finished, I asked, "Do you like it?"

"No!" Bumstabber barked.

Nutboy's lips worked for several seconds before he said, "I, um, it was different."

"Different? What do you mean by that? Did you recognize the tune?"

He shook his head, "Uh, 'I Cannot Achieve Fulfillment'?"

"No, guess again."

" 'Beneath My Big Toe'?"

"No, it's not a Tumbling Rocks song."

Bumstabber growled before saying, "It sounded like the mass murder of several rats."

Nutboy paused a second before he nodded his agreement.

Fine. Obviously, my travel companions were not highly trained in the arts like me. Princess Frederica was out chopping wood at the time or else she would have defended my tremendous musicianship.

The travel for the next three days was cold and miserable. Several times, I thought about turning back. It snowed for two of the days and made the roads slow going. Finally, on the evening of the third day, we camped just on the Fringolian side of the border before crossing over into Duragath.

The next morning, if anything, grew even colder. It made me long for the warmth and humidity of Immia. As I watched my breath billow out in front of me, it got me thinking. How could there be a giant spider infestation in this awful cold? I'd heard about woolly spiders in the far north from Nonac but they weren't supposed to be large nor this far south in the Twelve Kingdoms. Did they migrate? Or was this giant spider story just an excuse so that the Tumbling Rocks wouldn't come to Fringolia?

We broke camp and headed over the border into the lands of our traditional enemies. Our first clue that something was wrong was the abandoned guard station. Yeah, it was cold in the mountains, but there was usually a garrison there year-round. We poked around a bit and it looked like whoever was there left in a hurry a few days earlier. They traveled light, too, since many of the weapons were left behind.

A high-pitched, panicked shriek pierced the chill air. At first, I thought it was Nutboy until I realized it had come from my throat. In front of me, between two buildings at the guard station, stretched a giant web. It looked kind of pretty, with the morning sun shining through ice crystals hanging from it, but it was definitely created by something huge.

"What is it, Myrick?" Nutboy asked as he rounded the corner. I'll just say, his scream was louder, higher, and longer than mine. And he fainted. Frederica found us and carried Nutboy back to where our camp had been the night before. We restarted the fire and waited for him to wake up. An awkward silence filled the chill air was we all reflected on what we'd seen.

Bumstabber broke the silence. "We need to get outta here. Thems webs ain't natural."

The princess shook her head. "But if whatever things created those webs are this close to our border, they can easily cross over into our kingdom. We need to stop these spiders before they grow in numbers and invade our lands."

"Spiders?" Bumstabber asked. "No one said nothin' 'bout spiders."

"You didn't ask," I said.

He growled and shook his head. "We should go back and muster our army. There ain't enough of us to do anythin'."

The princess shook her head. "That will take too long. We first need to find out how big of a threat this is. Besides, we have Myrick and his magic."

Bumstabber snorted.

I stayed silent as I tried to figure out what I should do. I wanted to go home or at least get as far away from that place as I could. Did I want to see the Tumbling Rocks that bad? No. It wasn't worth my life.

At the same time, I did have magic. A lot of it. And I sort of did now know how to use it. Also, for once, I was prepared with combat spells and the mixed components to cast them. I could, conceivably, take care of this by myself.

Or, just as conceivably, I could be in way over my head and die. But if the threat was as bad as I feared, many good Fringolian soldiers could die, too. No, I needed to at least see how bad the infestation was.

Nutboy groaned as he regained consciousness. He looked up at the burning fire and shook his head. "Wow, I had a terrible nightmare. I dreamed that we entered an abandoned city and there was this giant spider web with crystals in it."

Before I could think of some way to soften the blow, Bumstabber said, "That wasn't a dream, you nit. It was real."

Nutboy's eyes went wide and his whole body tensed up. Before he could take off screaming into the woods where he'd either freeze to death or get eaten by a giant spider, I said, "It's okay. I've got some spells to handle them."

He looked at me, his eyes still wide, "You didn't say anything about spiders. You just said we were going to Duragath to see the Tumbling Rocks. Did you know about this?"

"Well, maybe a little."

"A little! Whatever spider made that web is HUGE. And you *knew!*" He pointed an accusatory finger at me. I feared the little guy would pop one of the veins in his forehead.

I tried to put on a confident expression. "Oh, don't worry about it. It's just a few spiders blocking the path. I'll get them all blasted out of here by lunch."

"Then it's settled," the princess said. "We'll gear up and push forward into Duragath to see how bad this is. Get your spells ready, Myrick."

I swallowed. "Um, yeah." I reached into my pack and pulled out *The Book of Myrick the Magnificent's Awesome Magic Spells and Recipes* and brushed up on the incantations.

I had my good ol' binding spell, *Durg the Browless's Fire Spout* spell, *Jangan's Spell of Long Pokey Objects*, and *Warner Dynock's Amazingly Spicy Chicken Strips* memorized. That last one was for the victory celebration feast afterward, of course.

Fifteen minutes later, we marched forward. Nutboy bravely decided to hang back to guard the camp, watch the horses, and keep the fire going. It was probably just as well. The chicken still needed to thaw.

Princess Frederica and Bumstabber had their bows out and ready with arrows. They were prepared for combat. I, though, feared I was getting into something I'd never get out of. We continued up the road for 300 yards when we came to our first obstacle: a large web stretching across the entire roadway. The strands were thicker than my thumb and difficult to cut. We drew our swords and hacked our way through.

As we finished and stepped through to the other side, the trees exploded with activity. At first, we couldn't see them because they blended in with the snow on the trees. Five enormous spiders, each of them the size of a cottage, stretched their long legs to the ground and came toward us.

Frederica and Bumstabber released their arrows but to no effect against the tough, white fur and hides covering the woolly spiders.

Since I didn't want to burn the forest down, I first cast the long pokey object spell. I pulled out the component vial, cast its contents forward, and shouted *"Jectsob yekop glon tihw oyu bats ot oingg m'i!"* Nothing happened. Instead, a savory, spicy aroma struck my nose as the components spread onto the closest spider. So, it appeared our celebration dinner would be just regular roast chicken.

Meanwhile, when Frederica and Bumstabber realized their arrows were useless, they unstrapped their spears from their backs and advanced, forcing the spiders to back away from me.

"If you're going to do something, I suggest you do it now!" Frederica shouted.

"Uh, yeah." I searched around in my pack and realized I had the herbs and spices section on the wrong side. I pulled out the fire spell vial and cast that spell: *"Toups Eirf."*

A long stream of fire leaped out of my fingers and into the closest spider. It burst into flame. I swept the fire spout about until it engulfed the other four. We backed away due to the heat. The spiders tried to follow us but were soon overwhelmed by the flames. The one with the spices smelled quite delicious, too.

We retreated to the camp. Nutboy jumped to his feet when he saw us. "You're not dead!"

"No thanks to 'im," Bumstabber grumbled, pointing at me.

"Hey, I vanquished those spiders rather well, if I don't say so myself," I said. "In fact, it was pretty easy. I think we should have no trouble making our way through into Duragath."

"That did seem to go rather well," Frederica said, "once you got the right spell figured out."

Bummstabber snorted. " 'Cept Myrick could set the whole forest on fire, if he ain't more careful."

Nutboy rolled his eyes. "And he usually isn't. He's already burned down several things he wasn't supposed to."

"Hey, that old building needed to come down anyway. And melting an entire glacier doesn't count as burning. Technically."

Frederica nodded. "Still, it would be wise to be cautious. Any fire started here could easily spread into our lands, too. Do you know any other spells that will work that don't involve as many flames?"

"Not really. I don't have many combat spells entered into *The Book of Myrick the Magnificent's Awesome Magic Spells and Recipes* yet. Most of them are for teeth cleaning, laundry, and clearing ants away from picnics." I made a mental note that I needed to add a few less-flammable combat spells into my collection. "I do have the binding spell memorized so I could bind them and then have the three of you jump in and stab them while they can't move."

Nutboy shook his head and took a couple of steps back. "Nuh-uh. Not me, I'm not going anywhere near those things."

"I ain't, either," Bumstabber muttered.

"We'll do what we have to do," the princess said. "Myrick, go ahead and use your fire spell where it seems safe, like in the roadway, and use your binding spell whenever the spiders are in a flammable location. I'll do the killing if no one else will dare." She stared at Bumstabber. "But let's break camp and move forward. We'll eliminate any that are near the roadway."

"Sounds good," I said, even though it really didn't.

Nutboy shook his head, looking pale. "I'll stay right here, as far from the spiders as possible."

I raised an eyebrow and pointed at the trees surrounding us. "Sure, you *could* do that, but those spiders like to hide in trees and crawl out to find their victims. I'm sure you'll make a nice meal, or actually in your case an appetizer, for any nearby spiders."

That convinced him to come, though we did have to wait for him to regain consciousness. Again.

Once packed, we mounted our horses and made our way into Duragath lands, keeping our eyes open for any more spiders or webs. We went for several miles before we came to the next web. This time, we didn't bother hacking through. I just burned it away. It still summoned three more spiders that charged out of the forest toward us. One fire spray quickly took care of them before they came anywhere near. Nutboy still passed out, though. We just slumped him over his horse and continued on our way. I cast a sleep spell on him, too, since we figured it would be better for him to sleep through it than to constantly be screaming and passing out. The horses were nervous enough without all that racket.

We encountered two more small nests I easily dispatched before we came to a massive mess of webs. If the number and size of the webs across the road were any indication, there were a lot of them nearby. We paused to evaluate our options.

"We don't want all of them coming at us at once," Frederica said. "I'm just not sure how to do that."

"Maybe Bumstabber could scout out and see how many there are," I suggested.

His eyes narrowed and he thumbed the tip of his spear to check its sharpness. "I don't think so, runt."

My rear right cheek twitched as it remembered how sharp that spear was. I stepped away from him. I next glanced at Nutboy but he was busy snoring on the back of his horse. Since I couldn't ask the princess to do it, I sighed and said, "Okay, I'll go." Yeah, I know, it was the most logical choice since I was best equipped to get out of trouble, but still, the thought of venturing into a nest of giant spiders didn't appeal to me.

I slipped around the webs, being careful not to touch any of the sticky threads or make any vibrations that could summon my eight-legged friends. It grew difficult to tell how deep I was into the web maze and I couldn't see an end to it. With each web I passed, my heart beat faster. I was *not* in a good strategic location if they decided to attack. And my magic running socks wouldn't help me escape if I got stuck in a web.

A noise sounded from over in the trees. I stopped and looked at the source. I saw a smaller spider, only the size of a horse, wrapping something up. The victim looked human, and it wiggled as the spider spun sticky tendrils around them.

"Help!" came a muffled cry from inside the newly-spun cocoon.

Now I had a dilemma. Rescuing the poor soul could bring an army of giant spiders down on top of me. But could I let the spider kill that hapless person?

No. But how do I save him and not die in a like manner?

I grabbed the correct vial of components this time, stretched my hand forward, and said, *"Listl yats."* Yellow tendrils sprang from my fingers and wrapped around the spider, putting it into a glowing, yellow cocoon of its own. Once the spider was sufficiently trussed up, I went over to where it had dropped its victim and drew my short sword. I sliced my way into the thick material, trying not to cut the person inside. I soon had the torso exposed (without any blood, I'm happy to say), and continued with care until I had his face cleared.

A man, not much older than me, was inside. He had shoulder-length dark hair, rather large lips, and a clean-shaven face. Once he could see, he said, "Oh, thank you, kind sir. Thank you for saving me."

"My pleasure. Myrick is my name. Myrick the Magnificent."

He nodded. "My name is Jhik."

My brain staggered for a moment. I couldn't believe my ears. "Jhik, as in Jhik Maugger, the sackbut player for the Tumbling Rocks?"

He nodded. "In the flesh."

"No way! Can I have your autograph?"

Jhik stared past me and went even paler than he was before. "Uh, uh, uh. Spider!"

I smiled at him. "Don't worry about that. I have him wrapped up good and tight. I *am* a wizard, after all."

"No, no, no. Look!"

I humored him and turned around to examine my magically mummi-fied monster. I froze in place, unable to move for several seconds.

Don't ask me how, since I'd never seen it before, but the spider was working its way *out* of my binding spell. It had pushed off the individual strands and was now halfway out. And I had wrapped it extra well.

"Get me out of here!" Jhik begged.

I nodded and went to work freeing his legs. I wasn't as careful this time.

"Ow. Hurry, ow."

"Sorry." Finally, his legs came free but his arms were still wrapped up. I figured he didn't need those to run. I helped him up and we dashed into the maze of webs.

"Where to?" he asked.

"This way." I grabbed the fire spell components, uttered the incanta-tion, and sent a stream of fire forward into the webs, melting a path through them. "I know a shortcut." We took off toward my companions. I knew this might bring the whole spider army on us, but I wanted to get to a more defensible position before they reached me.

Sure enough, as we ran through the smoldering webs, several large, white shapes emerged from the surrounding trees. And yeah, there were more than five this time. *Way* more.

We emerged from the last web to where the others waited next to the horses. Nutboy lay on the ground at the side of the road. "Run!" I shouted.

Frederica and Bumstabber looked around and saw the activity in the trees. They both nodded and tried to grab their horses. The horses, seeing the army of spiders, panicked and pulled away. They galloped off before any of them could be mounted.

Heavy bodies approached from behind. Fortunately, I was ready with another fire spell. I spun around to see at least thirty spiders heading toward me. The smallest was still as big as a large dog. I sent my fire spray into them, roasting the closest few. After seven of them curled up into blackened husks, the rest backed away, heading toward the webs again. Once they were no longer charging, I turned and ran to where Frederica waited with ready spear. Bumstabber went to chase down the horses.

"Who is this?" Frederica asked, pointing at Jhik.

"This is none other than Jhik Maugger, the greatest sackbut player alive and member of the Tumbling Rocks."

He inclined his head. "Barely alive, but I am in your debt. Thank you for saving me back there." He turned to look toward the burning webs. "Oh, those spiders won't be happy about that."

I shook my head. "It breaks my heart to destroy all that hard work." The princess and I then commenced getting the rest of the sticky webs off of him.

As we did, Frederica asked Jhik, "What were you doing in there?"

Jhik shrugged, "Well, I had this brilliant idea of sneaking into the nearby village where the spiders took my friends. I thought I could rescue them."

I stopped working on the strand around his left arm. "No way. You mean the rest of the Tumbling Rocks are trapped nearby?"

He nodded. "Yeah, unfortunately. I had fallen behind the rest of the group when they reached the village we're supposed to play at tonight. Spiders ambushed them. I hid and waited for the monsters to leave and then foolishly tried to follow. I didn't see the one they left behind until too late."

"Do you have any idea how many there are?" Frederica asked.

"There were at least a hundred that abducted my group."

"Cabbage," I swore as I started rummaging through my pack to check on my spell vials.

"And we don't know if that is all of them." Frederica rubbed her chin as she thought.

I looked up from my pack. "Well, I have good news and bad news."

"What's the good news?" Jhik asked.

"Well, I found another vial of the spicy chicken seasoning."

"And the bad?"

I grimaced. "I only have one vial left of the fire spray spell."

Frederica turned toward me. "How many can that deal with?"

"Maybe thirty or so, at most."

"What about your binding spell?" she asked.

I looked at Jhik. "Well, they seem to have the ability to squirm out of it. It will slow them down for a bit, but we would have to act fast to take them all out."

"And you don't have any other useful spells?"

"No. As you saw, my projectile spell couldn't penetrate their thick hides."

Frederica shook her head. "It looks like Uchdehn may be right. We should go back to Fringolia and get an army."

"What about my friends?" Jhik asked, gesticulating toward the village. "We can't leave them. I'm sure those spiders will start eating them soon . . . if they haven't already." The blood drained from his face as he said it.

Bumstabber ran back toward us. He'd lost his spear, and his whole body quivered with fear.

"This can't be good," I muttered.

When he arrived, he gasped for air and looked back up the road, pointing. His mouth worked up and down but nothing came out except strangled noises.

"Speak up, Sergeant Uchdehn," Frederica ordered. "What is it?"

I had a pretty good guess but it was confirmed when Bumstabber stammered out, "Spi-sp-spiders!"

"How many?" she asked.

He just shook his head and put his arms out wide.

Frederica examined the area. "They're surrounding us. They see us as a threat."

"This doesn't make sense," I said. "How can spiders be that smart. I mean, they're *spiders*."

"Someone must be controlling them."

Jhik snapped his fingers. "I did see someone else with the spiders. I think. I didn't say anything because I wasn't sure, but I thought I saw a shadowy figure moving between them."

"What kind of shadowy figure?" I asked.

"Human-sized."

"Great. Probably a wizard or necromancer or something. Just what we need." I had fought a few wizards before and sometimes came out triumphant, but this guy was an unknown quantity. All I knew was that he would have to be pretty good at his craft to control that many giant spiders. "I wonder what he wants."

"What we need to do is figure out a way to escape," Frederica said.

I looked for a way out as well but didn't see anything. The road was surrounded by trees and hills on each side. The forest was thick enough that there was no way to see very far ahead to detect any threats. Our best option was to pick a direction into the forest and hope for the best. Or use what I had left of the fire spell components and blast our way back along the road. But if there were as many as Bumstabber's arms indicated, I wasn't sure if I could.

By this time, we could see the spiders coming up the road. Those huge boogers could move fast, too. And there had to be over a hundred. There was no way I had enough fire spell components left. I instead pulled out my binding spell and cast some of the yellow powder toward them. *"Listl yats!"* The tendrils emerged. The spell wrapped around all of them but they started squirming their way out immediately.

"This way!" Frederica barked. We followed her into the woods and away from the village as she carried Nutboy on her shoulder. I hoped the direction was safe but there was no way to tell.

The ground inclined steadily and we could see some cliffs up ahead through the trees. I kept looking above and around us for any spiders lurking about but we lucked out. We reached the cliff face and Frederica started climbing. There were enough hand and footholds for us to climb to a ledge fifteen yards up.

Once there, we all collapsed to the rock and tried to catch our breath. Except for Nutboy; he just moaned and turned over to his side after Frederica put him down.

Frederica climbed to her feet and unslung her spears. The spiders emerged from the forest, surrounding the base of the cliff. "Now would be a good time for you to think of something brilliant, Myrick."

I sighed. "I don't have enough fire spell left. And if I set the forest on fire, it will kill us too." Of course, burning to death might be better than getting eaten to death. I don't know why, but at that moment, my main regret was that I would die before I got my chance to perform with the Tumbling Rocks. Or learn how to play the recorder.

A thought struck me then: the infusing spell Chuggit taught me. Except, I needed an object to infuse the fire spell components into. I smiled when I thought of the perfect one.

I reached into my pack and pulled out the recorder.

Frederica watched me as I did it. "Myrick, I don't think this is the time."

"It's always the time for music." I pulled out the fire spell components and placed the vial alongside the recorder on the ground.

Now came the hard part, remembering the right incantation. This spell mostly used pure magic, but it still wouldn't work without the right word. Was it *"Esufin"* or *"Esufnoc"*? I picked one and went for it. I didn't have time to ponder since the spiders had reached the base of the cliff. I summoned my magic, aimed it at the components and the recorder, and intoned, *"Esufin."*

At first, all I felt was the magic draining rapidly from my socks. Too rapidly. I feared I'd used the wrong incantation until I saw the components from the vial disappear and the recorder start to glow. It worked, but would there be enough magic in my socks to complete the spell? Was I about to be left defenseless? What good would it be for me to succeed with the spell and then not have any magic left to defend us? I still may have doomed us all to spidery deaths.

The magic stopped flowing and the recorder dimmed to a soft glow, similar to the way my socks glowed but with a red tint to it. And I still had some magic remaining in my socks though not much. It didn't feel like enough. Maybe for only a couple of spells, at best.

"Are you okay, Myrick?" Frederica asked.

"Yeah, maybe, but I don't have much magic left." I picked up the recorder. It was a little warm to the touch.

"How does that work?"

"I assume I hold it and say the incantation." I put it in my left hand and located the closest group of spiders coming our way. *"Toups Eirf!"*

Nothing happened.

"I don't see nothin'," Bumstabber griped.

"Wh-wh-what's happening?" Nutboy asked, sitting up from his nap. He looked down at the spiders climbing up the rock wall. He shrieked. At least it was loud and high enough to cause the spiders to pause for a few seconds.

"Well, I have good news and bad news," I said. "The good news is, I still have some magic left. The bad news is, I have no idea how this thing works." I frowned at the recorder in my hand.

"I knew you was gonna be the death of me," Bumstabber said with a growl.

Jhik examined the recorder as well. "Maybe you have to use the recorder the way it was designed."

"You mean, play it?"

He nodded.

Bumstabber's head dropped. "I think I'd rather be kilt by spiders."

I ignored him and put the recorder to my lips. I tried a note.

A bolt of searing-hot fire erupted from the end, whizzing just past Bumstabber's ear. "Whoa!" I said.

Bumstabber grabbed his nearly-singed ear. "Ya almost killed me, runt! Watch where ya pointin' that thing."

"Sorry, not sorry." I stepped over to the cliff edge and pointed the recorder at the oncoming hoard. I played different notes with each one resulting in a bolt of fire and the death of one or more spiders. In addition to that, I didn't feel my magic socks draining. "Awesome!" I yelled before I started singing and playing my favorite song. You guessed it.

> I cannot achieve fulfillment
> I cannot achieve fulfillment
> No matter how much I try
> I cannot achieve, I cannot achieve
>
> As I sit down on a grassy hill
> To seek cosmic connection
> A noisy wagon rumbles by
> And I lose all my reflection
>
> I cannot achieve, oh no, hey it's so
> That's all I know
> I cannot achieve fulfillment
> I cannot achieve fulfillment
> No matter how much I try
> I cannot achieve, I cannot achieve
>
> I lock myself in a quiet room
> And try to feel the sky
> But what do my seeking ears?
> I'm locked up with a fly!
>
> I cannot achieve, oh no, hey it's so
> That's all I know
> I cannot achieve fulfillment
> I cannot achieve fulfillment
> No matter how much I try
> I cannot achieve, I cannot achieve

As I travel 'round the Kingdoms
Looking for souls to help
A peasant boy kicks my bum
And I yell at the little whelp

I would sing a line, play a riff in between, and sing the next line. I may have danced around as I did it, too. Before long, all the spiders were piled at the base of the cliff. They lay on their backs with their white, furry legs twitching in the air.

Once the last of them were down, Frederica put her hand on my shoulder. "You did it, Myrick!"

I smiled and nodded. "Yes, I did."

Jhik winced and shook his head. "That was the most, uh, interesting rendition I've ever heard of that song."

Wow! A musician of Jhik's level found my music interesting. I was definitely on the right career path.

Jhik examined the carnage below us. "Would it be possible for us to go rescue my friends, Myrick? Do you think your recorder will keep doing what it's doing?"

"Sure," I said, smiling. "And I have a whole bunch more songs to do it with."

Nutboy groaned. I won't repeat the words Bumstabber used. Artless morons.

We climbed back down the cliff and to the ground. A few of the spiders were still alive but either a toot from me or a good jab from Frederica's spear took care of them. We were soon back to the road and on the alert for more eight-legged monstrosities.

There were none in sight.

Nutboy glanced about, ready to bolt at the first sign of trouble. "Uh, maybe I should watch the road or something. Or maybe go back to our camp."

Frederica shook her head. "I wouldn't advise it. There could still be others hiding in these trees. You are safest staying with us."

Nutboy gulped but nodded. At least he wasn't passing out anymore.

I led the way onto the trail that Jhik told us led to the village where he believed the rest of the Tumbling Rocks and their entourage were being kept. We soon reached a clearing around an unwalled village. There were webs stretched between every building and we could see some of the spiders crawling around on roofs. And there were a lot.

"Well, Myrick, this is it. I have your back." Princess Frederica held spears in each hand and gently guided me forward with her elbow. For some reason, my legs didn't want to move.

A few spiders along the perimeter noticed us and came shambling forward. One verse of "Beneath My Big Toe" took care of them.

We made our way forward with me in front, Frederica with her two spears behind me, Nutboy and Jhik in the middle, and Bumstabber taking up the rear. Those other three looked as nervous as I felt, but at least I had *Myrick's Resplendent Recorder of Fiery Death* to protect me.

More spiders emerged. More died to the melody of "Big Toe". I left a few for Frederica to give the final death blow to so that she wouldn't feel left out because, well, I'm just that thoughtful of a guy.

Spiders came at us from everywhere as we entered the village. Nutboy, Jhik, and Bumstabber ended up crouching on the ground while Frederica and I circled them. We soon had piles of dead spiders spread out around us, making it seem like we stood in a hole.

The spiders finally quit coming. We'd killed only about twenty, so I knew there were more. With the piles of dead around us, though, I couldn't see anything.

Frederica muscled some of the smaller ones aside and made us an opening to squeeze through. I shuddered as I pushed through the spider bodies, even with them being dead. I had to do a little dance to work out all the squibblies I felt, too. I also craved a nice, hot bath.

In the webs stretching between the various buildings and cottages, we saw several bodies in cocoons. I feared we might find dead people in them, but we went to work cutting them down from the webs and opening up the cocoons. Everyone we found was still alive, thank goodness, but some of them were sleepy as if on a drug.

"Woodney!" Jhik yelled as he removed the webbing from the face of one of the victims.

"Hey, whoa man, what's happening?" Woodney asked. "Am I dead?"

"No," Jhik answered. "I found help and we came to rescue you."

I spun around from where I was helping another person out of their webs and shouted over to him, "Awesome, you found your drummer." So with at least me, Woodney, and Jhik, there were enough of us to reform the Tumbling Rocks. The show would go on!

"Hey, finish helping me, here," said the woman I'd been cutting free.

"Oh, sorry."

Once her arm came loose, she finished removing the sticky strands from her face. "So, Jhik is alive. Is that Woodney?"

"Yes." I looked at her for a moment. "Wait, you're Rita Kichards, the recorder player!"

She grimaced. "That's me."

"Awesome. I have some great ideas on how we can weave two-part contrapuntal lines into the existing repertoire."

She looked up at me with her green eyes. "And you are?"

I smiled at her like a proficient musician would. "I am Myrick, Myrick the Magnificent. Wizard, swordsman, scholar, and professional recorderist . . . uh, recordist? Recorder player!" I stuck out my hand to shake hers.

She looked at it and frowned as she stood. "Wonderful."

Once a few other villagers were freed, they helped us to quickly open the rest of the cocoons. And to our great relief, all six members of the Tumbling Rocks were found unhurt. Seven, if you counted me, of course.

A woman screamed.

I pulled out my trusty recorder and jogged toward the noise. I know, that sounds uncharacteristically brave of me, but I was the only one who possessed *Myrick's Resplendent Recorder of Fiery Death*. I soon saw what caused the village woman to scream. The entire village was surrounded by the giant, woolly, white spiders.

Except they just waited in the clearing, watching us. I tell you, there aren't many creepier things to look at, besides Bumstabber with his shirt off, than a circle of giant spiders staring at you with their multiple eyes.

"Myrick, what's going on?" Frederica asked as she came up behind me.

"I have no clue." I held my recorder close to my mouth in case they resumed their attack.

A few seconds later, a path opened up through them. A figure wearing a black robe with its face hooded emerged to stand before us. It didn't even appear to be walking. It just stood there, examining us with a face that couldn't be seen under the blackness of the hood.

As you know, I don't like long silences. "Uh, hi there. My name's Myrick. Myrick the Magnificent. Sorry about killing your spiders. They seemed kind of, a little, sort of threatening. And they were capturing people who didn't want to be captured. But I should warn you, I am a *very* powerful wizard and could destroy the rest of your spiders if I desired. So, if you want to keep the rest of your pets safe, I suggest you back off and go away."

The figure didn't react and remained silent.

Just in case, I recalled my magic defense shield spell and got my copper bracelet ready if the figure in black started slinging magic at us.

I tried again. "Um, you okay, there? Need a drink of water or anything? I'm planning on cooking some chicken here in a bit if you're hungry. You're welcome to have some with us." I gave the hooded figure the best smile I could summon at the moment, which wasn't very good, I'm afraid.

Still, our friend in black hadn't made any other move. It seemed like they were evaluating us. Evaluating me.

As I tried to think of something else to draw them out into conversation, Frederica stepped forward, drawing her mace from her hip. "Speak before I beat it out of you!"

The spiders parted again and the figure drifted back through them. OFIB (for Our Friend in Black) didn't even turn around but kept their hooded face toward us the whole time. The path closed as soon as OFIB was out of sight.

"What was that all about?" Frederica asked me. "Is this some kind of strange wizard ritual?"

I shook my head. "I don't know what this is. At least the spiders aren't attacking. Yet."

They must have been listening because, at that moment, they rushed forward as one.

"Everybody, to the middle of the village!" Frederica shouted. "Grab weapons if you have them."

I put the recorder to my lips and started playing "Leapin' Lizard Flash" as I backed into the village again. I don't know how many spiders died from my deadly notes but they kept coming and coming. Before I realized it, Frederica stopped me from falling backward into the nonfunctioning central fountain.

"This is where we make our stand," she said. She leaped forward between two buildings and stabbed her spears at the spiders as they came. Other villagers with spears, swords, and pitchforks defended the other openings.

I climbed on top of a nearby platform to get a better view. Several other people were already huddled there, along with most of the members of the Tumbling Rocks. I went to work playing every song I could think of: "I Cannot Achieve Fulfillment", "Beneath My Big Toe", "Leapin' Lizard Flash", and "Begin My Ascension". After a while, I got to the point where I tooted whatever note I could. The spiders just kept coming.

I focused my attention on where the spiders were about to overwhelm the defenders. Soon, bodies built up between the buildings, forming barricades that slowed the spiders down. I also took out any spiders who cheated by climbing over the buildings. So far, we were holding our own, but it was only because of my magic recorder. How much magic did it have? What would I do if it ran out? All I could think of was to have my binding spell components ready.

It seemed like years before the number of attackers subsided and finally stopped. Due to the exhaustion that penetrated my bones, I had given up dancing. I tooted one final triumphant G-flat and sent the last spider to its creepy demise. Since I didn't see any other enemy coming, I sank to my knees to catch my breath.

As I tried to get my strength back, an eerie, high-pitched voice sounded. *"You win this time, Myrick."*

I climbed to my feet, looking around for OFIB but there was no sign of the dark figure. Only tired, frightened people and lots and lots and lots of dead spiders were around.

I later learned the platform I stood on was a temporary stage the villagers had erected for the Tumbling Rocks performance. The troubadours didn't do their scheduled concert and instead, we all pitched in to clean up the village. Fortunately, all the spiders appeared to be either dead or gone. We didn't have that triumphant dinner with the spicy chicken, either.

Two days later, once the village and the troubadours had recovered, the Tumbling Rocks prepared for their concert. I went up to Jhik as they started toward the stage. "Hey, I would love to sit in with you guys."

Rita stood nearby and frowned. "You haven't practiced our set with us."

"But you've heard me play. I performed every one of your songs I could think of while I was destroying the spiders. I know a lot of your songs already."

"Oh, is that what those were? No, thank you, we'll do just fine." She turned her back on me and climbed onto the stage.

"That was rude," I muttered.

I turned and said to Jhik, "But I also have this awesome magic recorder. You should see what I can do with it."

"We've seen what you can do," Jhik said. "And we're very grateful and all, but . . ."

The truth finally occurred to me. "Oh, I get it." I nodded. I then said in a softer voice, "You don't want me showing up the rest of the band with my superior musical skills. And it probably wouldn't be good for Rita's self-esteem if I out-played her on the recorder."

Jhik's jaw worked for a second before he nodded and said, "Uh . . . yeah, that's it. I'm afraid you're just too good for us, Myrick."

I sighed. "I understand. Maybe it would be best if I just formed my own group to demonstrate my incredible skills. Have a great concert."

"Thanks, Myrick." He turned and joined the rest of the group on the stage.

Despite me not playing, it turned out to be an awesome concert.

Don't look at me like that. I didn't lie. I *did* perform on stage with the Tumbling Rocks. It's just that none of the rest of them were playing at the time. Sheesh.

The Cave and the Lyre

DJ Tyrer

It was said that there were really only two seasons in Tarovia—mud and summer. It was summer and although Bradsin loathed the dust tossed up by the wheels of the convoy of carriages and carts as it bounced its way along the rutted dirt highway and the clouds of fat flies that swarmed about the horses' rear-ends, it was better than the wet and the cold of the alternative.

A cry went up and the convoy moved off the track to cluster about one of the shrinking ponds that remained amongst the undulating hills. Men jumped down and began to raise tents, which would shield them from the oppressive glare of the sun. Bradsin slipped down from the carriage, glad to be able to stretch his legs.

"A song," called Merrienne as one of her handmaidens assisted her down from her own carriage.

"Milady," he said with a nod. If the princess required song, she would have it.

Bradsin reached for the lyre that lay in a case on the floor of his carriage and unboxed it. He checked the strings, then strummed it and began to sing.

Merrienne held a tiny white dog tight to her bosom as she gazed about with an air of boredom and slight irritation. The princess was the reason for their journey: To ensure good relations with the neighbouring country of Bezov, she was to marry its new king. In Bradsin's estimation, she was not very keen on the prospect of the union. But, then, if the rumours of King Warra's gluttony were true, he supposed he was not quite the charming prince she might have dreamt of.

"Walk with me," she said. Merrienne always complained that the noise of the men getting their camp ready gave her a headache, which only made a long journey seem longer. Whilst they worked, she would seek to put herself some distance from them. It was his duty to soothe her with his music and song.

Slowly, they made their way to the edge of the camp and a little way into the wooded hills beyond, a handmaiden trailing after them. He was never quite certain which ones were which.

The dog began to wriggle in the princess's arms.

"Do you need to relieve yourself, do you?" Merrienne cooed as if to a baby. "Very well."

The princess set the dog down beside a tree and told it, "Don't stray."

Bradsin almost laughed when, immediately, the dog did just that. It took a sniff of the air and hurried off into the woods.

Merrienne gave a shriek. "Come back!"

Then, she turned to Bradsin and her handmaiden. "Well, don't just stand there, fetch Lolo."

Bradsin sighed and slung his lyre over his shoulder and set off into the woods, the princess just behind him. He could hear the dog making high-pitched excited sounds as it explored, chasing who-knew-what scent through the trees.

This isn't my job, he wanted to say, but, of course, it was. His job was to do whatever the princess told him to. He supposed he couldn't really complain; he was paid well enough.

There was a sudden yelp from somewhere ahead of them and the sound of panicked crashing through undergrowth.

"Oh, Lolo!" exclaimed the princess.

"Probably a wolverine," said Bradsin. "Vicious beggars."

"Oh, no! You have to save him."

He sighed and began to jog in the direction from which the sounds had come. "Yes, milady."

The ground was steeper here, rockier. He was puffing.

Glancing back, he saw Merrienne was close behind. He was a little surprised. For someone in long skirts and used to a life of pampering, she was really rather spry. Her handmaiden, in contrast, was trailing further and further behind. He could imagine there were many men in the kingdom who had dreamt of just such an opportunity of getting the princess away from her attendants, and, had he shared their inclinations, he might have relished it.

"Here, Lolo," he called. "Here, girl."

Rounding a tree, he stumbled to a halt and let out a curse that surely offended the ears of any gods who were listening and would earn him some time in theThird Hell upon his death—a possibility that seemed suddenly quite imminent.

He fumbled for the knife on his belt, wishing it were a sword and that he had a squad of guards near to hand.

"What is it?" called the princess. "It's not a wolf, is if? Is Lolo—"

She fell silent as she, too, rounded the tree and saw the band of half-a-dozen goblins that stood before them on bandy legs, the product of lives spent riding shaggy steppe ponies. Although they were squat beings with thin limbs, their appearance was deceptive, for they were said to each possess the strength of three grown men. Bradsin didn't know if that were an exaggeration, but he did know they could use their long serrated knives with deadly skill.

They grinned horribly.

The princess said something almost as indecorous as he had and he snapped out of his shock at the words.

"Run!" he shouted. Then, he added, "Goblins!" for the benefit of the handmaiden who had yet to see what faced them.

Bradsin and Merrienne turned and began to sprint.

The goblins were just behind them. Despite their awkward-looking gait, they were swift and easily covered the distance.

They were also smart. Had they not been, no amount of strength would have prevented the men of Tarovia from defeating them. But, they were masters of the swift raid, parting shots and ambushes, always one step ahead of the plodding armies of men, and he realised they were employing the same skills now, herding them as they ran.

Bradsin didn't know where the handmaiden had got to—he prayed to all the gods he could think of that she'd escaped back to camp and was raising the alarm—but, he did know they would soon be captured, or worse, if they didn't do something.

The problem was, he didn't know what.

"Lolo!" Merrienne cried, darting sideways between some rocks.

Typical! Here they were about to be seized by goblins and she was still thinking about that damn ball of fluff. With a curse he followed her.

Perhaps, if they were lucky, the random change of direction would confuse their pursuers.

He heard the princess shriek ahead of him and, as he rounded a rock, he too gave a cry of surprise as the ground disappeared from beneath his feet and he tumbled his way down into a gravelly ravine.

"Curses," spat Merrienne as she stood, "my dress is ruined."

"I doubt that tumble did my lyre much good, either, princess, but we can be glad we didn't break our necks and haven't yet been trussed up as slaves for the goblins."

He looked about them. "This way, I think."

She shook her head. "No, Lolo went this way."

"Forget the dog. We need to get back to the safety of the camp. She'll find her way back, I'm sure."

"I'm not leaving without Lolo. Look, there she is."

He didn't see he had much choice but to follow her. If anything happened to her and he had done nothing . . . her father would be far from forgiving.

How he hated the little dog!

"Grab her and let's get out of here. Those goblins might not have wanted to risk their necks throwing themselves down that slope after us, but they will surely find a way down and soon."

"Here, Lolo, come to mummy! Look, she's going into that cave."

"I am not going into a cave," he said, with all the firmness he could muster. "There could be a bear in there, or worse."

That was the wrong thing to say. Her hands flew to her mouth, smothering another cry as she bolted for the dark entrance.

"Just call for her to come out. Oh, come on, we don't have torches, we'll break our necks or get lost . . ."

"It's not too dark."

"It's not too dark . . . oh, my!"

It was true. Thanks to the occasional hole in the cave ceiling, shafts of light stabbed through the darkness, helping to illuminate the interior just enough for them to see where they were going and avoid concussing themselves on stalactites or tripping over stalagmites.

"She went down here," Merrienne said, taking a side-tunnel. The dog's startled yip echoed back toward them.

There was a sudden rumbling sound that made him duck his head.

"Careful, milady, the ceiling is collapsing!"

"Lolo!" She darted forward.

Infuriated, he lunged after her, grabbing hold of her arms with every intention of dragging her back to safety, regardless of the breach of royal protocol. Instead, he froze.

Before them, a huge reptilian head had risen from the floor of the cave to gaze down with rheumy eyes at the small white dog, which was trembling before it. The head was attached to a long, serpent-like body from which protruded four spindly legs ending in clawed feet. There was no doubt in his mind that this was a dragon of some kind.

He, the princess and the dog all stared at it, frozen in fear.

The dragon looked down at the dog and began to open its jaws.

"Do something," hissed Merrienne.

"What? I'm not a warrior."

"Play!"

"Play?"

"Play. Your music soothes me when my head hurts, maybe it can soothe this beast."

"I don't know I'm . . . oh, very well . . ." He unslung his lyre and began to play, crooning soft words like a lullaby, the sound of the strings echoing about them in an ethereal manner.

The dragon shut its jaws and lowered its head. Bradsin said a silent prayer of thanks and continued to play.

"Here, Lolo," the princess called softly, and the dog hurried over to her and jumped willingly back into her arms.

"This way," she hissed, and he began to follow her out of the dragon's cave, always playing.

Then, she halted and he heard her curse. From behind them came the sound of goblins. They were trapped.

He looked desperately about, then saw where a wide and lumpy stalagmite sat just below one of the openings in the cave ceiling. It looked like it might just be big enough for them to fit through.

He gestured Merrienne toward it, whilst he continued to play, and nodded up at the hole. She gave a grin of understanding and began to climb.

Once she was through, he stumbled awkwardly onto the stalagmite, not daring to stop playing for a moment, then looked up at the hole. Merrienne and Lolo were both looking down at him through it. The princess reached down with her arms for him. The problem was, he didn't think his lyre was going to fit through the gap without catching.

The sound of the goblins was close, now. There was almost no time left.

"Over here, you horrible things," he shouted. He didn't know if they would understand the words, but he knew they would come running regardless.

The dragon looked up at him, confused.

"Sorry," he said, "the show's over."

He threw the lyre at its head, then leapt up to seize the princess's hands, praying she was stronger than she looked. The dragon gave an angry roar just as the goblins burst into the cavern with enraged cries of their own.

Merrienne heaved him up enough that he was able to grasp the edge of the hole and, with her help, pull himself through.

Beneath his feet, he felt a rush of heat, and he heard the goblins shrieking. He doubted whether any would survive in the confined space. They just had to hope the dragon wouldn't come in search of them before they could leave the area.

"Your lyre," gasped the princess as Lolo licked at his face. He patted the dog.

"You can buy me another one," he said, standing and shaking himself. Yes, he was alive. "Besides, I think it was out of tune after our tumble."

Merrienne laughed. "Good, I shall; because, in the stories, heroes who rescue princesses usually expect a specific reward, and I don't think my father and my betrothed would be very happy about it."

Bradsin laughed. "Don't worry, you're really not my type. But, speaking of which, here come some brave warriors to escort us back to camp."

Clearly, the handmaiden had escaped to summon them.

"What in all the Hells was that unearthly sound?" called the captain of the princess's guard as he and a band of his men approached.

"A dragon," said Bradsin.

"No, don't scoff," said the princess, "he tells it truly. First, goblins, then a dragon—what a day! But, loyal Bradsin here saved me and helped me rescue Lolo." She bent her head to kiss the dog's nose. "But, I don't think we should dally. We should move camp just in case the dragon comes looking for us, or more goblins are about."

Merrienne shook her head. "Who would ever have thought that a wedding procession could prove such an adventure?"

"Not me," said Bradsin. "What about you, Lolo?"

The dog yipped.

"I'll take that as a 'yes'," he said with a chuckle.

Merrienne laughed, then commanded, "Let's go."

Milo Piper's Breakout Single that Ended the Rat War

David Hankins

Lieutenant Milo Piper sat in a torched donut shop that smelled of caramelized sugar and ash. Kinda like his mom's kitchen. He'd been sent on a supply run, but shamming was a time-honored Army tradition. He wasn't expected back for hours. Over-ear headphones and laptop blocked the howling winds of Chicago's abandoned Exclusion Zone as Milo mixed tracks on his breakout single, "The Warrior's Anthem."

This song would get him discovered. He *knew* it. Milo had only joined the Army Reserves to pay for college. He wasn't cut out for soldiering. He was a musician. But then the Rat War had broken out in Chicago and he was activated. Writing music was limited to stolen moments like these.

Milo's head bobbed in time with the beat, lost in his music, fingers absently playing chords on the ash-coated countertop. The chorus rang in his ears.

Fight for what's right and your song will live on. Oh, your song will live on.

Milo was snapped back to reality when a snarling brown rat with a hunting knife leapt onto the counter. The muscle-bound beast was the size of a terrier. Milo shrieked and threw himself back. His headphones yanked free of the laptop.

A screaming guitar solo filled the ruined donut shop. Two smaller rats, a white and a gray, bounded across the checkered tile floor with sheathed knives on their backs. The massive rat on the counter crouched to leap and then . . . stopped. Its murderous snarl faded and the others stopped running.

Milo froze, heart racing. The rats never stopped. Idiot scientists had seen to that. They'd tested neural implants on lab rats who then organized, escaped, started a war, and renamed Chicago 'Ratatopia.' They'd been unstoppable ever since.

The big rat sat on its haunches, twisted its neck from side to side with little *pop* sounds, then spoke in a thick cockney accent. "Hey mate, you gotta cigarette? I'm jonesing something fierce!"

Milo's eyes flicked from the rat's earnest expression to its knife. "No," he said slowly. "Don't smoke."

"Bloody hell," it muttered and sheathed the knife on its back.

"Bruiser, language!" the white rat snapped in a cultured soprano.

"Sorry, Princess."

Milo shuffled back as Princess and the gray rat approached. He wished he hadn't left his rifle in the Humvee. If he could keep them talking, perhaps he could escape. "Look, I don't want any trouble."

Princess leapt onto the counter and sniffed at his laptop. "What are you broadcasting?"

"Nothing. It's just my music." Milo bumped a metal chair in his slow retreat. It scraped the tile and he froze, but the rats didn't appear to notice.

Princess cocked her head, whiskers twitching. "Something is disrupting Alpha's signal, so it must be the music. I didn't think anything could do that." She turned beady black eyes on Milo as he settled his headphones around his neck. "We need your help."

"Who's Alpha and what signal?" Could he reach the Humvee before they caught him?

"My brother," Princess said, snarling. "His subsonic broadband signal controls our neurotransmitters. Makes us killers. With your music to disrupt his signal, we can stop Alpha."

That got Milo's attention. He stopped edging away. "You can end the Rat War?"

"*We* can. You'll have to carry the laptop."

Milo's mind spun as his recorded guitar solo led into a reprise. He wasn't a fighter, but he *did* want to end the war. No war meant no activated Reserves and he'd be free to chase his dreams. To write music.

Could he trust a rat?

For the chance to end the war? Absolutely.

"I'm in." Milo extended a hand. "Milo Piper."

"Charmed," she said and gripped his fingers in her paws. "I'm Princess. You've met Bruiser" --the muscle-bound brown flicked a cocky salute-- "and this is DJ." The scrawny gray rat beside her was missing one eye. He had a feral look about him.

Milo nodded. "Nice to meet you. Let's go end a war."

IN THE HUMVEE, MILO SET HIS LAPTOP TO CYCLE THROUGH HIS PLAYLIST before dropping it on the passenger seat. If music disrupted Alpha's signal, then music he'd play. Classic rock by Def Leppard made him smile as the rats climbed in. He'd written "The Warrior's Anthem" in the style of the old rock ballads.

"Rockin' tunes, mate!" Bruiser said. He jumped onto the gunner's platform between the seats and played air guitar. Milo's rifle lay on the platform, but Bruiser danced around it.

DJ sneered from atop the passenger's seat. "Give me poetry, spoken in rap, not this"—he waved a disgusted paw—"crap." He dropped to the seat and tapped at Milo's laptop, scanning his playlist.

"Hey!" Milo said but DJ just flipped his middle claw and perused. Princess climbed onto the military radio mounted on the dash and made an impatient 'let's go' gesture. Milo pursed his lips, threw the vehicle into gear, and tore out of the parking lot. "Where to?" he asked, heading toward downtown.

"The Willis Tower. Alpha tapped into the radio antennae on the roof to broadcast his subsonic signal," Princess said.

Milo turned onto a main thoroughfare and punched the gas. "How'd he do that? No offense, but rats aren't known for their skills at electronics."

Princess bared her teeth and hissed. "Humans are blind. We were intelligent *before* the neural implants. Alpha and I were in the same lab. He studied implant technology and learned how to use it for control. To bend his fellow rats to his will."

The venom in her voice sent shivers down Milo's spine. "Were you all in the same lab?"

"No lab for this rat," DJ piped in, single eye still glued to the playlist as his claw flicked the touchscreen. "I ain't down with that. Stolen from the street and chipped against my will. I struggle through this life. I wasn't born to kill."

Bruiser turned his air guitar into a drum solo on the edge of DJ's seat. "I was on special loan from McCartney Labs in London. Bloody scientists needed a rat hopped up on a lifetime o' steroids and nicotine to test their chip. I turned out bloody brilliant. Better than the rest o' this lot." Princess muttered about language and DJ snapped at Bruiser's drumming paws. The street rat missed as Bruiser resumed his energetic air guitar during the song's bridge.

The music abruptly changed, heavy bass and electric guitar replaced by angry gangster rap. Milo had forgotten he even had DMX songs. "Oi!" Bruiser said, dropping to all fours. "I liked that one! Change it back." DJ gave him the middle claw and Bruiser leapt at the scrawny rat with a snarl that made the hair on Milo's neck stand on end. They tumbled into a hissing, biting brawl on top of the computer.

"Hey. Hey!" Milo yelled, trying to grab the laptop as he drove. He almost got it but snatched his hand back when DJ bit at him. Bruiser used the distraction to grab DJ in a suplex and slam him into the keyboard.

The music went silent.

Milo's gaze snapped to Princess. She twitched then snarled and drew her hunting knife. DJ and Bruiser stopped fighting and did the same.

Crap.

Milo slammed on the brakes and spun the wheel hard to the left. The rats and his rifle tumbled into the passenger floorboard as the Humvee rocked to a halt. Milo grabbed his laptop and threw himself out of the Humvee.

His elbow hit the pavement first. Pain flashed up his arm and numb fingers dropped the computer. All three rats appeared in the open door-way, programmed murder in their eyes. Milo scrabbled back, heart racing.

He hit the curb and jumped to his feet. The rats climbed out and stalked past his silent computer on their hind legs, knives held like broadswords.

Milo turned and ran.

They'd stopped near a crumbling strip mall and he bolted for a pawn shop. It wasn't the closest store, but he couldn't make himself hide in the lingerie shop that was nearer. He'd never even been *in* one of those.

He hit the unlocked glass door at speed and popped it open. He spun and slammed it shut just as the rats reached it, bounding toward him with the knives in their teeth like furry pirates. Milo flipped the lock and stepped back, trying to catch his breath.

Bruiser sheathed his knife and grabbed a chunk of broken cement. Steroid-fueled muscles bulged and he heaved. The glass door shattered. Milo backed away and looked frantically at the piles of random crap. Skis, radios, jewelry . . .

Radios.

Milo leapt for the shelf and grabbed a radio boombox. He flipped the power switch and cranked the volume.

Nothing. No batteries.

He grabbed another, glancing over his shoulder. The rats weren't running now. They stalked forward, separating to surround their prey. Milo flipped the radio over. It was an old survival model with a crank handle on the back. He tuned it to the only station still broadcasting around here and spun the handle as fast as he could.

Low static rose as power built inside the radio. Milo cranked harder, found the volume knob, and flicked it all the way up.

Country twang filled the pawnshop.

The rats stopped.

"Bloody hell!" Bruiser yelled, spinning on DJ. "Look at the mess you made. We almost killed our pet human!"

Wait, what? Pet human?

DJ snarled. "The fault is yours, you muscle-bound freak. Speak more lies and I'll cut you deep." He brandished his knife.

Princess smacked DJ on the head and grabbed Bruiser by the throat, yanking him down to her eye level. "Stop this, both of you!"

"Why should I?" Bruiser pointed his knife at DJ. "He started it!"

Milo slapped the checkout counter with a crack, getting their attention. "Because we'll all die if we don't work together!" The rats cocked their heads at him. Milo knelt and set the radio on the floor. "Alpha is the enemy. He made you killers. Channel your rage at him, not each other."

Whiskers twitched as the rats eyed each other before they nodded and separated. A growl rumbled from Bruiser. "I ain't listening to DJ's crap music and I *definitely* ain't listening to *that*." He pointed a derisive claw at the emergency radio as the singer drowned his sorrows in whiskey.

Milo shrugged. "Too bad. All the stations out of Chicago went dark when the Army cut the city's power. This is the only one from outside the area that reaches this far."

"Then we'll listen to your laptop."

Milo shook his head. "I've been thinking about that. High volume uses too much battery power. We need to conserve that for our trip into the Willis. In fact . . ." He scanned the electronics shelf and snatched a wireless speaker that looked like a miniature '80s boombox. That would come in handy. "Come on, let's go," he said, heading for the door.

BACK AT THE HUMVEE, MILO RETRIEVED HIS LAPTOP AND SET IT BACK ON the passenger seat. Bruiser followed with the small emergency radio, a pained grimace on his face at the blaring country music.

"Why do I gotta carry this thing?" he said.

Princess, who'd made him take it, answered. "To keep you out of trouble. Crank it again, the battery's dying."

Bruiser grumbled but obeyed, climbing inside and setting it on the gunner's platform to work the crank with both forepaws.

Once everyone was back in the Humvee, Milo eyed DJ. He needed something to keep the street rat occupied and not taunting Bruiser.

"DJ, you know music, right?"

The scarred rat nodded.

"Great. I've been mixing a new song and I'd love your input." He tapped a few keys and brought up his mixing program. "You can use my headphones."

"That's not fair!" Bruiser yelled, working the crank.

DJ threw a furry grin at the big rat as Milo hooked up the headphones. They were too big for DJ, but he rested his head against the ear cup and was soon lost in the music, tail twitching in time with the beat.

They drove in relative silence, everyone else trying to ignore the country music that filled the Humvee. Bruiser was nearing tears but kept cranking the handle.

Milo drummed his fingers on the steering wheel, weaving around debris and abandoned vehicles. "So, Princess, what'll you do once the war is over?"

Her ear twitched. "I will return to a lab if they'll have me. Not for animal testing, I hated that, but there's joy in science. I would discover the wonders of the universe as an equal partner with the human scientists." She glanced over and caught Milo's arched eyebrow of disbelief.

She shrugged, her fur rippling across her shoulders. "Perhaps it's a lofty dream, but it's mine. What about you? Will you stay in the Army?"

Milo drew a deep breath and blew it out. "No. I never should have joined. It was a concession to my family so I'd have 'marketable skills' as I pursued music. My dad still wasn't happy with me. Wanted me to be a plumber and take over the Piper family business. I'd rather have a guitar in my hands than a wrench. Music is my life."

They fell into companionable silence and Milo considered the rats. They were a strange band; a 'mischief' he remembered a group of rats was called. They fought like, well, rats, but that reminded him more of family squabbles than anything. Army propaganda said rats were evil murderous beasts to be put down for their own good. Solve the rat problem through extermination.

Attempts at genocide wouldn't solve anything, especially now that the rats had proven their sentience. The war would just become an ugly urban brawl between species, and Milo wasn't entirely convinced that humanity would win that kind of war.

The problem was Alpha and his signal. If the rats were free, they'd have a chance to determine their own fate. Work with humanity instead of fighting them.

A blocked bridge ahead focused Milo's attention. Overturned cars and piled trash filled half the road; a fire truck on its side blocked the other half. "Um, Princess? Which way should I go?"

Her tail twitched. "This is the edge of Ratatopia, the rat-controlled heart of Chicago. The only way around is through."

"Excuse me?"

"She means floor it, ya plonker!" Bruiser yelled. He leapt from the emergency radio and pushed down past Milo's legs. Fifteen pounds of furry muscle slammed into Milo's right foot, throwing the accelerator to the floor.

The Humvee jumped forward.

"Whoa! What are you doing?" Milo clutched the steering wheel and kicked at the rat. Bruiser bit him just above his boot. "Ow!" He kicked some more but had to focus on the road as Bruiser lay on the gas pedal.

Princess leapt to the passenger window and pulled the lever, dropping it open. "Milo, open your window. DJ, that radio's dying again. We need music. Full volume! Let them hear it." She clambered to the other doors, dropping their windows as DJ yanked the headphones free. "The Warrior's Anthem" drowned the fading country music and reverberated through the vehicle. The scrawny rat had connected that wireless speaker.

Milo clenched his jaw as they bore down on the roadblock. Rats scurried across it, pointing bladed weapons in defiance. He cursed when he saw the barrel of a captured .50cal machine gun poking through the fire truck's missing windshield.

Flame burst from the .50cal with a deep *whump-whump-whump*. Tracers flew haphazardly as the gun's recoil overwhelmed the small rat gunners. One round shattered the driver's windshield, covering Milo in glass. He screamed, aimed between two cars, and smashed into the roadblock.

He didn't break through.

Screeching metal tore at Milo's ears and his forehead rebounded off the steering wheel as they crashed to a stop.

Debris and armed rats fell through the open window and into Milo's lap. He panicked and shrieked like an old lady who's seen a mouse in the kitchen.

Milo flung dazed rats out the window as fast as he could grab them.

"Stop! Milo, Stop!"

Milo froze, a struggling white rat in hand, and stared wide-eyed at Princess. Her empty forepaws were held out, beseeching. She scrambled off the military radio and guided Milo's hand to set the rat on the gunner's deck. Milo drew deep breaths, forcing himself to calm down.

"Mother?" Princess caressed the other rat's fur. The elderly white rat was plump. Scraggly gray tufts dominated the tops of her ears, brows, and chin.

DJ and Bruiser climbed up from the floorboard, saw the old rat, and prostrated themselves. Milo glanced at the rats outside the Humvee. One by one and then in rows they bowed as well. Milo turned a confused expression toward Princess. She gestured to the old rat.

"Lieutenant Milo Piper, this is Loretta, Queen Mother to Alpha and me."

Milo inclined his head. There wasn't much else he could do. "Pleased to meet you, uh, your majesty. How is it that the Queen Mother is pulling perimeter guard duty?"

Loretta snarled and rose on her haunches, stiff and regal. "I challenged Alpha's megalomania and my *darling* son linked my chip with the common rats receiving his signal. Sent me to protect his Ratatopia."

"So his signal doesn't affect all chipped rats?"

"Only those he selects. He rewards his sycophants with freedom. All others are fodder for his war on humanity. Even his mother." Loretta turned to Princess. "How are we free? What changed?"

Princess gestured toward the mini boombox speaker. "Music is the key. It disrupts the signal's reception in our chips."

Milo added, "But the second the music stops, you revert." *That* thought sent shivers down his spine. It was bad enough with three rats. He was surrounded now by an army of potential little murderers. He drew a deep breath. "We're going to the Willis Tower to stop Alpha. End the war."

A menacing smile spread across Loretta's furry face. "Then we shall escort you. It's time I had a word with my son."

Milo felt like the pied piper as he led the procession of rats down Chicago's empty streets. Princess and Loretta rode on his shoulders and he held his laptop open before him. He'd left his rifle in the Humvee. Bullets hadn't won the war yet. Time to give music a chance.

Bruiser marched beside him, portable speaker held high in both paws. He and DJ had almost come to blows again over music selection for their grand entrance. Milo had ended the argument by putting his playlist on shuffle. He had a little bit of everything.

Wagner's "Ride of the Valkyries" seemed a fitting song to start with.

Downtown Chicago was pristine. Milo had visited as a child when his mother took him to a summer concert series. That was when he fell in love with music. At the time, he'd thought the city had a comfortable, lived-in feel. Clean thoroughfares with the dirt and grime swept into the alleyways.

Not so in Ratatopia. The dirt was gone. Alpha's rats had been busy since capturing Chicago's heart, cleaning the city more thoroughly than the human residents ever had. It even smelled cleaner. As Milo and his entourage approached the Willis Tower he saw a wrecker, driven by rats, towing away an abandoned vehicle.

The tower's lobby was brightly lit and filled with comfortable couches and eating nooks. He glanced at Princess and pointed toward the lights. "I thought the Army killed Chicago's power months ago?"

"They did," she said. "Alpha truly is a genius. He rerouted every backup generator in the city to power the Willis, but only uses the electricity he needs. With solar panels to augment the generators, he can power this building almost indefinitely."

Milo glanced around. "If he's worked so hard to make the Willis his fortress, where are the guards?"

Princess shrugged. "He hasn't needed them, since no rat has broken his programming before. Any guards he has will be with him on the Skydeck."

They climbed a broad expanse of steps and Princess directed Milo through a museum of Chicago as it had been before the Rat War. The dim halls felt ominous with the interactive displays shut down. An ugly band of street rats stood guard outside the elevator.

Milo expected a fight, but the guards took one look at the mischief of rats carpeting the hall behind him and abandoned their posts, scurrying away. That made Milo smile. But then he considered the elevator and his smile dropped. "I don't think we'll all fit in there."

Princess snorted. "Rats are comfortable in tight spaces. We'll fit." She leapt from his shoulder, hit the elevator call button, then scrambled back up to her perch.

But Milo didn't *want* to be in an elevator with hundreds of rats. He'd never suffered from claustrophobia or musophobia—the fear of rats— but his stomach flipped at the thought of being trapped, one moment of silence away from a grizzly murder.

The elevator dinged, opened, and Milo forced himself to step in. Rats poured in after him, piling on top of each other in a writhing mass that reached past Milo's knees. A writhing mass of fur, claws, and teeth. And knives. Mustn't forget the knives. Milo's breath came faster and faster.

"Peace, warrior," Loretta said into his ear. "You are safe."

Milo wasn't so confident. Their ascent to the 103rd floor was the most nerve-wracking ride of his life. The elevator was bigger than he'd expected and he focused on the large display counting up to their destination. Tiny claws gripped his uniform's legs, pulling at him, and Milo felt a small whimper escape.

The music kept him safe.

He looked at Bruiser, who was mostly buried but held the speaker high and proud. "Ride of the Valkyries" was replaced by classic AC/DC and the big rat whooped in joy, waving the speaker in time with the beat. Tiny paws lifted from the elevator mosh pit with chitters and hisses as the rat army pumped itself up for battle. The screen above the door finally reached 103. The Skydeck.

The door chimed open and the rats poured out in a screeching, angry mob. The Willis's top floor was mostly open and surrounded by windows. A mass of cables and wires dangled from the room's ceiling, leading to an elevated faraday cage made of chain-link fencing. Folding tables lined the cage, piled high with electronics, monitors, and computers. The nerve center of Alpha's Ratatopia.

"That's . . . new," Princess said, indicating the cage that her army of rats surged toward. "Alpha's paranoia has grown."

Lab-coated humans hunched over the computers, watching the approaching rodents with fearful eyes. Milo realized that these were prisoners. Scientists forced to help Alpha.

A squad of guard rats, each almost as big as Bruiser, turned tail like their counterparts downstairs and ran for the faraday cage. They jumped inside, swung the door shut, and one slapped a large red button.

Electricity crackled in the air and Milo's hair stood on end.

"Stop!" he yelled, but the charging horde didn't hear him. They threw themselves at the cage in their battle fury. Crackles filled the air and the lights dimmed. Electricity arced from the cage, blowing some rats back and cooking others on the spot, their dead bodies sizzling on the wire.

A smell like burned bacon filled the room. Milo's gorge rose, but he forced it down.

The remaining rats pulled back. They circled the cage, knives out, screeching for Alpha to come out and fight.

A fat white rat rose from behind a laptop and waddled to the edge of a table. "What is the meaning of this? How are you ignoring my signal?"

Princess answered from Milo's shoulder. "Music. We are no longer your slaves."

"Impossible!"

One of the seated scientists pumped a fist in the air. "Yes! It worked!"

Alpha rounded on him. "*You* changed my signal?"

The man's eyes bulged. "No! It was already flawed. I found the flaw, but I wouldn't . . . please . . . no . . ."

The fat rat gave a screaming snarl and leapt claws-first into the man's face. He wailed and tumbled from his chair as the rat savaged him. The other scientists cowered back, averting their eyes from their comrade's misery.

Alpha hissed at the sobbing man then jumped back onto the table with a fleshy wobble. His gaze flicked between Princess and Loretta on Milo's shoulders and his whiskers bristled. "Your first chance at freedom, and you scramble back to a human. Pitiful."

Loretta and Princess leapt down and stalked forward. The Queen Mother growled at her son. "You are a disgrace to rats everywhere. You promised paradise, then stole our free will. Even the humans treated rats better than you do."

"I created Ratatopia! Without my guiding hand, we'd be a rabble. Victims for the humans to cage."

Princess joined her mother. "But at too high a cost." She gestured to the mischief of rats chanting for Alpha to come forth. "You've lost their trust. They will never follow you."

"They will once I've fixed my code so you can't override it with *music*." He hissed that last word.

The rats glared at each other and a brief silence fell as the AC/DC song finished. The chanting horde outside the cage all gave a synchronized twitch in the extended silence between tracks, and Milo's heart sank.

Alpha's subsonic signal spoke to them in the silence.

Milo took an involuntary step back before the mournful opening notes of Beethoven's "Moonlight Sonata" rang out, once again disrupting the signal. Minor melodies and intricate harmonies cast a calming pall over the circling rats. They slowed, tails twitching, beady eyes focused on the source of their rage. On Alpha.

Milo's laptop gave three very insistent beeps.

His eyes flew to the screen. A low battery warning blinked at him. Two minutes.

Cold dread settled like an anvil in Milo's gut. Two minutes before Princess and the others turned on him. If they didn't get Alpha out now, Beethoven's mournful sonata would be the last song he heard. A sad, final testament to Milo Piper's stillborn musical career.

Screw that.

If he was going to die, it would be on *his* terms, listening to *his* battle song. Milo tapped at his screen and switched back to "The Warrior's Anthem." He set the laptop down and stepped forward, fingers twitching in time with his rapid-fire opening guitar solo.

"Look at what Princess has done, Alpha," he said. "Rats and humans, working together as partners. Equals. You have every reason to hate us, but give humans a chance. We can find common ground."

The rat snapped his jaws and screamed, "I will not be caged!"

Milo raised his eyebrows and gave the electrified cage an exaggerated examination. He eyed the door and his breath caught.

The door wasn't latched. The guards hadn't pulled it fully shut. Only the electrified wire separated them, cooked rats hanging upon it as a grizzly warning.

Milo needed to open that door; give his rats access to Alpha. But he couldn't touch it without getting fried.

His laptop beeped again. Thirty seconds.

Alpha gave an ugly smile and rubbed his paws together. "I recognize that sound. Your music is about to die, and you with it."

Milo blew out his breath. Death by rat or death by electrocution. What a choice. He met Alpha's gaze and let his music flow over him. The Warrior's Anthem. "Fight for what's right and your song will live on," he sang. He loved that line.

Milo grabbed the chain-link door, wrenched it open, and rats rushed into the cage. Electricity pulsed up Milo's right arm, through his chest, and out his right heel. The world went white then dark as he spasmed. The power cut off and he collapsed to the floor. He landed awkwardly, his arm above him, twitching fingers still clenched around the fencing. The taste of blood and the smell of bacon filled his fogged brain. His heart gave syncopated beats.

Rats swarmed past him. The clash of steel and squeals of death echoed dully in Milo's ears before the room filled with silence.

True silence, without music.

A rat's weight landed on Milo's chest. His pulse pounded in his ears and he forced his eyes open. Princess looked down at him, blood staining her pristine white fur.

"You're alive," she said, sounding relieved.

"Am I? Doesn't feel like it." His throat was raw, his voice rough.

"Alpha must have used low amperage. Enough electricity to kill rebellious rats, but only injure his pet humans. That was very brave, Milo. Rat-kind shall forever be in your debt."

"Alpha?"

"Dead, along with his subsonic signal. I am the Alpha now."

"Oh, good. We won. Glad to hear it." Milo's eyes drooped and his muscles sagged as exhaustion and pain overwhelmed him.

THE NEXT SEVERAL WEEKS PASSED IN A BLUR FOR MILO AS HE LANGUISHED in a hospital burn ward. Princess had repatriated him and the scientists, sending them with a message to sue for peace. Negotiations had started while Milo recovered.

He half-watched the news on TV and absently rubbed at his throbbing right forearm. The doc said his heart would eventually recover, but the nerve damage in his arm was permanent. And he'd lost two fingers.

He'd never play guitar again.

The talking heads on TV were debating the benefits of a treaty between species when two furry heads popped up over the foot of his hospital bed. DJ and Bruiser blinked at him, ears perked up, whiskers twitching. Milo smiled.

"What are you doing here?" he asked. "I thought you were restricted to Ratatopia until negotiations ended."

The rats climbed up and sat at Milo's feet. Bruiser unslung a small satchel and retrieved cigarettes and a lighter. "Negotiations are done, mate. Signed and official. Princess and your President are announcing it tomorrow. We're full citizens now. And we get to keep the Willis." He flicked the lighter.

"Um, you can't smoke that in here," Milo said.

"Says who?"

"It's the rules." Milo pointed at a no-smoking sign.

"Bloody hell. Humans and your rules."

"They're your rules too, citizen."

Bruiser snorted but returned the smokes to his pack. DJ's whiskers twitched and he wouldn't meet Milo's gaze. He opened his mouth, then snapped it shut and wrung his forepaws.

Milo frowned. "What's wrong?"

Bruiser grinned and punched DJ in the shoulder. "My little friend's nervous. Afraid you're upset."

"Upset at what?"

Both rats blinked at him and Bruiser asked, "Haven't you heard the radio?"

Milo shook his head. "Don't have one in here. Just the TV."

DJ looked even more nervous and Bruiser barked a laugh. "You're a big hit, mate! Your song. It's on the radio!"

"Wait, what? How?"

Bruiser slapped DJ on the back, making the smaller rat stumble forward. "DJ went online, said he was your agent, and submitted "The Warrior's Anthem" with the story about your music freeing the rats and ending the war. You've been number one for the past two weeks. You really didn't know?"

Milo realized that he was gaping at them and clicked his jaws shut.

Bruiser cackled again and leapt off the bed. There were some screams and protests before he came bounding back, dragging a clock radio. He plugged it in and scrolled through the stations until Milo heard his own voice singing from the cheap speaker.

Fight for what's right and your song will live on. Oh, your song will live on.

Milo laid back and listened in wonder to his breakout single. The song that ended the Rat War.

Muzik Man

Wulf Moon

Muzik stepped in a clump of flowers that resembled daisies, growing on a distant hillside overlooking the capital city of planet Fendor. His servos hummed as he backed up and adjusted his stance, careful to avoid damaging any more.

He bent over them and whispered, "Sorry little fellas."

Muzik took a deep breath, filling accordion bellows within as he savored the aromatics without. What wonderful smells engulfed him in this good land! This scent like crushed lavender, that one like ground cloves, so refreshing compared to the recycled air of the ship that had just brought him here. He might be clunky metal on the outside, but his array of senses were hard won, and Muzik had vowed he would never take sentience and the gifts that came with it for granted.

He stood up and tilted his titanium head toward the powder-blue sky. A crystalline transport was making its ascent, engines whirring softly as it angled toward the heavens. Muzik waved at the ship, almost invisible to the eye.

"Buh-bye!" he hooted through his polymer lips. "See you in ten years!" And then, as an afterthought he trumpeted, "This time I won't screw up!"

Oily moisture formed at the corners of Muzik's eyes as he watched the vessel vanish. In the brightness of the morning sun, his irises contracted; golden-brown and of intricate filigree, they resembled delicate rosettes overlaid on the sound holes of ancient lutes. Tears spilled down his synthetic cheeks and he wiped them away with silver fingers. The transport vanished.

Muzik was alone.

"Whoever said 'parting is such sweet sorrow' deserved a firm kick in the gearbox!" He sighed. "Ah, well, the will of the Maestro and all that jazz. Not like I don't know the program."

And with a wheeze from his accordion lungs, he realized he didn't know the program. Not really. Not the big one. Oh sure, he had achieved the sentient Minstrel 1000 series by comprehending that *muzik*—the Maestro's complex compositions—weren't just exercises in teaching musical nomenclature, they were intricately designed symphonies designed to teach his neural network the language of emotion. But that had been two hundred and sixty-three years ago, and he preferred not to count all the backwater worlds since then that he had done initial pioneering on, prepping them for the arrival of the elite Minstrel 2000s and their teams. Muzik's life's work, it appeared, would never rise above the lonely routines of a *solo* galactic minstrel operative.

"Field agent," Muzik said, practicing his freshly downloaded Fendorian. "Just a fancy name for a sodbuster. I'm a musical clodhopper."

Shame fountained up; Muzik hung his head. This was no way to start a mission! He was a member of the special forces, an advance operative in the Maestro's expanding galactic task force where musical seeds were planted to transform rigid ideologies of alien species—like the cursed Archalon—into ascending harmonies of thought, peace, and cooperation. Not all invasions took place with armies—the most effective could be the injection into a culture of a word, a concept, a belief, or even . . . a song.

Muzik stared at the mushroom domes of the distant city. A faint veil of smog hovered over buildings gilded with amber sunlight. He stroked his chin. "Hmmm. Reminds me of the Cycanthlopan Mosques. Man-o-man, did those cats have rhythm."

With that, Muzik smiled, his teeth rows of ebony and ivory. He clicked his heels together with a clang. "If this culture is anything like the Cycanthlopans', I'll be jammin' on easy street!"

His irises dilated and contracted in rhythmic succession as he accessed his directives, hidden somewhere in a virtual reality labyrinth that materialized as a hedge maze, a marble manor glowing at the end. Ach! The Maestro and his games! But if he succeeded, everything the Maestro had collected about this world would now be his, and he had practiced this maze over and over on the flight in. Muzik flashed through the pathways, avoiding every wrong turn. Through the vast arrays of gathered knowledge, through the endless corridors of subroutines stacked with pearls of Fendorian wisdom, Muzik would be able to leap through megaflops of calculations and personalize his strategy for awakening another tone-deaf society to the wonders of music!

As the maze opened up to the steps and pillars of the glowing manor, Muzik leaped forward and caught his prize box just as the timer on its surface ticked to zero and it was about to float away.

"Gotcha!"

He popped the lid, looked triumphantly within . . . and his lips flapped with a frustrated gasp. The prize proved to be a few static-riddled radio transmissions. No detailed cultural studies from prosthetically disguised undercover operatives; no surveillance holos taken from cloaked satellites; not even FTL transmissions from a covert tap into the civic mainframe.

"Schmutz! Budget cuts!" Muzik looked up at the manor's double doors of burnished triluminar and shook his fist. "You could have left me with the funnies section of their newspaper. That, at least, would have been something! Next time, poke a stick in my eye!"

The door chimed. Upon the surface materialized a Securazon keyboard, patterned after the enlarged wings of a Bytillian buzz-bug. Muzik had been working on the lock for decades with no success. So many color cells to those wings, and the sequence included chromatic scales, tonic frequencies, symphonic scores, and complicated emotional cues. The manor was a vault; the lock sealed its contents from Muzik. He had only cracked this safe once before—that was the day he had transcended from the computational android psyche . . . into the sentient 1000 series.

Muzik shuddered, which sent his virtual avatar into a cacophony of discordant notes. A dark feeling wormed through his consciousness. This time, he suspected if he didn't succeed on this world he'd be demoted, and the lock would slowly fade away. He had seen it happen before to comrades who had failed to convert restrictive alien cultures to the enlightenment of music. Horrible confinement, hideous torment, the most excruciating agony a star-jumping Muzik Man could ever be afflicted with: tenure as minstrel-in-residence, teaching junior-level band to tone-deaf, flipper-fingered Purpluppians or some similarly encumbered race.

Muzik shuddered. He would never allow that to happen. And this time, he had a bold new plan. He called it *Big Splash*.

THE SUN NOW HUNG OVERHEAD AS MUZIK APPROACHED THE CAPITAL'S suburbs. As he moved, his head bobbed on the stalk of his neck, matching the swing of his gait. His neck was covered in silver valves shaped like hieroglyphics adorning ancient temples. The valves opened and closed and whistled as he walked. His torso was polished silver splashed with synthetic swirls dark as chocolate. His sides were open and had accordion-shaped bellows within, inflating and deflating in steady rhythm. Along the front of his shoulders ran scroll-shaped sound holes, radiating a beat that matched the cadence of his step.

Ooom pah-pah, ooom pah-pah, ooom pah-pah-paaah.

He was close to the suburbs now, and his receivers picked up a transmission. Local television. How quaint. The capital's single station was broadcasting video of a flowing brook with a chant repeating over and over: *"One thought, one way, one mind."*

Definite nuances of Archalon influence. The Maestro wasn't the only seed planter in the galaxy. Which was why Muzik was here, of course.

He spotted what appeared to be a farmer working rows of feathery plants and waved. The Fendorian four-footed it out of there. Muzik wasn't surprised. On most worlds, those in the fields tended toward conservativism, and those in the cities tended toward progressivism. He needed to find just one curious soul to begin his work. Besides, *Big Splash* called for big conversions, and teaching a few agrarian workers how to play the spoons just wouldn't do. He needed free thinkers! Bigger conversion numbers! Impressive field reports! Surely this was the way to advance in the Maestro's labyrinthine system of android development.

Muzik crossed a vacant lot and stepped onto a sidewalk. Civilization! His arms swung at his sides, the acoustical joints moaning like strings on a bass. He loved all forms of music, but he had a particular fondness for Earth instruments and compositions. After all, his masters study that helped him advance to the 1000 series had been *Planet Earth's Evolutionary Progression of Music and Its Ripple Effect upon Funkterfusion*, and it was then that he absorbed much of Earth's cultural nuances at the genesis of his persona.

The domiciles along each side of the street were white domes, uniform in size and shape, resembling rows of mushrooms clinging to a tree limb. So silent. No locals out and about. Wait! There was one, a flash of white as the curtains were drawn.

Muzik had just the bait. He clinked his fingers together, added percussion to the melody of his gait, and raised a few valves in his neck, playing the sweet enticements of a trihorn.

As he crossed into the next block, a door in one of the domiciles cracked open.

Muzik stopped. Faced the door. Flashed his piano-key smile. "Why, hello there!"

Silence from within.

"Aw, please come out. I don't bite." Muzik bowed, his joints sighing like a bow drawn over cello strings.

Still nothing. *Archalon influence, eh?* Muzik tried a new lure. "I am a priest bearing the gift of truth!"

That did it. The resident came out its door and stepped across its perfectly manicured moss lawn to the sidewalk. The being's torso was a long stalk with four stubby legs and feet at the base, two in the front, two in the back. It wore a gray cloak with draping sleeves as it waved spindly white arms. It tipped its mushroom-shaped head from side to side, revealing drab gills under its head dome. Three eyes blinked in unison along the curve of its head, it had a bump of a nose, and it wiggled cauliflower-looking ears.

Rows of fleshy rings that made up the stalk of the Fendorian's neck rippled; two of the segments separated, forming lips through which it spoke. "What in great Gorunskian's gorballs are you?"

Muzik's body trembled with excitement. First contact! Okay, remember the Golden Directives: to the extent possible, show respect for alien customs (even when they are eye-pokingly stupid); wipe your feet on the doormat before entering a domicile (except on Karasite, where the doormats *are* the husbands); and never ever play Lazazarian funkterfusion unless the crowd is drooling drunk (even though it's the coolest).

Muzik smiled and tapped his head; it rang like a church bell. "Why, I'm a Muzik Man 1000."

"A wutza whaa?"

"Muzik Man 1000. Universal harmonic android." He rolled his tongue into a cylinder, blew a whistling note, gave a snappy salute. "Muzik. At your service!"

The Fendorian flapped its arms. "Shhh. Try to keep it down. It's Sabbabah."

Muzik glanced left and right, lowered his volume. "Gotcha. And who do I have the pleasure of meeting on this fine Sabbabah afternoon?"

The Fendorian wiggled its torso. A handshake or bow? Maybe a nervous twitch? "I'm Hoagley of the maintenance guild."

Muzik wiggled just to be on the safe side. "A pleasure! Forgive my inquisitive nature, but does your species have gender designations?"

"Waah. You're missing a few bolts, that's plain to see." Hoagley pointed to his brown gills. "Male." He scratched some flakes from his creamy-white head. "Are you that new invention of the sultans? I heard we were getting boomer boxes on street corners to recite the sacred words, but you seem mighty flashy for the sultans."

"I am not a radio, Hoagley. I'm a Muzik Man."

Hoagley leaned closer, his tone hushed. "So, what's a Moo-zik Man do?"

"A Muzik Man makes music, *music, music* . . ." Muzik liked using the reverb with that line. Added a nice touch.

"What's mu-isic?" the Fendorian asked in his croaky voice, trying to pronounce the word correctly.

"Magic, my boy. Pure magic!"

The Fendorian scratched more flakes from his head. "What's ma-a-a-gic?"

Muzik's body sagged like a spent bagpipe. "This world is gonna be a tough nut to crack." Muzik rotated his head in a three-sixty. "Woo-hoo-hoo! What's magic? What's music?" A glissando of harp strings rolled from his sound holes. "Here, let me show you!"

The top of Muzik's head unscrewed, rising with a whine of hydraulics on a thin pedestal, fanning out into a disk. Muzik put his hands together, cracked his knuckles. "Gimme some bones!" His fingers extended into long drumsticks that he lifted up to the cymbal balancing atop his head.

"First, you gotta have rhythm," Muzik said, doing a quick tap number with his feet.

The Fendorian's bulbous gray eyes were blinkless and blank.

"Beat, man," Muzik said. "A beat!"

Muzik rapped his fingers against the cymbal.

Tssssss-tss-tss-Tsssssss-tss-tss-Tsssssss-tss-tss-Tsssssss

Hoagley blinked rapidly.

"You like that?" Muzik said. "You ain't seen nothin' yet."

Muzik's abdomen glowed bright. The black stripes swirled together, and a wide cylinder with a flat surface extended out from his chest as a snare drum. With one hand striking the cymbal, he lowered the other to his abdomen and drummed his fingertips against the taut surface.

Tappita-tappita-tappita-tappita

Then the cymbal.

Tssssss-tss-tss-Tssssss-tss-tss-Tssssss-tss-tss-Tssssss

"Feel the rhythm?"

Hoagley blinked his eyes even faster.

"Well then! Don't just stand there, man! Tap your feet!" The Fendorian gave Muzik what could only be interpreted as a dumb blink. "Like this," Muzik said, tapping his foot, the metal toes jingling like sleigh bells.

Hoagley gave a hesitant tap with his left forefoot. Blinked. Tapped again.

"That's it, that's it. You're getting the hang of it." Muzik slowed the tempo.

Hoagley tapped again and again and again, then alternated between all four feet, awkwardly matching Muzik's rhythm. His eyelids fluttered like butterflies. "I feel it," he said. *"OoooWaah."*

"Hey," Muzik said, flashing a smile, "you're getting the hang of it. There's hope for this world yet."

Muzik scanned his repertoire of songs, chose something with an easy beat, a *rachta* from the Kintanna system. He shifted the tip of his tongue into a small round ball, struck it against his teeth. Resonant marimba tones spilled from his mouth, swirled sweet as melted chocolate down the street.

"OoooWaah, OoooWaah, OoooWaah," Hoagley said, bobbing up with each "Oooo" and down with each "Waah." He tried tapping his teeth with his purple tongue, but no sound resulted. "How do you do that?" he asked.

"Ith eathy. Ooopth, thowwy." Muzik shifted his tongue back to speaking mode. "It's easy. Here, grab that waste receptacle lid, and that one from your neighbor. Go on!"

Hoagley hesitated.

"Go on. I have more *truth* to show you!" Sometimes, the Archalon made it too easy.

Hoagley grabbed the lids, brought them back to Muzik, holding them out like plates.

"Okay, now hold the handles in each hand. Good. Now hit them together every time you tap your foot. Try it!"

The Fendorian gave them a little knock against one another, and a hollow clang joined the medley.

"A good start! Now, a little harder."

A loud clang rang out. Hoagley stopped, wide-eyed. "I'll disturb the neighbors' meditation. I better not. It's Sabbabah."

How could Muzik work with a sacred day? "Do they let you sing on Sabbabah?"

"Sah-ing?"

"Sing. As in 'singing.' Vocalization of musical sounds? Speaking words with melodic tones?" Muzik demonstrated by alternating his pitch. *"Loooow. Hiiiigh. Buuuut* with *words* like *thiiiis."*

"Hmmm . . . the *Chants of the Archalon* we speak at temple on Sabbabah morn sound a little like that."

"Well, there you go! You do chants on Sabbabah. We're just going to spice them up with a bit of musical accompaniment. Go on, give it a try. If your neighbors come out, we can teach them too. They'll love it!"

Hoagley glanced up the street. "Uhh, I don't know."

"Come on! Work with me here, Hoagley. On three. And a one, and a two, and a three . . ."

As the Fendorian picked up the beat, Muzik bubbled with excitement. He leaned back and blasted air through the valves in his throat. The wail of a saxophone blared across the neighborhood, heady and wild. Music was happening; this is what he lived for. And with the Archalon seeding this planet for who knew how long, he tossed out the subtle approach— this world was going to need *a lot* of shaking up.

Hoagley's neighbors came out from their domes, a few at first, then more and more, seeking the source of the unworldly commotion.

Just what Muzik wanted. *Big Splash* was working! How many converts? How many marks could he add to his tally for the day? He'd convert this planet in record time. Perhaps this was how those mysterious 3000 series did it: one bold move that swept the planet by storm. Like the Beatles!

Hoagley's mate came toward them, lacy chartreuse gills swinging under her dome head like curtains in a stiff breeze. At least, Muzik assumed it was Hoagley's mate because one, she came out of the same dome, two, she had two little ones clinging to her back, and three, Hoagley seemed to be so purposely ignoring her. Muzik liked their baby 'shrooms, so cute with their little faces all scrunched up like they were about to fill their britches. He gave them a wink, and they bobbed down, only to peek out a few seconds later from their mother's sides to see if Muzik was still there. Muzik ran a stanza of *Universal Infant Phonics* through his melody—*gootchy-gootchy-gootchy-goo*—and the 'shrooms blinked in surprise.

Hoagley's mate was not so easily charmed. She cast a discordant note into the melody by clearing her throat, trying to get Hoagley's attention. When that didn't work, a jab to his side did the trick.

Hoagley turned to her, still crashing his trash lids together. "Darna! Didn't know you were there. Isn't this wonderful?"

Darna waved her fist, almost spilling one of the 'shrooms. Her voice was loud and shrill; Muzik thought she would make a good Bendorian piccolo. "Hoagley, what do you think you're doing? What's gotten into you?"

Hoagley blinked his eyelids rapidly, slammed his makeshift cymbals together. "Music!"

Muzik thumped his drum. "You're losing the beat, Hoagley. Concentrate. Concentrate. We have an audience."

"Sorry."

Hoagley slammed the lids together in earnest, and little toadstool children jigged in delight. Most of the neighbors that had come out were all goggle-eyed, some touching Muzik to see if he was real, some giving him the evil triple eye like Darna, and a few grabbing trash-can lids and making their own attempt to join the jam.

Darna's eyes grew dark. "Hoagley, don't you know this must be illegal?"

"How could it be?" he said as he slammed the lids together with a crash. "We don't even have a word for it!"

She jabbed him with her finger. "If the ancient worthies wanted us to make this . . . this . . . *noise*, don't you think it would have been written in one of the seventy-three *Tomes of Ascension*?"

Hoagley shrugged. "They must"—*Clang*—"have overlooked"—*Clang* —"something." *Clang*—"I always thought"—*Clang*—"the seventy-third" —*Clang*—"ended sort of"—*Clang*—"abruptly."

"Well, you're disturbing Sabbabah. There is a law against that!"

"But look at everyone. They love it! It's a chant with sounds!"

"Well *I* don't love it," she said. She waved her fist at Muzik, causing her shoulder to slope. A 'shroom slid off, dropping to the moss with a thud. It wailed in shock.

Hardly missing a beat, Muzik extended his arm and wrapped his fingers around the 'shroom. He hoisted the baby back to its mother's shoulder, then gave it a pat on the head. "There, there." He cooed. *"Gootchy-gootchy-gootchy-goo."*

Darna glared at Muzik with all the fury of her three eyes. "I don't know where you come from, mister, but I'm calling the constable!" She looked sternly at her mate. "Hoagley?"

He slammed the lids in sync with his other neighbors. "In a minute, my little puffball."

"Don't you *puffball* me! You know what's going to happen when the constable comes. You'd better be back in our dome before his patroller pulls up." She looked at the crowd. "All of you!" She spun around and marched back to her dome, the little 'shrooms bouncing madly against her back.

"Sorry about that," Hoagley said, pausing to talk to Muzik. "She's really quite nice once you get to know her."

Muzik smiled, clacking his tongue against the ivories. "I'm thur thee ithh. Nexth thime, I thry a lullaby on her. Thur to thoften even the tougheth nut."

"What's a lull-a-ba-by?"

Muzik shook his head, and his tambourine ears jingled. "Forgeth ith."

With that, Muzik spun in a circle and jigged like a piper. More and more neighbors poured into the street, arching their necks to see what in Fendor could make such wondrous sounds. *Big Splash* was *the bomb*! Giddy with the response, Muzik kicked in his amps, projecting synthesized chords from his sound holes. Everywhere, Fendorians murmured, *"Oooo-Waah, Oooo Waah, Oooo Waah."*

From the end of the street, a siren quacked and hissed. Muzik cranked up his volume and wove the siren into the performance. Some of the neighbors matched his jig, and a synergy of bounding rhythm rolled across the crowd.

Muzik heard a door slam, and moments later a red-cloaked Fendorian parted the masses, shouting at people to go home. Muzik saw him approaching, knew he must be the constable, but everyone was blinking so happily, he just couldn't stop. The constable shoved his way in front of Muzik and pointed a nasty-looking black cane in his face.

"Great Gorunskian's Gorballs!" the constable said. "What are you?"

Muzik kept playing and jigged from one foot to the other, but he rolled his tongue flat for better diction. "Why, sir, I'm a Muzik Man 1000."

"What's a Muzik Man?" the constable asked.

Muzik turned up the reverb. "A Muzik Man makes music, *music, music . . .*"

"Well I say you're funny looking."

"Thank you."

"I also say you're disturbing the peace, and on Sabbabah no less."

"I beg to differ, sir. I'm creating peace. Look at everyone's eyelids. See how happy they are?"

The constable's eyes bugged out. Muzik took it for a frown, a grimace, maybe gas.

"Inciting public assembly without consent of the sultans is illegal," the constable said, tapping the cane against his palm. "I'm going to have to ask you to accompany me."

Muzik flashed his ivories. "Of course, Officer. What would you like to sing?" He tapped his midriff drum and head cymbal. *Bum-bum, tsssss. Rimshot.* He snapped his fingers. "Hey, I've got your number! Wagner! See what you think of *Ride of the Valkyries*."

Muzik performed a raging sample.

"I've had enough!" the constable said. "Let the holy sultans decide your fate. You're coming down to the senate."

"The sun ants?" Muzik asked, shouting over the blaring music and the sudden crash of Hoagley's trash lids as he caught the new beat. Muzik beamed with pride: he had made his first disciple. This world would be a breeze, and he gave himself special marks for the way he had just laced the sound of a kazoo through Wagner's tempest. He'd have to remember that one.

The constable waved his cane like a baton. "No, no, no! The senate, you dope. Turn that racket down! You don't mean to tell me you haven't heard of the senate?"

Muzik lowered the volume. "Can't say that I have. Are there lots of Fendorians there?"

"Of course! It's the religious center of the universe!"

Muzik adjusted his linguistic program, and the Fendorian word he had been translating *senate* became *synod*. "Well then," Muzik said, excited by the opportunity to make more converts, especially religious ones, "lead on, Macduff!"

Hoagley lifted one of the trash lids between himself and the constable. He leaned forward, and his eyes were huge bulbs as he mouthed the words *You don't want to go there.*

Muzik tilted his head and pitched words off the trash lid so only Hoagley could hear them. "I'll be all right, sport. I'm here to reach as many Fendorians as I can. My job security depends on that."

The constable gave Muzik a shove. "Move it, bud!"

Muzik waved goodbye to Hoagley, then turned his volume back up and clashed his cymbal. "Keep practicing!" He waved to the dispersing crowd. "All of you! I'll be back. Promise!"

An adolescent Fendorian in that awkward, button-headed stage held her ground, refusing to leave. Tears welled in her eyes as she swayed to melodies stirred within her. Muzik knew that look on any world—teenagers were the most fertile fields for minstrel operatives. He gave her a knowing flash of the ivories. Seed planted. The roots would run deep in this one.

The constable jabbed Muzik with his cane, pushed him toward the honking car. Muzik marched in compliance, but thundering Valkyries led the way.

THE JOINT. THE SLAMMER. THE BIG HOUSE. THE CRUSHER. MUZIK KNEW all the terms in hundreds of languages from dozens of worlds. He didn't mind jail. Muzik did his best work with a captive audience.

This crusher was underground, white rock caverns sealed off with steel doors, with solid bars bolted over ventilation shafts. Horrible lighting —overhead fluorescents—but delightful acoustics with the high ceilings and stone walls. There were twenty Fendorians in Muzik's cell. After processing, it was lights out, and these cats slept like rocks. He had planned on spending the night working the puzzle lock to the Maestro's vault, but the labyrinthian maze had shifted, and he ended up spending the night chasing dead ends. He suspected he was being punished for letting his anger get the best of him. Probably not a good idea to tell the Maestro to poke a stick in his eye, because changing the maze sure felt like it.

After the morning trays—Muzik didn't need nourishment, but he had accepted a tray anyway—his cellmates had pulled their sleeping pads around to Muzik's, where he sat in a *sukhasana* pose. It was strange to see them mimic him, crossing four legs as they sat down.

A brown 'shroom Fendorian cleared the wattles of his throat and wiggled in greeting. "Name's Beez. Do that thing again."

Beez's sleeves were rolled up, revealing intricate scarification. Muzik translated one of the words marked in his flesh. *Momma.* He figured this would be a good one to start with, what with loving his mother so much and all.

"What thing?" Muzik said. He had changed his preferred lighter-pitched persona into a raspy, lounge-lizard character. Rule 337 in the *Galactic Minstrel Operative's Database*: *Reflect your audience. When they see themselves in you, their soil softens.*

Beez pointed a spindly finger at Muzik's neck. "That thing you do. Those sounds you whispered, in your sleep last night."

Another said, "He was just snoring, Beez."

Beez gave him the three eyes. "I know what I heard."

Muzik nodded, setting the metal discs in his ears jingling. "I was meditating. Sorry if I disturbed your sleep—that just happens with me. It's called music." He didn't add reverb—plenty of it in here.

"Do it for us, that moo-sick."

Rule 338: *Show personal interest before proselytizing.*

"Sure thing, Beez. But first, let's chew the lichen. Tell me what you're in for."

Beez fingered his neck wattles. "For painting my domicile."

Muzik wondered if he should adjust the definition of that Fendorian word to "home," but he had noted the dome was an intrinsic element to their dwellings—perhaps because it matched the shape of their heads. He let it be.

"What, you tagged your own home with graphic illustrations?" Seeing what appeared to be confused scrunching of Beez's eyes, Muzik tried again. "You painted symbols on it, like those on your arms?"

Beez leaned his head back and let out a hoot that lifted his gills. "You crazy? I would have been capped for that, not even a trial."

"Capped?" Muzik had no translation for their slang.

Beez drew a finger across his neck. Oh. Muzik understood *that* sign.

"You see, the painters' guild has rules on color. Domiciles must be pure white, inside and out. But this was my own dome, and me and the missus moved to the edge of the 'burbs to avoid all the scrutiny, know what I mean? Thought the civic inspector wouldn't catch us. This was inside, in our little puffball's sleep room."

"What color could be so offensive to get you thrown in jail?"

"Eggshell."

Muzik flapped his polymer lips, making the sound of a spent balloon. "Jeepers, creepers, Beez! What a constipated culture!" He snapped his fingers. "But I've got just the laxative! You know, medicine? I'm going to teach you the blues."

Beez held up his hands. "I don't want no trouble, man. I'm in it deep enough as it is just dipping my brush in the off-whites."

Muzik snorted through his trihorn. "No, not blues. The *blues*."

"Wutza whaa?"

"Okay, you know those sounds I make?"

Beez nodded. "Yeah, you called it moo-sick."

"Right. Music. Well, this is a name for a certain type of music. Music for sad times, but 'A shared sad is half as bad,' or so my Maestro says. And not all the songs are about one's troubles. They can sing about hope, too."

The others nodded at the word *hope*. One shriveled Fendorian said, "Mmmm-hmmm. We could all use a good helping of that."

Beez leaned forward, three eyes bright. "Teach me this color."

Muzik grinned. Twenty new converts today for sure!

"That's why I'm here," Muzik said.

Muzik thought way back, to his favorite planet, to his second-favorite musical genre, to a tune by Muddy Waters. Nobody sang the blues better than Muddy, not nobody, not on any world. And Muzik knew, sure as the marks on Beez's arms, this song would leave an impression on his heart. Forever.

"Okay, cats. Bring me one of those buckets against the wall—preferably one you didn't do your number in this morning. *Great*. Now who here has some spoons? No?" Muzik blared a *ta-dah* from his horns and held up two. "Why, would you look at this. I must have sticky fingers."

Forty-six planetary rotations later, after teaching his cellmates everything they needed to start a swinging blues band—including diagrams on how to create an acoustic guitar, double bass, drum kit, and harmonica—Muzik got his synod hearing.

Muzik stood in the center of a domed coliseum on a dais encircled by a stone banister. Could be a pulpit, could be a witness stand, but right now, it felt like a cage. He rotated his head in a slow three-sixty to take in the surroundings. Each shadowy tier was supported by colonnades of gray marble pillars, and upon the tiers were rows of solemn, gray-cloaked acolytes, still as stone. Tough crowd, tough crowd.

He focused his attention on the larger square dais before him. It was composed of three stepped-up tiers of hewn stone blocks. Upon the top rested eight nondescript gray chairs, and in these sat eight ancient Fendorians with crusty brown-splotched heads adorned with pointy gray hats. Judging by the gills, the holy sultans comprised four males and four females. Each held a thick staff in their withered hands and wore (thank goodness for the change of scenery) purple robes fringed in white sequins that sparkled under the bright spotlight shining down from the center of the dome.

Muzik tapped his feet, gave his head another spin, and let out a powerful wolf whistle that echoed through the tiers. "Gr-r-r-oovy! What a place to hold a concert!"

The sultans raised their staffs in unison and slammed the ends on the dais. A collective *boom* echoed through the coliseum.

"Silence!"

"If you want silence, why slam the staffs?" Muzik thumped his torso drum and clacked his head cymbal in a rim shot. *Bum-bum, tsssss.*

The staffs thudded in thunder. *"Silence!"*

Muzik raised his hands, fingers clinking together randomly. "Gotcha. It's thrillin' to be chillin'."

"Silence!"

"Sheesh!" he whispered, shifting his weight from one foot to the other, each movement setting off tiny violin squeaks and cello moans from his joints. "Best I can do, I'm afraid. Really."

Muzik lowered his gaze, tried to look submissive, and noted fist-sized stones that littered the floor. *I'd complain to housekeeping if this were my joint.*

One of the sultans stood up. Must be their leader, a prime. Muzik had to admit he looked imperious in that tall pointy hat. His staff, too, was different from the others, ending in a wicked-looking spear tip. The prime sultan cleared his throat, each of the sagging rings along it rolling in waves with the vibration, like someone jiggling a bowl of gelatin. His spindly limbs quivered as he croaked.

"You stand before the holy sultans, most right righteous reverends of the Way of Nothingness." He lowered his voice. "Who are you? Where are you from?"

I am from the realms above was the first response that came to Muzik, but he thought better of it. That one had already been taken. Muzik gave a piano-key smile and tapped his head with a clang. "Why, I'm a Muzik Man 1000."

"What's a Muzik Man?" the sultan asked.

Muzik turned the reverb *way* up. "A Muzik Man makes music, *music, music* . . ."

The sultan jerked as the word winged around the coliseum. "Where do you come from?"

Muzik played a series of horns and trumpet sounds through his throat, a little tantara used to announce royalty. "I'm from the stars." He paused, cocking his head. "Great acoustics in here, by the way. My compliments."

"Are you a prophet?" the sultan asked.

"Nope," Muzik said. "Something better. I'm a musician!"

The sultan's three eyes narrowed, and his tone sank to dark depths. "Who sent you?"

"Why, the Maestro, of course."

"Never heard of him. Who is this mah-mie-mie-my-Maestro?"

Good question. He'd like the answer to that himself. Muzik did know the basics, and he made it even simpler for the sultan.

"It means *master* . . . well, in this case, I think it means *mistress* of the house. I'm really not sure yet—gender is such a sticky issue when it comes to androids. *Ahem.* No reproductive parts. But I've heard at the 3000 leve—"

"Stop this babbling! Tell us who this mah-muh-Maestro is."

"Conductor of the orchestra? Queen bee of the hive? Teacher of the acolytes? Aha, *bull's-eye!* Your world, it appears, needs a little jazzing up."

"Nonsense! We are Fendorian, blessed long ago by the ancient worthies, the true prophets from the stars. We need nothing but their wisdom, recorded for us in the Tomes of Ascension."

"Ancient worthies? Oh, you mean the *Archalon.* Pinheads, every one. Not a creative circuit in their synapses. They've screwed up more worlds than I can count."

The sultan looked as if he had caught a bone in a segment of his throat. "You dare speak of the ancient worthies in such terms? Blasphemy!"

"Have you ever met them?"

The sultan paused, scratching behind the cauliflower bud of his ear. "Er, no, they visited our world a millennium ago."

"Well, I have. Their emissaries are specialists in stunting growing civilizations with their 'holy tomes.' Keeps the galactic competition down." Muzik smiled and blew a sweet note that matched the tremulous tone of a Baroque recorder. "But don't worry—that's why I'm here. We'll have you sultanships right as rain in no time."

The sultan bashed his spear-staff against the dais. "Stop speaking irreverently of the ancient worthies!"

Muzik noted the irritation in the sultan's manner, but his *Big Splash* initiative required *big moves*. Shock and awe. Truth will out. No pussyfooting around this time—Muzik was in the fast lane.

"Just speaking the truth. Don't get me wrong, the Archalon's methods work great for maintaining order, if that's all you're after. All those laws on shedding pleasures of physical life in order to ascend toward ultimate nothingness makes for some very docile, sheep-headed citizens. But it sounds like a pretty dull party if you ask me."

The sultan tilted his head and raised his voice, addressing the acolytes; the other sultans joined in the antiphon. *"The ancient worthies gave us u-ni-ty."*

Thousands of voices washed across the coliseum like waves murmuring upon a seashore. *"The ancient worthies gave us u-ni-ty."*

Muzik shook his head, setting his ears jingling. "You hear that? You've got tone, but no melody. Doesn't even have a beat you can dance to. It's not inspiring."

"It is to us," the sultan said. He spoke louder, and the other sultans joined him. *"One thought, one way, one mind."*

"One thought, one way, one mind," the acolytes returned in unison, their voices resonating under the dome.

Rotating his head, Muzik said, "Okay, cool it with the acolyte reverb for a sec, will you, pals? Thanks." He faced the prime sultan, decided *Big Splash* might need a bit of recalibration. Rule 776: *Flattery gets you nowhere, but sincere praise makes everyone's days.*

"Actually, that wasn't bad, Your Sultanship. You people have natural harmony, and *your* voice in particular, I must say, is *most* powerful."

The sultan bellowed as if to prove it. *"Silence!"*

"You know," Muzik said, stroking his chin, "we could work that sound into the benediction if you want. You seem to like it so much."

More thunder. *"Shut up!"*

Muzik hunched with a squeak and grimaced. "Okay, okay. Sheesh." A little panache, a little sincere praise, a little touch of melody into religious services—these had been his best tools in the past. What a bunch of stiffs!

The prime sultan shook the point of his staff at Muzik. "You will remain silent while the holy sultans adjourn to seek wisdom from the Tomes of Ascension regarding your case."

"Case?" Muzik said. "As in *trial?*" Muzik decided to switch the Fendorian word for *synod* back to *senate* and wondered if he'd made the right choice in getting himself sent here. His cheeks puffed out as he pumped the sound of a tuba through his throat valves. *Bum-bum-bum-bummm.* "I demand to know the charges!"

The prime sultan's voice croaked. "Unlawful assembly. Disturbing the peace. Interrupting holy Sabbabah. Blasphemy against the ancient worthies. Advocating apostate divergence from the Tomes of Ascension. These are *grievous* crimes."

"No more grievous than living in a world without music."

"We've gotten along just fine for a thousand years without your heretical sounds. Yes, we know this thing you speak of. A few Fendorians have tried to sway the populace in the past with such *noise*, but they were shown the . . . error of their ways. As the ancient worthies stated in the twenty-third tome: 'Peace rests in silence.'"

"So does death."

The prime sultan tugged the wattles of his throat. "Indeed."

Another sultan slammed her staff down. "You are ordered to remain silent until our return."

Muzik saluted with a clang. "Roger, that. Over and out."

The sultans turned, stepped down from their dais, marched to an arch, swept open a door. The last sultan slammed the door behind her, leaving Muzik on the coliseum's floor alone.

Muzik looked on the bright side. More jail time wouldn't be so bad. Archalon worlds practiced incarceration of creative thinkers—his best converts, as he had already discovered, would be found in their detention facilities. It would be all right. *Big Splash* hadn't failed—it was swiftly taking him back to his target audience!

And if the verdict came back worse, he'd play the ace up his sleeve. Worked every time.

Moments passed. Muzik sighed—this was certainly boring. The acolytes didn't twitch a muscle. They just stood in their tiers, rigid, gray, silent. Muzik sighed again. Rotated his head in a slow three-sixty. Tapped his fingers against the pulpit railing.

Tappita-tappita-tappita-tappita

He sighed again, looking up at the crowd. All those people.

Tappita-tappita-tappita-tappita

He stared at the dome, recalled the wonderful acoustics when they chanted. With a little practice, what a chorus these acolytes could make in such a structure.

Tappita-tappita-tappita-tappita

Deep in thought, Muzik extended the fingers of his other hand, stroked his chin, tapped his lips. Such a stifled people. Such a terrible waste of creative power. He thumped his synthetic cheek, stared into the distance, touched the cymbal atop his head.

Tsssss

He jerked at the sound. How it amplified in the acoustics of the stone chamber! He reached up again. Stopped. The sultans *had* ordered him to be silent, which, he supposed, fell under that irritating directive that, to the extent possible, show respect for local customs (even when they are eye-pokingly stupid). He closed his lips, tried to be silent. Pursed them a little. Whistled softly, an innocent little number, barely audible above the second or third tier. Muzik eyed the crowd again. Wouldn't they look great on his report?

Maybe just once more.

He tapped the cymbal.

Tsssssssss

Muzik smiled, ran his tongue up and down the ivories.

Oh, what the heck, I'm here to make music. Deploy Big Splash!

Tssssss-tss-tss-Tssssss-tss-tss-Tssssss-tss-tss-Tssssss

Tappita-tappita-tappita-tappita

Tssssss-tss-tss-Tssssss . . .

Acolytes surreptitiously leaned forward, trying to get a better view. He stopped playing for a moment, smiled up at them.

"This is called music," he whispered, releasing a melodious sigh. His words were soft as a mother's murmur to her nursing child, yet they rose with subtle power to the heights of the coliseum. "Music," he said again. "Remember it."

And then, Muzik broke out in song.

Tender and melodious, it breathed with the sweet harmony of an adolescent choir, matched by gentle stirrings from pipe organ chords as tubes rose from the top of Muzik's shoulders. From those pipes, Muzik sent up threads of mists, tendrils of silver that curled through the air. Slowly, the acolytes gathered to the edges of the tiers, swaying to the rhythm's enchantments.

The sodium spotlight jerked, swiveled from the dais to the pulpit, casting back the shadows. It limned the mist surrounding Muzik in the rays of a golden nimbus. He had their attention.

Just what Muzik wanted.

Muzik's thoughts flashed through a litany of songs spanning the galaxy that might complement this unique setting. He fought back a desire to go right over the top with his personal favorite, Lazazarian funkterfusion. No, that's what got him into trouble on the last world, thinking of his needs instead of the people's. Funkterfusion was an *acquired* taste. First, he needed to teach them *how* to taste.

He snapped his fingers, gave a raspy growl. "*Yeah!* Chamber music."

Muzik wove the sound of a violin into his improvised melody. He added another, and another, and another, creating a vivacious quartet. Setting his joints to moan with violin and cello string harmonics, Muzik swayed to a rendition of Vivaldi's "Spring" from "The Four Seasons," Opus Eight.

A myriad of eyes blinked.

"You like that?" Muzik said, never missing a beat. "You ain't seen nothin' yet."

Keeping the violins, Muzik added a Bandorian acoustic harp and tweaked some of his joints to moan with Cycanthlopan bass strings as he melded "Spring" into another brilliant allegro, this one by the Erkantha Cluster's greatest composer, Vierdig Zen Fadel.

Muzik twirled, waving his outstretched arms in fluid, serpentine motion. As he flowed with the melody, his very dance became song. Soon he layered in a bagpipe's moan with the rise and fall of his chest; flutes from three different worlds whistled through valves in his throat; Oltanian pipe organs resonated through tubes on his shoulders; Triskolian stream chimes rippled from his dangling fingers; Neerkathian twilight bells jingled from his tapping toes.

Fendorian eyelids blinked everywhere, like flurries of migrating butterflies. Muzik spun in dance as acolytes hummed to the creative lifeblood fused within the melody. He sensed this was his grandest performance to date, thought provoking and soul stirring, resonating with the visions of his persona. He gave himself over to the movement, his body swaying like a willow, rippling in the breeze of harmonics.

Thunder boomed, jarring thunder, that sliced through the chords suspending the melody. Muzik turned as he played—

"*Silence!*"

—and faced a dais of fuming, mushroom-faced sultans.

The spotlight jerked, shot to the dais, the sequins on the sultan's robes flashing. Acolytes bowed in obedience and backed from the banisters. Muzik tried to still his body's rhythm, but shudders of vibrations from all the instruments he had employed rolled from his limbs long after the melody stopped. His sides finally sagged with an accordion's moan, and he let out a relieved sigh, which, unfortunately, trilled like a trihorn. He tilted his head—which gave off a violin squeak—and scrunched his shoulders—which moaned with a Cycanthlopan twang.

"Sorry about that," Muzik said. "Just trying to pass the time productively."

The prime sultan pointed his staff. "We gave you orders to cease and desist!"

"I can't!"

"Why not?"

Muzik tried to hold back the reverb, but he couldn't help himself. "I'm a Muzik Man. A Muzik Man makes music, *music, music* . . ."

The lyric echoed through the coliseum like a shout from a canyon.

The prime sultan let the echo die and cleared his throat. "You have been brought before the holy sultans for inciting a riot on Sabbabah. We have no need of witnesses, for you have repeated this heinous crime before our twenty-four eyes. How do you plead?"

Muzik, though grieved by their tone-deaf hearts, turned up his piano-key smile.

"Forgive me. I apparently did disturb your Sabbabah, but I was teaching a musical chant, and was told by the locals that chants are an acceptable Sabbabah custom. I did not know your laws, and I promise to respect your Sabbabah restrictions in the future."

"Ignorance of the law excuses no one!"

"I kinda figured that would come next. I therefore plead upon Your Sultanships' mercy. As you can see, I was made for music, I can't sit still, and it's impossible for me to stop being *me*. But I will hereby refrain on Sabbabah, and I humbly beg this court's forgiveness."

The sultans thumped their staffs. "We have confession of the crime. The holy sultans shall serve as your judges, jury, and executioners."

Executioners? Muzik held up a glittering finger. Time to play that ace. "Uh, excuse me, Your Sultanships. I am just a simple Muzik Man, but doesn't the seventy-fourth *Tome of Ascension* clearly state that an off-worlder shall have th—"

The prime sultan cleared his throat. "There are only seventy-*three* tomes of Ascension."

"With all due respect, sir, I beg to differ. If I could just be given a moment, I would be happy to project images of the original obsidian tablets held on Archalon Primus, which will clearly prove tha—"

"Enough! We do not need some tinkling mechanized perversion lecturing us on sacred law. You are not from our world. You know *nothing* of the law."

"Oh, I could write a book on the *Tomes of Ascension*, believe you me, and I have faced more than my share of Archalon-based tribunals. There is no way even with, *ahem*, seventy-three tomes, that a governing authority can execute a sentient representative from another world, nor seize or destroy their property—either personal or disseminated—without first granting right of appeal and formal hearing. Additionally, you are required by Archalon law to allow adequate time for counsel to appear from the defendant's home world. Seriously, they wove that concept throughout the tomes to protect their own missionaries and eventual emissaries. I hereby invoke—"

"Enough!" The prime sultan gnashed his teeth. "We determine the will of the Archalon. Our decisions are infallible."

Muzik whistled. "Man-o-man, wish I never made a mistake! Practice, practice, practice makes perfect, I've always been told, and an honest heart is better than gold."

"The holy sultans have already achieved perfection in Nothingness, which is how, through our purity, we are able to judge you."

The sultan gave a pointed look to those crowding the tiers. "We have consulted the *Tomes of Ascension*, and they are quite clear about incorrigible deviants from the law. Death by stoning, by the hands of those who condemn you."

Muzik blared *aaaaruuuuuuuga, aaaaaruuuuuuuuuga.* His head whirled full circle, projecting his voice clearly throughout the coliseum. "You can't be serious! All I'm guilty of is being me!"

The sultans moved down the tiers of the dais, using their staffs as canes. Step, step, *thump.* Step, step, *thump.* Muzik fought down a desire to compose something with the rhythm.

They hobbled forward. "That is your crime," one said, picking up a stone and hurling it at him.

Muzik ducked. These cats could throw! "Hey, now! Your Lordships have taken the words of the Archalon *waaay* too literally. I'm sorry if I ruffled your gills, but I'm sure we can work this out."

Step, step, *thump.* Step, step, *thump.*

Another stone hurtled through the air. Muzik heard a chorus of acolytes whisper *"ohhhh"* as it clanged off the side of his head. Tambourine jingles spilled from his shattered ear and tinkled against the flagstones like fallen pieces of silver.

"Hey, cut that out!" Muzik said, pressing a hand to the side of his head. "Why are you doing this? You have nothing to fear. Music is wonderful. Let it touch your souls!"

"We need nothing more. We have all we need."

Bong-ong-ong. A large rock crashed into Muzik's chest. He had time to rebound it with his drumhead, but the impact knocked him off his feet. He tumbled to the floor.

"Please," Muzik said, sitting up, head askew. "Give me another chance. Listen before you judge."

Thuuunk. "We've heard enough."

Muzik's android psyche flashed RED ALERT and FLEE NOW FOR SELF-PRESERVATION across his internal readouts. He wanted to listen to its urgings. He still had tricks they hadn't seen. But even if he managed to escape, he would be a fugitive. He would never be able to reach so many Fendorians again. One touching melody, one moment of epiphany—that was all it had taken to open up his emotions and change his life ever after. Would he run away and deny them their chance?

"Here, you're obviously agitated. The zythyran pipes from Gambar's Opus Four are quite calming. Maybe this will help."

Valves opened in Muzik's titanium throat. His rosette eyes looked away from the sultans and up to the acolytes. *Please remember.* Blessed music spilled out, sweet trilling that rippled with the deepest emotions Muzik had ever experienced.

Muzik deflected a stone with his arm and played on, filling the chamber with melodies that twined through the air like incense. He poured himself into its creation, plumbing new depths of feeling as he gave birth to each note. He could almost smell the music, sweet and heady, like crushed lavender and cloves. He felt light as a feather, floating upon the thermals of sound toward the heav—

Bawang-ang-ang. Discordance slammed him back into the reality of the chamber.

"What? Oh, so the zythyran doesn't suit your tastes. You don't have to be so crotchety. Here, try—"

Kaa-luuunk. Tha-wong-ng-ng. Tsssss.

"Hey! Stop that. You're *damaging* me!"

Stones and staffs were everywhere. Muzik tried to dodge the jab of a staff, experienced failure at the shattering of his front teeth. A dark streak hurtled toward him. He ducked, but it caught the cymbal atop his head, snapping it off. A storm of stones rained down. Muzik held up his hands, tried to ward off the blows, but there were just too many. A lance jabbed deep; a hiss sputtered from his right side.

Muzik looked down. Green oily fluid dribbled from a pierced bellows and pooled on the stones. Sparks of power shuddered along his limbs. Discordant sounds born from instruments across the galaxy bled from his body; Muzik struggled with all his remaining power to draw them into harmony.

"Maestro," he cried, weaving the tones into a dark requiem. He lofted his voice to the top of the dome. "Forgive me, Maestro . . . I screwed up."

Muzik sagged like a spent bagpipe; he slumped against a baluster, slid to the pulpit floor. Valves on his neck randomly flicked open and shut. Shoulder pipes shot up and froze, bleeding silvered mist. A soft wail escaped his body, fading into nothingness.

Night had fallen upon the capital of Fendor. The world's twin moons were out in full bloom, illuminating the city's recycling center in a bright wash of silver. Zephrinna, the adolescent Fendorian in that awkward, button-headed stage, hunched beside a dumpster, looking left and right. Seeing no one, she carefully flipped the lid and climbed inside.

Trash clattered and squeaked as if seeking to betray her. She crouched on all fours, leaned forward, and rooted through the refuse with her spindly arms. If a constable caught her, she would have to endure another caning, but Zephrinna couldn't help herself. Sure, the district fathers had prayed over her, even claimed they had received a sign from the ancient worthies telling them to assign Zephrinna to the guild of seamstresses. Trouble was, Zephrinna didn't want to be a seamstress— she hated cloth. In fact, the less she wore, the better she felt.

What she loved was electronics, but the district fathers would hear nothing of a female working in an exclusively male guild. So, late at night when she was supposed to be sleeping, Zephrinna would sneak out. She and her friends had a secret shop in an abandoned warehouse where they pooled their resources. Their latest triumph had been her idea—a parabolic reflector through which they listened to radio signals that she believed came from the stars.

Zephrinna had been working alone this evening, wiring in a new amplifier in an attempt to boost the signals that seemed to originate from

Cluster 482. When she had powered it up and leaned over the feedhorn to adjust, a sudden urge struck her: she should go immediately to the recycling center. This in itself wasn't unusual, it's where she did her *woodjie* hunts—her search for trashed electronics. But she was working on *this* at the moment. She had dismissed the desire as she tweaked the feedhorn, but when the signal meter spiked, that urge grew to irresistible need. She strapped on her tool pack, trotted down dark alleys, and slipped over the recycling center's fence.

And now she was in a dumpster in the back lot. Zephrinna stopped digging and blinked wildly. Jackpot! Something silver gleamed under a pile of nutrient cans and loops of rusty wire. Lichen fryer? Boomer box? No, too round. She gripped the object with both hands, hunched with all fours, and tugged it to the top of the rubble.

A dented metal head faced her, eyes blank. It was connected to a body.

"The metal man!" she said, studying the mechanical marvel, remembering the miracle of all his instruments and the sweet sounds they had made when he walked down their lane. And then, as she pulled it up more, a gasp. "How could they have done this to you?"

She cleared the torso free of garbage. "Great gorballs, have you looked on brighter stars!"

She studied the dented arms and broken hands, fingered the oily gash in its side. Seeing the damage in its entirety brought tears to her eyes. He had been a wonder, a thing of intricate beauty and exquisite craftsmanship, whose wheelworks moved in rhythms beyond the knowledge of their world. Couldn't the constables and leaders have seen this wasn't a machine, this was a work of otherworldly art?

She halted and clenched back a cry from her neck rings. Of course they could. It's why they had to destroy him.

Filled with desperate purpose, she wrenched the body onto its side so the torn opening shone in the moonlight. Oil gleamed on the slashed bellows and slicked the crystalline components within. She leaned closer, careful not to block the moonlight. Ah, something she understood: an assortment of wires that had been severed. The sheathing looked like multicolored lizard skins, and the conductor appeared to be strands of gold, but wires were wires.

"Make way for the doctor," she murmured as she reached in her pack and pulled out needle-nose pliers and electrical tape. She stripped wires, reconnected those of matching color with quick twists, insulated the connections from the others with the tape. It was a long process.

A sudden spark! The metal man's eyes flickered and lit up. There was the wheeze of an accordion. Servos whined.

Zephrinna jumped back, banged against a side of the dumpster, fell on her bottom into a cluster of rattling cans. She watched the metal man's head rotate as he struggled to sit up and finally succeeded.

His head rotated again, slower this time, and it stopped as it faced Zephrinna. Twin eyes glowed, and the intricate irises shimmered soft brown in the moonlight, constricting and dilating like a steady pulse.

"Do you remember?" Zephrinna said, fear and awe mingled in her tone. She held the pliers in front of her; her hand trembled.

He blinked his eyes. His persona rose through a miasma of jumbled subroutines. Memories locked in place. Working his left bellows, he flexed his polymer lips, found they were still intact.

"Why, I'm a Muzik Man 1000," he said as he loosened his android psyche from its restraints so that it could run diagnostics and repair modes. "And who, may I ask, do I have the pleasure of greeting on this moonlit eve?"

"Zephrinna," she said. "Of the, uh"—she looked at the pliers in her hand—"electrical engineering guild." She blinked a few times. "Well, actually, they won't let me into the engineering guild, but I won't let that stop me."

Muzik studied her. He *remembered*. She was the adolescent that had stood there in the street, swaying to his music when the constable dragged him away. Perhaps all was not yet lost. He spoke as calm as the night's breeze. "A pleasure to meet you, Zephrinna. As far as I'm concerned, you should become whatever you wish to be."

Zephrinna lowered her pliers, released a long sigh. She scanned him up and down. "I've never seen anything like you. Where did you come from? And what is a music man?"

Muzik spun his irises. "A Muzik Man makes music, *music, music* . . ." He sighed—the reverb still worked. Muzik shifted his shoulders, shrugged off the last of the wires and can lids. "Would you like to hear something special?"

"Would I!" Zephrinna said. "Just keep your voice down. We don't want to get caught."

Muzik chuckled softly. "Voice?" He flashed a gap-toothed smile. "Baby, you ain't seen nothin' yet."

And he began to play. Low volume, but that didn't hold him back.

Muzik could almost see the jazzy rhythm entering her, fusing with her spirit. What must it be like to grow up in a world with so many restrictions? What if he had been wired to make wondrous music, and then they had stuffed him in an assembly line, screwing bolts to blenders? What would it feel like to have your unique persona ruled by the android mind, instead of the other way around?

Muzik didn't have to look at his shattered body to know the answer.

He played on, studying the glow in Zephrinna's eyes. He recognized that glow. It was the same glow, the same fire that first burned in him, the day he *felt* the music.

Zephrinna's eyes widened, grew brighter, and he realized that his playing could not possibly transfer this musical fire into his students if it didn't already rest within them, like coals waiting to be stirred. Muzik could feel himself identifying with Zephrinna in ways he had never felt before. She wasn't just a mark on his mission, someone to train and point to in proving his proficiency as a Muzik Man. She was a person, just like him, with problems, just like him, with hopes and dreams, just like him.

He wanted to help her, to help others like her become whatever they wanted to be, whether that be musician, electrician, explorer, farmer. After all, Muzik had risen above the confines of his original programming—surely these beings could too. He just had to be discreet with this world, play *a lot* more cautiously, and be careful whom he chose as his . . . *friends.* How that word sparkled in his mind.

Friends. Not marks. Not converts. Not stepping-stones to his own ambitions and goals. *Friends.* He had had it all wrong, all along. He was here for them . . . not they here for him.

Like those tears in Zephrinna's eyes. Muzik felt them as though they were his own. Though he had studied the composition for years, for the first time he truly grasped the Maestro's meaning in the lyrics of the Concerto of Divine Moonlight, Opus 27, No. 2: *"What is Empathy? Simply this. Your pain . . . in my heart."*

"That's incredible," Zephrinna whispered as Muzik drifted the melody into a slow fade. "What do you call it?"

Muzik came back from his revelation. *Right.* He had a friend to help. He tried to lift a hand to tap his head, couldn't, so he just opted for a bell tone by clapping a broken tooth with his tongue. "Lazazarian funkterfusion, my girl. Do you like it?"

"Oooo Waah," Zephrinna said, sliding close, brushing detritus from his body. "That's saah-weet! I'm going to get you fixed up—*Promise!*—show you to all my friends."

Muzik sighed, the sound of a bow gliding over violin strings. "I'd like that," he said. "I'd like that very much."

With those words, Muzik found himself transported.

He stood before the Maestro's manor at the end of the labyrinth. It surprised Muzik a little, but he assumed the damage had caused some sort of malfunction, jolting him into his VR program. But virtual had never felt so real, and he had to admit he suddenly seemed fit as a fiddle. He held up his hands, and the fingers were all there. He gave them a shake, clinking them together; they sang in wind-chimed tones. His first dream? A vision perhaps?

The doors to the vault were open. He stood there, wondering whether it was a trick, but nothing changed, so Muzik cautiously stepped inside. A nocturnal melody of chirping crickets greeted him, and everywhere stars flickered, like fireflies casting enchantments over a summer night. He took a deep breath.

"Maestro?"

The stars sprouted wings and soared through the expanse, spilling a wake of sparkling incense rich in scents of lavender and cloves. The wings gave off a myriad of vibrations, a symphony of sound, a chorus so wondrous, Muzik could only call it heavenly. He imagined that if all the spinning planets and all their celestial orbits and all the glowing stars spiraling around the hub of the galaxy could produce tones scored to music, it would sound something like this.

The symphony held him spellbound, played for what seemed an eternity. Maybe it came from eternity. Muzik stared into the night, breathless in the wonder of it all. This one song was the pinnacle of everything he aspired to create; Muzik knew he would be studying its intricacies for the rest of his existence.

The symphony rose to crescendo, flourished in absolute brilliance. Comets streaked and stars coalesced into a crystalline structure, a massive hovering sphere that radiated nacreous light. While Muzik basked in its glow, the sphere flashed with sapphire emblazonry, and the sweetest soprano sung out to his deepest desires:

SOMETIMES, MUZIK, OUR GREATEST FAILURES BECOME OUR ULTIMATE TRIUMPHS. WELL DONE, MY DEAR WONDROUS SONG. CARRY ON, MUZIK MAN 3000.

Muzik thwopped his forehead with a clang and raised his hands heavenward. "Minstrel 3000 series? Me??? I shot right past the 2000s?"

NOT PAST. THROUGH. WHEN WE RISK ALL, MOMENTOUS EVENTS CAN ACCELERATE US, LIKE A STARSHIP SLINGSHOTTING AROUND THE WEIGHTY MASS OF A SUN.

"Does this mean I get a—"

YES, MUZIK, I AM REDIRECTING A MINSTREL TEAM TO YOUR LOCATION.

"Wowza! I can't believe it. I'm really a 3000?"

YES, MUZIK. YOU ARE A COMPOSER NOW. CHOOSE A NAME FOR THE MELODY THAT IS YOU.

Muzik stood in stunned silence.

Then he did a tap number with his feet, thumped the drum on his chest, flashed his piano-key smile. The wail of a Lazazarian kazoo blared across the vault, heady and funkterfusion wild.

"*Oooo Waah!*"

finis

The Box

Bill Housley

One of my men pulled out the chair for her and she sat, glaring at me from across the table. I could see from her red eyes and dried tears that she'd been crying.

"I trust my men treated you . . . respectfully," I said.

"Of course," she replied in clipped tones. She shook the folds from her napkin and spread it on her lap. "They're more loyal than you are, General."

"We're all patriots here," I said with a smile. "Yourself included."

"Really? You were ordered to stand down with the rest of our military. Why didn't you?"

"What? Surrender? My dear, your father *gave* our planets to the Krathaal. Why should I be a party to that? No, when he betrayed us his authority was nullified, at least in my book. We'll still need to take steps, though, to secure our safety."

"Is that why you've kidnapped us?" She glanced back at her retinue as my men seated them and gave them each a plate of food to set on their laps. "Surely you don't think they'll allow you to escape in exchange for me?"

"Escape from what?" I laughed over my drink. "We're not going anywhere. I brought you here because you were in somebody's way. Perhaps you don't realize your part in all of this. You're far more valuable to me than any hostage."

I looked into her eyes and could see the wheels turning.

"I see. So you've rescued me? Somehow, I don't feel very rescued." The twitch on the right side of her lovely mouth gave away her sarcasm. "So now what? You'll feed us, let me thank you, and then allow us to leave?"

"As I said, you're very valuable to me and I need fuel for my ships."

She pretended to laugh.

"So that's it then, money? You disappoint me. I didn't think you were that shallow."

"What's the word from inside the court, Princess?" I asked, changing the subject. "What do the Krathaals plan to do about governing our people?"

She paused and looked down at her hands.

"Well, there won't be much change right away . . ."

"They've already dissolved our Parliament," I said, interrupting her.

"For now, I guess . . . but our former planets will still have representation in the Krathaal government in the form of our king–I mean, *former* king. My father has gone to the Krathaal homeworld and he'll serve in their parliament."

She resumed eating as if that were all there was to it.

"A seat in Krathaal legislature, Princess? Really?" I said. "That's awfully nice of them to give the former king of Gestuk such a high chair to sit in."

She looked up from her plate.

"Well, there's more . . ."

"You know it's only an observer's seat," I reminded her. "They might allow him to comment from time to time but he'll never have any vote. Yes, and I also know that they've assigned a Krathaal diplomat to sit on our king's throne as Governor of the Gestuk Realm of Planets. Did your tutors teach you as a child what happens to people with no real representation?"

"Slavery," she admitted, her voice cracking slightly. She took a sip from her glass.

I let that thought smolder in her mind for a couple of minutes while we ate. Did I know her as well as I thought, or would she disappoint me and ruin my plans? She obviously didn't yet know what her father had done. She'd passed that test at least.

"What about our military?" I said after a minute or two. "How do they plan to disarm us?"

"All of our conscript soldiers are already being released from their draft service, or from prison, and returned to their homes and families as citizens of the Krathaal Collective. The warships whose commanders obeyed the commands of our king, instead of following you, will return to port and eventually be dismantled . . . or absorbed into the Krathaal military. They've already started rounding up officers and imprisoning any of them who fail to pledge loyalty to them."

"Lovely, what about all those corrupt imperial family members like yourself and your father?"

Her face reddened.

"They . . . we . . . can renounce our titles and become Krathaal citizens, same as the military."

"Really? With their heads still firmly attached to their shoulders?"

She paused.

"Presumably."

"I see. So with so much opportunity ahead of you as an ordinary Krathaal citizen and all, why did I find you running from them? I mean, I'm glad you did–otherwise, you wouldn't be sitting here having dinner with me."

She took another bite instead of answering.

"Oh! And where is that ridiculous little brother of yours . . . the Beautiful Bard of Bestoreth?" I said with a flourish. "I must say I do miss his performances."

She laughed and her eyes twinkled.

"He's gone on tour."

"Oh, to sing more of his famous war ballads? I should think not."

She shook her head and smiled sadly.

"No, just love songs."

"And what about his wealth?" I said, dropping the money hint again.

"If he behaves himself he gets to keep it, same as all the rest of us . . .my father too."

I motioned to one of my men and he brought me the backpack. I could still smell the dried blood on it as I reached inside it for the box. Leaning forward I slid her half-empty plate out of the way and set the box in its place. Her hands fidgeted as she almost reached for it, but then she folded them in her lap.

"What is this?"

"Don't play games with me," I said.

"I don't have the slightest notion, General Traitor, what this box is," she lied.

"Yes, you do," I said. "This box has brought us together here today. I lost a squad of good men retrieving it from the Krathaal. Would it surprise you to know that I haven't tried to unlock it?"

She raised an eyebrow.

"Well if you went to so much trouble, then you already know what's in it."

"You didn't know the Krathaal had this box, did you?" I said. "I know that your father first showed it to you when you were a child. He showed you how to unlock it. Not only are you one of the custodians of that box, but you're also one of who used to be only a few who knows what it actually connects to and how it operates. You've read its programming many times and even enhanced the code a bit to enhance its security."

She casually retrieved her plate and placed it on top of the box, then took a bite of food.

"If you know so much, then you also know what this box protects and that I'd quite happily die, as slowly as you like, rather than unlock it for you."

"How did the war go against us, Princess Freeda?" I asked, changing the subject again. "You must have overheard your father talk about it at some point."

She waved me off and sat back, wiping her mouth with her napkin. "I have no head for such things."

"You have a head for math and technology, Princess," I replied. "I know how smart you are. Our military was larger than the Krathaal's and even more capable in various ways. We were winning."

"We *were* winning," she admitted, "until the Krathaal outmaneuvered us. Large groups of our units were captured in the last several battles."

I felt my face heat with anger.

"Not captured, Princess, *sold*! Your father *sold* those ships to the Krathaal, right along with the rest of the fleet. The Krathaal paid our king the value of those ships in exchange for ordering their surrender. Those warships were built with the wealth of the people of the Gestuk Realm of Planets and defended for years with our blood, and all the Krathaal had to do to remove them from the war was to simply slip some money into your father's wallet."

"You lie," she said, her voice cracking.

I leaned forward and pushed the box closer to her.

She paused for a moment to spoon another bite from her plate and then stared at it for a time. Then she pushed the box away, shaking her head.

"No," she said. "I refuse to unlock this box for you, not even to prove your lies. You're just saying those things to get me to open this box. If I did that, you could use it to steal funds from the Imperial Vault. That vault contains the only serious wealth that we have left and it could be used to relieve much suffering."

"Whose suffering, Princess? Yours?"

"You don't know me!" She stood and screeched in my face. "I am not the traitor here, you are! Our king commanded you to surrender your ships to end this horrible war and stop the killing of our people, but you selfishly fight on! You prolong a lost cause and expose us all to more danger! The Krathaal don't know about the Imperial Vault and if they did they would seek to plunder it, just like you do. I can't allow that! Someday, when the Krathaal are history, I or one of my clan or their descendants can use that money to rebuild."

"No, they can't," I said. I leaned forward, took her plate again, and pushed the box back in front of her. "They do know about the Imperial Vault and they do seek to plunder it. What they don't know is that it has already been plundered by your father, the king."

Her eyes went wide and her hands twitched again as she glanced at the box in front of her.

"All I want is for you to see the truth for yourself," I lied.

She sat and stared at the box for a minute, then she sighed and placed her thumb on the corner of it.

"Recognized, Queen Freeda," said the box.

Her eyes went wide again.

"Wait! Queen? What?"

"Makes sense," I said, sitting back in my chair. "Your father has abandoned his people and renounced his throne. By our laws, you're now queen and chief trustee of the Imperial Vault."

She sighed again and shook her head.

"And if my father has kept his wallet quantum linked to the box . . . then that's how it knows his location and status."

"Sure, he'd keep it linked," I said. "He wouldn't want to miss out on any pending deposits to the vault now would he?"

She looked at me and blinked.

"Did you know?"

"That your father's treachery had made you the rightful queen? Yes, I did. I wasn't sure yet the box would be smart enough to make that connection, at least not without some command from you. I must admit though, as smart as you are, I'm more than a little surprised that the box figured it out first."

"Well, things have all happened kind of fast."

"Mmm-hmm," I nodded, "By the way, the Krathaal have figured it out too. When your father abandoned his throne, I sent men home to secure that box, but the Krathaal had already seized it. It took me several more days to chase it down. If I hadn't grabbed you when I did, you'd be their prisoner by now—my spies learned from them where you were headed and that they have folks waiting for you there."

I pushed my chair away from the table and stood up.

"Anyway, I've told you about your father's treachery and gave you the key to your precious, empty, Imperial Vault. You can use it to view the transaction records directly from the king's linked wallet. We've refueled and reprovisioned your ship. Go ahead. Take your attendants and leave. Oh, and I suggest that you head somewhere other than where you originally planned."

The look on her face told me that she had no intention of leaving. If anything, she settled more solidly into her chair. A display had appeared on the top of the box and she used it to enter some commands. Her eyes grew cold as she read the money movement history. She grimaced and began to carefully activate other features on the box.

"That box knew to address you as queen," I reminded her. "So, it might still be linked to your father's wallet."

"Yes, I understand that," she said, glancing up at me. A small keyboard popped out of the box and she looked back down and began typing on it.

I didn't want to appear too eager, but she was taking too long. If her father noticed what she was doing he could break the link from his end. I needed him to not do that.

"The king's wallet . . ." I said.

"Yes, yes, I know, I get it. Now, give me a moment with this please."

She typed frantically and more lights on the box lit.

"Your highness, please hurry," I said.

"Hush!"

Her fingers flew over the keyboard. Then she reached into her pocket and pulled out her wallet, laying it carefully on top of the box as I watched. Her wallet lit, then blinked several times as she completed the transfer.

She'd taken the bait. The old former king had just lost all he'd stolen, every bit of it. All the vast wealth of our government, the bounties on our warships, along with all the various other bribes that he'd accepted from the Krathaal and others. I'd already seized much wealth in various ways since the surrender . . . but nothing like this. All the funds to run our government and military were in the queen's hands . . . and she was in mine!

"Have you broken the link to your father's wallet?" I asked.

"Of course," she said, leaning back and sipping her drink. "I can't lock him out completely yet, but that won't matter so long as we keep him away from the box. He'd need to touch it to get back in, and the vault is still empty anyway."

I had to act quickly or my victory could be lost. I turned and took my ceremonial sword down from the wall and stepped toward her.

She quickly stood and faced me, seeing immediately what I'd planned to do. The young queen, beautiful and popular, a skilled and intelligent leader, knew that as long as she lived the people would look to her. Also, though our laws gave Parliament the power, the crown holds the purse strings, and she had just complied with my plan and filled that purse.

"NO!" One of her attendants called out suddenly and jumped to her feet. Her dinner plate fell, shattering to the floor as she ran to try and interpose herself between the queen and I.

"Stop her," commanded the queen with a quick glance at one of my men. He nodded and stepped forward, blocking the path of the screaming, sobbing woman. She slapped him and scratched his face and tried to duck around him but he seized her and they fell together to the floor as they struggled.

"Gently," the queen told him as I stepped around the table. We locked eyes and exchanged grim expressions for a moment.

Then I knelt and extended the weapon out to her hilt first, bowing my head.

"I pledge my life and all of my fortunes to your service, my Queen."

She took my sword and I felt the bite of the sharp blade cutting into my hand as she slid it slowly from my grip, sealing my blood oath.

"Rise."

I looked at her standing there even more beautiful holding the bloody weapon.

"Please," I begged her. "Fund the retaking of your empire. Help me gather our Parliament out of hiding and put them back in the service of our people. Let me place you on your father's throne."

"It's not my father's throne anymore," she said, handing the sword back to me. "It's mine."

The Bard and the Invisible Witch

Elsa Nickle

A bard sat across the table from me. The long peacock feather in his bright purple Tudor cap swayed as he lazily strummed his fine white lute. The neck and pegbox had been intricately carved into the ornate head of a dragon.

"Did you know that being invisible is the most sought-after ability? Which, might I add, is ridiculous." I sat back, twisting the silver ring wrapped around my finger, wanting to find solace in its solidity. "I mean, really. Do you know how many times I've been walked in on while trying to use the privy? Trust me, it is not a blessing."

The tavern was filled with drunken men and women and loud laughter. People enjoying the company of one another. And yet, not a single glance was spared in my direction. I wanted to scream, but it would do me no good.

Basil and beef and the overripe smell of ale filled the air. "Would you like some stew, Ruby?" I asked myself. "Why yes, I'd love some." I mocked even though hunger was far from my mind. It was only that I missed at least being asked. I leaned closer to the stone hearth by my table to let the heat of the fire lick my permanently cold skin. It was the closest thing to an embrace I had felt in weeks.

I sighed, staring at the flames. "I don't know what happened. One minute I was sitting with the other women in my coven, laughing and eating and playing cards, and the next I was nothing." My head fell to my folded arms on the table.

"I know, I saw you," the bard said with another strum.

My head shot up. "You can see me?" A rush of excitement was quickly followed by humiliation. No doubt I had said something embarrassing. The heat of a blush crept up my cheeks.

"Why do you think I sat here?" he said.

"I don't know, perhaps you thought the table was empty?" I had lost count of the number of times I had been sat on. The bard chuckled as he maneuvered his lute to his side and sat forward in his chair, something like mischief twinkled in his pale blue eyes. He lowered his voice. "It sounds like what we have on our hands is a *vieille sorcière*."

"A what? And what do you mean 'we'? I seem to be the only invisible one."

He inclined his head to acknowledge the question. "A *vieille sorcière*, or hag for short, is a mix of vampire and a boohag. She sucks the life and energy out of a person until nothing is left of them. And you are correct, *seem* is the right word for it. There have been others before you and others that will come after. And worst of all, if the creature gets enough to, er . . . how do I put this delicately . . . eat—"

"I would not consider that to be delicate."

He shrugged. "Nevertheless, once she is no longer hungry, she will have adequate strength for the *congregatio* spell."

My blood went cold. I had read of such a spell. It was said to weave through large crowds, sucking out souls until nothing was left but dried out husks of skin. But I never thought I would be in danger of such a curse.

"And how do you know this?" I challenged his claim if for no other reason than I did not want it to be true.

"I am a bard, dear. I have traveled to every corner in every land in search of heroes to sing of. And do you know how you find a hero?"

I shrugged a shoulder and shook my head.

"You look for the monsters." He gave a wink. "Well, my dear, I must bid you *adieux*. Time to tune for my next show."

"But how do I find this . . . this . . . monster?" I panicked at the thought of him leaving.

He leaned toward me, lowering his voice to just over a whisper. "You should take a look at those who you surround yourself with and see which one hides a secret behind their smile. The one who seems to shine brighter while you are drained." He stood with the groan of a man well into adulthood who had survived many adventures.

"And what of the hero? Who will defeat this monster?" I needed to know where to find them.

He gave a smile, pity in his eyes. "One step at a time. But whatever you do, should you find the *vieille sorcière*, do not let it sing. That is how the spell begins. Have hope and you'll be all right." Hope? Such a fragile word offered no protection. I needed a word forged in fire. I needed a hero.

My fear was replaced with exhaustion, like I had run a mile through molasses. All I wanted was for everything to go back to the way it had been before.

Before. Now there was a magical word if ever one existed. But there was no turning back the clock. No way to stitch the *before* to the *after* without a ragged seam and so I was stuck in the middle, the red thread of fate dangling from my reluctant grasp.

I watched him leave before I stood, a thousand thoughts and a million doubts crowding my mind. How would I be able to figure out who was doing this let alone how to find a hero?

I dodged drunken sailors and snaked around tables where men and women leaned in to play cards until I came to the table where my sisters sat dipping their soda bread into their stew.

My usual seat was taken by Noxi, so I knelt in a gap between Adni and Eira, propping my elbows on the rough oak table. None of them turned toward me, which wasn't surprising considering I was invisible, but I couldn't help wondering if they even missed me. Did they care? Looking around the table, it didn't seem like it.

My eyes scanned the familiar faces, resting on each one as I did so. I wasn't sure what to look for. There was no way any of them were capable of hurting me like the hag was hurting me. Adni didn't have a malicious bone in her body. She was the brains and level head of the group. Her straight dark hair hung over her shoulder as she listened to Noxi talk, brow raised in both concern and concentration.

And it couldn't have been Noxi. I had been the one to introduce Noxi to the group when she had come to me, asking for help. She was theatrical, with her wild stories and tales of woe, but she was also fun and talented with a voice of an angel. Eira was the heart of us. Her hair cut short and a light in her eyes. Her smile was one that could brighten up even the darkest night. Lyana, with her fiery red hair, was the talent. She was focused and quiet, that is until you got to know her. Her skills with a quill were unmatched and I had to admit that I envied her gift to spin words into treasures.

Then there was fierce Ash, the one whose loyalty you had to earn. She had been through some battles but always came out stronger than before. Her chestnut hair was in a tight queue, her foot propped up on the edge of her chair. She smirked and shook her head at a joke I hadn't heard. Was I losing my hearing along with everything else? Would my mind be the next thing to go? Fingertips of worry crept up my spine and then settled back down in the pit of my stomach.

"There must be something we can do," Etya said, putting a hand on Noxi's shoulder. Etya was the spirit of our coven. The glue that held us all together with her words of wisdom and guileless heart.

But why was Noxi on the verge of tears? I had to hear what she was saying. I yawned, trying to pop my ears, and focused on her words by reading her lips.

"It's too late. Amelia tried to control my mind. She tried to ruin me." Her breath shook.

I couldn't help the relief I felt. Of course it wasn't one of my sisters. It was Amelia, the strong-willed witch from East Hollows who had bright white hair and a sharp tongue. How could I have doubted these ladies for even one second? A hint of dread hit me next. Amelia was coming after Noxi. I couldn't let that happen. We had to protect our sister. We had to stop Amelia.

"We must find her. Confront her," we all said in unison. Noxi's eyes locked with mine and I felt a jolt of joy that she could still see me.

"No!" she said quickly. "She will only lie. Say what she thinks you want to hear. Besides, I fear she has left town. There is no use searching for such a horrible person. We're all much better off without her." But what Noxi didn't know was that we did have to find her. We needed to trap her. To defeat her before her power grew.

I was about to say as much, but was distracted by a tingling in my hands. I closed them and then stretched them wide. When I looked down, my fingertips were fading. Soon I would be invisible even to myself. My head started to spin. My arms and legs went weak. I had to find Amelia before it was too late and force her to reverse her hold on me.

"Let us not think on the witch a moment longer," Adni said. "You have a show to prepare for." A show? How did I not know anything about a performance? They really were living their lives without me.

No one would notice if I left the table. No one would notice if I stood on the stage and danced a jig. The realization that nobody cared, nobody remembered me, cut like a million little paper cuts and suddenly I found the air was too thin. I couldn't breathe. With an exhaustion that nearly knocked me down to the sticky planks of the floor covered in day old ale, I stood and made my way outside.

The dusty rose and lavender sky was smudged with grey clouds. I breathed in the fresh cold air that smelled of chimney smoke mixed with sweet pine. How long until I was nothing more than a wisp, a memory, a whisper in the wind? My eyes stung, but there was no time for tears. I had to find Amelia.

Only I didn't know where to begin, what to look for. I searched the street but only saw horses and carts and little shops with teacups and pastries and colorful fabrics lining the windows. My eyes caught on a coach peeking out of the alley across from the tavern, black with gold trim. Noxi's. But what struck me as odd was that it was loaded, the horses hitched. She was leaving. More adventures I knew nothing about.

There was a white leather box buckled on the back of the coach, about the size of a toolbox, too small to be for her wardrobe, too big for trinkets. The city might have been safe, but not that safe. I knew I had to search for Amelia, but I couldn't let my friend's trusting nature rob her of something valuable.

I only meant to check to make sure that nothing valuable was inside, but when I opened the box, I leapt back in horror.

Skin, grey and withered, twisted and tossed inside. The familiar face of Amelia, now gaunt and ashen, looked up at me from her boneless body.

"Help," she mouthed the word. I couldn't believe my eyes. There was no way Noxi could have done this. I had been with this girl through difficult times. We had inspired each other. We had been best friends.

But then the other times came rushing to my mind. The times she had called and I had come running to carry her burdens. The times she had attached herself to me in order to be seen, as if she were swapping my life for hers. A sinking, anxious feeling swept over me, like flying in a thunderstorm.

"Noxi! Hurry! Your show is about to start." I heard Eira's voice ring from around the corner.

Her show. Oh, no. If her voice got to the others in the room, if her song slithered through their ears and wrapped itself around their minds, who knew what they would become?

"Just a minute! I'll be right there," her voice was sweet and innocent, but now I heard the shadow behind it.

I shut the lid, unable to buckle it, and dove under the coach. I saw Noxi's signature red shoes where I had been moments before. The sound of sniffing.

"You wretched woman. Who has been here?" Noxi rattled the box. "Tell me!" Nothing. Could Noxi read Amelia's mind? Did she know I was there, hiding under the coach?

Noxi gave a long breath out from her nose and then inhaled. Amelia shrieked, so weak it sounded like wind through a leaking window. Noxi continued on until the cry turned silent. I felt sick and numb and scared.

That would be me soon if I didn't find a hero. Stuffed in a box and drained of life.

Noxi held her skirt and started to bend down. The way she had looked at me earlier made it clear that she could, in fact, see me. I held my breath. I didn't even blink. Not daring to move even slightly. Not risking even the slightest sound.

"There you are." It was Etya this time. "You can't be late for your own show!" Noxi straightened and stumbled as if Etya were dragging her away.

Seconds sped by. Soon she would take the stage. How was I supposed to find a hero in that kind of time? I had to get to the bard, and fast. I counted to five to make sure the coast was clear then bolted from under the coach.

As soon as I turned the corner, I saw the bard sitting on some bales of hay just outside the tavern door, his lute held up to his ears as he tweaked the strings.

"What are you doing?"

"Getting ready for the show."

"Your show?" Was he in on it as well?

"You would think it would be my show, seeing as I'm the Master of Music. But alas, they have found another voice to woo the crowd. No. I am but background noise," he said as he lowered his instrument and began to expertly pluck the cords. It sounded as if he had five hands.

"Simple is not the word I would use to describe your talent, but maestro," I said, and he grinned at the name. "It's Noxi. She's the hag."

"The singer? Hm, that does pose a problem." He stroked his goatee but didn't offer any solutions.

"You have to stop her!"

"Me? Oh, dear child. What do you expect me to do?"

"You're the monster hunter!"

"I am."

"So . . . hunt it." I bounced on my tiptoes. I didn't have much time. None of us did.

"I did hunt it. And I found it. Well, I guess technically you found it, but I pointed you in the right direction. However, I do not destroy the monsters. Not anymore."

"But we have to do something." Why was he so calm? Did he not feel the urgency?

"Precisely," he said. I was nearly to the point of ripping out my hair. How could one person be so infuriating? "You see," he continued. "I may have slain quite a few monsters in my younger years, but now I am the one who whispers the secret to others. I allow them to defeat the demons." His gaze landed on me and he gave me a look as if he expected something.

"Why are you looking at me?"

"Because you must defeat it. You must use your unique strength to fight the creature." It felt like a dozen goldfish fluttered in my stomach.

"Unique strength?" What on earth was he talking about? He met me not even an hour ago, what did he know about my unique strength?

"I can tell you this: the best way to defeat it is by spreading your light."

"What light? I'm invisible. I'm nothing." Hot tears of frustration and fear began to sting the back of my eyes, but I would not let them fall.

"You are far from nothing. A snowflake may be small, but no one wants to get caught in an avalanche."

"What does that even mean?" I clenched my fists, helpless.

"It means you need to find your light, your voice, and make it grow. What is it you want these people to remember? What do you want them to feel?"

I managed to clear my scattered mind long enough to think about it for a second. What was the thing I needed the most at that moment? "Hope?" I said, my voice weak.

He gave a small nod. "All right then. That is what you need to spread."

And with that, he grabbed his lute and headed back inside, leaving me there, frozen in place. Right as he opened the door, he turned one last time. "Find the right words, the rest will come. And remember, you cannot fight darkness with darkness."

Fear climbed up my chest like poison oak and threatened to strangle me. Find the right words? But how? And even if I did find the right ones, how did I spread them?

I slid through the door and watched as the hag sat on a stool on the platform. The faces of the crowd looked pleased, eager even. They came to be entertained and she would distract them with just that as she sucked away their souls.

But as I looked closer, I saw the exhaustion behind the fake smiles. The emptiness. Gathering my courage, I went over to the first table. They couldn't see me, most likely they couldn't even hear me, there was nothing for me to lose.

Softer than a breeze, I went to each and every person and did the only thing I could think to do. I told them that they were enough. That they were loved. I said that they were needed and cherished and that their future was theirs. I whispered words of hope into their ears over and over again until my throat was like sand and my voice hot wind.

Noxi spotted me. Her brow creased in anger, but she kept singing, louder, faster. The people were drawn like moths to a flame. Their faces went slack, sad, in pain.

I looked inward, found the golden thread of my inner light and focused, urging it to grow. They had to listen, they had to believe, they had to feel.

I spoke hope as loud as I could. The beat of the word drummed louder and louder with each person and light began to flicker in their eyes. Noxi's hold weakened and in that moment, I saw hope in a new way. It wasn't delicate or fragile. It was rising each time you fell, bruised and bloody and broken. Hope was a beautiful battle cry.

The hag's voice cracked as people reclaimed their energy and fought to spread their light. She grabbed her neck, choking noises erupting through clenched teeth. Tears streamed down her pale skin as she began to shrink smaller and smaller until she was nothing more than a beetle on the stool. Faster than lightning, the bard pulled a tin cup from his belt and captured the bug with a bang.

My friends looked a bit dazed as they turned first to each other and then to me. The recognition in their eyes and the smiles on their faces was salve for my wounded heart. They stood then ran, embracing me.

"There you are, Ruby! Where have you been?" Etya asked, giving me one more squeeze.

"Not far," I said. "I just had to light a flame."

The bard took off his cap and bowed, exiting the platform to a standing ovation. The world would never know the impact that one man had on the world, the many monsters he had defeated. But I would never forget how he had helped me finally be seen again. How he had given me something I thought I had lost: hope.

Saving the Akagi

William Smith

The entire battle was engaged and lost in five minutes. Huitzilin slept through it. The blaring of the starship's call to battle stations awakened him for a moment, but a drill announcement immediately followed it. As a member of the morale branch, Huitzilin was exempt from participating in drills for 48 ship-board hours. His branch hadn't rested for a week while participating in Teuctzin Isabel's visit to the planet of Tenyaca for the Birth of Fire celebration, and Huitzilin thought his two days of relief were much deserved. He was in an escort fleet traveling through friendly territory, a parade leaving the field. Dangerous space was far away.

When the ship began battle maneuvers, the gravity-responders allowed him to remain asleep. When Teuctzin Isabel's flagship was destroyed with all lives lost, there was no shockwave for him to feel. Only when an enemy plasma slug passed through his own ship from bow to stern and cored the vessel out did he realize something was wrong, and by then he was already a statistic. He didn't know it, but in less than a second, his ship had gone from fully operational to marked for imminent scuttling.

Huitzilin dressed in a hurry and ran out into the corridor, leaving his shell-inlaid trumpet behind. His duty as a morale guard would not require music today. The gravity-responders gave out mid-stride and his momentum hurled him across the hall and into a wall. He recovered quickly and pulled himself along the wall using emergency handholds.

Halfway to Huitzilin's battle station, the lights gave out. Red emergency lighting replaced them. It suddenly felt like he was flowing through a blood vessel, and when he reached the sealed bulkhead that led to his battle station, he knew he was close to hemorrhaging. Through the bulkhead window, he could see what had once been the heart of the ship. It was now a twisted web of scrap metal and a cloud of flaking gold. A good portion of the ship's cosmetic trimming had become shimmering waste in the cold of space.

No orders had been given to abandon ship, but Huitzilin guessed the PA system was down. He pulled himself along through freefall to the nearest lifepod launch center and discovered a crowd of other crew had come to the same conclusion. They floated in a mass near where the lifepods should have been, the mass growing larger as more of the crew arrived. All of the pods had already been launched. Everyone was shouting and screaming.

"Where are the pods?"

"Watch where you push!"

"What happened?" Huitzilin joined in the shouting.

"An ambush!" Someone said. "They came out of nowhere."

"Did you see?" Someone else shouted. "The Teuctzin's ship exploded! She must be dead."

A shock went through Huitzilin's heart. Could Teuctzin Isabel really be dead? But the crowd was at too hot a fever to notice the news.

"WHERE ARE THE PODS!?" The same voice from before shouted again.

"The bridge is gone! The drive is dead! Are they going to scuttle us?"

"Did you say Teuctzin Isabel is dead?" someone wailed.

This time, the news got through. The fever died down and despair replaced the panic. The Teuctzin, sunflower and strength of their people, had been killed by the enemy. Their own ship was dead in space and whatever was left of their fleet would likely scuttle the ship to prevent it from falling into enemy hands. To lose a half-intact vessel to the enemy in such a way would be another unacceptable strike against the fleet's honor.

"We're all dead," someone moaned. "Our soul is lost, and our lives are soon to join it."

"NO!" a high feminine voice sounded behind Huitzilin.

A flurry of green robes and dark hair sailed past Huitzilin. His eyes went wide with surprise and renewed hope. The flurry settled at the edge of the crowd, adding a bright spot of color to the gray uniforms of the crew. A young woman was at the heart of that color, the Teuctzin herself! Huitzilin reached toward her, an unfulfilled promise on his lips.

"Everyone!" Teuctzin Isabel announced. "Do not despair! You have your lives as I have mine!"

Huitzilin pulled his hand back. A collective gasp ran through the crowd. Some drifted toward the Teuctzin as if they were being sucked, stopping themselves just short of what propriety forbade. Others performed the awkward freefall bow they had been trained in but never before used. The Teuctzin floated forward until she was right up against the crowd. A hulking house guard in dull yellow uniform followed close behind her, glowering at the crowd to keep their hands to themselves. A pistol hung on his hip.

"We will find a way out of this," Teuctzin Isabel said. "Have faith in yourselves."

A murmur built in the crowd, the crew wondering how the Teuctzin could have come to be in their presence. Her ship had been destroyed, and before that it had been on the opposite side of the convoy. Someone finally realized their good fortune. "We are saved! They wouldn't scuttle the ship with the Teuctzin aboard. Someone will come and save us." A wave of relieved agreement passed through the crowd, but the Teuctzin didn't seem to share their relief, even when all Huitzilin could see was her back.

"We *will* be saved," she said, "either by our own hand or by the hands of our fellows, but it's not as simple as you say. Only a select few knew of my presence on this vessel. If my flagship has indeed been destroyed, then those who knew were lost with it."

The tentative hope in the crowd lost its grip. Someone began to weep; no one offered comfort.

The Teuctzin was quick to react. "We cannot give in to death. I will say again, our health is still our own. We can move, we can think, and we can fight for our survival. There are bound to be more lifepods, but I do not know the way to them." She reached out a hand to the closest crewmember, a junior officer with a panicked look in his eyes. "Will you show me the way?"

The man shrank from her, his panic growing. This same sentiment was shared by the rest of the crowd. Touching the Teuctzin was heresy. Men and women had been executed for merely considering the possibility. But the Teuctzin was undaunted. She extended her reach and took the man by his uniform coat. The house guard grimaced but did not stop her.

"Do not abandon yourself or your crew for the preservation of my purity," the Teuctzin said, glaring at the man in her hand and then at the rest of the crowd. "Who will show me the way to more lifepods? If you must say it is to save me, then do so, but guide us to safety nonetheless."

"There will be more lifepods toward the bow of the ship," Huitzilin spoke up, his voice close to trembling. "We should all go there."

The Teuctzin turned to face him, still holding the officer's uniform. "Thank you, tepchyahqeh," she said, accurately identifying Huitzilin's rank. "Do you know for sure that the pods will not have been used by others?"

"It is unlikely," he said. "The damage—" his voice faltered. "The crew assigned to those pods will have been cut off. If they are still alive, they won't be able to make it there."

"Very well," the Teuctzin said. "Once we have found safety, we will send help for them. Sometimes those with the power to save themselves must do so, so that they can save others. What is your name, tepchyahqeh?"

"I am Tepchyahqeh Huitzilin Tlamqui, my lady," he said, barely keeping his voice steady under the assault of her eyes on his own.

"My thanks, Huitzilin," she said. "I ask you to lead the way." She turned again to the crowd. "Follow us now. Treat that as an order from your Teuctzin if you must."

Huitzilin hesitated, looking at the house guard. He had been staring at Huitzilin from the moment he had opened his mouth. Teuctzin Isabel noticed the look the two were sharing and slapped the guard on the arm. "There is no time for pointless observances of honor. Huitzilin, take us now."

"Yes, my lady," Huitzilin said, but still waited a fraction of a second until he saw the house guard nod his head. This time, Teuctzin Isabel did not notice.

Huitzilin pulled himself up to the ceiling and made his way over the crowd and past the Teuctzin, keeping plenty of distance between them. "It is this way."

The Teuctzin followed immediately, deftly using the same handholds as Huitzilin. She made up the gap he had created between them easily, and the house guard was right behind her. They were both well-versed in zero-gravity movement. The rest of the crew was slower to follow, still fearing they might infringe on the Teuctzin's honor, but their fear of vacuum death was even stronger.

The group moved through the dimly lit hall of the ship like a dislodged blood clot through a corpse, a barely registered last sign of life. Huitzilin led from the front, his thoughts on the pods that had already launched without their occupants. Some bug in the ship's system or command from a dead officer had sent the pods off prematurely. What were the chances the same mistake had not triggered all of the other pods in the ship?

He glanced back at the Teuctzin, who was herself looking at the mass of crewmembers behind her. Huitzilin could read her concern for them in the way she slowed; the way her head turned to watch carefully when a crewwoman lost her grip on a handhold. The woman tumbled into one of her crewmates, but they were able to recover and help each other to keep moving.

The promise was once again on Huitzilin's mind.

The Teuctzin looked ahead again and caught Huitzilin watching her. He refocused on the corridor before she could see his embarrassment. It was not his place to bother her now, no matter what promises he had made or to whom.

Their luck proved poor. Huitzilin came upon the next bay of lifepods to find them just as empty as the last. The gathering point for evacuation was bare. There were no discarded personal items and no blood of the wounded; no sign that any others of the crew had been there before him. Teuctzin Isabel and the house guard came up behind him, the situation as evident to them as it was to Huitzilin.

"You were wrong," the house guard growled. It was the first time he had spoken, and his voice made the vacuum of space feel closer.

"It is not his fault," Teuctzin Isabel chastised him. "Focus less on blame and more on a new plan."

"Yes, my lady."

The rest of the crew arrived. Despite the walls of dismay continually mounting around them, they were more controlled than they had been. There was no further mumbling or weeping. The crowd regarded the empty pods and then turned their attention to Teuctzin Isabel, waiting to hear what she would say. She looked at Huitzilin and then at the crowd.

"It is simple," she said. "We move on to our next option. I came aboard last night through a hanger bay. I did not notice how large it was. Would there be ships enough there to ferry us to safety?"

"It is a fighter bay, my lady," a man in the crowd said. "Single-person craft. And even if there were enough of them, they would have been launched at the start of the battle."

"We couldn't get there, anyway," someone else added. The crowd's tongue had been loosened by the Teuctzin's candor. "The damage has cut us off from the hanger."

"No matter," Teuctzin Isabel said. "There are still other avenues. Damaged as the ship is, it can still be an asset to us, and we have some thirty of the empire's finest here. Bring me your suggestions."

A junior officer spoke up. "My lady, the communications hub is within our reach. You could contact what remains of the fleet and bring them to save you."

"Save *us*," the Teuctzin corrected. "Do we know what remains of our fleet or the disposition of the enemy fleet? I will not call more souls to rescue us if they are likely to be lost themselves."

"I was in secondary navigation when power was lost," a crewwoman said. The Teuctzin's attention settled on her, and the crewwoman seemed to wither. Her voice shook as she continued. "Our map screens were not fully accurate, my lady."

"Speak freely," Teuctzin Isabel said, "what were you able to surmise?"

The crewwoman shuddered but pressed on. "The enemy force was small, only one carrier and four cruisers, but when the ship lost power, they had already inflicted significant damage. Many of our ships were destroyed before they could engage defenses; including your flagship, my lady."

"Do you know how many?"

The crewwoman shook her head. "Not a full accounting. When the map screens died, five ships had been lost. I do not know if any of our carriers were among them."

The Teuctzin was quiet and contemplative. The crowd joined her in silence for a time, but they began to grow impatient. The remainder of their fleet would not wait long to scuttle the ship. Even if friendly forces had been pushed far from the battle space, a single well-aimed plasma projectile or guided missile could still be fired from long range. It would take time, but the projectile would invariably reach them. It might already be on the way.

The crew mumbled and murmured again, if a little more productively. Someone would offer a suggestion on how they might help the Teuctzin escape, and a dozen other voices would tell them it was impossible.

"Quiet," Teuctzin Isabel's house guard said firmly, and the chatter stopped.

The house guard was not simply bothered by the noise. When the lifepod chamber was quiet again, Huitzilin could hear a subdued groaning and banging coming from the ship's hull. The others noticed it as well. Everyone was well acquainted with the ambient noises the hull of their ship might emit, even when it was under distress. This was new. It sounded like someone was clambering across the exterior of the ship.

"Boarders," the house guard said. "My lady, you must move toward the ship's center. If they breach here, they will decompress the chamber."

"Could it be rescuers?" the Teuctzin asked. "Perhaps our fleet has rallied and achieved victory."

"It has not," the house guard said flatly.

"I will trust your judgement. Come, everyone," she said, waving to the crowd. "We must get away from here." She addressed the junior officer again. "Yaoyehqeh, can you take us to the communication hub?"

"Yes, my lady," the man said. He started moving around the crowd toward one of the bulkhead doors, gesturing for the Teuctzin to follow him.

She stayed put a moment longer. "Tepchyahqeh Huitzilin."

Huitzilin hadn't expected to hear her say his name again and it startled him. He gripped his handhold tighter, drawing himself a few inches closer to the ceiling. "Yes, my lady?"

"Stay close. I may have further need of you." Only then did she follow the junior officer.

Huitzilin hung in freefall gravity for a moment longer, unsure if he should really stay with her. He was just a lowly trumpet player, no matter what promises weighed on him. Too much had been asked of him. He had always taken comfort in the knowledge he would never get the chance to act on his promise, but now Teuctzin Isabel was within his hearing, and she was ordering him to stay near.

He pushed off a nearby wall with his feet, gliding to catch up to her, but not gliding so quickly that he aroused the concern of the house guard. Just because the Teuctzin wanted him close didn't mean the guard wouldn't shoot him.

As he flew across the chamber, he glimpsed an odd shape lingering outside a nearby porthole window. He only saw it for a second and it was murky through the darkness of space, but the silhouette was clear; an enemy cruiser lurking within boarding distance, keeping pace with the drift of the derelict ship. It was a panther, frozen mid-pounce, fangs bared and ready to begin feasting on its kill.

Huitzilin reached a close but respectable proximity with the Teuctzin just as one of the panther's fangs pierced the skin of the ship. The bright end of a cutting torch burst to life on the hull, flooding the chamber with red and orange light. The torch worked its way around the side of the hull, marking the beginning of a neat circle. A hiss followed it. Air was leaving the room.

"Quickly!" the house guard shouted. "Through here. We will seal the bulkhead to slow their progress."

The crowd needed no further encouragement. They piled toward the door and Huitzilin and the Teuctzin had to move out of the way. They were separated from the house guard on different sides of the door. The house guard gave Huitzilin a look across the passing crowd that spoke of torture and death in the event Huitzilin did anything improper, but then put his efforts toward quickly guiding the crew to safety. For Huitzilin's part, he kept as far from the Teuctzin as was physically possible given the crowd's confinement. It was unsettling being so close to her, functionally alone together.

She made it more unsettling, drifting toward him until their shoulders were almost touching. "You seem to have some interest in me," she said.

"My lady?" he stammered. "I am of the people, nothing more. I wish to serve and obey."

"No, it's more than that," she said, and Huitzilin found himself wishing for the crowd to move faster so that the house guard could come and separate him from the Teuctzin. "The people of this crew regard me in many different ways, but I am familiar with all of them. Fear, admiration, loyalty, and a surprising amount of lust given our circumstances. Your interest seems special, as if you know me."

"I hope not to know you," Huitzilin said, which was the only response that seemed appropriate. It was the least likely to invoke punishment.

"The truth? I admit, I expected a lie, which makes me all the more curious. You do not wish to know me, and yet your mind lingers on me in a way that is not appropriate for your station." She gave him a sly smile and it chilled him faster than the cold of space ever could. "If— no, *when* we survive this ordeal, I will learn your special interest. Keep close or I will order Nezuapli to shoot you."

She said the last part coyly, like she would do no such thing, but she also spoke with the authority of the Teuctzin, which meant death at the hands of the house guard was a certainty if he strayed more than a few yards from her. It was more than he should have been expected to bear. If he had just fulfilled his promise right away, he could have been done with her and resumed his place as another anonymous member of the crew, waiting to die by other means.

He could do it right now. The crew was almost all through the door. He was trapped in the presence of the Teuctzin for at least a few more seconds. If he blurted his secret, it would no longer be his problem.

But it was not a happy secret. While it would give him closure, he felt certain it would give her pain. He was certain there was no right time to deliver on such a promise, and he was doubly certain this particular time was as wrong as wrong could be. Whether it was the end of their lives or not, perhaps it was better to take his secret to the grave.

Teuctzin Isabel waved the last member of the crew through the door and the moment passed. With its passing came an outrushing of air. Their enemy outside the hull had completed entry into the ship with a bang, and the ship's atmosphere vented to meet them. The passing air deafened Huitzilin and tugged him toward the door, but then the bulkhead slammed down between them and the intruders. The emergency life support system filtered more air back into their compartment.

"Lead on, yaoyehqeh," Teuctzin Isabel said, pointing to the junior officer who was looking like he wished he had avoided responsibility instead of taking it on. "We have very little time."

As they began to move again, the house guard—Nezuapli was his name—did not immediately return to the Teuctzin's side. Instead, he went among the crew, looking for anyone with weapons. None of the survivors were warriors, and therefore few of them carried even sidearms. The handful he could find he gathered around him, moving them to the back of the crowd where they could fend off any attackers. With the arrival of the enemy, it seemed he had put his trust in the Teuctzin to momentarily look after herself, though Huitzilin still caught a few of his ill-tempered glances. If any harm came to the Teuctzin while she was in Huitzilin's proximity, he would not likely survive for very long after.

So now the trumpeter was guide, promise-holder, and guard as well, when he only wished to be alive and aboard a lifepod.

While the junior communications officer was at the head, it was Teuctzin Isabel that guided the crowd quickly and quietly through the dimly lit halls of the ship. Now that the enemy's presence was known, a wariness settled over the group. They were surely being followed, and there were likely to be more boarding parties spreading from other points in the ship, raiding the carcass for valuable equipment or intelligence. The enemy may even have devised a plan to re-engage the ship's propulsion systems, potentially saving it from scuttling so that they could take it for themselves. Their success in such an endeavor would not be for the benefit of Teuctzin Isabel and the remaining crew. Death in the scuttling was better than execution or enslavement at the hands of the enemy.

They arrived at the communication hub without further incident, though the tension in the group had only heightened. Huitzilin thought he had heard enemy bootsteps or cutting torches around every dark corner, though it was just as likely he was hearing the creaking of doomed metal. His senses had tuned themselves beyond the ability to rationally analyze his surroundings.

Teuctzin Isabel terrorized the junior communications officer by patting him on the back. "Excellent work, yaoyehqeh. Now, how can we send a message to the rest of the fleet?"

"My lady," the man stammered, "I only knew the way here. This is not my station. I am a gunnery yaoyehqeh."

The Teuctzin gave him a lingering, flat stare. "Is that so?"

The gunnery officer shrank. When Nezuapli growled at him from the opposite side of the crowd, he was reduced to quivering jelly. Huitzilin knew how he felt.

Teuctzin Isabel raised a hand. "It is not his fault. I should have been clear in my expectations. Is there anyone here who does know the working of these machines?" None of the crew spoke up and Huitzilin felt personal dread again.

"Is there no one?" Teuctzin Isabel asked again. "Where have those stationed here gone?"

"My lady," Huitzilin said, regretting that his tongue remained in his mouth, but knowing it had to be used, "the crew that works in this chamber likely has a different evacuation point. They may be dead, off the ship, or just on the opposite side from us." His throat felt so dry. "However, while this is not my station either, I have operated some of this equipment before."

As a performer, he had occasionally been assigned to play his horn over the ship's PA system. He had never touched the long-range equipment, but the control schemes were similar.

The Teuctzin resumed her sly smile. "Is that so? What is your station, Huitzilin?"

"I am a trumpeter of the morale branch."

Despite the grimness of their situation, she laughed. "Excellent, show me what you can do." Huitzilin nodded and awkwardly floated around her to one of the machines. She took up a position at his shoulder, much closer than he was comfortable with.

"Again, you are drawn to my aid against your will," she said. "Perhaps it is not your own interest in me, but the guiding hands of fate and Huitzpeuchli." A small gasp escaped her. "It is even in the name! Though I would rather avoid such superstitious thinking."

Huitzilin fed power from the emergency supply into the equipment, trying to ignore the Teuctzin's proximity and her implications. If there was something divine in his meeting with Teuctzin Isabel, he had not wanted it. Then again, the divine cared little about the wills of their subjects, Huitzpeuchli in particular. The god of stars and war was well-known for his pitilessness. He was less well-known for using his hands to guide fate, but that did not change Huitzilin's position.

Nor did it change Huitzilin's inability to get the communication machine to work for him. Whatever he tried to do, errors got in his way. "My lady, something is wrong. I cannot send a message. I do not know why."

His admission of failure was punctuated by a deafening blast of gunfire. It echoed out of the nearby hall and through the chamber. Huitzilin jolted, looking in the direction of the noise.

One of the armed men the house guard had pressed into service was standing on the other side of the room's main door, clutching his stomach. He drifted backward and his hand fell away, revealing a blackened hole the size of a shafo melon. Someone screamed.

"Watch the corridor you fools!" Nezuapli shouted, thrusting himself toward the door and pulling the wounded man into the chamber. The man came limply. Huitzilin had seen death before, and he saw it now again.

With the dead man out of the way, Nezuapli drew his pistol and reached around the threshold to fire blindly down the hall. More gunfire answered, burning charred circles into the metal next to the house guard, but missing his exposed hand. The enemy had managed to bypass the locked bulkhead and maintain pressure in the ship as they went.

Nezuapli pulled his hand back and set to organizing the other armed crewmembers. They bounced into action, none of their previous despair showing in the way they charged into the hall, finding little spots of cover in the alcoves of the corridor and in another room across from the communication hub. Their ship had been slain, that was out of their hands, but the ones who had slain her were within reach of a bullet. There was also a Teuctzin to protect.

"Perhaps you could solve the problem?" Teuctzin Isabel asked, directing the question at Huitzilin.

"I will try," Huitzilin said, and then added, almost as an afterthought, "my lady."

"Perhaps quickly," Isabel added.

"Yes, quickly."

Huitzilin bore down on the machine, working his mind against the jargon-laden error messages that one of the ship's commtechs would easily understand. *Cannot transmit via VAS. Unacceptable bandwidth load. Error 37: infrastructure failure. VAS malfunction, consult a technician.* A string of automatic gunfire interrupted his already jumbled analysis. So far, only the one crewman had died, but the firefight was intensifying.

It was starting to feel like he had done this already. There had been firm soil under his feet the last time and fate had attached a man to him rather than this woman, but most of the important details were remarkably similar. Gunfire, a confined space, and a voice in his ear that wouldn't–

"This is not quick enough," Isabel said.

The manual, Huitzilin thought. He bent over and pulled a book from a dusty metal drawer at the bottom of the machine, awkwardly thumbing through unfamiliar paper meant for low-power emergencies, until he found terms defined at the back of the text. There was more gunfire. Someone screamed in pain.

"The manual?" Isabel asked. "Now?" She pushed Huitzilin to the side while he rifled through pages. "What do these errors say? What in the Ancient Mistress does VAS stand for?"

Huitzilin looked up from the manual in horror. What had she just said? Had a Teuctzin of the empire just taken the name of a goddess in vain? It wasn't even blasphemy, just unexpected, as if she had spoken in a foreign language.

She looked at him. "I see! The index. Let me see that." She took the manual out of his limp fingers. "Here it is. VAS: versatile antenna system. Does that mean there is something wrong with the antenna. Hey! Attend!"

She slapped Huitzilin on the side of the head, jarring him back into the moment. "Um, yes, sorry, that sounds right." He pressed a button on the machine and the same error appeared. *VAS malfunction, consult technician.* "The ship-to-ship antenna is likely damaged." He thought about the giant hole that ran the length of the ship. If the antenna had been in line with that hole, it didn't exist anymore.

"We just need to reach the antenna and repair it," Isabel said.

"I am not sure this is our most productive path," Huitzilin said. "The ship is badly damaged. It is possible the antenna was destroyed."

She put her hand under her chin and gently rubbed her neck in thought. It was a gesture Huitzilin had seen before, and not just on supraluminal video broadcasts, but in the flesh two years ago. The reports of the guns did not faze her. Somehow, despite living the pampered life of a Teuctzin, she was in her element, performing at peak efficiency.

"Do you know where the antenna is?" she asked as her house guard again leaned around the threshold and fired three concussive shots at the enemy.

Huitzilin pictured the ship in his mind, trying to remember its silhouette from all the times he had seen a vessel of its class from afar. Living in the bowels of the ship had not given him a good picture of the exterior. But there was a distinct antenna-like feature that stuck out in his mind the same way it stuck out of the middle of the ship.

"Amidships," he said, "not quite out of the path of the damage, but maybe far enough away to have been spared. We could get there from here, but no one—"

"Then we go," she interrupted, then turned to where the house guard was fighting for his and their lives. "Nez! We must go amidships. Is it possible?"

"If you demand it, my lady," Nezuapli called back, not taking his attention off the skirmish at hand.

"It is demanded," Isabel said.

The house guard took the fallen sidearm from the dead crewman and got to his feet. Standing just on the safe side of the door's threshold, he shouted to his newly acquired subordinates.

"Your Teuctzin wants to see the center of your ship!" He pointed down the hallway, toward the enemy. "Amidships is that direction. I will lead a tour. All who are armed will follow me. Any who neglect the call are no longer of the people. Am I understood?"

He had no problem making himself heard above the cacophony of the firefight. The men and women around him had no problem standing up to his call. Waiting for a friendly ship to callously destroy them was difficult, and so was holding a tenuous position against the assault of an enemy, but charging into the enemy's teeth? Choosing death on one's own terms? That was as easy as breathing.

There was no dissension among the ranks. Even some of those that were unarmed took up positions to follow their comrades. If and when their armed brothers and sisters fell, they would be there to pick up dropped weapons. Either that, or they would reach the enemy's position and beat them with fists and feet. Even the lone trumpeter of the group was not immune to the fever of a charge. Huitzilin felt the draw to battle as well.

"Remain where you are," Isabel said, somehow reading his desire. She moved to stand next to her house guard. Nezuapli tensed as she came closer to the hallway and the bullets flying down it.

"I will not tolerate recklessness," she told him before he could ward her away. "Are you sure it can be done? Do not waste these men and women on a pointless task."

"The enemy number but four," Nezuapli said. "They are well-equipped, but we can take them if we are swift. I have already killed one."

"Do it then."

The house guard smiled and let out a high yip. "YEOOOWW! To me, friends!"

His sudden excitement caught Huitzilin off guard. Where had the stoicism gone? The other conscripts were not as surprised. They let out yelps of their own. For a moment, the gunfire stopped. The enemy had heard the gleeful shouting and were just as confused as Huitzilin. In that lull, the house guard found his advantage.

He jumped through the threshold of the door and charged out of sight. The armed portion of

the crew went after him. A merciless din of gunfire followed. From where he floated by the communication equipment, Huitzilin couldn't see any of what transpired, but he heard it well enough.

Isabel drifted back to him and waited by his side.

"My throat is dry," she said after a moment. "Too much shouting and oration. I'm used to making speeches with more humidity in the air."

Huitzilin stared at her, unsure what to say or do. He didn't have water, though a part of him wished he did so he could satisfy her thirst. But she wasn't asking for anything. Every word out of a Teuctzin was either a request or a demand, and yet this was neither. It was merely a statement, as if she was equally unsure what to say in such a moment.

She was quiet after that, letting the battle play out without comment. Huitzilin fiddled with the equipment, making sure he wasn't missing something obvious. The gunfire continued for only a few seconds longer, not even long enough for him to start worrying about his own safety. His concern remained with the men and women fighting. If he was willing to admit it, he also worried about Isabel's feelings should her house guard fall. It was clear the two were close.

Only when an unwounded Nezuapli came back through the door and informed the Teuctzin that the task was accomplished did Huitzilin realize that, if the house guard had failed, Huitzilin himself probably would have been shot by the enemy, along with Isabel. Perhaps he hadn't worried about it because he was more worried about the scuttling, or maybe he was too preoccupied with his promise.

He should have told Isabel during the fight. It would only have taken a moment. She would have been forced to listen to him and then, once the fight was over, there wouldn't have been time for her to ask questions. No, she would have found a way to ask questions.

Now Nezuapli was rushing them into the hall and toward the middle of the ship. There was no longer time for promises. But Isabel stopped them all in the corridor. There were eight dead bodies. Five of them were the enemy, wearing black space suits and light armor. Three were from the crew. Isabel let herself float in their midst, producing three small silver disks from somewhere beneath her robes: plastic ritual candles, initially meant to be used at sea but repurposed into chemical lights for space travel.

"Nez," she said, "secure the way amidships. I will join you shortly."

The house guard hesitated only a second before he snatched up a fallen enemy rifle and shoved it into Huitzilin's arms. The weapon gave Huitzilin a certain amount of comfort, probably in the same way the charge had given the others of the crew courage.

Nezuapli ordered two of the crew to stay behind as guards and set off down the hallway with the rest of the crew. He did not look back. Suddenly, it was just Isabel, Huitzilin, and the two guards.

Isabel gently shook each of the discs and then partially cracked them in half. They began to glow with dim white light. She placed one disc next to each of the three dead crewmembers, careful to make sure the candles floated in relative stillness next to the bodies.

When the discs were in place, she bowed her head and closed her eyes. Her lips moved, but she made no noise. A moment later she straightened, smoothing out her dress. Huitzilin and the two other crew members stared at her in awe, and at least, for Huitzilin's part, love. Every subject of the empire loved their Teuctzin because it was required of them. That was simply how the empire worked. Now, watching her grieve for the men and women that had sacrificed themselves for everyone else's survival, Huitzilin found himself in the presence of personal evidence that his love was justified. It was still uncomfortable to be so close to her, but only in the same way that it was uncomfortable to hold his hand close to a sunlamp.

"Let us go," she said, and pushed off in the direction the others had gone.

Her three guards came after her, falling naturally into guarding positions in front and behind. Huitzilin purposefully put himself a few steps ahead of her, but she matched his pace anyway.

"Do you think I wasted time?" she asked quietly.

Huitzilin thought about it as they moved. "No." She had immediately accounted for any lost time by sending Nezuapli ahead, and even if she had made everyone wait during her ritual, it would only have cost them a minute. Huitzilin did not think that their survival would hinge on a single minute.

"Thank you," she said. "I was not certain."

They caught up to the rest of the group quickly, and together they made it amidships without encountering another firefight. They were lucky. There would be more than just five boarders, and the ship was not that large. Unless they were scuttled in the next few minutes, they would run into more of the enemy soon.

It was not easy finding the antenna. Huitzilin's picture of where it might be was external only. It was the same for the rest of the crew. Given a model of the ship, they could point to the antenna with ease, but being inside the model made it more difficult. Huitzilin knew there would be a console or wall control panel that connected directly to the antenna for internal repairs, but he didn't know what it looked like.

Isabel was the one to find a window that gave them a view of the antenna outside. It looked intact, and she was able to intuit where the panel would be based on the antenna's location on the hull. The rest of the crew took up defensive positions, spreading out through the rooms and hallways that converged at the antenna station.

Huitzilin slung the rifle over his back and went to work trying to figure out this new, unfamiliar system, scanning over the control panel's digital screen and examining the cabling next to it. The communication maintenance systems weren't remotely similar to the communication transmission systems. All of the errors were different and came with a whole new jargon. The interface was even a different color scheme, with orange being the dominant indicator of an error rather than red. Worse, there wasn't a manual to turn to. Others of the crew gathered in around him, attempting to offer their own perspective. None of them were part of the maintenance crew, and so all of them were as confused as he was.

Suddenly, Huitzilin felt annoyed that so much of the equipment on his ship required extensive education to operate. He had always scorned the ground forces for their commitment to equipment that anyone could use, regardless of talent or intelligence. The dumbest grunt could operate the most advanced piece of ground forces technology. It was a point of pride for every sailor in the imperial navy that they were the only ones who could do their specific job. This was especially true for Huitzilin as a trumpeter.

He hit buttons at random, hoping to trick the system into working for him or maybe trigger an error message he could understand. The interface grew more orange and filled with indecipherable error tags. He was making things worse.

"Did you try hitting it?" Isabel asked, leaning over his shoulder.

"And jostle loose something important? I don't want to break it any more than I already have."

"Maybe it's *already* been jostled loose, perhaps as a result of an enemy shell tearing out the guts of the ship?"

That was possible, but Huitzilin was suddenly more concerned with how familiar the two of them had become. He had stopped addressing her as "my lady" somewhere along the way, which should have earned him a beating from the house guard.

"I'm hitting it," she said, raising a palm.

"Don't hit—"

She smacked the side of the panel before he could finish speaking. The digital screen came loose from the rest of the panel, all of its connecting cables popping out of their sockets. It hit the floor and the screen cracked.

Huitzilin stared at it. He should have grabbed her hand. No, he was glad he hadn't. If he had touched her, he would have been shot, though that would probably have been preferable to anything else that might happen to him.

"Oh," Isabel said. "I shouldn't have done that."

Huitzilin didn't say anything. He picked up the screen and looked it over. The screen was dark with a spiderweb crack starting at the corner where it had hit the floor, but the cables dangling from the back weren't damaged. The plugs were intact as well and seemed to correspond to simple inserts on the control panel.

"The antenna just retracted itself!" a crewwoman shouted from a nearby window.

Huitzilin looked at her for a moment and then started plugging the interface back in. When he had inserted all of the cables and mounted the screen to the panel again, it powered up on its own. The image was distorted, but after a few seconds a message appeared on the screen.

Initiate system reboot? Yes/No?

A shiver at the base of his neck rippled to his right shoulder and became a signal to his right finger to touch the button corresponding to *Yes.* A loading bar and more technical jargon scrolled across the screen, split in half by the crack.

"Wait," the crewwoman by the window said, "it's coming back out now. Was *that* part of the antenna always extended?"

Huitzilin couldn't see what she was talking about, but a few seconds later the regular system interface returned without any orange errors. It was functioning normally, as much as he could judge what normal looked like.

"Does that mean it's working?" Isabel asked.

"I think so."

"Huh," she grunted. "Then maybe I *should* have done that. Good work everyone. Let's get back to the communication hub now, and quickly. We don't have much time."

The crew broke from cover and began to move back the way they had come. They floated around Huitzilin, who was hanging still in the air. He was trying to figure out if Isabel had gotten lucky or had been given some divine favor. The safe assumption was that everything a Teuctzin did was divine by association, but that was just a little hard to believe.

"Come on, Huitzilin," Isabel said as she followed the crew, "don't worry about it too much. The antenna was just inspired by my brilliant leadership."

He smiled, then frowned, and then he unslung his rifle and followed after her brilliant leadership.

No further intruders appeared on the way back, but the group heard echoing gunfire from elsewhere in the ship and came upon a few straggling survivors, some of them wounded. It was a wonder to see the life come back into them when Isabel approached. Rescue by a large group of the surviving crew didn't spark any life in them at all, but when their Teuctzin approached and asked about their condition, it was as if shining star-matter had dripped off her and filled them with light. A man who first sullenly declined medical treatment for a burn was suddenly happy to be salved and bandaged when she smiled and put a hand on his head. The sight of her or a simple touch was enough to reignite the spirit of survival in men and women that had nothing left.

Huitzilin knew he was feeding off her light as well. He was beginning to think they might actually survive. If things continued the way they were going, he was going to have to fulfill his promise. But then there was more gunfire echoing from the direction of the communication hub.

The crew was spread out, checking hallways as they moved, keeping Isabel at the center of their loose formation and as far from danger as was realistic. Nezuapli had gone ahead again with a few others of the crew to clear the way. When Huitzilin and Isabel rounded a corner and found him, one of the house guard's subordinates was motionless and drifting, a cloud of smoke blooming from a burn wound. Nezuapli was shooting into the communication hub. He jumped back just in time to dodge return fire. Instead of burning away his face and melting his chest, the rounds made two black scorch marks on the wall behind him.

"Stay back," he mouthed to Isabel, waving his hand to emphasize what his voice dared not. He clearly didn't want those inside the hub to know someone important had appeared outside. In addition to valuable materials, boarders would be looking for high-profile prisoners.

Nezuapli's eyes landed on the rifle Huitzilin still carried. It had mostly been a cumbersome obstruction since the house guard had first given it to him.

"Toss me that," Nezuapli mouthed.

Though it left him without a means to defend himself, Huitzilin was all too happy to comply. He pushed the rifle gently toward the house guard who caught it easily in zero-gravity.

Huitzilin and Isabel watched as Nezuapli fiddled with the rifle, adjusting the power controls. More of the crew came up from behind and were shushed to silence. There wasn't any noise coming from inside the communication hub, making Huitzilin wonder if the enemy was still alive, but then he heard creaking metal and plastic from within, as if someone had put too much pressure on a flat surface.

Nezuapli seemed to have tuned the rifle to his liking. It was humming with extra power. That wasn't usually a good thing on a pressurized starship, but Huitzilin trusted the house guard's judgement.

Nezuapli pushed away from the wall and aimed right at it. Only then did Huitzilin realize his full plan.

"Wait," he started.

The house guard fired the weapon through the wall and into the communication hub. The heightened energy level of the rounds in the rifle meant they had no trouble burning right through the metal between them and the soldiers inside. Nezuapli fired several more times and there was more movement from inside. Someone shouted in surprise, their voice muffled by a vacuum-sealed helmet. Then there was silence.

Nezuapli peeked through one of the burn-holes he had made and gave a single satisfied nod. "They're dead. It's safe."

He had forgotten there were more than just enemy soldiers in the communication hub.

"I think you may have killed us as well," Huitzilin said without thinking.

Nezuapli gave him a sharp look. "Watch how you speak to me, tepchyahqeh."

Huitzilin's heartbeat increased tempo. He should have been more tactful. He was losing his sense of social place. Talking to royalty, even their guards, was a bad idea. Talking without thinking was a nightmare.

"Gods, he's right," Isabel said. "The equipment!"

She rushed into the communication hub and Nezuapli's eyes widened. He raced after her. Just because he had said it was safe didn't make it so. Huitzilin eased in slowly after them, taking in the damage. There were five dead enemy soldiers adrift in the air, but that, although a grim sight, was the only bright spot in the room. It smelled of burning plastic.

The machine Huitzilin had been working on before had a smoking hole right through its center. One of the dead soldiers was floating just next to it, blood pooling out of him and into the exposed circuitry. Huitzilin pushed the soldier gently away from the machine and looked over the damage.

Here was something he truly had no experience with. At least the antenna maintenance panel had a user interface. The inside of the communication machine was just wires and circuit boards. He immediately gave up on the idea of fixing it and tried to power the machine on. It sparked and caught fire the moment he reconnected it to emergency power.

Nezuapli was quick with a nearby extinguisher to put the fire out, but the fire-retardant foam sealed the fate of the machine—not that it had had much fate left in it.

"What about the other equipment?" Isabel asked.

"It is all for internal communication," Huitzilin said. "Inside the ship only, for entertainment and crew use. Nothing else can reach the rest of the fleet."

"Oh," Isabel said. Then she was silent, but only for a moment. "What are our other options?"

Huitzilin, Nezuapli, and the rest of the crew were quiet. The ship was a corpse, after all. It couldn't talk. It couldn't move or fight. Emergency power would soon run out and then they would just have what little oxygen was left in the ship. That would probably bleed away in short order. But of course, their own troops would blow them up long before oxygen became a problem.

"Oh, gods," a crewwoman said, but she didn't have a solution to contribute. Instead, she had a computer-pad in her hands. "My tactical display just lit up."

Isabel walked over to her and examined the screen. Huitzilin didn't bother following.

"What are these dots?" Isabel asked.

The crewwoman with the computer-pad took a deep breath. "It's messy, but it looks like the ship detected a salvo of missiles from the direction of the system's star. They are on course to impact us."

"Ah," Isabel said. Huitzilin could see the neurons firing in her head. She was still looking for a way out. "If we can't communicate with the rest of the fleet, perhaps we can dodge the attack. If we get thrusters back online or even just one boost out of the main drive, we could avoid the missiles and signal our forces that we're alive."

"The main drive is gone, my lady," Huitzilin said. "There is nothing there. Thrusters wouldn't help us dodge a guided missile, especially without enough power to get them working."

"Could we commandeer one of the boarding craft?" she asked.

"Impossible," Nezuapli said. He seemed in a daze, his eyes distant. "Our soldiers have tried it before. The enemy ships cannot be flown without special genetic access. They explode if improper use is detected, and enemy marines will risk death before being coerced into helping."

"Fine," she said. "What about lights? Could we rig the ship's running lights to blink and send a visual code?"

She was reaching, scraping the edge of a cliff and hoping she could hold everyone's weight with just the tips of her fingers. Huitzilin could tell she knew it as well.

"Don't answer that," she said. "We're much too far away for running lights to make a difference, I know that. How much time do we have?"

"It is hard to say, my lady," the crewwoman with the computer said. "The sensors are too damaged to determine when the missiles were fired or how far away they are. They're slow movers by space travel standards, but we still don't have long to impact."

"My lady," Nezuapli said. "It is my fault. I should have been more careful. Please, take my weapon and–"

Isabel smacked him on the side of the head "If you dare ask me to take your life, I will revoke your status in my house and re-title you as tlac."

Nezuapli's head sank. "Yes, my lady. I apologize, my lady."

Everyone was quiet. The despair they had managed to banish was creeping back in. Huitzilin could feel it too. The scramble for a solution had distracted him from his fear. He could tell Isabel hadn't yet given up, but there was nothing left to try.

The ship itself had given them a sign. The vessel's damaged sensors should not have been able to detect incoming weapons fire, let alone show it to them on an over-the-air computer, but it had done them the service of ensuring they knew the end was coming. In the silence, the surviving crew dispersed to the corners of the room and nearby hallways. Some found secluded spots to be alone. Others went as friends or couples to be alone together.

Huitzilin remained in the communication hub. He wanted to sit down and rest against something, to make himself small. He put his back against one of the useless machines and tried to rest his backside on the floor, but he ended up awkwardly floating away from everything. The lack of gravity made it impossible to get in a comfortable position to die. It would have been easy to fold in on himself and become a ball, but that would have been undignified.

In one last assault on Huitzilin's delicate sense of social self, Teuctzin Isabel pushed over and floated next to him. It seemed he wouldn't get to die without one last chance to fulfill his promise. If only the plasma slug that had killed the ship had taken him with it earlier and saved him the embarrassment. Nezuapli remained vigilant in the center of the room, floating in place, perhaps still looking for some method of escape.

Isabel spoke first. "'Not long to live' is too long when there's nothing to do but wait."

"It will give some the time they need to prepare themselves," Huitzilin said.

"That is good, then."

Huitzilin opened his mouth to spill his secrets but said something else instead; something he should not have.

"Why do you insist on breaching the code of honor with me? I know it is your right, but it has distressed me greatly at a time I would rather have rather spent finding peace. Any of the other crew could have done what I did. They can all read a manual. You reset the antenna on your own. Yet you insist on keeping me close. Even now, it seems you wish to spend your last breaths speaking to me. You must know how much it upsets me. It would upset any of the people."

He said it loud enough for both Isabel and Nezuapli to hear him. Huitzilin expected to be choked to death for his impertinence. Instead, the house guard just gave him an unhappy look and a half-hearted growl. Isabel grew more thoughtful.

"Do you believe we have breached honor?" she asked. "Or have we simply ignored ritual in the face of peril?"

"Ritual is essential to maintain honor," Huitzilin said.

"Ritual is essential for rote memorization. It forces the people of our empire into the positions we have set out for them and ensures that other possibilities do not occur to them. Often times, that is a useful outcome. It keeps the empire running smoothly and the greater part of the people enjoy happier lives for it. But ritual can be taken too far, particularly when life and death are in contention. When thirty men and women are more concerned with proper freefall bow etiquette than the continuation of their own lives, ritual has failed."

"Very well, 1 can agree with that," Huitzilin said. At any other time, he probably would have been shot for admitting a possibility existed where he might disagree with her. "But why me?"

"You spoke up. You volunteered to help, and that instantly made you more qualified than anyone else. Nez can do many things, but he cannot do everything. And if I'm being honest, I could feel my death was close and you were the only person in the room who seemed capable of seeing something other than their Teuctzin. It was nice to think someone might know Isabel had died along with the Teuctzin. It was selfish of me, I know. I would have released you from your discomfort and simply endured, but I realized you were holding something back. It seemed like you wanted to tell me something, but for some reason you refused to say it."

Huitzilin remained quiet, staring ahead and away from her. He did not want to know his Teuctzin. He was much happier being of the people. But he knew he couldn't abide by that feeling, not when this woman was next to him, experiencing the same fears and misery as the rest of the crew. If she wanted to be treated as human, was it right to deny her that?

"Why not tell me?" she pressed. "If it's something truly blasphemous —well, given your apparent devotion to ritual and honor, I doubt that could be it."

"I," Huitzilin began, his voice quiet. Something on the other side of the room caught his eye, floating loose in freefall with everything else. "I . . . I see a cable."

"That is not what you were going to say," Isabel said.

Huitzilin pivoted in the air and kicked over to the other side of the room. He passed Nezuapli on the way. The house guard gave him a confused look. When Isabel went to the far side of the room as well, he followed them both.

The cable that had caught Huitzilin's eye was very familiar to him. He used it every week during morning Quiztli, the call to general assembly. It matched an electrical port on his trumpet, an amplifier pickup. Such things were more useful on stringed instruments, but the device allowed him to play his trumpet for the entire crew without significant degradation of sound. It also had a connection to the ship's communication antenna in the event that a musical performance would be broadcast from the ship to the rest of the fleet, to a planet, or to a space station. He had never used it for that, but he knew it was possible.

"I need my trumpet," he said.

"Now?" Isabel asked. "One last song to send us off."

"I can play for the whole fleet with this cable. It goes right to the antenna. We could send them some kind of message; get them to deactivate the missiles."

Isabel's eyes widened. "It doesn't use the destroyed machine?"

"I don't think so. I mean, the two systems are on opposite sides of the room."

They were quiet for a moment, contemplating their own ignorance. There could be a thousand wires in the wall connecting the two points. Huitzilin's assumption was founded on proximity only.

"Where is your trumpet?" Nezuapli asked.

"In my quarters," Huitzilin said, "toward the stern of the ship and the lifepods where we first gathered." It was well past the antenna station. The ship was barely longer than 1000 yards, but the distance was magnified by the presence of boarders.

"The enemy must know the scuttling salvo is coming," Isabel said. "They may have abandoned this ship. We have to try." She turned away from Huitzilin and Nezuapli and approached the nearest concentration of surviving crew. "There is another way off the ship. We must retrieve Tepchyahqeh Huitzilin's trumpet."

None of the crew responded. They didn't even look at her. Their enthusiasm depleted, they weren't willing to expend energy on a new plan. Huitzilin could see it well. In their hearts, they knew they were doomed.

"Please, we can do this," Isabel said, turning to a different group of crewmembers. "We can survive."

"Can we, my lady?" a crewwoman asked. "If even you cannot save us, perhaps it is a sign that it was not meant to be. At least we can die knowing the enemy won't use us or the ship to any advantage."

"I *will* save you," Isabel said. "If you won't come with me, it will just be the three of us. Remain here and stay safe."

"Tepchyahqeh Huitzilin and I will go, my lady," Nezuapli said. "You will stay with the others where it is safe."

Isabel glared at him. "Giving me orders? Encroaching death has made you bold."

"It has always been my prerogative to command you when there is a threat. I am trained for combat and Tepchyahqeh Huitzilin knows the way. There is no time for discussion."

The house guard grabbed Huitzilin by the arm and hauled him away before Isabel could protest further. She didn't try to follow them as they went out into the hall, but Huitzilin could feel her eyes on his back.

A few of the crew looked up as they passed. No one moved to join them. Too much failed effort toward survival had left them spiritually exhausted.

Nezuapli let go of him and followed him through the ship. They moved quickly, only stopping at corridor intersections to see if any boarders were lying in wait. The enemy, no doubt, had better information on the incoming salvo than the crew did. If they weren't already gone, they would be soon.

"I am sorry I snapped at you," Nezuapli said. "It was my mistake shooting that machine, and I knew it. In my pride, I lashed out."

Huitzilin was shocked to hear him say anything at all, let alone to hear him apologize for something that had been well within his rights. Huitzilin had reacted with barely disguised hostility when the house guard had fired into the communication hub, and that was not how a man of the people should behave around royalty or their guards.

"I can tell you are a good man," Nezuapli continued. "You have been dutiful to the Teuctzin despite the extreme circumstances and her erratic behavior."

It was another shock to hear him speak ill of the Teuctzin, and Huitzilin knew the words would disappoint Isabel.

"Her leadership inspires dutifulness," Huitzilin said. "I cannot help but love her, and I am sure it is the same for the others, even if they are incapable of showing it anymore."

Nezuapli gave him a sharp look.

"Dignified and royal love, of course," Huitzilin amended. "I harbor no romantic feelings."

Which was the truth. He had no interest in seeing Isabel after this day, in the afterlife or otherwise.

"That is good. Many confuse romance and duty. How close are we?"

"My quarters are just around this—"

Huitzilin peeked around the corner that would lead to his room and pulled his head back quick enough to strain a muscle. There were a dozen enemy soldiers gathered at the end of the next hallway. An airlock door had sealed in front of them, and they were trying to open it. Their voices, stern but verging on panic, were muffled by their suits. Nezuapli watched Huitzilin's reaction and did a quick check of the hallway himself, barely exposing a single eye.

"They don't appear to have noticed us," he said quietly.

"Do we wait for them to move on?" Huitzilin asked, matching his whisper.

"That airlock is sealed for a reason. If they open it, the compartment will empty into vacuum. And I don't think we have time to wait."

Huitzilin didn't have a time piece. He had no way of knowing how close the missile salvo was to hitting them.

"What do we do?"

Nezuapli's head pivoted, observing his surroundings. A large piece of the interior hull the size of his chest was floating nearby, shaken loose by the shot that had killed the ship. He grabbed it out of the air, gripping it by a torn bit of wall-strut. He dialed the power down on his rifle and handed it to Huitzilin, then he drew his pistol. He looked like an ancient ocēlē knight, girded for battle with shield and with a pistol in place of a short sword.

"Cover me. Once the enemy is dead, retrieve your trumpet."

"There are 10 of them," Huitzilin said. "You don't stand a chance."

"Their numbers are not an issue."

"You'll get yourself killed. Isabel wouldn't want that."

Nezuapli gave him one last stern look. "The Teuctzin does not always get what she wants."

The house guard dove around the corner, holding his makeshift shield out in front of him. Huitzilin watched him go and then steadied the rifle on the edge of the hallway corner. If he couldn't stop Nezuapli, he could at least support him.

The enemy soldiers, still focused on the airlock, did not notice their approaching attacker. Nezuapli floated silently closer and closer and Huitzilin waited, finger on the rifle's trigger. One of the soldiers turned around. Huitzilin shot him, taking him in the arm. The soldier spun from the force of the impact, flailing his limbs and bumping into his comrades. Nezuapli opened fire, hitting two of the enemy soldiers in the head.

Huitzilin fired one more time, the shot just missing Nezuapli and hitting the spinning man in the chest. He stopped flailing. Huitzilin took aim on another soldier, but then Nezuapli was among them, and opportunities vanished for a clean shot.

Nez was like a jaguar among startled goats. He fired twice more with his pistol, dispatching two soldiers with headshots. Then he threw the empty weapon at a third soldier, knocking the combatant's helmet back. The remaining soldiers fired their rifles at him, but they either missed or hit the shield. The power on their weapons wasn't dialed high enough to burn through the metal.

Nez drew a knife and charged one of the five remaining soldiers. He stabbed the man in the throat but exposed himself to the rifle of another. He was shot in the right leg. A human in freefall had plenty of other ways to maneuver, and it seemed Nez did not feel pain. He pivoted around the man he had just stabbed and took his weapon, firing it back at the dead man's comrade and riddling him with burn marks. At the same time, he pivoted his shield toward the other three soldiers, blocking several more shots.

But the shield was losing its usefulness. It had been cooked and warped by the heat of punishment. Nez threw it at the three remaining soldiers and then threw himself at them, leading with his knife. They became a tangle of body parts, and Huitzilin found his chances to intervene complicated even more. Nez's knife moved in and out of the human mass as he found soft flesh to stab. Blood filled the air around them.

More rifle shots went off. There were muffled screams and unmuffled grunts.

Two of the soldiers stopped moving. Another pushed away from the tangle, leaving a thick line of blood behind. It streamed out of his chest, but he was still raising his weapon for one last shot. Nez wasn't moving anymore. He didn't react as the last dying soldier lined up on him.

Huitzilin shot the soldier in the head. The hallway went quiet. The different bodies drifted in the directions they had been going when they became corpses. Nez remained still.

Huitzilin slung the rifle on his back and propelled himself down the hallway as fast as his arms could take him. He stopped himself with a handhold just before running headfirst into Nez's floating form. Huitzilin awkwardly worked his way around the house guard's body, trying to check his pulse. He found a left leg that was barely attached at the calf. He found a singed, bleeding hole in the stomach and chest. He found an arm that was severely burned where it had nearly fused to a hot metal shield.

He also found breath, but it was weak. The house guard was still alive. Huitzilin could tell it would not last for long. The blood in the air was thick, and much of it was bubbling out of Nez.

"Ahhh," Nez wheezed, and Huitzilin wasn't sure if it was an acknowledgement of his presence or a death rattle. "You . . . Got . . . Him." There was a long pause. "Good . . . shooting."

"I told you it was suicide," Huitzilin said, his own voice barely coming. He grabbed the man's hand and held it tight. "Why did you do that?"

"Not . . . done . . . yet. Get . . . the trumpet."

"Isabel would have told you not to do this. You know that."

The house guard smiled. For just a moment, his lungs were strong, and his voice came clear. "So she would. Get your trumpet, boy."

He died. Huitzilin was alone, still holding his hand. He wanted to stay there with Nez. It felt like the right thing to do. But he knew there was no time. There might not even be time to make it back to Isabel if he went as fast as he could fly. He quickly opened the door to his quarters, found his trumpet and mouthpiece, and rushed back to the communication hub, leaving Nez's body behind.

On the way, he encountered one more group of enemy boarders. They fired a few half-hearted shots at him and then left him alone. They were probably as concerned about the missiles as he was. That they hadn't abandoned the ship yet was a good sign. Maybe there was enough time left.

He reached the communication hub. Isabel's eyes lit up as he entered the room. The light vanished when she saw that he was alone.

"Where is Nez?" she asked.

"Gone," Huitzilin said quickly, knowing a single word for Nez's death was harsh but necessary. He went to the instrument station and plugged the cable into his trumpet. A panel on the wall lit up with green text. It looked like the transmission would work. "What do we send?"

Isabel stared at him for several long seconds. He could feel the missiles getting closer and closer, but he didn't dare say anything. He couldn't force her to ignore the death of her guard, even if all of their lives depended on it.

"I worked out a code," she finally said, picking up the computer-pad the crewwoman had given her. The tactical display was gone and replaced with a note-taking program. Tiny circles and short lines were written across the top. Huitzilin instantly recognized the code form. It wasn't a common form, but still saw limited use by the imperial navy. The enemy was unlikely to understand it.

"This should work," he said. "What does it say?"

"*Teuctzin Isabel is alive and aboard this ship*," she said.

Huitzilin checked the connection between his trumpet and the ship one more time, then he wet his lips and pressed them against the trumpet's mouthpiece. He followed the code's instructions, blowing a short note for each circle and a longer note for each line. It went quickly, and when it was done, he repeated the code. Then, he played it a third time.

Some of the crew looked up at the noise, but quickly lost interest. They either didn't understand what was happening or didn't care to know if it would work.

"Now what?" Isabel asked when Huitzilin lowered the trumpet. There were tears forming at the edges of her eyes. They pooled into two balls, refusing to fall in zero gravity. She wiped them away with a soft sniff.

The computer-pad was showing its tactical display again. Huitzilin was unfamiliar with the readout, but it was clear enough to see their doomed ship at the center and eight little white dots blinking toward them. They were very close now. The image was distorted and occasionally flashed out of sight as it lost connection with the ship's damaged sensors, but the missiles couldn't have been more than a few minutes away.

"Light delay," Huitzilin said. "And they need time to decode the message. It doesn't mean anything yet. The message was sent." He didn't know that for sure. The machine the trumpet was connected to seemed fully functional, but he didn't know what fully functional actually looked like.

One of the crewmen spoke—the gunnery officer that had led them to the communication hub. "They think you're lying. Everyone knows Teuctzin Isabel was on the flagship."

He had apparently been paying close enough attention to make everything worse with his cynicism, though Huitzilin couldn't blame him. Why be anything but cynical when death was certain.

"No," Isabel insisted. "You are wrong."

She turned around and floated to the destroyed communication equipment. "All I have to do is tell them we're still here. I can do this."

She reached into the hole Nez had burned open, pulling out burned wiring and wiping away the blood of dead soldier. She would not give up and started pounding on the top of the machine with a flat hand. It was obvious the machine would never work again. Luck or divine favor would not step in to save her this time. Huitzilin remained where he was. He held his trumpet in one hand and the computer-pad in the other.

What could be done in a few minutes? He had the ear of everyone in the system, even if they couldn't understand him. What did that let him do? How much time did he really have? Was it even time enough to play a song for the crew?

A melody struck him. It was one he had played many times before. He knew it by heart. Every member of the royal family had a song composed for them at birth. The tune would receive adjustments and variations as the child grew older and earned recognition, but the core melody was always the same.

Huitzilin fixed Isabel's anthem in his mind and did his best to tune the trumpet after playing just a few bland notes. He was first chair trumpet of the morale branch band. If he was going to play this song, he wasn't going to play it poorly.

He made one last check that he was still connected to the ship, and then he began to play. It was a slow melody. Long notes gave way to short, dramatic pauses. Huitzilin felt every new measure coming and put all of his breath and heart into buzzing out each brilliant note. The trumpet wasn't the ideal instrument for such a song. A softer wind instrument or something with strings would likely have fit it better. He did his best with what he had and hoped the rest of the fleet could hear him trying.

He got lost in the music. The song was just under two minutes in length, and for two minutes there was nothing left in the universe. He wasn't trying to save anyone, not even himself. He was just playing his instrument; this was what he had always been best at. If he was going to die, it would be with his lips on the mouthpiece and his last breath funneling through brass pipes.

There was more to the song than the melody, but he couldn't put any of it into his trumpet. It was all secondary, anyway. The lyrics were repetitive and trite. There was usually dancing, but the slow and boring kind. The music, though? That was beautiful; more beautiful than he remembered now that he was belting it out for the last time.

When he was done and out of breath, he found the entire ship was looking at him. The despondent crew had gathered around. Isabel had left the broken machine and floated next to him. Huitzilin hadn't noticed any of them moving. If no one else in the vastness of space had heard him, at least these few people had. Whatever else he had done with his life, this had been good.

He looked at Isabel. She wanted him to tell her what he knew. Could he really do that? She was very likely in the last moments of her life. Did he want to make them even worse by telling her something so upsetting? But it had been in the last moments of someone else's life that he made this promise. Did he grant a dying man's wish to be heard, or did he grant a dying woman's wish to pass away without learning the horrible truth?

"I knew Tlatena Pedro. I was with him on 52 Acatl c."

The sound of her older brother's name brightened Isabel's face, but it darkened when she heard the name of the planet.

"I only knew him for a week," Huitzilin continued. "We were stuck in the same trench with forty other imperial soldiers. The enemy pummeled us with artillery on the ground, bombs from the air, and plasma from orbit. You know the story, I'm sure. You know it was Mactlin incarnate. We spent a week in the underworld, expecting every whistling shell to be the last thing our ears would hear. I was trapped there with all of them, serving in my biennial combat position. I didn't even have this trumpet with me.

"Tlatena Pedro kept us alive. He saved us when the enemy tried to kill us. He saved us when we tried to kill ourselves. I would have died two years ago if it weren't for your brother, I am sure of it. I never spoke to him until the very end, but I knew he was the best man in the universe. I would have followed him out of that trench and into a million cannons.

"The only time we talked was at the end of his life, on the last day of the battle. I won't mention his condition at the time. You probably know exactly what happened to him. It doesn't bear repeating. It was also the only time I doubted his word. He gave me a message to give to you, verbatim. I'm sure he never expected me to be able to deliver it."

He paused. "You knew your brother better than I. Are you absolutely sure you want to hear this message?"

She gave him a knowing smile. "I'm quite sure I know what he was going to say, and I'm quite sure I want to hear it."

Huitzilin looked down and said, "On the final day of the siege, when I came upon your brother in the last few minutes of his life, he gave me this message for you: 'You are going to make a terrible ruler. You were always worth little as a teuctzin, and you'll be worth even less as tlihtoeni. I should hope father outlives you so that someone more worthy can take his place.'"

Huitzilin looked up expecting to find Isabel's expression had turned sour. Instead, he found that her smile had only grown wider. The rest of the crew was staring at him in horror. But Isabel began to laugh. At first, Huitzilin thought it was a deranged laugh, but he quickly heard joy in her full, throaty bellows.

Her laughter went on for thirty seconds more. When she finally stopped, Huitzilin wasn't sure if it was because the approaching missiles reoccurred to her, or she had finally realized her brother's message wasn't funny.

"You remembered the message well," she said, and suppressed yet another surge of giggles. "It was very specific."

"I apologize, my lady. He told it to me twice and made me repeat it back to him while the surgeon tried to save his life."

The man had been nearly cut in half at the waist, but he had been so enthusiastic and insistent that Huitzilin had thought he might pull through.

"That big polnokoyo," Isabel said, and a few people in the room gasped.

How her language could shock anyone after what he had just told her, Huitzilin didn't know.

She continued, "It's nice to know he was thinking of me at the end."

"Again, I apologize, my lady, but how are you not furious?" Huitzilin said. "At your brother or me?"

"You were just relaying his message, and he was always protective of me."

"His words weren't protective," Huitzilin said, though when Tlatena Pedro had delivered his message, it had been with an incongruous amount of heart.

"Pedro hated his position," Isabel explained. "He did his best to excel, but every day that he lived under the responsibility of being tlatena was two days off his life. It is the same for our father. It is draining work, and my older brother always wanted to spare me from it. This is his way of trying to deter me. I don't know why he thought it would work, but he also never understood my relationship with my position.

"I didn't speak to him for two years before he died. I thought there was some rift between us, and that I had done something to alienate him. I thought he might really have come to the conclusion that I was not worth his time. What you have given me today is proof that I was wrong. You may hear an insult, but I hear a plea for my health.

"Let me tell you something, Huitzilin." She took the computer-pad from his hands and faced the screen toward him. "I love to serve."

The screen showed the same tactical display as before. The dots that indicated the missiles were almost right on top of the ship, all seven of them. Huitzilin cocked his head to the side. There had been eight dots before.

Isabel went on. "Every day I live as teuctzin is two days added to the value of my life, and while you were giving me my brother's message, one of the missiles self-detonated."

Huitzilin took the computer-pad from her. The missile dots weren't on top of the ship at all. They had passed the ship. One blinked out of existence and the remaining six continued away. If he was right about the orientation of the display and its relationship to the space around them, the second missing missile had just hit the boarding ship he had seen earlier outside. Not only had friendly forces not scuttled their teuctzin, they had also eliminated the closest enemy combatants instead.

Huitzilin raised the computer-pad over his head like it was a trophy. "We aren't going to die!"

It took a few moments for the crew to realize he wasn't delusional. He showed the screen around, pointing at the trajectory of the missiles. As a group, they all went to the edge of the ship where the hull met space. They gathered next to tiny windows, trying to see outside. Indeed, the enemy ship had been reduced to scrap and embers.

The crew erupted into cheers and grateful sobs. Isabel approached Huitzilin again.

"Tepchyahqeh Huitzilin," she said, "you're pretty good with that trumpet. How would you like a promotion to house guard?"

Huitzilin looked at her, stunned. "Absolutely not."

Freedom's Song

Cray Dimensional

Finn O'Sullivan sat strapped to one of two chairs in a wee office at Belfast Asylum. His guitar lay on the wooden desk, out of reach of his bound hands and feet. The blokes running the asylum weren't allowed to use restraints, but the alienist, otherwise known as mad-doctor Edward Ward, didn't follow the law. After all, the man incarcerated him even though he wasn't mental. So what if he sometimes saw the future. It didn't mean he was delusional. He just wanted to be free, living the life of a bard. He would've escaped months ago if it weren't for his guitar. But he couldn't leave his musical mistress. Her strings inspired the future tales.

Edward Ward sat across from him, with only the desk between them. He wore a fine black vest and oversized slacks, not his usual attire. But no matter how fancied up he was, the scowl on his face told Finn all he needed to know. "Finn, my boy. I need you to be on your best behavior today for the Overseer."

Finn wasn't a boy, and there was no way he would make Ward look good without payment. "Will I, yea?!"

Ward slammed his fist on the desk. "Listen to me, you will behave, or I will make your life miserable."

"I could behave if you give back me guitar."

"Only if you admit that you do not see the future and that your visions are delusions spawned by the devil."

"Well, aren't you de Holy Joe? What's wrong? You don't like the jig I wrote you? How'd it go again?"

"Now Ward is locked in Granisis Tower
Where he no longer has the power
To lock away those with magical gifts
Imprisoned, he listens to Finn's music and sits."

Edward Ward slammed his fist on the desk. "Lies. Another year for you, then." That was Ward going back on his word again.

Finn had been here for donkey years and didn't expect to be released. He wanted to finish that song, but without his guitar, he couldn't. It was his muse. "Sure, look, I wouldn't believe you if you said otherwise. You have no plans to let me go. Why not a bit of music to pass the time?"

"Sing for freedom for those
Whose gifts give them different woes . . ."

Ward interrupted. "Stop! You don't play music. You spin tales."

The conversation was going nowhere, but this was the closet Finn had been to his guitar. If he could get Ward to take off the restraints long enough to grab it, he could leg it out of there. "Stall the ball, Ward, I got to hit the jacks, or things will get messy. You don't want me to stink up your clean-smelling office."

Ward threw his hands in the air. "Of course, you do. I'll let you loose, but I'm going with you to make sure you don't get into trouble." He made his way across the closet sized room to Finn.

Finn didn't make a move while Ward untied the restraints. Instead, he pretended to be the scrawny bard with no fight. Once free of the straps, Finn dropped to the hardwood floor next to Ward's feet. Ward was too busy looking out the window to notice what Finn was doing. Grand. The bloke wore brogues bound to his feet by leather laces. Finn exploited Ward's fashion mistake and tied the laces to the chair.

Ward turned away from the window and reached down to grab him. "Get up."

Finn sprang to his feet and grabbed his guitar off the desk. Ward fell over the chair, giving Finn enough time to leave.

Finn ran down the empty cinderblock corridor, glancing behind him to check for Ward. He heard clanks and banging from the office echoing through the walls. Shortly after, a bell rang to signal that an escape was in progress.

Finn picked up the pace, making his way through the hallways to an exit. The door to the gathering hall was to his left, and on his right was the entrance to freedom. He looked around the corner to find a muscular attendant that blocked the exit. He couldn't take on a man of that size. A guitar in the gathering room played "The Feast of Bealtaine," giving him an idea. He had heard rumors that the new Overseer planned to bring in art and music to calm the savage inmates. Maybe he could use that. So, he straightened his shirt, combed his red hair with his fingers, and walked over to the exit with his guitar strapped to his back. "Dia Duit. Me shift is over, and I'm looking for the way out of here?"

The attendant scowled at him. "No one leaves during the lockdown."

Finn pointed to his guitar. "Look here. I have a show to get to in a candle mark. I'm not a threat."

The attendant crossed his arms. "No exceptions."

Finn looked behind him to find Ward getting closer. He could attack, run, or hide. The tune "Maguire's Lamentation" played from the gathering room across the hall.

He ran into the sanctuary-sized room. Other patients sat on chairs encircling a green-eyed lass with a guitar. Why was a noble lass in a room that smelled like body odor? Usually, they wouldn't want to mess up their hair done up in coiffures. But this one didn't seem to mind. Instead, she sang to her guitar music, smiling at him. After she finished the folk song, she beckoned him to join her.

A female voice spoke in his head.

"Why are you here? You're not sick like the others. You're gifted like me."

Finn jumped. Grand. Now he was hearing voices. Was he becoming one brick shy of a full load? He ran his hand through his hair, panicking that Ward was right. Then the woman winked at him. Ah, she was behind this. Regardless, he didn't like people probing his head, even if they were pretty.

"Get out of me head, lassie. I got enough problems without your meddling."

She winced. *"That's gratitude for you. I was going to ask you to grace us with a song."*

He smiled. *"Favor me with your name for it."*

"Molly Magee, what's yours?"

"Finn O'Sullivan, at your service, lassie. Can't wait to see ole Ward's face when he hears this one."

Finn proceeded with another verse from the song he sang earlier, creating more lyrics as he went.

"Finn O'Sullivan, on his quest for freedom,
Ran from Edward Ward at the asylum.
Trying to prove to all that his songs
We're not ramblings of an insane one.

"Sing for freedom for those
Whose gifts give them different woes
For someday, they might prove
That their magical gifts are of use."

Several patients, including Liam and Ronan, stood up and swayed to the melody. Liam stomped the rhythm, followed by Ronan. They were humming to the chorus. With each additional clap and voice, Finn's heart swelled with pride. It was his job to entertain. His troubles diminished as he was carried away by the melody. By the time Ward waltzed through the door on the second verse, Finn had forgotten he was locked up in an asylum.

Ward pulled the guitar out of Finn's hand and lifted it over his head as if to smash it. "It's time to put an end to this nonsense."

Finn's eyes bulged. Ward had gone too far threatening his lady guitar. "You're a bugger. How dare you threaten me lady!"

Molly stepped between the two men. "My Lord Edward. It would please me to have this instrument. It has a rich tone that mine does not possess. It's just the right sound for The Lucky Shamrock Pub."

Ward kissed Molly's hand. "Whatever you wish, Overseer," he said, handing her Finn's guitar. "Let me secure Finn, and then I'll escort you out." Ward placed shackles on Finn's wrists and walked with Molly out of the room.

Finn's stomach turned. Molly betrayed him. How could he be so stupid as to trust a noble? Nobles didn't mix with the common folk. Maybe he didn't have foresight after all. He didn't have the strength to stand anymore, so he sat down. With his guitar gone, he had no reason to stay. He needed to escape to get back his musical mistress.

Finn looked around the gathering room but didn't see any attendants or alienists hanging about. But thanks to Ward, who had shackled his wrists, he'd have to find another way out. He shuffled his feet, kicking a thin metal hairpin. What luck! A new plan emerged. Using his feet and hands, he picked the lock of his shackles, freeing himself. But that wouldn't be enough. He needed to create a distraction. So, he released Liam and Ronan and sent them out to the hallway. Finn tried to explain to them what they needed to do. "Run. Don't let the blokes catch you."

Liam spouted verses from the book of *Revelations*, catching the attendant's attention at the door as he ran. Ronan screamed like a robin in distress and ran in the opposite direction. "The rats are coming."

Ward chased after him, leaving the front door unguarded. Finn had a clean line to venture out of the door where freedom awaited.

The multi-story asylum loomed over the football-field-sized lawn, casting a dusk shadow on a Brougham carriage. The air smelled like cut grass. Finn debated whether to run or hop onto the back of the carriage.

The asylum door opened, revealing Ward. If Finn ran, Ward would undoubtedly catch him. But was the other option better? The driver cracked the reins, prompting Finn to decide. He jumped onto the back of the carriage and waved to Ward. Ward chased the carriage but couldn't keep up.

AFTER A HALF-HOUR, THE CARRIAGE STOPPED AT THE LUCKY SHAMROCK Pub across from the riverfront, giving Finn a chance to hop off and hide behind a bush before its unknown occupant got out. He wished he hadn't 'cause the stench of fish guts from the market next to it turned his stomach. To his surprise, Molly exited the carriage. What was she doing in this section of town? She pulled out two guitars and then entered the pub.

Finn followed her in, scanning the pub for Edward Ward. A few sailors congregated around the bar, and green-eyed Molly sat at a table opposite the bard's stool. Fortunately, Ward was absent. Finn relaxed. He had another hour or two of freedom before Ward discovered him. "Lassie, give back me guitar."

She smiled at him. "I thought I'd save it for you. I will give it back if you finish your song."

Finn tapped his leg. Could he finish the lyrics from his premonition? Ward wasn't here, and Molly already knew of his gifts. What was the harm? He strummed a G-chord, weaving the rest of the future tale.

"At a pub, Finn met a lass from afar
Who lured Ward by pretending she was an Overseer.
With a kiss, she distracted while working her magic.
Releasing his suspenders, so his pants fell.

"Sing for freedom for those,
Whose gifts give them different woes.
For someday, they might prove,
That their magical gifts are of use.

"Ward tripped over his pants and fell to the floor.
A piece of parchment skidded close to the door.
The princess now had the proof she needed
To stop the kidnapping of the gifted.

"Sing for freedom for those,
Whose gifts give them different woes.
For someday, they might prove,
That their magical gifts are of use.

"Now Ward is locked in Granisis Tower.
Where he no longer has the power.
To lock away those with magical gifts.
Imprisoned, he listens to Finn's music and sits."

When done, he sat next to Molly. "Did you enjoy it?"

"I did, especially when the princess unbuttoned his suspenders. Is it a true tale?"

Finn coughed. "Not yet. Curious. Why is a lass like you alone?"

"Oh, Lord Ward told me to meet him here. He'll be in soon."

Finn's palms sweated. He rubbed his wrists, remembering the restraints. "That's me cue to bugger off." He bolted, but Molly's mind voice interrupted.

Wait. I know what Ward did to the gifted. Help me prove it.

Ward entered the room, eyes fixed on Finn.

Molly, unbutton his suspenders. I'll distract him.

Finn stepped back. "We meet again, Ward."

"O'Sullivan, you don't look well. Come with me."

All eyes were on Finn. "No, I'll stay here."

Ward stepped forward, tripping over his pants. A piece of rag paper dropped out his pocket and landed on the floor. The bar erupted with laughter.

Molly picked up the letter. "This is proof that Lord Ward kidnapped the gifted. As princess of Granisis, I order you to take him to the tower."

Ward dusted himself off. "Read what's on the page. You don't have what you think. I switched the lists. I knew about your ruse thanks to Finn and his song."

Molly grinned. "So you admit that you believe Finn has foresight and you imprisoned him anyway. Your confession proves you are guilty and these sailors who are citizens of Granisis are witnesses." She turned to the bar. "Sean and Aiden, do you have what you need now."

"Yes, my lady." Sean said. The two sailors made their way over to Ward to pick him up and bind his hands behind his back.

Molly nodded to Finn. "You can come with us to Granisis. There you will meet the other gifted."

Finn picked up his guitar. "Aye. I'll give it a lash. I'd like to help free other gifted with you, but first I have me show to finish. Join me in a chorus of *Freedom*."

A week later, after a boat ride to the hidden island of Granisis, Finn and Molly stood in the courtyard of the castle. The spring festival brought the savory scent of bangers and mash. But eating would have to wait until after they played *Freedom*. When they got to the chorus, the gifted audience sang loud enough for occupants of Granisis Tower to hear.

> *"Sing for freedom for those*
> *Whose gifts give them different woes,*
> *For someday, they might prove*
> *That their magical gifts are of use."*

A Song of Smokeless Fire

Elise Stephens

Uncle,

I write these words because you refuse to listen when I sing them.

You think me too prying, too stubborn. You make choices for me as if I'm still a little girl, but I can no longer ignore the gnawing questions about another life from which you rescued me. I believe an event in our shared past is the root of our nomadic wanderings, you chasing after rumors like today's, of a strange death that befell a flutist and her friends while they sat in an open field. Their bodies were found burned, but no cause of fire found.

My memory holds clues to a home I barely remember, and it too is edged by flames. Why did you rescue me and from what? Today I've made myself a promise: I'll seek answers that I'm old enough to know. You cannot stop me.

Your niece,
—Amal

When the swallows shifted their migration and flew patterns contrary to nature, when the lilies bloomed months before their time, and when the blood-feud rivals warmed overnight to friends, the jinni took notice of the music that had inspired this upheaval.

The singer, a young man named Hasan, was the eldest son of the Assad family, a well-established merchant bloodline. Hasan's music spanned the space between flesh and spirit, and once the jinni knew, he had to witness the gift firsthand. Such music as Hasan possessed could change the world, if properly nurtured.

When the jinni secretly entered the walled courtyard of the merchant's home, he found Hasan tending the jasmine vines. Still concealed behind the fountain, the jinni gathered his plans for aiding this mortal ascend to greatness, then assumed human form. Hasan turned as the jinni approached and a coppery beam of sunset spilled through a window, turning his curls to fire.

"Welcome," Hasan said, slanting a glance from beneath dark lashes.

Between them stood a small table with two glass cups of tea. Hasan gestured to a chair with an embroidered cushion, folded himself onto the other, then told his guest,

"I don't fear angels, demons, or jinn, nor do I care which you are. I only ask: what do you seek, and do you come as foe or friend?"

The jinni's human-shaped heart lurched with imperfect rhythm. He saw centuries passing and wind eroding stone even as he stood fully in this one precious moment of eternity. He whispered, to keep the thunder of the jinn out of his voice. "I seek your songs."

Hasan arched an eyebrow. "To steal them?"

"To breathe them in."

"Very well. As to my second question . . .?"

"I wish only good for you."

Hasan grinned, showing a mischievous dimple. "Very well, jinni. You may stay." He rose again to tend his jasmine, limbs alive with mortal youth. As the jinni watched, he considered that Hasan would walk but a few years under the sun, then wither like the loveliest of flowers. All men did.

They talked late into the night, drained three pots of tea, and burned eight hours of lamp oil. Hasan shared scraps of verses from the song he was writing and the jinni sang a few lines with him, searching for the way to blend spirit voice with human.

When the jinni slipped away at last, he calmed his worries by telling himself that this was only natural: that a human who could alter the world's natural order with his songs would summon the love of a jinni.

Dear Uncle,

My first memory of home is also the memory of losing it. Fragrant flowers, I believe they're jasmine, the babble of a fountain, candlelight, and a glittering green jewel that I grip in my fist. You play a song that night and I understand the notes as words you speak to me. Resonant strings and a smooth wooden voice. I wonder, was that oud that you played the same one you carry now?

The music and the beauty break when a man screams for the song to stop. He drops his cup and wine splatters the tiled courtyard. Wind roars indoors and the hot, crackling air hurts my skin. Everything is on fire. The flowers blacken. The fountain turns to steam. The people scream as their hair ignites and their flesh chars. The smell is evil.

I weep, but the fire doesn't take me. I don't know why. You carried me away from it all.

Why did we live? Were we lucky, or spared? Guilty or innocent?

Is there blood upon my hands—our hands?—is there an unknown debt in my name that you're hiding from me? This is my history and my right to know.

—Amal Who Remembers

"W̲ʜᴀᴛ ɪs ʏᴏᴜʀ ᴛʀᴜᴇ ꜰᴏʀᴍ?" Hᴀsᴀɴ ᴀsᴋᴇᴅ ᴏɴᴇ ɴɪɢʜᴛ, ʜɪs ʜᴇᴀᴅ ɪɴ ᴛʜᴇ jinni's lap while the jinni ran fingers through his lover's hair.

They sat in a high tower overlooking the city while a crescent moon smiled down on their secret happiness. Hasan's final notes were gently fading on the evening breeze. He'd been teaching the jinni to sing with him, their voices blending in a pleasure the jinni had never tasted in all three hundred and ninety-seven years of his life. Hasan was not the first human he'd loved, but he was the first he'd wanted to die beside.

"The closest thing you'd know to my form is fire," the jinni said. "But without smoke."

"Fire that wouldn't sting my eyes or burn my lungs? Sounds perfect."

The jinni cupped Hasan's cheek in his hand. "I'll show it to you someday."

Hasan sat up, dark eyes outshining the stars. "I've been writing a new song. For us."

"Is it ready? Can I –"

"Not finished yet. Soon."

When the jinni kissed Hasan, he wished with all his being that he were not a being of smokeless fire; that together they might age at a shared pace, that their music might mature the way time intended, or at least that their song might last beyond a few short stanzas.

That night, the jinni gave Hasan his ring of mastery.

His lover strung it on a gold chain with the vow, "Though I possess a jinni's ring, I am not your master. I will not use this to make wishes that bind you. Love must have the freedom to go or stay, and I shall never force your obedience."

Uɴᴄʟᴇ,

I stepped into my past today. The ruins of the Assad house, once belonging to a merchant family, its courtyard charred. The fountain still stands, and some floor tiles retain their color. It is the place where my earliest memory turns to flames.

A friend of mine, a librarian, took me to this place after I described my recollection. My friend explained the tragedies that span more than a decade, and in each one a demon who descends upon a musical festivity and slays all present, consuming them in a fire that yields no smoke.

I connect these horrors to the night you carried me away from the fire that claimed the people of this house. The memory echoes with music, taunting me with shreds of meaning. What was this song? If anyone knows it, you do.

I can already imagine the chords you'll use to chide my uncouth curiosity: dissonant combinations to underline your annoyance. But can't you hear the building crescendo? Can't you see that I never fully forget a song, once I've heard it, and I will search until I learn the musical prelude to the fire on that tragic night?

—Amal of the House of Assad

WHEN THE JINNI ALIGHTED ON THE UPPER BALCONY OF THE MERCHANT'S house to meet Hasan beside the potted orange tree, the singer greeted him in a brocade vest and linen tunic, rather than his usual soft robe with its braided belt. Hasan no longer wore his ring around his neck, but on his little finger. An evil premonition rippled through the jinni, but he kept his smile warm as he drew near and said, "What's the special occasion?"

Hasan stiffened and pulled back. The jinni's heart became cold mist.

"We must stop seeing each other." Hasan's words were toneless and flat, stripped of all music. His eyes were dull stones at the bottom of a lightless pit.

The jinni saw an abyss gape between them, centuries-old, littered with bones of dead men and whistling with the screams of anguished spirits. He didn't reply.

"I've spoken to my father," Hasan went on. "He's made me see what is wise and prudent. You and I are from different worlds, and I must make choices to establish myself and provide for my family." Hasan straightened his shoulders, looking every inch a prince. "I'm engaged to be married."

The jinni tried to find his voice, unsure whether he wished to be a vapor or a thunderstorm. At last, he said, "I will share you, if I must."

"No, it must be a clean break. I'm to inherit my father's business, after all, and my focus must be directed to this end."

"Then you don't mean to sing?"

"For a living? No. A hobby, perhaps. But I must be practical."

There it was. The jinni heard the pain that Hasan was trying to hold back. It was a faint mewling, like a kitten as it drowned.

The jinni whispered, "At least let me visit you. If only to comfort you when your wife is absent, to listen to your songs when you sing them, to cherish you in the shadows if that's all that's left to us."

Hasan's eyes flashed once with longing and the jinni felt his hope, stoked by a hundred years of waiting, try to rise again, but then Hasan shook his head.

"No. Such conduct would not be proper. It's long since time I grew up." Hasan glanced down at his ring and, in the moment before Hasan broke his vow, the jinni's heart turned to ash.

Hasan said, "I wish to hereby banish you from my presence. You may not come near unless I explicitly summon you."

The jinni fled. He could do nothing else. He was a spirit bound by the power of his ring, and he had believed, like a foolish mortal, that he would not be betrayed. Nothing but the ring's mastery could have parted him from Hasan. He knew he would spend the remaining years of Hasan's mortal life waiting, praying, and begging to be summoned back into his beloved's presence.

Uncle,

You've taught me hundreds of songs, held back the One that
means more than all the rest: the Song that woke my primary
tongue, for I sang before I spoke, as you've told me many times. I
knew musical harmonies before I understood grammar. This is
that Song.

You saved me from the fire that took my home. In a way, I'm the sole heir of that fallen kingdom, a princess of sorts, and you were once our minstrel.

I've visited the archives in the capital. I've lied, disguised myself, and stolen into restricted sections; all things you didn't raise me to do. The archives told me the story of a merchant, Hasan al Assad, born with a legendary voice of honey-and-silk, who forsook his talent to follow in his father's business. How he was known to wear a large emerald ring on his finger and when his household perished in a mysterious fire, his daughter's body was never found.

This is what I suspect: that you played a song that night of the fire and it somehow summoned the fire-spirit that killed my family. I escaped death via my chance possession of this emerald ring, the one I still wear today because you've made me promise never to take it off.

If that's true, then I know why you chase these rumors of death. You loosed a cursed song onto the world, and have been serving penance ever since, trying to stop more people from learning and singing this same song. And yet, you have no voice with which to persuade them.

The first to die was my family, and the ring that protected me is a jinni's ring. The jinn are spirits of fire—is a jinni burning all these people because of that Song? Why does the song enrage the jinni? Do you know?

—Amal of House Assad, Bearer of a Jinni's Ring

THE JINNI FLED TO THE MOUNTAINS, SEEKING PLACES AS COLD, SHARP, and barren as possible. For, though he could not die, he hoped to numb his mind with pain. All the while, his ears remained tuned to Hasan, hopelessly hoping. He was startled to attention when, only an hour after his exile, Hasan stood on his balcony and sang alone to the empty sky.

The jinni could not come, for he'd not been summoned, but he listened from afar. The music was their song, the one Hasan had mentioned but never sung for the jinni, a duet for two voices, raw and beautiful and incomplete.

The jinni's tears burned pocks into the mountain stone beneath him. He knew, without being told that, after this, his lover would never sing again, and the thought of Hasan silencing his divine gift was a pain that wounded the jinni more than his exile.

Uncle,

I love you. You taught me to parse the chords of human life, to absorb its intricate range of sadness, joy, and toil. You sheltered me from every threat you could imagine. Because of you, I hear birds sing and know when they hunt food for their young and when they worry about nest-building. I can parse the notes of an old man's whistle—the melancholy nostalgias from his contented thanksgivings. I speak music more fluently than anyone I know, and you have shut this part of me away from the world, for you will not let me sing anywhere but in a closed and shuttered room. But while this demon-jinni still prowls our land, all who sing are endangered.

I must find the angry jinni and this Song. If the killings are to stop, if there's a cure for the jinni's rage, it lies within the Song itself.

—Amal of House Assad, Bearer of a Jinni Ring, Singer

No dreams, no music, only silence. In just the blink of an eye for jinn, Hasan would die, and the jinni's fragile hope of being summoned could be buried beside Hasan's corpse.

But then, decades later, the jinni was bewildered, for he heard the summoning song. It didn't issue from a human throat, but from an instrument, the notes sliding on the rich curves of an oud and it was undeniably Hasan's unfinished duet.

The jinni followed it like an arrow, unsure what he would do when he arrived. A hundred humiliations might await him, but so also might a tender reunion. And yet, it was clear, even before he reached the song's source, that the musician was not Hasan.

This intimate melody, sacred as a lover's body; this duet meant only for the jinni and his singer, was being played by another for cheap entertainment.

The jinni became a storm cloud, boiling with thunder, rage, thwarted joy, and descended on the scene, prepared to shred the music, note by note, that it never again be played. With a touch of bitter poetry, the setting of the song's performance was the same tiled courtyard with jasmine vines in which the jinni had first met Hasan.

It was an elaborate feast, candlelight flashing on gold jewelry, rich tablecloths with shining threads, tender cuts of meat, and gleaming gemlike fruit. The guests were listening to the music of a slender minstrel.

Flames filled the jinni's mind. Tonight would be this minstrel's last performance and the last night for everyone. The jinni plummeted in a torrent of wrath, burning the life from each guest, one by one, swallowing all in a smokeless fire that flamed with indiscriminate passion.

He recognized the man he adored only after he'd slain him. Hasan had grown a belly and covered his handsome face behind a large beard. Even his voice was ruined, roughed by years of hookah. The jinni shouldn't have been able to kill Hasan under the ring's protection. But it wasn't on his hand.

After he'd finished with the guests, the jinni found a survivor: a small child sucking on the ring's emerald as though it were a sweet, its magic shielding her.

The jinni saved the minstrel's death for last. He paused on the verge of turning the man to cinders and ripped out the minstrel's voice instead. There were many fates worse than death, the jinni told himself, and a singer who could not sing seemed a fitting punishment.

Uncle,

Forgive me, for I've ransacked your papers and found the Song, transcribed in your child's scrawl. I can read the story in the melody and feel the broken edges of its unfinished harmonies.

You said you lost your voice when you were a young man, and I think I can piece together the rest: First, years before you lost your voice, when you were still a street beggar, you overheard the enchanting farewell song that my heartbroken father sang from his balcony. The melody was so haunting, you knew that it would bring you glory if you could one day attribute it to your name.

Years later, when my father was a rich merchant, and you were a young and budding minstrel, you were invited in to play at his house party. My mother liked the song you chose. She didn't know its nature or that my father had written it. My father recognized the notes once you'd begun performing it and tried too late to stop you—this is my memory of his shouting—and then the fire-jinni came for us all. The ring spared only me.

I lost my family. You lost your voice. The jinni is still angry. But I know the solution now. That incomplete song is pain, loss, and betrayal. It must be finished, and I must help that come to pass.

I was born for this.

—Amal of House Assad, Bearer of a Jinni's Ring, Singer and Music-Speaker

A TRANSCENDENT TALENT SUCH AS HASAN'S MUSIC WAS NOT SO EASILY smothered, to the jinni's disappointment. Like a disease, the unfinished

duet found its way into the world. It seemed someone had overheard it during the brief performance of the now-mute minstrel.

This eavesdropper had gone on to sing it at a dinner party. The jinni heard it and burned each and every dinner guest, but didn't think to burn down the house as well.

A few years later, a transcript of the duet was found by another with a musical ear who arranged it for two instruments and held a small concert in its honor. A musician needed only to hear the melody once to absorb it and, despite the jinni's efforts, he couldn't stamp out the song. Thus, the jinni's grief outlived his beloved, born over and over by the notes of their incomplete song. He'd managed to destroy one with his rage, but not the other.

Then there was the night the song clawed its way into a fresh wound of its most recent iteration. The singer was a young woman. Her choice of stage was poignant, for charred jasmine vines and a soot-streaked courtyard fountain were her only audience. The winds of an approaching storm screeched from above and warped her voice. No one else would overhear. She was not singing for human ears. None but a jinni whose life was woven through those notes could have heard her.

The jinni hovered before the woman in his form of smokeless fire, prepared to take her life, but curiosity slowed his vengeance. Her face, ringed in dark curls, put him in mind of another face. Her voice's honey smoothness was like another voice. The way she looked up through her dark lashes brought to mind a moonlit meeting in this same courtyard. Then he saw the emerald ring on her finger.

His ring of mastery. The child who he'd spared the day of Hasan's feast. He'd thought her just a child, worthy of sparing if only for her innocence. But now, in her voice and face, he saw Hasan. She was the singer's daughter, the incarnation of the life Hasan had chosen apart from him.

The woman sang Hasan's song like a native tongue and shaped each note to its truest color. Her voice shimmered with the sadness of loss, the ecstasy of pleasure, the mirror-shine of wonder, and she sang as one who understood the world first through song.

And then, more music, this time with an instrument's voice. The strings squeaked at first, like frightened throats. A man leaned against the scorched wall stones, storm winds tossing his silver hair as he cradled a battered oud in his arms.

Human age hid little from a jinni's eyes. This man was the minstrel who'd audaciously performed Hasan's song here in this same courtyard at Hasan's feast, accidentally summoning the jinni and murdering the guests, then lost his voice as punishment.

The jinni felt his heart sink. These two lives he'd let live on that night had returned to torture him again with the same song. It seemed mercy had done no favors.

The jinni prepared again to kill them, or at least the minstrel, since he had no ring to protect himself, but the jinni was arrested by the woman's voice, as no music had done since Hasan had first sung to him.

His lover was dead, as was the fate of all mortals, but here, in the voice of his daughter, whose very existence was betrayal-made-flesh, he heard Hasan singing again.

Urgency filled the woman's song. With open vocal sounds, she pleaded, drenching the notes in compassion, grief, and beckoning kindness. She held out her palm, and in it lay the jinni's emerald ring, granting him self-mastery once more. She was surrendering the ring's protection, showing she did not fear him. Just as Hasan hadn't feared the jinni's power on the night they first met.

The jinni took the ring, then rumbled in his thunder-voice to see if the woman would cringe. The minstrel fumbled his chords, but regained composure and held his part. The woman began the song anew, eyes fastened to the jinni's face. She sang in true song. There was no deceit in this music. Somehow, she knew the jinni's love story and his sorrow. Had she learned it from the song itself?

Unlike the others, this woman wasn't stealing the unfinished duet and using its majesty to elevate herself; she was giving it back to the jinni, its proper co-owner.

My love, the jinni thought, *your child is asking me to finish what we left undone.*

The daughter with no family, the minstrel with no voice, the jinni with no hope.

This woman's song invited the jinni to enter its melody, to find his rightful place in the duet.

The jinni thought again of moonlight on fountain tiles; of jasmine blossoms and hot tea, of bitter laughter and joyful tears, of a mortal's music that could have changed the world and a spirit's thunder-voice that had barely begun to tune itself.

The jinni began to sing.

A Power in Ink

Max Florschutz

She was near the end of her set when she saw them coming in the front entrance of the pub. Two of the Predict's enforcers, easily identifiable by their shockstaves and gilded armor, slitted helmets looking right in her direction. It was something she appreciated about their designed-to-be-menacing look. It was, but it also let everyone see right where each enforcer was looking.

Her fingers flew up and down the strings of her violin as the two began making their way slowly into the back of the crowd, prodding bodies aside with slow but purposeful movements. A few patrons turned to question the shoves, only to immediately recoil as they took in the red and silver colors. Gradually the two enforcers worked their way forward, the crowd breaking around them like waves before a ship.

"Mynessa, enforcers."

The words echoed in her head as her companion spoke, flitting across her mind like bubbles on a fizzy drink. *I see them,* she thought back, shifting the position of her fingers to throw her music into a minor key. Most of the crowd wouldn't get it, but the owner of the alehouse would. *Obvious, though.*

"There are probably more at the back exit."

She couldn't nod, not without giving away that something was amiss. Instead she kept her eyes forward, fingers flying over the strings of her fiddle while her other arm worked the bow back and forth at a feverish pace. The crowd, already loud and energetic, let out shouts and whoops as her hands became a blur, the song building to a frantic crescendo. *Good thing that's not how we're getting out.*

The enforcers were halfway to the stage now. There were probably more coming at her from her blind spot, timing their pace so that they'd arrive just after the enforcers coming from the front, ready to spring the trap when she rabbited. With more pairs stationed outside the doors in case she got past the ones inside, shockstaves at the ready.

"They're getting close."

I know, she thought back, letting her eyes slip to the far side of the alehouse's main room, where several patrons were leaning over the bannister of the second level, clapping in time with her frantic tune. She picked up the pace, fingers burning as they danced across the strings. *One more bridge and then the big finale . . .*

"Any second now . . ." Her partner was getting impatient. As were the enforcers, their shoves to move people out of the way growing more aggressive with each passing moment. Mynessa rose as the song neared its end, putting her whole body into a draw of the bow across the strings and taking advantage of the moment to check the rest of the crowd, looking for any individuals that were enforcers in disguise.

"There," came her partner's voice, echoing through her mind. *"By the bar."* Mynessa zeroed in on the woman immediately, the only one there who was watching the show but scowling. She was in casual, nondescript clothing, but the side of her scarf had slipped, revealing the beginnings of a tattoo.

I see her. She also noted the alehouse's owner reaching beneath the bar with a look of concern. They knew what was coming.

With the final, resounding shriek of a high note Mynessa raised her hands high, holding them and the fiddle above her head as the crowd erupted in cheers. Her rise called forth a reaction from the enforcers as well, both of whom began openly shoving their way through the crowd, tips of their shockstaves glowing.

"You've been a wonderful crowd!" Mynessa said, projecting her voice as the assembly continued to cheer. "Thank you, and remember!" She let her words echo for a moment as she dismissed her instrument, the polished wood breaking into clouds of colored smoke that slid up her arms, sinking into her dark skin and taking shape as tattooed representations. The two enforcers were almost at the front of the crowd. "The Predict is a fraud and a magrel's asshole besides!"

The crowd roared its approval even as the two enforcers abandoned all pretense of subtlety, slamming people aside as they both began to charge.

"Two behind!" came the warning, but Mynessa was already moving, racing across the alehouse's small stage—more of a low bar against the back wall, really—and heading for the far side of the room opposite the bar. The crowd, well familiar with her escapes, parted before her like grass, making way while also surging toward the enforcers. From behind there came the sharp *crack* of a shockstave discharging alongside a howl of pain.

"She's going for the stairs!" The shout hadn't come from the direction of the two enforcers she'd seen. A second pair then, as warned.

But the enforcers were wrong. The crowd parted before her, opening a path toward the stairs to the second level, but she wasn't heading that way. Instead she extended her arm, the tattooed bracelet around her wrist shifting and growing into three dimensions. A fleshy protrusion shot out of the base of her wrist, wrapping around the banister of the second level landing and tugging hard. Several nearby patrons recoiled in shock and surprise as Mynessa sprang into the air, the retracting muscles of the fleshy tongue jerking her upward toward the second level. She dismissed the tattoo just before impact, the muscle melting away into colored smoke that sank back into the skin around her wrist. Fingers locking around the smooth wood of the bannister, she pulled herself up and over the railing to land on the second level, the sounds of the crowd behind her growing louder—now more akin to an angry mob than the cheering fans they'd been just a minute earlier.

Of course with the enforcers being the new "show," that didn't surprise her. Especially given the number of non-humans she'd seen in the crowd and the Predict's crackdowns.

She bolted along the landing, heading for the hall at the far end that led to the alehouse's guest rooms. She felt a sudden sense of alarm at the back of her mind—pure emotion, spilling over from her partner—and threw herself into a slide, dropping to her knees as a crossbow bolt slashed through the air where she'd just been. A glance down at the crowd showed that the suspicious woman at the bar was now holding a crossbow, another bolt matching the one embedded in the wall materializing from the smoke around her arm.

"Nice dodge."

Next time say something, Mynessa shot back as she rose once more, rushing down the landing as below the crowd moved even closer to a mob. She could smell the tint of ozone from the shockstaves now, but the enforcers were being overwhelmed, shoved back by the angry citizenry. From the corner of her eyes Mynessa saw the plainclothes enforcer lift her crossbow once more . . . only to crumple as a nearby patron slammed a bottle against the back of her head, crossbow and ammunition fading into smoke.

Mynessa was about to enter the hallway when the door of the nearest guest room parted and another red-and-silver clad enforcer stepped out, sweeping the business end of their shockstave at her head. She ducked, again sliding across the polished floorboards as the blow swept past overhead, curved end sparking. She snapped her elbow up, striking the enforcer's leg armor at the weaker knee joint and using the jolt of the impact to spin and get her legs beneath her. The enforcer let out a shout of pain, knee buckling, and Mynessa rose as they dropped, driving her own knee right into the enforcer's helmet. Their head slammed back, hitting the wall with a loud *clang*. She was already turning the motion of dropping her knee into a spin, sprinting down the hall as the enforcer recovered their wits. As much vision as the helmets blocked, they *were* good at their job of—

"Dodge left!"

Mynessa jerked her body to the side as the shockstave flew past, thrown by the enforcer and missing her by a gap so small she could *feel* her skin prickle at the charge it held. The curved tip hit the floorboards with a sharp *snap*, the wood around the dull blade charring as the weapon discharged.

Thanks. That was better. She danced around the instrument, well aware of the shouts and cries at her back as she counted each door. *Three, four, five—That one!* She practically threw herself through it, wooden latch snapping upward as she powered past the door to reveal a dark room not even lit by an electric bulb, though there was an oil lamp on the nightstand, a sign of the alehouse's budget and clientele. But the light wasn't what interested her. What did was the small panel in the side wall, as well as the unlocked window that looked out over the rooftops of the underbelly. That was her exit. *But first . . .*

The panel slid up easily, exposing a tiny lift that led to the kitchens below. Instead of a hot meal the lift held a small bag of coins—her payment for the evening, most of it collected from the crowd.

"Good haul tonight."

Her partner's voice echoed through Mynessa's head as she lifted the coin pouch, feeling its weight in her grip. She slipped it into a pocket on her vest and rushed for the window, already keenly aware of the stamp of heavy boots rushing down the hall. The window slid up easily, and a second later she was running across the rooftops, cheap tarpaper providing sure footing despite the late evening mists.

"She's on the rooftops!" The cry came from somewhere nearby, and a moment later she caught sight of a figure moving through the mists nearby, thin and lithe and wrapped head to toe in reddish cloth.

"It looks like you're getting special treatment tonight," her partner said as Mynessa raced across the rooftops, boots pounding out a furious staccato rhythm. One that was being echoed. *"Chasers."*

I'm well aware. She could see the faint sparks of electrical energy glimmering in the fog as her pursuers activated their weapons. Ahead a narrow gap loomed as the rooftop ended and she leapt, crossing it with ease. *Any ideas?*

"Mynessa Odivar!" Her name echoed across the rooftops from somewhere below, amplified and scratchy. That meant an enforcer car. At least one. Maybe more. "For treason against the Emperor—"

It's never just "revolution," she noted idly as she jumped again, once again calling on her bracelet to aid her leap. *Just treason against the Predict.*

"—and for consorting with traitor royals, you are under arrest! Surrender!"

Not likely! I didn't ask for this, but that doesn't mean I'm going to turn myself over!

"And I appreciate that."

Mynessa winced, less at the rough landing she'd just made as she cleared another rooftop, or the sound of her pursuers, and more at the uninvited words doubling down on her own thoughts. But there was no time to dwell on it. *I need to get off the rooftops, and fast.*

"I'm seeing three behind you, Mynessa, though that term doesn't feel quite right. But they're there."

Chasers?

"Yes."

Ahead the mist was mixed with smoke and soot, and she ducked around a chimney adding to the latter. *Three chasers is unusual. Must be a raid.*

"Or they've increased your level of interest. They're openly accusing you of consorting with royals, so they must suspect we're connected."

Mynessa winced as she leapt over another alley gap, passing above shanty rooftops and lean-tos below. Her fingers caught at a windowsill, the roof of the next building a story above her, and she extended the tongue of her bracelet once more to pull herself the rest of the way up.

Something *whistled* out of the darkness, striking the side of the building beside her as she rose with a sharp *pop* then falling down into the alley. Stun-bolts. At least they weren't trying to kill her.

"That would be the drop, I think. And it wouldn't just be you."

Quiet. The smoke of her bracelet dissolving back into her skin mixed with the mist as she pulled herself atop the next rooftop. Unlike the flat roofs she'd just left, this one was steep and pitched, and she scrambled on all fours up the slope. She needed to get as high as possible as she neared the edge of the underbelly.

Something rattled behind her. *"That would be a chaser coming up the building. They're quite fast."*

I know. She scrambled over the roof's peak, dull moonlight leaking through the mists and smoke, and slid down the other side. Her clothes were going to be filthy later, but it beat the damage they'd take from an interrogation. Again her feet left the ground as she jumped another alley, landing on another steeply sloped roof and making her way upward. She was high enough now to see the rising cliffs that marked the edge of the Underbelly, along with lights that glimmered from thousands of structures that had been carved and built into the stone over the centuries.

The steps behind were getting closer. An electric whine sounded from nearby, a siren from one of the enforcer's armored cars, probably trying to track her from the streets. It was terrifying . . . but at the same time strangely exhilarating. Again she slid down the side of a rooftop, leaping just moments before she would have dropped into the yawning chasm of a street. The tongue lashed out once more, grabbing at the rooftop on the other side and aiding her jump so that she landed amid the tarpaper on the far side rather than coming up short.

"That's still gross."

You're welcome to walk. Another stun bolt bounced off the nearby roofing, skittering up the slope and vanishing over the peak. Mynessa scrambled after it on all fours, throwing herself over the peak in a roll moments before another bolt flashed by, vanishing into the mists.

"They have gliders."

Counting on it, she replied as she spread her weight, coming to a halt on her back just over the peak. A flick of her wrist and a mental command saw smoke billowing from her right arm, the familiar comforting weight of her wooden staff dropping into her hand as the smoke condensed. A moment later a shadow flitted over the top of the roof and she swept the stave upward, bracing one end against the rooftop. The weapon vibrated under an impact as the tip clipped her pursuer's foot, their skillful leap immediately turning into a tumble with a shout of alarm. They hit the roof once, bouncing once . . . and then plummeted over the edge of the next alley, their scream sounding for only a second before terminating in a faint chorus of thuds.

"The others won't fall for that."

"I know." This time Mynessa said it aloud, letting a little of her annoyance seep into her words. "Say something useful?" She dismissed the staff as she pushed herself down the roof, the smoke seeping back into her arm as she picked up speed again, pushing off at the last moment to sail over the next alleyway. Below she spotted the chaser, lying at the bottom of the alley in a tangled pile. *Good riddance.*

Another stun bolt missed her by inches as she scrambled up and over the next peak, and she let out a curse. These chasers were *fast*. Worse, the building she was atop now was a large one, the space over the peak a massive flat depression full of chimney-pipes and seepage drains, ringed on all sides by the steep peaks of the edges. *Why* it had been built like that she couldn't say.

But if I'm going to have to fight, it's as good a space as I'm going to get. She ducked behind one of the chimney stacks, feeling the warmth of the bricks press through her shirt as she summoned her staff again, the smoke solidifying in her grip.

The footsteps of her pursuers slowed, but she heard no cries. They must have noticed that the sound of her own boots had ceased and signaled one another. A series of quick, shortened impacts came from behind her, one of the chasers making their way down from the peak into the depression. A second set of footsteps came a moment later, but echoing from a different location. They were spreading out, then. They knew she was nearby.

It was hard to keep her breaths controlled after such a prolonged sprint, but she did her best anyway, trying to keep her exhalations below the ambient sounds of the Underbelly, which were now quite loud by comparison.

Tarpaper *scritched* as someone took a step off to her right. Close, but not quite close enough yet. Could they have seen tracks or marks from her boots? Did they know where she was?

The panic wasn't entirely hers. *Relax*, she intoned. *I got this. I'm not just good at running away.* Another *scratching* sound echoed across the rooftop, this one closer, and she tightened her grip on the stave.

"We know you're here." The voice was firm if a bit reedy. Out of breath, perhaps? Maybe chasers weren't as good as she'd thought. More footsteps sounded from the other end of the roof. "You can't hide forever."

No, just long enough. The faint scratching of leather on grit to her right was getting closer now, the voice nearing her position. "Just come quietly, and this can be over by morning. All we want to know is where the princess is."

Right. The steps were close enough now. She counted to three, readied herself . . . And swept out from behind the chimney stack, the tip of her staff humming through the air as she swung it at what she hoped was head level. The chaser, wrapped head-to-toe in red clothe, was only a few feet away.

To their credit they got their shockstave up in time, barely blocking the impact—though the blow did knock their defense back. Mynessa spun, using the rebound of the impact to whip the staff around her body and bring the other end up fast and low. Again her target managed to see the strike coming, the butt-end of their shockstave coming up just in time to block the brunt of the strike, but not enough to keep the rest of the attack from bouncing up and into their thigh. The chaser let out a grunt of pain, but Mynessa didn't relent, already spinning her staff back to strike with the other end. Again her assailant tried to block, but this time the strike struck home, hitting the back of the chaser's hand with a sharp *crack.* They let out a cry, dropping their shockstave to the rooftop—and a moment later the butt-end of Mynessa's staff slammed into their temple, dropping them like an empty sack.

"Behind and high!"

She spun at the cry of warning, ducking to the side as a downward blow from the other chaser's shockstave slammed into her hasty block. She felt the strength of the impact resonate down both her arms as the curved metal blade skipped off to the side, smacking into the rooftop and discharging with a *pop.* Mynessa brought one end of her staff down on her attacker's shoulder, eliciting a grunt of pain, but after the block her arms felt almost limp.

Still, she didn't need to use her staff. She danced back as the chaser recovered, crouching and holding her weapon in one hand, the other low to the rooftop. As expected the chaser leapt forward, sweeping their stave in a blow meant to overpower her block.

Save that it didn't connect, staff dissolving into smoke as Mynessa slipped to one side, the heavy blow *just* missing her and slamming again into the rooftop.

Just as her other hand came up, brandishing the shockstave her first foe had dropped and driving the charged end right into her opponent's gut. There was a *snap* as the weapon discharged, and the chaser was blown back across the tarpaper, dropping their own weapon as they hit the ground, twitching and shaking.

"Oh, that was well done. Well done indeed."

Mynessa tossed the shockstave aside with a clatter. *Thanks.* She kicked the already recovering chaser's own weapon away as she stalked over to them, and before they could raise a guard slammed her fist between their eyes once, twice, then three times, stunning them. It probably wasn't as effective a deterrent as the concussion she'd given the other, but at least neither of them would be chasing her anytime soon.

Then she set off across the rooftops, making for the Cliffs and the end of the Underbelly.

A half-hour later she was halfway up the side of the Cliffs and back on the streets—though due to the steep nature of the streets that meant she was still atop the buildings below, horizontal space on the cliffs being at a premium. Still, she wasn't *running* over the rooftops, not like she had been earlier. She'd donned a cloak from her small side bag—not too uncommon on the Cliffs and the higher Heights, where the winds peeled away the fog and smoke of the Underbelly but also carried with them a chill—and did her best to look just like anyone else out for a walk. Twice an enforcement car rolled by, humming and buzzing with energy as it rolled down into the Underbelly. There were definitely at least a few raids going on. With luck none of the safe-houses had been hit.

She'd know soon enough if they had. She and her "partner."

I really didn't realize what I was getting into. But by the time she had, there had been little other choice. It wasn't that she didn't like the royal family —they were fine, insofar as decent people went. They'd made the city— and the rest of their small empire—a haven among the remaining Royalist nations, adapting laws and controversial ideals from the more progressive republics. And Mynessa had certainly never seen any reason to see the other, non-human races as "sub-human."

"That was, I think, the Predict's breaking point," came the voice of her strange partner, fizzing through her thoughts. *"He opposed that change. I suspect my father never suspected how staunch a position he'd taken on it, nor what it would drive him to."*

For a moment Mynessa wanted to rebuke the voice for intruding on her thoughts, but the mention of the late king softened and then waylaid her response. *Sometimes you really can't tell with people,* she thought instead. The response felt weak, but she wasn't sure what else to say.

Besides, her partner could feel the sincerity of her words. That much Mynessa was certain of. She'd learned a lot over the last few weeks as they'd adjusted to this new strangeness.

"We both have."

There it was again. A reminder that her thoughts weren't quite her own.

"I'm sorry. I don't mean to pry. But . . . you think quite loudly. And—"

You don't have a choice in things, Mynessa thought back. *I know. It's just how the magic works.*

Ahead she spotted the front doors of the manor that was serving as the current safehouse for Royalist meetings. Nothing looked out of the ordinary, but she chose not to move straight for the doors, instead stepping to the opposite side of the street, dodging a few rolling carriages on the way and making for the barrier that kept traffic of all kinds from plummeting over the edge and down to the next level of the Cliffs. Chimneystacks poked up along the edge of the road, some designed with decorative brick or stone benches, others merely unassuming grey slabs emitting faint wisps of smoke that were stolen away by wind into the night.

She let out a sigh as she leaned against the barrier, the events of the evening pressing against her now that she was away from the raids. Down below she could see lights breaking through the fog and smoke that shrouded the Underbelly, crimson smears of what were likely chemical flares used by the enforcers to call for backup or signal a capture.

"You're tired, aren't you?"

Mynessa nodded. *Yeah. That much magic takes a toll. Manifesting an instrument for an evening is one thing, but repeatedly manifesting and returning a tattoo takes it out of me.*

"I feel it too."

That's . . . less comforting than it sounds, really.

"My apologies—"

Mynessa cut her off, turning away from the tableau before her and instead choosing to look across the street at the home *next* to the current headquarters. *Don't be. It's not your fault. Not anymore.*

There didn't *appear* to be any signs of trouble or distress at the headquarters, and the curtains on the fourth floor had been drawn in the proper order to signify that everything was undisturbed. If even one of them had been out of order, then there would have been nothing to do but go to ground in another safehouse and hope the enforcers didn't catch up with her. A simple system, but one that had kept the Royalist meetings from being raided so far—though there had been a close call in the early days.

She turned and looked out over the Underbelly once more, watching the fog slowly roll and curl against the base of the cliffs, almost like waves at a beach.

"You should probably head in. They're very likely worried about you."

Worried about you, you mean, Mynessa fired back, only to feel the emotional wince as the barb struck home. *Sorry, that was out of line.*

"No," came the reply. *"I'm afraid you're not exactly incorrect."*

At least *she* meant it. She could feel the sincerity behind the comment.

"Well," she said, pushing away from the barrier and making for the edge of the street, watching for any wagons coming from either above or below. "Let's get this over with. I could use some sleep."

"I thought you bards were never-ending founts of energy."

"That," she said quietly as she crossed the street, "is a clever ruse designed to pull more money out of our crowds."

"Do you miss it?"

The question caught her by surprise. "Being a bard?"

"No no, I mean life before . . . this."

Course I do, she thought, keeping her voice internal as she stepped onto the sidewalk on the other side of the road, turning and making for the manor. The sidewalk was deserted, but if anyone materialized out of any shadows to question her, it would be a simple matter to pretend to be a hired hand coming in late in the night. Simple right up until it became complex, of course.

Before this, I didn't have to worry about whether or not a disguise would save my life, just how the audience would react to my using it to tell a tale. Before this I played at alehouses to pay my rent and earn a little money, not to help fund a resistance. And before this . . . Well, I didn't have to fight quite as much. There were no front steps up to the main door, just a slightly raised and covered porch barely a foot and a half across. She came to a stop on it and gave the bell two short, quick pulls.

"But you did fight?"

The Underbelly isn't always a nice place at the best of times, and it's downright nice compared to some places I've been to.

"They sound perilous."

Eh, they make for good stories. A curtain twitched off to her left, almost invisible in the gloom but a twitch all the same. A moment later the door opened, lantern light spilling out across the porch.

"Oh, you've finally arrived, have you?" The steward's stern visage glowered down at her—even as tall as she was, the steward was taller. "Well you know the deal, get in and get telling tales if you want to be paid."

"Thank you sir," she said quietly, bowing slightly as she stepped past him into the dark interior of the house. It was a spontaneous act, different every time just in case someone happened to be walking by. Not until outer and inner doors were shut did the steward's stern look drop, his expression immediately becoming one of concern.

"Mynessa, by the Graces! Where have you been, we've been worried sick—"

"See? He cares."

That's because he's attracted to me.

"So? He still cares."

The steward—Raddel—was still talking in a quick but hushed voice as he illuminated their path through the home with an electric lantern. "Word's come in from four different sources. Raids all over the Underbelly and a few on the Hills. There was a rumor you'd been caught—"

"Well, I wasn't," she said, trying to stem the flow spilling from his lips. "Though they tried. They just weren't good enough." She gave a little flourish with one hand as she spoke, a lifetime of working a crowd not easily shaken off. "And I even got paid. Is there a room ready? Maybe one with a meal? I've been running across rooftops tonight and taking down chasers. I could really use a hot bath."

The steward hesitated only for a moment before replying. "I understand that you're tired Mynessa, but the colonel is here and—"

"Oh *great*."

Her words didn't stop Raddel. "—and he needs to speak with, well . . . you know." Raddel glanced around the hall as if there were enforcers in earshot. "*Her*. As soon as possible."

She fought back the urge to let out a groan. "Can't it wait? At least until I've gotten some food?" The steward's course changed, taking them up a flight of stairs. "I took down three chasers tonight and did a lot of manifesting."

"Three?" Raddel almost came to a stop as he looked at her. "At once?"

"What? No. No one fights like that unless they have to or they're stupidly overconfident. All the heroes you've ever heard about lived and won because they *didn't* try to fight a bunch of people at once without making sure they'd only face one at a time. I tripped one over a rooftop, then fought the other two one at a time."

"Incredible."

"No, not really." She was too tired to want to deal with Raddel's misplaced flirting or whatever it was. "But I'm really tired and—"

"I'm afraid it can't wait." The new voice came from the top of the stairs. The colonel came into view as Mynessa hurried up the last few steps, standing with his hands clasped behind his back, the sternness of his expression nowhere near as fake as Raddel's had been. His head was long since bald, a shining dark dome above a stern, firm jaw that almost never featured anything but a scowl. At least where she was concerned. "I apologize, but it truly can't. There's someone here who wished to see her highness."

"*Who?*" Mynessa voiced the query a second later.

"Deputy Askello."

Who?

"The deputy is responsible for *all* government oversight of trade and shipping," the colonel added, reaching into the inside pocket of his jacket and pulling out a small flask. "She wants to meet with her highness, to see proof for herself that the royal family is not entirely deceased as the Predict claims. If so, she has promised to ally herself with our cause, which will make preparing for our coup *much* easier. So do as you're told, musician."

Mynessa scowled and extended her hand, the tongue bracelet taking shape with a thought and lashing out, snatching the flask from the colonel's hand and delivering it to hers. The colonel scowled but said nothing as she popped the top off and took a whiff. Wine, likely a decent vintage. She sucked it down, ignoring the flavor and letting out a gasp when she finished.

"Fine," she said, tossing the now-empty flask back to its owner and noting his deepening scowl. "But I get a meal. And a bath. And then some sleep."

"You don't get to make demands—" the colonel began, but then he shook his head. "If her highness agrees to it."

He's a real magrel isn't he? Mynessa thought as she took a quick look around.

Raddel motioned to a nearby door. "In there. You'll have your privacy."

"He's just under a lot of stress," came the reply from her partner. *"But even father echoed your words more than once."*

Well, I'd be surprised if I was the only one, Mynessa thought as she followed Raddel's gestures into what was clearly a small sitting room. Once the door was shut behind her she peeled off her cloak, followed by her small bag.

It had all been an accident. Pure happenstance that had bound her to the princess's fate. She'd met the Inker, Paggel, in an alehouse far to the south, shared a few too many drinks, and somehow been convinced to let him show her what he was working on. Later she'd woken up with a hangover and a new tattoo—far from her first, but rather the first of *its* kind, as she'd discovered when she'd manifested it and seen with shock a living thing shoot across her room. Paggel had explained that he'd discovered something new, a way to bind *living things* in ink the same way others bound inanimate objects like her fiddle or her staff. A whole new, undiscovered school of inking, infinitely more complex than conventional tattoos. He'd shown her his first attempt, a set of literal wings from a Carbardian Great Condor, which while not enough to let him fly had enabled him to at least glide somewhat reasonably, though he himself had suspected other magic at work in the binding.

Though strange, she'd quickly grown accustomed to the strange bracelet and its myriad uses, and agreed to journey with him northwards as he searched for a sponsor.

After all, she thought as she pulled her shirt over her head, leaving it on her arms and catching glimpses of the *massive,* complex tattoo crawling and shifting across her back. *It would have made for a good story.*

"It's still a good one," came the princess's voice. *"You're just still in it."*

Mynessa nodded as she unwrapped the supportive binding around her chest. She didn't have to remove *everything* from her back, but experience and experimentation over the last few months had shown her that it certainly made things easier.

There had been a lot of experimentation. She and Paggel had arrived in the capital after several months of travel, the Inker constantly testing deeper applications of his discovery and looking to gain sponsorship for his research. It had taken weeks, but he'd worked his way up to an audience with the royal family's daughter—not quite the crown prince, but no mere aide either.

That had been when everything had gone wrong. Halfway through the presentation the Predict's coup had begun, men-at-arms loyal to his cause seizing the palace and slaughtering the royal family. Trapped, with no way out, the princess had asked both Mynessa and Paggel to do the unthinkable.

Her back exposed, Mynessa focused her thoughts, feeling the strain as smoky ink boiled from her back, the tattoo there—more complex and involved than any she'd ever seen—lifting from her flesh, spilling out in colors and shades that mixed and flowed around one another. She could *feel* the magical ink leaving her skin, more than with any other tattoo. The presence at the back of her mind faded, drifting away as more and more ink boiled from her back. Fatigue took its place as the last of the tattoo lifted free, and she fought to stay awake. If the wielder slept or became unconscious, the binding would return to its place. She *had* to stay awake.

Free of her back, the smoky inks swirled in the air, taking on a vaguely humanoid form before condensing—skin, eyes, lips, and limbs all forming and gaining solidarity. Within moments, Princess Navo Tedeca stood atop the couch, still wearing the same formal garb she'd worn the day they'd met.

Princess Tedeca—Navo, really, as close as they were now—looked down at the couch and frowned. "Drat," she said quietly. "I really thought I'd manage to come out sitting that time."

Mynessa shivered as the expenditure of magic rolled through her and covered herself once more. "You're standing at least. It's better than you managed before."

"And I still can't change my clothes," Navo added, looking down at her voluminous sleeves in disgust as she stepped off the couch. "It has to be possible. I'm sure of it."

Mynessa just shrugged. She wasn't so certain, but how could she be where Paggel's magic was concerned? He hadn't even known, and any theories were as lost as he was, the exertion of binding the princess to Mynessa's back having killed him. In a daze, Mynessa had snuck out disguised as herself, none of the Predict's forces stopping her past checking to confirm she wasn't a member of the royal family in disguise.

They'd burned the palace wing behind her. A funeral pyre for Paggel and his knowledge.

Navo's hand touched her shoulder. "I'm sorry," the princess said, looking down at her. "I know you're tired."

"Of course you know," Mynessa replied, giving her a fake smile. "You feel it. You're in . . . there." She couldn't bring herself to say "me." It sounded—and felt—wrong. "All day. I know you know." Just another oddity that they'd had to accept. But it meant the princess was alive, in a way. She was no mere echo. Mynessa knew that. She was a living, breathing, sapient being, bound to the magical ink tattooed on her back. She wasn't just memory, she was alive and real.

"Do you want to stay here?" Navo asked, gesturing to the couch.

Mynessa shook her head. "No. I'll just fall asleep partway through your meeting, and you know what would happen then."

"My meeting with the deputy would be far more memorable." Navo smiled, and Mynessa mirrored it as the princess offered her a hand up.

"That's one way to put it, certainly," she said, rising and holding back a sigh as a stiffness in her legs made itself known. She must have winced, however, because the princess nodded.

"Sore."

"Yes. A bit."

"It'll make a great story someday."

Mynessa just nodded. "Thanks for the warnings, by the way. You're getting better at calling them out." The first time Navo had tried, she'd confused right and left, and Mynessa had spent the next few days nursing a lump on the side of her face from an errant enforcer's fist.

"I do hope I'll get good enough at this that you won't have to disrobe when I'm needed," the princess added as Mynessa reclaimed her bag and cloak. "And that we—I mean I—can figure out how to adjust my garb. At the very least leave a few layers behind."

"Just be glad you're not coming out naked," Mynessa replied. Her response made the princess's brow furrow, as if something about her statement had stirred her thoughts past a simple joke, but before she could ask a knock at the door drew both their attentions.

"Your highness?" It was Raddel. "Are you prepared?"

Navo let out a sigh so quiet Mynessa was certain she was the only one that had heard it. "I'll try to make this quick," she said with a backward glance. "I'm tired as well."

And with that her demeanor shifted, growing serene and impassive. "I am," she called, and Raddel opened the door, bowing as the princess swept by.

"My lady," Mynessa heard the colonel say. "This way." She caught a glimpse of them through the doorway, heading down the hall, and in a strange way she still felt as though she could *feel* the princess's position once she was out of sight . . . but that was probably just her mind playing tricks on her. Though sometimes she'd felt like she'd known where other manifested items were, and the bond they shared was unusual . . .

She put her thoughts aside and stepped out into the hall, Raddel's face lighting up as he saw her. "And you, Lady Mynessa? What will you do while her highness meets with the deputy?"

Mynessa glanced down the hall just in time to see the colonel guide Navo through a set of doors, closing them behind him. No doubt the remainder of the Royalist leaders were present at that meeting—and oddly enough she felt *certain* of it at the moment.

"A meal," she said, turning back toward Raddel and then stepping to one side, putting her back against the wall before sliding down it to sit with her legs crossed. The fatigue she'd felt earlier was more pronounced now, but she needed to keep herself awake. And maybe glean some words from the princess's meeting if she listened carefully.

Not that she needed to listen closely at the moment. It wasn't hard at all, even through the closed doors, to make out someone's astonished—and loud—gasp of Navo's name, likely followed by a quick genuflection. She almost imagined that she could feel a momentary flash of embarrassment from Navo. Though again, that had to be her imagination.

Raddel was still waiting, and she shook her head, covering her momentary distraction with a smile. "Sorry," she said. "Really tired. But a hot meal would be nice. Then a bath once the princess is done with her meeting."

Raddel nodded. "I'll see to it personally."

Mynessa nodded but didn't give him any further encouragement as he strode off, heading for the kitchens. *Raddel. You keep trying, but you have no idea what you'd be getting into.* It wasn't that there weren't elements of attractiveness to him—a quick glance at his backside as he left was more than enough to confirm that—but he was city-born through and through, while she was a traveling performer. Raddel was put-out enough by some of the non-humans that had showed up at the various Royalist meetings —not to a truly aggressive or dismissive rate, not like the Predict—but more than enough to show that he didn't perform well in unfamiliar situations. If he ever left the city, even to one of the neighboring towns, she was certain he'd return within a few weeks at most. Some people were just sedentary.

And I'm not about to give up my traveling ways if I can help it. Assuming I ever can again.

She and Navo had both wondered about what the future might hold—whether or not the Royalists succeeded in restoring the throne.

Was there an Inker out there that could undo the bond that Paggel had created? Or would their lives be forever tied? They presumed Navo would age, as bound items showed small changes over time, like the tuning of her fiddle or the replacement of the occasional broken string, but neither of them truly *knew*. The colonel clearly intended to see the princess back on the throne even if it meant Mynessa was captive in a nearby room—imprisoned in lace and gold, but a prisoner all the same.

She shoved the endless questions from her mind, pushing them away and off for another time. Muffled voices echoed from the princess's meeting, but the speakers were keeping their tones low, making it hard for Mynessa to make out much of note.

A mouth-watering scent caught her nose, stomach rumbling in response and stealing her focus from the meeting. A member of the staff followed the scent into the hall, a tray held in his hands. With a bow they presented it to Mynessa, and she took it, setting it across her lap. A stew and bread, as well as a pastry of some kind. She dug in with fervor, the servant stepping back and waiting.

The meal was gone in minutes, the servant quietly taking the tray and retreating to leave her alone in the hall. The minutes passed, and she kept herself from falling asleep by thinking back on the events of the evening, from her performance to the force of the raids sweeping the Underbelly.

Might be a good idea to hold off for a few days and let things die down. Perform in some other parts of the city. Maybe even the Hills. There wouldn't be alehouses there—the nobility were above such things—but there would be "drinking establishments" she could play at, and maybe even stir up a little trouble in.

Of course, there would be a heavier enforcer presence so close to the palace. And a good portion of the nobility had, publicly, at least, sided with the Predict after he'd seized power, which might make some of her messages a little less well-received. And if anyone recognized her, disguise or not . . .

Especially after they'd called out her name during the raid. She'd been named before, but something about earlier had brought with it the feeling of a snare slowly closing around her. Before it had felt like happenstance. Now there could be no coincidence.

Down the hall the conversations ceased, and short time later the door to the meeting room opened. Navo glided out with a regal step that almost made it look like she was floating. She hated the step, having confided with Mynessa that it was stiff and almost painful to perform if done poorly, and she'd never been good at it. But royalty had certain expectations, even if much like a bard many of them were theater.

"It was good to see you again, your highness," a woman who had to be Deputy Askello said as she followed in the princess's wake. "I had feared the worst, but with you truly having a hand in things, I would be honored to lend my support."

Navo nodded. "My people will be in touch. There is much we can do to weaken the Predict's power. Your skills and talents will be needed."

Askello bowed. "As you command. By your leave, your highness?" Navo nodded. "Then I bid you farewell for now." With that the deputy turned and walked down the hall, vanishing into an adjoining corridor a moment later.

"Well done, your highness," the colonel said quietly as he stepped out of the room, Mynessa just barely catching his words. Despite the smile on the princess's face, somehow she knew Navo was annoyed with him. "You handled that well."

"Colonel Bastava," Navo said as she turned, walking down the hall toward Mynessa. "Did I understand correctly when I heard you explain to the deputy that you planned only to aid those taken in the raids that were aligned with us or from the upper reaches of the city?"

Mynessa didn't miss the way the colonel's eyes narrowed. "You did, my lady. Our resources are not without limit, and we need to focus on helping our people first. The Underbelly—"

"Is as much a part of this kingdom as any other. Should I ignore my loyal people in Fcisfel because they are not here?"

"I . . ." The colonel frowned, but lowered his gaze. "No, my lady, but—"

"But what?"

"Your father would have understood—"

"My father let the Predict's ways fester until the rot saw him burned alive," Navo shot back, anger clear in her voice. "If you mean to simply repeat the same mistakes that led to the Predict taking power, then this movement is already doomed to failure. You *will* see to it that our agents, few though they may be, work in the Underbelly. And I may watch personally to see that it is done. If it is not, then you will be forced to consider yourself a Royalist without a royal."

The colonel let out a faint hum of displeasure. "You play a dangerous game, your highness."

"I'm sorry, I thought we were revolutionaries." Navo stopped and faced the old military commander, matching his stern look with one of her own. "I will *not* condone withholding aid from those who need it simply because some might consider them beneath my station. I serve *all* my people, not some. Am I understood?"

The colonel nodded. "You are, highness." Though it was clear from his tone and expression that he still disagreed. "May I take my leave?" Navo nodded and the colonel immediately moved off, his stiff gait somehow even more uptight than usual.

The moment he was out of sight Navo's regal posture collapsed, the princess letting out a sigh as she looked at Mynessa. "Thank goodness that's over."

"I really don't think he likes you, highness," Mynessa said, pushing herself up and wincing as the stiffness returned.

"Navo," the princess corrected, one corner of her mouth quirking upward in a small smile. "Again, you've earned that right. You didn't *have* to do any of this. You could have fled the city and never deigned to manifest me."

"Not really," Mynessa replied with a shake of her head as a member of the staff appeared at the end of the hall. "Tried, maybe, but . . ." She shook her head again, her tight braids bouncing against one another. "You'd have never forgiven me, nor I myself."

Navo walked alongside her as they moved down the hall, the servant offering a deep curtsey as they both neared. "The lady Mynessa's bath has been drawn," she said.

"Could I trouble you to draw one for me as well?" Navo asked.

"Of course, my lady!" The servant's curtsey deepened, and she backed away before turning and gesturing, her eyes still downward. "This way, if it pleases you."

Mynessa ignored the formalities as they followed the servant's lead, instead giving Navo a curious look. "You're going to try it again?"

"No offense," Navo replied, "but I feel stiff and sore as well, almost like I was running with you. And I haven't had a proper bath in months. Having one with you—as strange as that sounds, you know what I mean —isn't quite the same."

"No, I'd imagine it isn't."

"Besides, I want to try something new."

"I might fall asleep."

Navo shrugged. "If you do, then you do. I'd still like to try." She brought one hand up, covering her mouth as she yawned. "To tell you the truth I'm tired as well, though I'm unsure why. But it's why a bath seems so appealing. I'm determined, even if I have to take it in my clothes."

Ahead of them the servant almost stumbled, clearly listening with confusion to their discussion.

Try living it, Mynessa thought with a wry spark of amusement. *And having a living, breathing person bound to your skin.* One who, thus far, had been unable to remove more than a few small items of clothing without triggering a failsafe in the enchantment and returning her to her place on Mynessa's back.

Even that, they had both noted in the early days of their partnership, was unusual. Unlike other tattoos, Navo's would change and shift, not just from manifest to manifest but while in place on Mynessa's back.

"Was there any other interesting news brought up in your meeting?" she asked, changing the topic for the moment.

"Only that Askello has heard rumor of another potential supporter against the Predict," Navo replied. "A steel magnate named Toshil. Apparently they've become inebriated at a few small social functions and expressed displeasure with the Predict's new taxes compared to those of my father. An opening, perhaps."

"Indeed," Mynessa agreed as the servant led them up another level.

"We might be able to bring him into our fold. His contacts and supplies would be very useful." There must have been an odd look on her face, because Navo then gave her a curious look. "What?"

"Just thinking," Mynessa said as ahead of them the servant opened a door to a spacious looking bath. "In stories and tales that I tell, so much is glossed over when it comes to raising a rebellion. It's all inspiring speeches and big, pivotal moments. No one talks about the meetings behind closed doors unless there's an immediate importance to one of them."

"Oh, that." Navo smiled as they both stepped into the bath chambers, the flooring beneath them changing to wooden slats over shaped stone. Several large metal tubs sat in the center of the room, one filled with steaming water. "Yes, it's far from the life of action most tales paint it as, isn't it?" The servant swept past them, opening the taps by another tub and then moving to cupboards at the back of the room to pull out bars of soap and large, fluffy towels. "But they leave out these bits too."

"Mmm," Mynessa said, her eyes fixed on the hot bath before her. "That they do. Not to say there aren't tales of baths in stories, but they're not the kind one tells in polite company."

"Do you need anything else, your highness?" the servant asked Navo.

"No, thank you. I'll attend to my own wash," the princess answered. With another curtsey the servant left the room, closing the doors behind her.

"You said you wanted to try something new?" Mynessa asked as she peeled her clothing off, dropping it on a provided bench.

"Yes," Navoo said, grasping the clasp of her robes. "Two ideas. Both *may* require your help."

"Oh?"

"I've tried merely removing my clothing before, and only found myself back on your, well, back," Navo said. "But that was me simply removing it, as if it were just a piece of clothing. But what if I attempt to manifest it?"

Mynessa blinked. "As if your clothing were inked?"

The princess nodded. "Exactly like that. Except . . . I've never been inked. My only knowledge of the process is seeing others use it, and well, our current situation. So . . . how do you manifest or call something back?"

Mynessa thought for a moment before replying. "It's . . . different. It's been so long since I haven't been inked that it's hard to say. I suppose that the first thing I do is recognize that I am bound to whatever I'm inked to. It is part of me. I then . . . will, I suppose . . . that item to come forth, into my hand or where I need it. It takes practice, but that *is* all it takes."

Navo nodded. "At the very least I can try. If nothing happens, then I have lost little." She closed her eyes, forehead furrowing in concentration. A second later, she began to open the front of her outer garment.

Only for the robe—along with everything else—to fade into smoke. Mynessa shook her head as the smoke swirled and circled before heading toward her, already wondering whether she'd have the energy to manifest the princess once again, only for a sudden shout of elation to cut through her resignation like a blade.

"It worked!"

The smoke settled into Mynessa's back, swirling past her to reveal a fully nude Princess Navo standing without a single stitch of clothing on her. A second later she looked down, cheeks going red. "A little too well."

Mynessa, stunned, still managed to pull her gaze away to check her own flesh. Even over her shoulder, what she could see of her back now sported a very different tattoo than the one she'd become accustomed to. Then Navo spun, and Mynessa's surprise was stolen by another observation. "Your back!"

"What?" Navo twisted, turned to try and peer over her shoulders, a hint of alarm in her voice. "What about it?"

"Stop moving," Mynessa said, ignoring the developments on her own skin in favor of stepping over to the twisting princess. She had a hand on Navo's shoulder before she'd even considered that she was laying a hand on royalty . . . but no sooner had the thought slipped across her mind than she dismissed it. *We're basically sharing a body these days. A hand is nothing.*

"Your back," Mynessa said, gently pressing Navo's shoulder and turning her to get a full look. "It's covered in ink. I thought you said you'd never been inked."

"What?" Navo twisted, shaking off Mynessa's hand and stepping over to one of the provided mirrors. "But I . . . that's new. I swear it. I've never even felt a needle before, or at least hadn't until Paggel did this. But . . . he didn't make this."

The mirror's surface was slightly misty, but it was still clear enough for Mynessa to make out the sweeping sprawl of tattooed pathways inscribing a massive circle on the princess's back. A circle, she noted, not unlike the one around her own wrist. Only a thousand times more complex, with lines so numerous they were almost solid.

"Have you—?"

She already knew what the princess was going to ask. "No," she said early, "I don't. I've never heard of anything like this before." She stepped up close, getting a better look at the thousands of lines inscribed across the princess's back.

Inscribed? Or part of her?

What was more, some of them almost looked like they were . . . *moving.* Shifting, slowly but surely. *Like her own tattoo does when she's on my back.*

Where did this come from? "Was this under your clothes all this time?"

Navo gave her a flat look, turning to face her. "How would I know? I've never disrobed until now."

"Right," Mynessa said, chiding herself mentally. "That's fair."

"Also, are my clothes tattooed on *your* back?"

Mynessa twisted, then turned so that she too could get a better look at her back in the mirror. Bright ink stood out against the darker shades of her skin, unfamiliar symbols and shapes she was certain hadn't graced her flesh mere seconds ago.

"I think," she said after a moment's consideration, "that we are both in far over our heads here. Swimming dark waters, to borrow a phrase from the coralfolk." *And with Paggel gone, there's no one we could ask.*

"We should get someone to make a copy," Navo said, standing beside Mynessa and eying both their backs. "There might be something to these shapes that another inker could understand, maybe even use to help figure out what's happened to us and how to undo it. If we summon someone . . ." She stepped away, toward the bell that would ring the servant's quarters.

"Wait!" Mynessa said, her tone drawing the princess up short. "Not now."

"What? Why not?"

"A few reasons," Mynessa said. "First, I'm tired and still want my bath before I fall asleep. But second, we don't *know* what we did. Not yet. We don't know if the ink on your back is connected to you dismissing your clothing, or if it was already there. We can check tomorrow. Maybe those are your undergarments or something."

Though it seemed unlikely, as complex as the moving circle was.

"But secondly," she said, stepping back over to the tub. "Your—our—situation is known only to a few, and we'd better keep it that way. Notes, sketches of obvious inker marking, anything like that is something that might make it to the wrong person, or clue the Predict into how Princess Navo really got away and where she might be."

Navo nodded and lowered her outstretched hand. "That's a fair assessment. Good thinking."

"Besides, you'd miss your own bath."

Navo spun, her gaze going to the tub with the active spigots. "And by the Graces, I want that." She leapt across the room, the action most unprincesslike, and swung one leg over the edge of the bronze basin, letting out a sigh of contentment as her toes touched the water.

"I've missed this," she said, letting her whole leg slip down into the tub. The rest of her body followed a moment later, another contented sigh filling the room the princess sank to her chin in the steaming pool.

Mynessa finished removing her own clothing, breeches and undergarments gone at last. Then she too let out a sigh of satisfaction as she lowered herself into the hot bath, the heat immediately soothing her stiff and sore muscles. For a minute or so she just sat in silence, letting the warmth sink in.

However much she was tempted to close her eyes and sleep, eventually reason won out, and she followed the princess's example, scrubbing herself free of grime and soot. She left her clothes where she'd laid them for the staff to launder, opting instead to wrap herself in a robe for the journey to her room. The princess made the trip in-person as well., thrilled to be clad in a robe of her own, a welcome change from the formal attire she'd until now been trapped in. None of the staff questioned Navo asking to speak with Mynessa in her room rather than the neighboring quarters that she was supposed to be using—and in fact, Mynessa noted, most of them probably had to have noticed that the princess's room was never actually *used*.

Granted, they were likely drawing their own conclusions about that. But it was better than exposing the truth, at least for the time being.

"All right," Navo said once they were alone. "I'm ready."

Mynessa nodded and focused her thoughts, willing the princess to return. Before her eyes Navo's body broke apart into cloudy smoke that swirled through the air before sinking into her back. With it came a wave of fatigue that was overpowering. The princess was gone, her robe lying empty on the floor.

Did it work? Mynessa "asked," for a moment worried that their earlier experiment had broken something.

"I'm here," came the reply. *"And nothing feels different. Outside of the satisfaction of having had a bath."*

That's great, but . . . She swayed, eyes sliding to the bed. *Talking about it is going to have to wait until morning.*

"I understand," Navo replied as Mynessa sank down into the cushions of the mattress, wrapping a heavy blanket around herself. *"In fact, I think—"*

Whatever the princess wanted her to hear was gone as the world faded into blissful sleep.

THE NEXT MORNING BROUGHT WITH IT NEWS OF INCREASED ENFORCER activity, the colonel himself informing Mynessa that neither she nor the princess were to leave the building for the time being. Navo accepted the decision with understanding, while Mynessa had to grudgingly admit that the decision made sense. Instead of going out, she spent *some* of the day performing for the staff while the princess met with other members of the Royalist movement and coordinated their plans.

But not all of it. When she wasn't the "vessel" for Navo, as the colonel seemed to consider her, he seemed not to care at all what she did as long as she didn't venture far enough for the princess's manifestation to break down. Not that she wanted to for either of their sakes, and didn't dare think of what might happen if she attempted it with the princess given how much effort it took just to manifest her.

Still, as long as she stayed within the house she seemed fine—something she'd proven once by leaving her fiddle at the entrance and going all the way to the other end of the residence without issue. Her range was surprisingly long, though she had felt the pull of the instrument by the time she'd reached the fourth and final floor.

But with the whole of the headquarters to make use of, Mynessa quickly manufactured an excuse for herself and retreated to the one space that might contain answers, or at least some theories, to her and the princess's current predicament: the library.

Much of it, she'd discovered by the end of the first day, was barely organized, more for show than actual reading or reference. Which wasn't too surprising.

The raids lessened in frequency over the next few days, but Navo found herself needed for more Royalists meetings, binding both of them to the house as she planned and schemed. Mynessa didn't complain, choosing instead to return to the library once more and pore through the books there under the guise of "research" for her job as a bard.

As the days passed, however, all she'd really discovered were a few books discussing the basics of inking, much of which was common knowledge, and a single instance of one author discussing the steeply rising difficulties of bonding increasingly complex items and machines such as firearms.

Not a single text had mentioned binding anything living. To the contrary, it was as if each writer had considered it so impossible as to not discuss it. There were mentions of other forms of magic across the texts as well, from the modern powers of electricity—though one book asked if it, or other forms even were technically magic and not just science misunderstood—to the alchemical creations of the coralfolk and the western continents, among others.

The one item of use she found was a listing of basic "runes" that were used in the binding process, but *none* of them resembled the symbols on either of their backs.

There was no way around it. If they wanted to solve or even understand what Paggel had done, they were going to have to find an Inker who knew as much about the magic as he had. And while common inkers weren't rare, one capable of binding anything more complex than a staff or a stave, like an instrument, was.

By the third evening, as she returned to her room to find Navo waiting, all she'd earned for her study was a headache and a mounting sense of frustration.

"Nothing," Navo repeated once Mynessa had relayed her findings. "That isn't surprising, but it is unfortunate. It confirms what I'd feared: We'd need to look outside of the city in order to find someone with the knowledge to understand Paggel's work."

"Or bring one here," Mynessa replied from her position atop the bed. "And I doubt that's going to be within your power unless you're the one *in* power, so to speak."

"Or at least have access to my family's rightful finances."

There was something to the princess's words, and Mynessa rolled her head to one side to look at her. "What's that supposed to mean?"

"I mean that despite the aims of the colonel and many of the Royalists, I'm not certain my taking the throne is the solution everyone needs," Navo replied, her expression solemn. "It's what the most powerful of the nobility want because it lets them keep their power. But that same centralized authority is what made it so easy for the Predict to organize his coup in the first place."

"Careful, princess," Mynessa said with a grin. "You're starting to sound like a representist."

"Is that such a bad thing?"

To Mynessa's surprise, both the princess' tone and expression were serious, and she forced down a glib reply before it could escape. "No," she said with a bit more thought. "I personally don't think so. I've been to the republics, and they're far from solving every problem. But you're not wrong that centralizing the power led to the Predict being able to take over in the first place. It's not my place to advise you—"

"It's not? When I live on your back?"

"—but if you were to push for more representation of the common folk, you'd need your throne to do it. And assurance that your former Royalist allies won't immediately decide to take the same path as the current Predict."

"A fair worry."

"Why's it on your mind? Royalists a little zealous?"

"A bit," Navo confirmed with a nod. "More like divided. Both sides are willing to use me to further their own ends, belief in the royal family or not, but both have different ideas of what those ends may be." She sighed, leaning back against the wall. "At least both of us will be able to leave the headquarters tomorrow."

"Oh?"

"That magnate Askello was curious about? Toshil? She contacted him through a third party and heard back. He's interested, but only if he can—"

"Meet the princess and confirm there's a royal behind the movement."

"You're quick," Navo said with a smile.

"Bard. Have to be. Even when tired. So we're meeting Toshil tomorrow?"

"In a neutral location, yes. It's short notice, but we could really use his support."

"Sounds good to me. I could use the air." She rolled onto her back. "As fair trade, maybe I could go perform somewhere? See if I can stir up a little extra support and cash? People will be unhappy after the raids, and I can push that."

"It sounds reasonable," Navo replied, rising. "But for now . . ."

She held out a hand, and Mynessa took it. A moment later there was a swirl of smoke, and Navo vanished.

"Goodnight, Mynessa."

Goodnight, Navo.

"Suspicious, aren't you?" Mynessa asked the colonel as she climbed inside the third carriage they had switched to in the last thirty minutes. He gave her a grim look as he closed the door behind him, before rapping at the roof for the driver to set off.

"You disagree?" he asked as they began to move forward. "The Predict's enforcers clearly have identified you by name and sight. And the posters—"

"I know," she said, a bit more forcefully than she'd meant to. "Their artist was terrible." For starters, he'd made her nose much too thin. But the text had been clear: She was being sought due to connections with possibly surviving members of the royal family and the Royalist movement.

In other words, even if the meeting with Toshil went well she wasn't going to be making appearances on the Hill anytime soon. Not without a good disguise, not with the reward the Predict was offering.

"But as suspicious as you are, I'm surprised you don't worry this is a trap," Mynessa added as the wagon rounded a corner, jostling over cobblestones.

"Believe me, the thought has crossed my mind," the colonel replied. "But we need Toshil's resources and connections too badly to pass up the chance. With Askello and Toshil combined, we'd have enough of a hold over the markets and trade to strangle the Predict's income. Subtly at first, and then openly. Sellswords aren't loyal once they're unpaid. That would tip the scales."

He shifted, pulling his coat to one side and revealing the revolver strapped at his hip. "But rest assured, bard, if Toshil is dealing dishonestly with us, he'll have the Grace's own blood to pay. Pavest, my driver, is armed, as is Tando in the back. The meeting place is a neutral warehouse near the docks—"

"That explains the fishy smell."

"—and we've both agreed to only bring ourselves."

"And if Toshil lies?" Mynessa voiced the princess's question.

"Then your orders are to retreat with myself, Pavest, or Tando and make for the nearest safehouse. We . . ." He paused. "We're slowing."

"I noticed," Mynessa said, reaching for the window shades.

"Don't," the colonel replied, slapping her hand away. "Just in case. I'll do it." He cracked the door open, blocking the light with his body and drawing his revolver. "What's the hold—"

There was a sharp *crack* as something blew the colonel's body back, the scent of ozone filling the air. Mynessa had a brief glimpse of a stun bolt falling to the floor of the wagon as the man flew back, twitching and jerking, and then echoing cries came from the front and back mixed with other sharp *cracks* as someone took down their escort.

"Ambush!"

Mynessa was already moving, rushing for the door on the other side of the carriage. Only for it to be wrenched open just before she could reach it. She had the barest glimpse of the curved end of a shockstave— and then her world exploded, every muscle in her body tightening and dancing as she was blasted back across the carriage. She hit the far side with a *thud*, vaguely aware that someone was screaming with pain inside her head. Or maybe it was audible outside as well.

Someone spoke, the sound muffled. Her whole body ached, muscles twitching. The colonel pushed himself up, lifting his revolver, only for an enforcer to bat it aside and jab the man in the chest again. He lurched, shouting as he convulsed.

A sweet-smelling bag dropped over Mynessa's head from behind, tugging her back as the world seemed to float . . .

. . . and slid into a black void.

She awoke with a gasp, jerking her head up as burning scent invaded her nostrils and calling forth a rough, dry cough.

"Mynessa! You're awake!"

I . . . What's—? Her hands were bound behind her back, around a post of some kind.

"Hmph," grunted a still somewhat blurry figure in front of her. "The bard the Predict wants so badly."

Mynessa tried to speak as the coughs faded, but only succeeded in making a croaking groan. Her throat felt dry as a bone.

"No princess." The voice was deep. "That's what I get for rushing things, I suppose. Still, there's always a chance someone will talk."

"You got her," another voice said as Mynessa's vision continued to clear. "Now let us take her."

"Not yet," the first voice said. "Rule of business, friend." There was something to the way they said the word that made it fail to sound endearing in any way. "Never let go of something until you're *certain* you don't have a better use for it. Don't forget who's paying for this little excursion right now."

"Mynessa!" Navo sounded alarmed. *"They gassed you, and you were gone and I was all alone and—"*

Reality crystalized. Ambush. Someone, likely Toshil, had betrayed them. That was probably who was speaking. She pushed aside Navo's frantic relief, focusing on the still-blurry figures and voices in front of her.

"—to the Predict."

"Which is better for your boss, hmm? A gift he has to assemble, or one that's fully together?"

Her vision was improving with each passing second. She couldn't make out any detail yet, but the suit the speaker was wearing looked expensive.

"I'm familiar with your 'assembly.' She'll be no good to the Predict dead."

The other figure laughed. "Don't you worry. She'll still be alive."

"So you said, but the colonel—"

"You blame me for that? I warned you the man was old. You fools were the ones who insisted on using shockstaves cranked up to dangerous levels. Something I'll mention to the Predict, so *your* name in his ear, when I give my report. Unless, of course, you can think of any reason why I might forget."

Not friends, then, Mynessa noted, her thoughts quieting Navo's near-panic.

"What?"

Toshil set a trap for us, but he's not in it for the Predict—

"Oh, that. Yes, I gathered that the moment he had his men bring us here."

You were awake? Mynessa asked as in front of her, the enforcer gave a scowl of displeasure at the man in the suit.

"And you weren't. It was awful. I never want to go through it again. But I could hear and see things. It's how I know where we are."

Which is?

"A warehouse only a few blocks from where we were taken. But Mynessa, the colonel is dead!" Even if only in thought, she could hear the concern in Navo's voice.

She closed her eyes, focusing. *Okay, first? Don't panic. They might be saying that just to try and trick me into saying something. This whole thing could be an act.*

"You're . . . right. I suppose that makes sense."

It might surprise you, but I've done this before.

"What?"

I owed a small-town crook money.

"What happened?"

I paid him. I actually did owe him, and it was a lot easier to just pay and leave town. Now give me a moment. I need to think.

The world was still swimming when she looked up, along with her thoughts, but she did her best to look right at the blurry suit. "You." Her voice was a croak, but it had the effect she'd hoped for. The suit shoved the enforcer to one side.

"Get out." The enforcer hesitated, probably scowling, but then they turned and left the room.

The room. With her sight finally coming fully back she took a better look at her surroundings. It looked like an empty storage room, the wood rough and untrimmed, and the floor covered with the dust and dirt that tended to build up in an older structure. Navo had claimed it was a warehouse, and that did fit with the bare walls and thick boards. The ceiling above her was likely another floor, the supports bare and exposed with notable gaps between the boards. Light was coming from two sources—a bare electric bulb hanging from a wire that had clearly been tacked in place after the room had been built, and a line of dusty, dirty windows along one wall. There was another post opposite the one she had been tied too, and for a brief instant she wondered why.

The question fled, however, as the suited man who'd ordered the enforcer away stepped in her direction.

"That's Toshil," Navo said, confirming what Mynessa had already guessed. The magnate's suit was crisp and trim, cut along sharp lines with a wide, almost splayed, tail to the coat that was the current high fashion. His hair had been slicked back, the black peppered with grey, and the twin tufts of his beard had been treated to jut forward like a small pair of tusks.

Every inch of him screamed money. Except for his eyes, which held a hunger that made Mynessa's skin crawl.

"So," he said, coming to a stop a few feet away. "Mynessa Odivar. The wanted bard. I must admit, I do find your presence a bit perplexing." Toshil clasped his hands in front of his waist. "I was expecting to meet with Princess Tedeca. The colonel I can understand, but why *you?*"

"Maybe I look a lot like the princess? I'm told I do a pretty good impression."

Toshil frowned. "Spare me your wit, bard. You don't look a thing like her. Anyone who buys that ruse wouldn't be fit to be included in a plot against the Predict. Why were you along?"

"Lie!"

I know. "Decoy. The princess was coming in another carriage, and we were to make the swap right before meeting you."

The frown deepened. "No, I don't buy that. We ambushed you just before the meeting point. By then there wasn't any good location to make a swap."

"You're pretty up-to-date on secret meetings for a steel magnate."

"You'd be surprised how much business is better done in secret. And should be pleased, since it's working in your favor right now."

"Oh?"

Toshil grinned, the expression empty, like that of a hungry shark. "Indeed. The enforcers wanted to take you and the body of the late colonel to the Predict immediately. If not for my oversight, they would have. I've heard stories of the methods the Predict uses to extract information. Straightforward and brutal. I am a businessman first and foremost: I have simpler ways of acquiring information. At first, at least."

"Let me guess: money?"

"Exactly. Tell me everything, and I'll pay you accordingly, then let you go."

"Into the arms of the enforcers."

"Nothing so cruel." The smile was still cold. "No, if you tell me what I need to know, give me information that I can *use*, I'll provide you with a way out of the city. I don't know what the Royalists promised you, but surely you can see the wisdom in an exit with a fat purse in your pocket."

Unless I just disappear along the way.

"All you have to do is tell me a few things. Where the Royalists meet, for example, and why the colonel *really* brought you along. Why you're involved at all."

"They like music while they ride to meetings," Mynessa said.

Toshil's eyes seemed to grow colder. "All of them?" A cold, icy chill worked its way down Mynessa's spine. There was something about the man's words . . . "Or just meetings with *her*, like the day the Predict staged his coup?"

Panic flooded through her, though it wasn't entirely her own. *Stay calm. Don't panic.*

"But he knows!"

No one was in that room but us and Paggel. No. One. Knows.

"Touched a nerve, I see," Toshil said, his smile widening. "I'll admit I don't know what happened that day, but clearly something important came of it. Was the whole meeting a ruse? The inker perished, I know that much. And now I find you in a wagon instead of the princess. And you *are* inked. Hmm."

Navo, I need you to stay calm. If he figures out what's really going on . . . The panic in her head lessened, but she could still feel it pressing against her mind.

"Maybe a very clever, advanced disguise you can summon?" Toshil asked. "Makeup and clothing that you can use like an inked actor or actress on stage, but the best money could buy?"

She tried to keep her face neutral, but it wasn't a bad guess. At least Toshil didn't seem to know what Paggel was truly researching.

"You do have a lot of ink," Toshil continued. "Don't leave me standing here guessing, girl, tell me! Why were you with the colonel? What's your place in this? Where are the Royalists meeting?"

"The colonel liked my jokes."

Toshil's slap was like a hammer-blow, knocking her head to one side and leaving her cheek stinging. "That's enough of that, bard. I've given you the easy solution: Tell me what I want to know. I'll pay you, give you your freedom, and you can leave with no harm done. Make this difficult for me . . ." His face hardened.

"I . . ." *What do I do? Lie?* No, he'd see through that.

"Can you escape?"

Toshil's smile deepened, though beneath his dead eyes it only made the chill at her back stronger. "I have others to talk to right now who might be more willing to speak. Why don't you think about it for a little bit? If you're willing to speak properly when I get back, then I think we could be friends. If not . . ." Again his grin reminded her of a shark. "There are a lot of bones in the average body. It can take *days* to break them all."

"He's going to torture us!"

Obviously.

"Think about it." Toshil turned to the room's lone door and gave it a quick knock. Someone opened it for him and a second later it closed with a *click*, leaving her alone in the room, the still air stifling and hot.

"Mynessa . . . What do we do?"

I don't know. You've been awake longer. Any ideas? She took a quick look around the empty room, but there wasn't much to see aside from bare walls and the two posts. Shifting against the ropes, attempting to move her arms and fingers, did nothing. Whoever had tied her up had done a good job. She barely moved, and rope had been threaded between each finger.

"I . . . I don't know. Can you manifest something? A knife?"

I could, but it'd drop to the floor. They tied my fingers up. Standard practice with someone that's inked.

She paused for a moment, perking despite the stiffness in her shoulders and neck. *But* you *could.*

"What?"

Manifest. And untie me. Our one advantage is that no one else knows you're here. I manifest you, then a knife, and you cut me free. Or just untie me.

"And then?"

We work on that bit when we come to it. But if we're both free we're a step further ahead than we are now.

"I understand, but can you manifest me? Your back is covered."

That's going to be the tricky part, Mynessa thought with a frown. *Because I can't take my shirt off, and I've not been able to manifest you with any of the control of my other tattoos yet. So for this to work, I'm going to need to make that happen.*

"I understand. Can I do anything?"

Just try to keep your emotions in check, if you can. She could feel the faint pressure of Navo's mind riding just on the edge of her consciousness, a storm of fear mixed with sadness, panic, and pain. *I'm sorry about the colonel. Mourn him once we're out of this.*

The emotions pulled back, anger the last to go. Not directed at her, she knew, but Toshil.

She closed her eyes, trying to tune out all distractions, from the hot, muggy air of the room, to a faint cry of pain from somewhere nearby, just audible through the door. A faint spike of worry cut across her mind as the cry echoed, followed by an apology from Navo as the emotion vanished.

Mynessa didn't reply. *Shut everything out, focus on the manifestation. Envision it. Will the ink to activate.* She could *feel* the presence that was Navo on her back, the image shifting and crawling around her skin. She just needed to will it *outward*, urge it to *take shape.*

Come on . . . She could feel it starting, feel the ink beginning to lift from her skin. Only for the process to stop as the smoky ink pressed against the shirt at her back.

No! Pass through! She could feel Navo's mind growing distant as the cloud of ink tried to move, but then it came back with a mental *thud*, Navo's emotions and disappointment colliding with her own as the ink returned to her back.

Mynessa let out a frustrated grunt. *Why won't this work?* On a whim she manifested the bow of her fiddle, the ink seeping out from the ropes around her arms and forming the familiar shape on the floor. With another thought she recalled it, the motion just as easy. *Why can't I do that with you?*

"Maybe the magic is different when it's a living thing?" Navo suggested. "*Have you ever tried to manifest that tongue anywhere else?*"

Mynessa frowned. *Only once, after Paggel first inked it. It can't, because it needs to be connected to me.*

"*Perhaps that requirement is the same for anything living?*"

I . . . I don't know. The thought honestly hadn't occurred to her. *If so . . . then we're well and truly stuck.*

"*What about your knife? Could you manifest it beneath these ropes?*"

No. She shook her head. *The ink won't manifest where there isn't space. It can't push things out of the way to take shape. It's just smoke. There's no leverage.*

The door shifted, latch clunking, and a moment later Toshil strode back into the room, the muggy air almost seeming to cool under his smile. Two enforcers followed him, their own expressions grim counterparts to the magnate.

"Get to it," Toshil ordered, and Mynessa felt a momentary spike of fear, hers or Navo's, maybe both; she wasn't certain, as the enforcers flanked her position. A third entered the room as the first two grabbed her arms in tight, firm grips.

"I know I didn't ask," Toshil said, idly rubbing the knuckles of one hand. There was blood there, fresh and wet. "But I assume you don't intend to talk?"

"I'll talk," she replied, and for a second Toshil's eyes widened, the enforcers on either side of her stiffening. "What do you want to talk about?"

Toshil's expression soured. "Bards," he intoned, motioning for the three enforcers to continue. The ropes around her hands and arms began to loosen. "So glib." The ropes came free, and the enforcers jerked her around, pressing her face up against the post that had been at her back a moment ago.

"The *other* way," Toshil intoned, and the enforcers yanked her around the post so that she could see him if she bent her head to the side. Again they began tying her tightly to the wood, her arms wrapped around the rough beam in front of her instead of behind.

"All the way down to the wrist," Toshil instructed. "Leave her hands and fingers free." The enforcers worked quickly, following his orders and pinning her whole body against the post. "Good. Now leave."

"Yes sir." The trio moved out of the room with haste, closing the door behind them.

"Now," Toshil said, the cold smile back on his face. "It seems you're the most useful potential at the moment, and I'm certain you're not being honest with me, since you are a bard, and that is your job. But . . ." He extended his hands, adjusting the wide sleeves of his jacket as smoke began to pour down them. "Since you rejected my first offer, we'll jump right to the next step in this process."

The ink swirled around his hands, forming a pair of pliers and a small, sharp-looking knife. "I find that most people become quite cooperative when you go after what matters to them," Toshil said with another cold smile. "As a bard who plays the fiddle and sings, I believe that would be your fingers, followed by your voice."

Revulsion from Navo swept past the edges of her mind as Toshil took a step forward, the feeling mixing with a cold chill that was raising goosebumps down her arms.

"Let's not be hasty," she said quickly, tucking her fingers into fists when her arms wouldn't move. "What do you want to know?"

"Oh no," Toshil said, his smile growing wider as he stopped in front of her. "See, you don't understand how this is going to work. We're not in the bargaining phase right now."

"No no no no no no no—" Mynessa tried to shut out Navo's sudden panic.

"What's going to happen is that I *am* going to ruin your fingers," Toshil said. "Permanently. That's the only way for you to take this seriously. Then, if you tell me what I need to know, I'll leave you your voice." Still smiling, he reached forward, grasping one of her hands in his and wrenching the fingers apart. "Now, where to start?" He pressed the edge of his knife against the joint of her pinky finger, and Mynessa screamed as it began to slice through flesh.

Smoke boiled from her clothing, and Toshil let out a laugh as it swirled past him. "Really?" he asked as Mynessa looked on in dumb shock, stunned even beyond the stabbing pain coming from her little finger. "What are you hoping to do, girl? You can't control what you manife—"

With a sharp *crack* the end of Mynessa's staff collided with the back of Toshil's head. For a moment the magnate stood there, a dull, unfocused look in his eyes, and Princess Navo swung the staff again, striking the back of his head once more.

Toshil slumped, his body collapsing to the floor, his tools fading into clouds that streamed back up his arms. Mynessa stared at the princess in shock, jaw opening and closing. Navo was holding *her* staff like one would a club, panting heavily.

"How . . .?" Mynessa managed to croak out. "You . . . *manifested.* With my staff."

"I . . ." Navo dropped the staff, as if suddenly aware that she was holding it. It clattered against the boards. "I don't know. I just wanted to stop him so badly from hurting you, and then I reached out and . . ."

"I think," Mynessa said carefully, reaching out and summoning her staff back into her arm just to indeed confirm that it was hers. "That we are both far past our realm of understanding."

"Agreed."

The pain came back, a burning heat emanating from the pinkie that Toshil had cut. "We can figure it out later," Mynessa said. "Untie me, quickly. And then get back on my back. I don't want anyone else to see you."

"Can you get out of here alone?"

"I can try," Mynessa replied as Navo loosened the knots. A few seconds later she was free, the ropes dropping down around her as she stepped away from the post. The cut on her pinkie was still bleeding, and she winced as she eyed it. It was deep, but it hurt worse than she hoped it was. She ripped a piece of cloth free from her shirt, wrapping it around the base of her fingers on her right hand.

"Here," Navo said, helping her tie the strip in a knot to stem the blood. The injury let out a fresh wave of pain as she tightened the cloth, blood staining the fabric.

"Thanks." Mynessa eyed the door and then held out her hand. "Back in, quickly. No chances." Navo nodded, and a moment later dissolved into a smoky cloud, vanishing up Mynessa's sleeve.

You said we were close to where we were ambushed?

"Yes. A warehouse just a few hundred yards away."

Good, Mynessa thought as she summoned her staff to her hand once more, moving for the door. *Then I know roughly where we are.* She moved quietly, coming to a stop beside the door.

"Shouldn't we tie Toshil up?" Navo asked.

No, she replied. *A blow like you gave him? If he wakes up, he won't be in any shape to do much. He might die.*

"Oh."

And I won't feel bad if he does. Mynessa rapped the knuckles of her good hand against the door, mimicking the rhythm Toshil had made. A few seconds passed before the latch gave with a *clunk.*

"Yes si—?" The enforcer's wide-eyed look of astonishment was interrupted by the end of her staff slamming into his chin, rocking his head back. She tapped the side of his temple, and then before he could react wrapped one arm around his head, turning and using her body as a fulcrum to hurl him into the storage room. He bounced as he hit the boards, and before he could even attempt to rise she drove the tip of her staff against the side of his skull once more.

"I'm glad you know how to fight," Navo commented as Mynessa divested the enforcer of his stunstick. No stave for this one.

Me too, and not for the first time. She turned the stunstick to full power, the weapon humming. *Let's find our people and get out of here.*

A quick look out the door showed a vast, dimly-lit space, broken up by stacks of dusty wooden crates with no labels. *Smuggling?* she wondered off-hand as she took a few cautious steps out. *Or just forgotten supplies?*

The side of the building had a whole selection of back rooms that stretched for a good half the its length, but none of the doors had enforcers deployed outside of them. *So where are the others?*

"I didn't see where they took them, but—"

A nearby scream of pain cut off Navo's comment. Mynessa spun, lifting her staff. The shout had come from the other end of the warehouse. *There must be more rooms.*

She moved quietly through the stacks of crates, confirming her guess shortly thereafter when she picked out what looked like offices in the back, separated from the main warehouse by walls of glass windows. Through them she could see two enforcers beating what had to be one of the men from the carriage. *But where's the—Oh, up.* There was a second story to the offices, and second figure there being "tended to" by another group.

"I count five. Can you take on so many?"

I have to if we want to get those men out.

"Do you?"

She thought about it for a moment before replying. *You're in my head. You know I couldn't.*

"I'm very fortunate to have been bound to a woman of moral principle, Mynessa."

Yeah, I know. She crept forward, keeping her head down as she moved through the stacks, and then crouching low as she moved across the open space between their end and the start of the offices. There wasn't even a guard posted, but then Toshil's enforcers probably hadn't expected to need one.

She risked a last glance through the glass as she knelt by the door. Three enforcers, two familiar-looking, and none of them watching the door. Plus one bloody prisoner tied to a chair between them, face barely recognizable.

Mynessa took a deep breath and then yanked the door open, stepping into the room. She'd hurled the stunstick before any of the enforcers had even looked up, striking one of them in the back with a loud, electrical *snap.* A forward step brought the tip of her staff whipping up against the head of their companion, slamming him in the temple before clipping the shocked fellow as well, dropping them both. The third began to let out a shout, only for the sound to cut off as she shoved her staff forward, the tip striking the center of his forehead and snapping his head back. Like the other two, he dropped as well.

The driver looked up at her, dazed. "Odivlar?" he muttered through bloody lips.

"Ovidar, but that's not important," she said as she crouched, undoing his bonds. *Did they walk us here, or were we driven?*

"Driven, actually!" Navo replied. *"There's a carriage!"*

Good. Where?

"Through the back of this office, I think."

She looked down at the driver. "Stay here. I'll be back soon."

It wasn't hard to find the stairs that led up to the next level of offices. Nor relieve the unconscious enforcers of their stunsticks to repeat her previous trick. The pair of enforcers working the man above went down quickly, electrocuted and then battered by her staff.

"Lean on me," she told the footman, helping him down the steps.

"There," Navo said, directing her toward a door at the rear of the offices. *"Through there."* Mynessa went first, using her last shockstick to take down a single guard that had been left with the carriage.

Which was a very nice carriage, though impressively unremarkable to the eye. *All the better for sneaking around the city.* She guided the two battered captives into it, only to pause slightly when she spotted the colonel's still form lying inside. The cool skin of his neck confirmed that Toshil hadn't been lying.

There was no time to grieve. The magrel harnessed to the wagon snorted as she took the driver's seat and lifted the reins, shaking their heads and casting glances back at her as if sensing her tension. With a twitch they moved forward, battering the warehouse doors out of the way and moving out onto an empty dock.

All it took was a glance at the Cliffs to work out a rough position. She snapped the reins, driving the carriage forward and into a narrow back alley. A moment later they were on a main street, surrounded by traffic of all kinds as they melted into the city's ambiance.

Still, it took several minutes for the pounding of her heart to ease and the rush of their escape to fade. There was a hat with a wide brim below the driver's seat, and she donned it, concealing her face.

"Now what?"

Mynessa turned their course again, putting the still-high sun at her back and further covering her face. *We take this wagon to one of the safe houses, like the ones we used on the way here. And then . . . Wait, why are you asking me?*

"Because," Navo replied. *"The colonel is dead, and I'm humble enough to admit that my appearance was largely a figurehead for them to rally around. The colonel was the glue. With him it was going to be hard enough to pull support against the Predict. Without . . ."*

What about Askello? Mynessa turned the wagon onto a main road, moving with the traffic. *She supported you.*

"*She did, yes, but many of the Royalists gave the colonel their support for the idea of the royal family because of the ideal we represented.*"

Mynessa frowned, and not just because another wagon laden with what smelled like fish had cut her off. *Then don't be what he represented.*

"*What?*"

You trust me, right?

Momentary amusement flowed at her. "*Do I have a choice? But in seriousness, Mynessa, I do.*"

Remember what you said about being for the people a few days ago? Do that. The colonel is gone. But that doesn't mean the rebellion has to die. So he paraded you in front of a few nobles and merchants. So what? You can still parade in front of them. But you can appear other places too.

"*The Underbelly.*"

I was thinking the common folk, but yes. Certainly you might lose a few supporters from your current members—

"*Maybe even drive them to the Predict.*"

Not if you're careful. Neutrality would be preferred. But you sought the colonel and let him take charge.

"*That is true.*"

But you *are the princess, and unless I misunderstand how things work here, the rightful queen. The colonel and his associates may have been loyal, but they still referred to you as the princess. I'm not saying we can't walk away. At a word I could take us anywhere. We could find a way to break this bond, and you could find a place in any other nation as an exiled royal. You wouldn't be the first. But . . .*

"*You don't want to do that, do you?*"

The feeling that came with Navo's question made her smile. *No, I really don't. And not just because I'm morally opposed to autocrats like the Predict.*

"*Technically my father, the king, was an autocrat.*"

Fine. Self-serving autocrats. But either way, you aren't *an autocrat. You want to help your people. And by chance, you're bound to me, and can't do that if I don't help. Which I do, and not just to be part of a story other bards might share someday.*

She pulled the reins up as a busy intersection neared, slowing the carriage. *You can't do this without me. But I think you could without the colonel. If you want to.*

"*I do.*" The response was almost immediate. "*They are my people, and I still have a responsibility to them, if you'll allow me to act for it.*"

I'd be a lousy friend if I didn't. There was a pulse of warmth from Navo. *So then,* Mynessa thought. *Back to the headquarters?*

"Yes. We will need to find medical treatment for our men, as well as attempt to prevent any breakup. I will call a meeting, and . . . Mynessa, I will still need a second. Someone to take the colonel's place. I want it to be you."

Me?

"I want you in every meeting, everywhere I go. Not just as a friend, and a confidant, but as a representative. I've had three months now to watch you aid our cause in the Underbelly. If we want to bring them in, I can't think of anyone better to lead that push." There was a pause. *"If it helps, think of the stories. Will you do it?"*

Well, I can't really say no, can I? You do need my help.

"Fair. But I would feel better if I knew you wanted to take part."

Mynessa smiled. *I wouldn't have tried to talk you into it if I didn't want some part in it, Navo. Let's do it. It'll be a strange partnership. But, like I tell the crowds sometimes . . .*

She flicked the reins again, one of the safe houses she knew of nearing. *All stories start somewhere small. Ready to start yours, Queen Navo? Officially?*

A laugh. *"Ours, you mean? I am, Mynessa."*

She smiled, guiding the carriage onward down the street . . .

. . . and into history.

The Song to Save a Cursed Kingdom

Kate Dane

I f Princess Secharelle's song failed again, her kingdom would fall.

Not today. Maybe tomorrow or a month from now. Maybe next year. The kingdom would fall.

She kept her eyes closed, unwilling to look at her music master, and pressed her hands together in front of her waist. Strength and determination would lift her voice this time. Not like the last . . .

Her throat went tight as Robineau's image floated into her mind, stopping her breath. His face, his confidence, his lips promising her all would be well. Then her voice had cracked. Magic tore through the spell chamber, burned him, charred his face into black and blood.

He'd died because he trusted her, an eighteen-year-old girl.

They would all die when the kingdom fell. Her parents, her horse, her dog, the court, the very grass and rivers and trees. All would be sucked dry of life and wither.

"Breathe." Music Master Mayoret's voice floated through the air with a musical lilt even through the sharp command. "Without breath, there is no song."

She breathed, a heaving inhalation, as if more air would gift her the ability to stay in tune. Magic came to the call of music. The princess's blood let her harmonize with past spells to reinforce the kingdom's shield against angry ghosts.

"Open your eyes," Mayoret commanded.

She looked away, anywhere but at the music master's face. A square room with each side twice as long as a horse, a door of iron strips with a cross-bar. Rock walls, bare. Soft colors for hard stone, with yellows, greys, shading into white. They'd removed the tapestries and placed her in this room, rather than one with a wooden door, after her first attempt. Metal sconces wanted torches and openings let sunlight stream from green trees stretching upward.

"Look at me," he said.

She flinched and dragged her gaze to Mayoret, Her crown weighed heavy on her head.

The music master was pinch-faced and fussy, a head taller than she, a martinet in a pale green silk and gold-trimmed coat, long breeches with a green-on-green stripe which made him appear taller. He rapped heads of those who did not meet his standards, though limiting himself to the knuckles of royalty. The greatest voice teacher from Iridon who'd traveled to train her voice.

He was a tyrant, but she couldn't stand the thought of his flesh searing.

Her stomach surged and she pressed both hands against it. "Tomorrow. We should practice more."

"You are ready." He gave that assessment with a snap. "Delay no longer."

He wanted the prize. A castle, jewels, a royal title. All promised to entice another music master to risk his life. He didn't want to die. He must believe she could do this.

She nodded, her stiff neck making the bob difficult, and swallowed to try and moisten her dry mouth. It didn't help.

"I'll hum the sequence. All you need to do is sing with me."

She nodded again.

He hummed, the sound loud and tugging her on.

Princess Secharelle opened her mouth and sang. *Don't think. Sing.*

The syllables poured from her mouth, words in a no-longer-spoken language imploring the earth to shield those she loved and her kingdom. Her voice soared loud and sure. She couldn't waver.

The shaking began in her stomach and traveled through her body, setting her bones thrumming. The world answering her call. Breezes played with her hair, water rippled down the stones, the air itself sparkled as if beads of frost burst. Noise grew from the rustle of leaves to the spill of water to the roaring of a waterfall while snow fell about her. Her song rang out.

Mayoret's lips stayed tight. He must be humming.

She couldn't hear him.

They'd practiced so many times. She could do this alone. She sang on, heart hammering, hand rising to her breast, gaze fixed on him.

His lips began to quiver and his face paled.

She must be slipping out of tune. No. She couldn't. Each note had to sound exactly the way they had rehearsed over and over. She strained for the feeling, the sense she was managing the tune. Memorized syllables, sung in small pieces and now chained into one enchantment.

Was her voice going up or down?

She didn't know. She'd lost the hum which let her match.

The magic around her gusted, growing stronger. Flames spurted in air and from stone walls. Water fountained from the floor in one spot and another.

She sang faster, struggling to reach the end. Stopping would loose a hurricane. Even a poor completion of the spell would be safer. Her voice cracked.

The wind exploded into a spinning whirlpool, the fire flashed, splitting around her, splashing the stone walls, dodging the blasting fountains. The music master's pants burned with the speed of an oil-dipped torch.

She struggled for the notes, singing with all her heart, loud and unmelodious.

Her music master turned into a pillar of fire.

She fell to the floor, sobbing, burying her head so she'd see no more. Her crown clanked against stone, staying stubbornly attached to her head, while raw magic raged all about. "Why not take me?"

After minutes, the magic storm stopped, silence fell.

Princess Secharelle stood, panting, and stared at the body before her. Blackened flesh with blood in spots, hands in charred claws, his lips remained untouched. Lips which could sing music. His clothes were burnt rags which would have him muttering about the decline in court dress. A choked laugh burst from her lips.

Another music master dead.

If only she could throw herself from a window, drown herself, walk into a fire and burn as she deserved for these deaths.

If there were another heir with magic and music, she could stop trying instead of killing those around her when her magic exploded.

As the lone blood-princess, she had no choice.

She would serve her kingdom until it fell and kill a thousand music masters with her feeble attempts at song, dying with each one though she walked the castle as a living ghost.

A fortnight later, Princess Secharelle had no music master. She'd sung phrases loud and soft, but couldn't tell whether she hit the right notes. Trying the entire spell alone could be deadly if the magic had no other target. It hunted singers. Her death would mean the kingdom's end.

Today she'd come to the royal audience, as usual, in search of another teacher who might be lured by her father's promise of riches and nobility. The audience room had walls of stone covered with elaborate tapestries chronicling the history of the kingdom. Singers short and tall, in court dress changing over the ages, detailed with loving care. All princesses of the realm who'd done their duty. Spare princesses, never risking the ruling queen or king.

Her mother had unkindly birthed only one princess, though five princes. Magic answered only to the call of female voices of the royal blood. The queen, gossip whispered, had angered the gods by marrying a foreigner.

The court was filled with familiar faces, standing and talking and moving from one conversation to another while they awaited her parents. No one new whose voice lilted, no one carrying an instrument or wearing a musician's mark. They didn't speak to her or even acknowledge the princess of doom.

Politeness, her mother said. They didn't want to break her focus on the spell to save the kingdom. Fear or disgust or anger, she thought. So she stood, alone and unspeaking, in the waiting crowd.

The chatter of voices and the sounds of the bells on their court dress jingled and rang as they maneuvered for status. The noise fell on her ears like crows clacking and festival merriment mocking. Another week with no help and fading hope.

Perhaps she should head into the world seeking a minstrel. Her father would never give her leave. The king believed royalty stayed in place and let the world come to them. Besides, her spell might not even work if cast beyond the castle.

She stared at the oldest tapestry, a woman standing on a cliff above waves, drenched by the sea, a golden halo rising from her hands into a dome. Yes. The first princess who fended off the dark had no castle, only her voice. No music master, no training. Only her gift and desperation to save her people from her father's bargain with death. His kingdom's souls so he could live forever.

I have the desperation. Not the gift.

A young man's voice rose through the room with the command of a player. "Carambotte sought a music teacher. I am here."

The princess shifted sideways so she could glimpse him.

A guard held his shoulder.

Despite his arrogant words, he didn't belong at court. The man wore a peasant's tunic and breeches, ill-cut hair, and shabby boots. No musician's badge. "You need someone to teach a braying princess." He jerked the thumb of his free hand toward his chest. "That's me."

Braying princess? Princess Secharelle's fingers curled tight into her palms. The kingdoms laughed at her and the music masters who died. They were all a joke outside the cursed kingdom. She lifted her chin and spoke up. "I don't have four legs and I don't bray."

"Excuse me, honored princess." He brought his arm across his waist and tried to bend into a bow, but managed only a crooked tilt in the guard's grasp.

"Release that boy." The king's voice fell softly from the private royal entrance at the back of the hall. He and the queen stood, their faces lined and old-looking. Pained by the spell's failures.

The guard loosed the peasant, who staggered free.

"No boy I, but the solution to your problems. If the rewards are as promised." The peasant fished a bedraggled parchment from inside his tunic, checked the words and looked up expectantly. "Title not needed. Castle and lands, fine. Gold and jewels, excellent. Do we have a bargain?"

"My father's word is not in question." Secharelle stepped closer. "Tell us of your training and accolades. And your name."

"I'm Raven. I have learned from the birds, the frogs, the donkeys, the wind, the rain, and the snow. All who listen know my skill." He pulled a flute from his tunic. Wooden with holes and not entirely straight, as if he'd stripped the bark from a tree branch. He tootled several notes.

"We have no need of a musician." The queen sounded weary. "We need someone who can teach—"

"Teach a donkey to sing?" Raven marched toward the king and queen, the court parting as if a tide pulled them either side of the grand chamber. "They wouldn't let me bring the beast in. Could we go outside?"

"I'll not—" The king's refusal was interrupted by the queen placing her hand on his arm. "I'll not have this audience turned into a spectacle. Stand aside while I deal with court business."

He actually brought a donkey to prove his musical skill? The princess stifled a giggle. The poor lout was the joke. Not she.

Raven bowed and moved to join the nobles. They shifted away, leaving a ring of space around the peasant. He stood, comfortable as a tree in a clearing, and replaced the flute inside his tunic.

The king listened to disputes while the princess studied the peasant with his straw-colored hair and dirt-brown clothes. Cheap colors. The kind of man who looked more like a groom who'd clean stalls than one who would tutor a princess.

He raised an eyebrow at her.

She nodded and edged backward. Her parents wouldn't care if she escaped the audience. She was going to see this claimed singing donkey for herself. Raven would have to remain in court.

"Stay, Princess." The king didn't look her way.

She stilled in place. The private viewing she'd planned and sending Raven away wouldn't happen. He would have to pay a pretender's price. Likely nothing more than a few days hard labor, since he would lack funds to pay the fine. His choice for mocking royalty.

The disputes brought for royal decision had never seemed so petty or the audience so long. Finally, they reached the end of the last one, a border dispute over who owned one-half meter of boggy ground. Court was formally recessed.

The queen summoned Raven and Princess Secharelle to join her and the king on the procession to their private royal exit.

Raven wasn't much taller than her. His shoulders were considerably broader.

Once they left the court floor and reached the secluded anteroom, the queen and princess removed their crowns and set them on nearby tables. The princess felt no lighter. Stone walls locked her in, though here the room was softened with wood tables and chairs with cushions. Wood and fabric which would burn better than flesh.

The king halted and surveyed Raven. "If your donkey does not prove your worth as an instructor, you will be branded an imposter. Do you wish to depart?"

"That would depend on whether the terms offered for success remain." Raven scratched his jaw. "The poster said you were seeking someone to teach the princess to sing a complicated tune precisely. I can succeed."

"From your accent and your words, you are not from Carambotte," the queen said. "Do you know why this song matters?"

"No." Raven shrugged. "I don't care. The reason does not influence the singing."

"The reason defines the price of failure." Princess Secharelle stared into his eyes. Blue, the color of a poison frog, mottled to lighter blue and dark blue shading toward black. Foreign eyes. She refused to let her voice waver. Pitch she might lose control of. Not poise. "The song is magic. When the song fails, magic explodes. Seven music masters have died while I sang."

Raven's face was serious as he spoke directly to her. "Do not worry your kind heart. A traveling musician faces death on a daily basis. Angry patrons, jealous husbands, bandits."

"A wise traveler can avoid all three. Magic storms cannot be ducked.".

"Do not fear, Princess. I shan't leave you facing another corpse."

"I'm not scared." Her chin lowered. "I'm never the one to die."

His eyes narrowed. "Surviving can be harder."

She forced a laugh which came out raspy. "Most would prefer to be alive."

"Most," he said.

He saw too deeply. She looked away, breaking the connection. He ignored her warnings. Let the stubborn peasant prove himself unfit. "Show us this singing donkey."

Raven bowed to her, deeper than before. "The donkey awaits outside the stable."

"Should this donkey have disappeared," the king declared, "you will be considered to have failed."

"Lily wouldn't leave me, and she can be stubborn about being moved." Raven stepped to the side to allow the king to lead.

The king strode down the hall toward the stables.

The princess was shaking, half with laughter, half with a fizzy feeling as if she'd spun in circles until dizzy. "You named your donkey Lily."

"I've never understood the desire to attach ugly names to animals or people." Raven's smile could have charmed an angry goat.

Did he think her name ugly? She looked at her mother.

The queen looked back, her lips tight and her face white and weary. She waved a dismissal and nodded slowly. "Go. See this donkey. You must sing. You must complete the spell." She moved away, wobbling.

What was wrong with her graceful, determined mother? She seemed old, broken in spirit. *Because of me.*

"Does she need you?" Raven's quiet question shook her.

"She doesn't need me." Her voice came out raw and ugly. "She needs me to sing."

Raven offered his arm as any courtier might. "Let's not keep the king waiting."

Princess Secharelle placed her fingertips delicately on that arm. Her kingdom had waited far too long already for her to sing the spell. If a donkey could sing, she could. Surely.

THE BROWN DONKEY STOOD OUTSIDE THE WOODEN STABLE, HEAD lowered, belly hanging, big ears splayed outward. The summer sun warmed its coat.

Stableboys bustled about, moving faster than they normally would under the king's gaze. The yard smelled of horse and dung with the used bedding stacked high. Wooden stable and straw. Another place her loss of control could set aflame. Chickens pecked for bugs. All as usual but for the donkey.

Raven moved forward and Princess Secharelle let go of his arm, standing alone beside her father.

"Lily," said Raven.

The donkey turned her head toward them, opened her eyes, black ringed with white, and white-tipped muzzle, ears swiveling as if searching for sound.

Raven moved toward her and patted her nose. "Sing."

The donkey made a snuffling noise.

Raven tapped her on the nose. "No cabbage for you. Sing."

The donkey trumpeted long and loud.

The princess sneaked a peek at her father. His face was shading to red.

Raven stepped back. "Lily needs an audience. And music." He pulled out the crooked wooden flute and blew a few notes.

The donkey's ears twisted and angled toward him.

"We will not be mocked." The king had slipped into the royal we. Not a good sign for Raven.

"Donkeys can't really sing." Princess Secharelle didn't want the peasant flayed. Her father's temper grew more unstable by the day while the reports of ghost sightings grew. Her lips twitched and she giggled. "Lily brayed on command. That's like singing."

"That is not singing." The king turned slowly to face her. "He mocks you."

"I don't feel mocked. I should get to decide."

Raven's flute trilled a high, fluttering sound.

The donkey snorted, lifted her head. After a whistling intake of air, she uttered a high pitched squeaky noise, one short burst after another.

The king twisted to face the donkey.

Raven played a deep long sound.

Lily uttered a lengthy, deep bray.

The music played on, bard and donkey, she uttering sharp, short sounds or longer, deeper ones, until his notes and her braying entwined in a melody.

The princess clapped. "Music to my ears."

Raven ended with a bowing flourish. Lily snuffled and whiffled as she bent one leg under in a donkey version of a bow.

"I disagree," said the king. "But you have chosen your music master."

He would die if she lost control again. The clever peasant. "No! I don't—"

"You admired his musical abilities." The king sounded pleased. "I will accept him as your teacher."

Her father left.

"You should run." She studied Raven's face, the dimple in his left cheek, the way his left eyebrow quirked up and his eyes. Eyes bluer and brighter than gems with dark shadows, the kind of eyes she could spend a century falling into. If only she could escape her world. "Take Lily and go. Please."

Raven shook his head. "I taught a donkey to sing. You said so."

"This isn't like being a traveling bard. People throwing rotten turnips, chasing you out of town with their dogs. That's nothing. This is different. Here you could die. You *will* die."

"Have you so little faith in me?"

"No," she said. "In me."

Seven weeks later, Princess Secharelle sat on a chair in her mother's bedroom fidgeting with her dress. She poked at the embroidered flowers, the ones which never faded or died.

The sky showing through the windows was dark, though it was midday and no rain fell. Ghosts were closing in on the kingdom, shadowing her people. Animals died. Healthy and young, they would falter and fall. Not people. Not yet.

She had to complete the spell.

Raven's image flashed before her. Making sad faces, happy faces, strange faces, imitating Lily's noises. The walks they'd taken, the countless attempts to teach her by listening to birds, squirrels, horses, the sounds of guards moving, the clink of their weapons, the shrill of a whistle, the thumpity-thump-thump of sword drills.

Raven's constant flute practice and questions. Up, down. Longer, shorter. Note—where did that sound fit into the spell she'd learned? Too many wrong answers.

She'd try to match the sound and she could, as long as she could hear him.

That had worked with Mayoret, until the magic roared. Then she lost her cues. Raven claimed the donkey learned the sounds. He'd showed her, how Lily could sing in tune to the movement of his hand. He'd put her hand on her stomach, had her practice breathing, while her breath caught and skipped.

Her stomach flipped under that teaching touch. Her voice locked up and squeaked when he rubbed calming circles. When he touched her hand, ah, then, her voice soared, the phrases which would make the complete spell coming out easily. He said she could do this. He trusted her. She loved him.

If she tried again and failed . . . Raven would die. She'd warned him. He believed in her. She didn't.

The world could die at the hands of ghosts before she killed him.

She looked at her mother, sipping chocolate from a dainty cup with a tray across her lap.

The queen had never seemed fragile before. Now her hand trembled until she replaced the cup on the tray.

"I can't do this, Mama. I'm broken. You say a musical note is higher or lower. Listen harder. I can't hear it. I've never heard the difference, not in all these years." Not unless she heard through Raven's ears. With him there, coaching, she felt it in her bones. "If I can't hear it, how can I sing true?"

"Bargains must be made, if necessary."

Princess Secharelle stared. "A bargain brought the curse upon this kingdom."

"A selfish bargain." Her mother's voice was sharp. "I bore your father five princes. We needed a princess to sing the ghosts away."

"You had me."

"I offered my blood and life if it would save my kingdom." The queen held out an upturned palm which bore a large, puckered scar.

Of course, her mother was a woman of royal blood. The queen, not the expendable princess who had to sing the kingdom's shield. She could strike a magic bargain. "How did you dare?"

"Your father never knew. I needed a princess. I bore you, but you didn't hear music. I'd failed."

The princess was her failure. Another cursed bargain. That's all she was. Cursed.

The queen continued. "I heard the true price, then, humming through my head. The magic—only a youthful princess could save my kingdom, not a mother. I could sing the spell, but the notes from my lips would have no enchantment. I offered my voice."

"You never sing." The princess sat, stunned. Never. No hum, no note of music.

"I told your father I'd lost my voice. Spent too many hours singing lullabies to you. He ordered me to sing. I croaked like a frog. We never spoke of it again. Or sang."

"He never knew you'd dealt with gods."

"Gods or demons." The queen laughed, sharp and short. "Your father thought he loved me. He was a foreigner and would not have believed. He would have thought me deluded or a witch. I will save my cursed kingdom." The queen looked into the princess's eyes. "I know you can do this. I gave you my voice."

"But not your ear." Princess Secharelle laughed, her laugh scaling up and down higher and lower than any notes she'd sung. "A fool's cursed bargain. The voice to sing, but a princess who can't sing. For want of a singer, your kingdom shall fall."

"I feared so." The queen picked up her cup again. "Until I heard you walking and laughing and singing with Raven. Now I know. He has given you the gift of song. With his help, you can sing the spell."

Her mother didn't understand. "He taught me. I'll sing alone. Without him in the room." Where fear for him would make her voice crack. She needed him far away.

"The kingdom needs every chance." The queen's eyes narrowed. "I've given up too much."

"I don't want your voice."

"The price has been paid. I won't let you fail."

Princess Secharelle smiled and nodded. "I understand now. The safety of the kingdom matters more than any person."

Let her mother believe that. She'd bargain away her life for the kingdom but not the life of the man she loved. She would cast this spell alone.

THE NEXT DAY WAS EVEN DRYER.

Air sucked sweat from human and beast alike and left the ground crumbly. Last night's storm hadn't helped.

Princess Secharelle had to send Raven and his donkey away. They didn't belong in the kingdom. They could go barding somewhere else. They'd live, whatever happened here.

Princess Secharelle stood in the empty room rubbing her dry eyes, glancing from stone to metal door and back. Her tongue slipped out to moisten her lips. Raven talked about tongue position to shape syllables more clearly.

He was walking closer now, down the hall to this chamber of death.

Usually, she'd meet him in the garden. Not today. Another rosebush died. She couldn't stand beside death.

"Princess." He dipped his head as he reached the door and walked into the room.

"You need to leave. Today." Her heart thudded dully in her chest. He would be safe, if no one else.

"What? No. You need me to signal you when you fall off pitch."

She forced a smile. "You've trained me well. I can do this alone. All I have to do is sing the way we've done a thousand times."

"Are you trying to save the kingdom a fortune?" He took both her hands in his.

"No." Her lips quivered while she pulled away. "This kingdom's problems aren't yours. You've done your part. You and Lily should move on to see all those places you tell stories about. Go everywhere, to the places over hill and river and ocean, the ones you haven't yet seen. Sing your songs through country and town and castle."

"I've seen enough to know my heart belongs to this kingdom." He stared into her eyes. "To this castle. To this—"

"If it's the money, don't worry. I brought jewels." She tugged a pouch from her bulging stomacher and handed it to him. "And a note gifting them to you as well as a note extolling your abilities as a music master. I've recommended you to the guild in Iridon as outdoing Master Mayoret. A reference if you wish to continue teaching."

"You've got my future planned out." He tossed the pouch to the floor, where it thudded and fell sideways. "I don't take money I haven't earned. You haven't yet succeeded in casting the spell."

"I never will with you here."

"Why not?" He moved closer, stroking her hair. "Am I a distraction?"

She jerked back, her teeth biting into her lip. "You know the magic has escaped me to strike down every other master. Why are you insisting on staying? You could be safe."

"Missing a heart is not safe."

"You're not missing a heart."

"I will be if I leave you." He held out his hands. "I would rather die than let you die. I would prefer we both live where I could see you safe, even if only from afar. Besides, you have a better chance of succeeding with my help."

"I'd rather you leave than you die."

"My leaving is not your choice, Princess."

"It is. I won't sing with you here." She marched to the far side of the room, her slippers smacking the stone floor with each step, and spun to face him. "Get out."

"The king and queen will be interested to hear you say that. Their decrees override yours."

"You can't tell them."

"I will. They won't put you into the dungeon, but me?" He shrugged. "I will be blamed for seducing their daughter away from her duty."

The queen would see it that way. Definitely. She'd sacrificed her life, her voice, to give the kingdom a singing princess. The only way Princess Secharelle could keep Raven safe would be to complete the spell. He was right. She had a better chance of succeeding with him to coach. He'd trapped her. Better to sing now, before the kingdom grew drier and her nerve crumbled. "You blackmailer. Fine, let's do it."

He shut the door of metal strips, sealing them both into the stone-walled room. "I love you."

Air and outrage burst from her. "I know."

She couldn't admit she loved him. Not when so much could go wrong. This time, if someone died, it would be her. She'd call the magic to strike her dead.

Princess Secharelle took her spot, the one she'd practiced in those thousand times, and sang.

Raven stood with his back to the door. When she sang, his hands rose to gesture, louder here, softer there, hold that note longer, cut that one off. The same way he'd trained Lily.

Breezes rippled through the room and water skipped from stone to stone. Flowers perfumed the air and light glinted like sun hitting a sword blade.

All Princess Secharelle had to do was watch his hands and follow their direction. His hands, warm flesh, not seared and charred.

Her eyes closed to block the images of Mayoret's blackened corpse overlaid on Raven's living body.

Her voice faltered and heat burst while she struggled through the next two lines.

Raven's hands clasped hers, tightly. "You can do this. Look at me and *sing*."

She opened her eyes, stared into his face, and sang.

He pulled one hand away and signaled a higher or lower pitch.

She watched those gestures as if her life depended on the precise placement of his palm. Not just her life.

The kingdom's existence, the life of the man she loved.

Magic gusted, swirling and buffeting her into a spin.

Raven circled her back with one arm while with the other hand, he motioned for volume and a higher note.

She sang with all her heart, pouring herself into every syllable.

Flames spurted around them and spun in imitation of their waltz. Water fountained and plummeted in arcs. Rainbows exploded about them.

Her throat grew tight and the syllables she sang choppy. A wind tore her from Raven and twirled her until she was dizzy. She'd lost sight of him and his hands.

Fire split the room, a wall she could barely see through. Her back was against the door. He was trapped against the wall. Raven screamed her name, but she couldn't stop singing to listen.

Princess Secharelle fought on, through the remembered melody and words she didn't understand. She was losing the fight. The ghosts would win and eat the kingdom's life. Her ancestor's bargain had cursed the kingdom. Her mother's bargain had cursed her.

She needed a new bargain. What did she have to trade? She had nothing. Her voice quavered. She couldn't, wouldn't quit and doom them all. She would save Raven.

Her arms reached out, embracing the wall of flame which leaped and cavorted, orange and yellow and red and burning, furious white, tearing strips from the magical fire. Her skin didn't burn, the magic armoring her. Still she sang, nearing the impossible crescendo.

She crossed the flames and shoved Raven toward the door, pointing.

He shook his head. "Take me. All of me. I will not leave you."

You are mine. The words rang inside her head while she sang. *My love, we are one heart, not two. One single heart.*

The fire curled about him, licking, tasting the way a cat might lap at water.

Water thundered down, soaking them both.

For the first time ever, the princess could hear the notes, the melody, the way it all entwined, the way the notes had to end.

Each syllable and sound struck music. She understood what Raven tried to teach. The swords clanking, whistle shrilling, birds chirping, squirrels chittering higher and lower, every sound a beat of music. She could hear melody in her heart, her breath, her mind. The kingdom's people, animals, land all chanted together. *Life.*

She finished the soaring final phrases with a long-held high note that shrilled and echoed through the spell room and out the windows, soaring louder than any thunderstorm.

The flames vanished, the water dried, and the room fell silent.

Rain fell. Gentle, soaking rain pattering outside.

Princess Secharelle ran to the window.

People turned in circles, heads tipped back so the rain washed their faces.

"We did it! You and I. We saved them all. Together."

Raven patted her back, pulled her to face him. "We did it." His voice was loud.

"That's what I said." She pressed her hand to his cheek. "We think alike."

He shook his head. "I can't hear you."

She stared. He'd told the magic to take all of him. She'd claimed him as her own. Said they were one heart. Without meaning to, she'd bargained to save him from her magic.

The way she heard music. She was hearing with his ears. With her unintended bargain, she'd stolen his talent.

How could he play music if he couldn't hear?

His world would be silent forever because he'd stayed to help her.

He'd saved a kingdom. "I'm sorry. So sorry. We have to fix this. Maybe your hearing will come back. I'll pay any price. Trade away my voice, my ears, my life. We'll find a magician who can fix you."

"I don't understand. I don't need to. You're safe."

"I love you." She shaped the words carefully so he would understand what she said. "I love you."

Raven pulled her into his arms and kissed her, hard.

She leaned into his kiss. They were one. She and her love. Forever joined. Let the princes marry princesses, she was going to keep her wounded Raven. Two hearts beating as one forevermore. She would be his ears, translating his songs, his voice into music which would make listeners weep.

A chirp sounded in her ears.

"Did you hear that?" He pulled back, his face alight. "I heard a noise."

"I did." She traced his ear with her fingers. She sang a phrase from the song they'd worked on so long. The notes sounded precise and vibrating to her ear, the higher and lower range clear. "You can hear music. So can I. The magic bent around you because we were one heart. The flames wouldn't burn you."

"My music belongs to you now, as do I."

"Our music and our ability to hear."

They clutched each other tight and tighter, souls blending, while around them the kingdom played the sounds of life growing.

One Last Gig

Martin Greening

"He asked to see you," my daughter said on the holo. I didn't even know she'd had a kid. "You still on Mars?" she asked.

I leaned closer to the public terminal to smother to echoes of magboots clanking on metal grates as miners passed by to and from work. "Yeah."

I'd told my wife it was a once in a lifetime opportunity. I'd only be gone two years. Six months there, twelve months on tour, six months back. She begged me not to go, but I did anyway. Then the tour got extended, two years became three, and three became five. Going on fifteen, sixteen years now. Each year took me further and further from my family. Each year took me to more notoriety and larger venues, and more vices. Each year made it more difficult to return home.

"You look good," I told my daughter. She had the same gray eyes as she did last time I saw her, except for a few creases at the corners. Several white strands now striped her auburn hair.

"Mom still hasn't forgiven you."

She'd sent divorce docs a few years after I left, and an ultimatum, the tour or them. I'd like to say I took my time to sign, but I'd be lying.

"And you?"

She looked down for a moment, then said, "He found a vid of you in Mom's stuff. Wouldn't stop asking."

"What's his name?"

"Not sure you've earned that."

I could almost feel the slap from a hundred fifty million miles away, and I probably deserved it. "Yeah."

"He wants to know if you still play."

I told her I played all the biggest stages on Mars. Everything from the Elysium Arena to the Grand Bazaar in Ares Prime. I told her about the feel of the bright lights, the roaring crowds, and the rhythm of being part of a great band. I told her I even played for the King of Sabaeus once.

I didn't tell her the tour ended ten years ago, or how my agent dumped me the year after. I didn't tell her the only gigs I could land now were in tarnished clubs in the dock district or dusty bars out in the mining colonies. A far cry from the Grand Bazaar. I didn't know what had changed, but I knew I could get back on top. I had to get back on top. It'd be hard work, like it was back on Earth at the start. Small gigs, one by one, each bigger than the last.

The more I told her, the less she spoke. Each tale parched me, both physically and emotionally, as I realized none of those tales included her. "Liv?" I said.

"It's Olivia now."

"I'm sorry."

Her face hardened and she looked like she was going to say more, but all she said was, "Yeah."

"Can I talk to him?"

She looked away again, then said to me, "Don't make promises you won't keep." She motioned for someone to come closer. A boy came onto the screen, maybe six years old. His eyes were the same gray as Liv's, but his broad nose and high cheekbones reminded me of my own face when I was his age.

He said hi then asked, "What should I call you?"

I hadn't expected that and wasn't sure what Liv would want me to say. "Call me Myles for now."

We chatted for a few minutes about school, and his friends, and the flute he's learning to play, until Liv said it was time for bed. He protested a bit, then asked "When can I see you?"

The words caught in my throat. "Soon," I said. "Maybe nine or ten months."

The smile he gave me was like a thousand suns that burned into my heart. I knew then I had to finally go home.

Six months later I found myself broke on the moon having spent
every credit I had for a ticket from Mars. I had none left for a shuttle to
Chicago. Only a satchel with some personal items, my sax in its battered
leather case, a pair of decades old magboots, and a black suit with the
start of bare threads at the edges. If I was going to make it to Chicago, I
needed money, and the only thing I knew how to do was play.

I sent a quick holo to Liv telling her I'd made it to the moon and
would be there as soon as I was able. She sent a quick reply and finally
told me his name, Aron. A good name. She didn't say much or why she'd
told me. Maybe it was because I'd shown her I was on my way. Or maybe
some other reason I couldn't figure out. I thought about asking her for
money to buy a ticket, but that wasn't fair to them, not after being gone
for so long, and I didn't even know if she had money to spare. So that left
me finding a gig.

I walked into an underground joint with a toy rocket above the door,
flickering orange lights pretending to be the engine blast, and asked the
olive-skinned bartender if they had any spots for me to play. "We're full
up," he said. "Try Tranquility Base."

The moon's meager gravity seemed to tug me down more. "Already
did." I'd hit up every bar and club on the near side of the moon, or at
least those that would even let me in the door.

When I left the place, I walked through the dim tunnels cut into
moon rock and tried not to think too much. My magboots grew heavier
and heavier with each step, until I came to a rail station. A wave of air
pushed past me like it was escaping, a massive flute announcing a train's
arrival. A constant stream of miners, scientists, tourists, and who knows
who else, departed and boarded the trains. None of them paid me any
attention, so I did the only thing that ever brought me any joy. I set down
my satchel against a square pillar, set down my case to retrieve my sax, set
down all my grief, dejection, and despair, and began to play.

Some people say playing a sax is like making love, but they've either
never played the sax or have no idea what love is. Playing a sax is more
like falling deep within yourself and cutting off the world until it's just
you and the sax together as one being.

I started with *Careless Whisper,* an old song, before transitioning into something more freeform. My fingers hopped from key to key to bring the notes to life.

The gentle thud of something landing in the velvet lining of my case prompted me to open an eye. Someone had tossed a credchip inside. Several people stood still among the flowing masses, but I could not tell who had left it. Maybe they'd already moved on. I closed my eyes again to focus on the rhythm.

Soon the credchips multiplied with each passing puff from an incoming train. In each group of passengers some stopped to listen, some paid their respects, most kept shuffling to their destinations without a second look.

A few songs later, a boy called above the din, "Look out." A teen in a red jumpsuit weaved through the crowd toward me. Two others followed behind. They all seemed to float between the people, as if they'd turned their magboots off, or didn't have any. Swift as birds they passed by, the lead boy piercing the crowd like an arrow. The second runner was already past me when I realized he'd picked up my case. It had been some time since I'd done any busking, and with my thoughts preoccupied I didn't consider trying to guard it. I cried out, but before I could reach the thief, the tail boy had already blocked my path. And then they were gone.

I didn't know how much they stole. Never had a chance to count it. Maybe it was enough to book a shuttle. Maybe not. But what I knew for certain. I was broke again and now down one sax case.

I spent the night cycle sleeping on a station bench until a cop ordered me to leave, then wandered the tunnels. When people began to wake, an idea came to mind. Maybe the takings would better at a high-end spot, instead of in the station. Maybe safer too. I checked a public terminal directory and found the Ritz Carlton wasn't too far away.

With my case gone, I needed something to collect the tips. I rummaged through a trash receptacle on my way to the hotel and found a wide plastic cup. White and brown residue clung to the inside. I wiped it down with dirty napkins as best I could. It wasn't pretty, but it'd do.

The hotel sat under a geodesic dome filled with windows so you could take in all the majesty of the starlit sky and the swirling blue and white of Earth. It'd been a while since I'd seen the planet so close, and I stood there letting the colors seep into me. Chicago hid somewhere under the clouds, but I'd get there soon.

Fewer people walked the plaza in front of the hotel than the crowds at the station, but their clean attire attested to greater wealth. Wealth I hoped to part them from. At least a little. Again, I set my satchel down, this time at my feet so I could step on the strap, placed the dirty cup before me and began to play.

My notes flowed around and up, toward the windows above and along the plaza tiles. Not even the clank of boots or dozens of simultaneous conversations could drown out my music.

"The nerve," a woman said.

"They'll let anyone in," another said.

"I'm calling the police."

That got my attention. Last thing I needed was a fine, or worse, incarceration. A few couples walked by, giving me wide berth. Some glanced at me with their chins held high and their scowls clear. Others wouldn't even give me that. And not a single credchip in my cup.

That's when I saw the princess leave the hotel.

I'd seen pics and vids of her on Mars. Princess Yazmina of Sabaeus. Tall, bronze-skinned, beautiful. And rich. She wore a long silver dress and a group of square-jawed men in dark high-necked suits orbited around her as they walked through the plaza.

Should I call out to her? No, she'd probably ignore me. But a song, a great song. Maybe that would get her attention, earn her patronage. I wracked my memory for what I'd played for her father those many years ago. Maybe she'd been there. Maybe she'd heard and would remember.

Then I began to play. The notes flowing through me and pulling me deeper and deeper from the present. I could feel the distant stage lights warm my skin, the clink of glasses, and the thunk and scrape of magboots as people moved about the club while I played. The applause when I'd finished, especially the king's, felt like a mother's long embrace.

When the last notes of my performance faded, I opened my eyes to find the princess gone. I wanted to sit and close my eyes and wish myself to Chicago, but a lone officer strode toward me. He carried a taze-stick and a not-so-friendly face, so I picked up my satchel and fled.

I found another station bench to spend the night cycle on and thankfully was not run off by police. After a few hours of rest, I decided to try the plaza again. All it would take is one or two benefactors and I'd be off this rock. The likelihood of my cup still being in the plaza was not good, so I fished another out of a trash bin on my way. This one was narrow and tall and smelled like coffee and cream. My stomach growled in response. I had the remains of a protein bar in my bag and ate it to placate my gut as I walked to the plaza.

The Earth waned through the windows above the hotel, half of it obscured in darkness. I'd be there soon, I promised. A few people were up and about in the plaza, still scowling, chins up, or ignoring me. No sign of the cop with the taze-stick. I found a spot close to the one I'd had the day before, set up, and played.

Not long after I began, my cup still empty, I saw her again. The princess and her entourage emerged from the hotel. I couldn't believe my good fortune. Another chance, and this time I had to get her attention. I looked straight at her, not closing my eyes, and played a loose jazz run, loud and clear. She did not respond, and her guards maintained their vigil around her as they walked by. My chance was slipping through my nimble fingers. Desperate, I folded in the chorus of the Sabaeus national anthem. It was a gamble since it didn't fit well with what I'd been playing, but I couldn't think of anything else.

She stopped and turned toward me. I met her gaze and one of her men stepped up to me, his face stern.

"It is all right Mikhail," she said and moved closer. "You look familiar. What is your name?"

"Myles Jaxon."

The guard, Mikhail, said, "Your Highness."

She waved a hand at him. "He is not one of my subjects," she said. "Yazmina. Princess Yazmina if you must."

"I played for King Fayez once. At the Grand Bazaar. Your— Yazmina."

Her eyes opened wider in recognition. "Ah. I was young, but my father brought me to that concert." She looked me up and down, taking in my ragged suit and the used cup on the ground before me. Did she see me as some sort of low-life vagabond now?

"Mikhail, leave him some credits. Good day Mr. Jaxon."

Mikhail tossed a credchip into my cup with uncanny accuracy and stalked back into position as they walked away. How much had she left? Enough for a shuttle? I wanted to check but didn't want to be rude. Whatever she left, it was more than I had since those teens stole my case.

"On second thought," the princess said. Her entourage halted and she reversed course. "Would you consider a private concert in my father's court on Mars? You would be well compensated."

Well compensated? How well? Enough to book a ship direct from

Mars back to Earth? Now that would be fantastic. And the prestige of playing for the king could jumpstart my career again. Open new venues back on Mars.

But what about Liv and my grandson? Taking up the princess's offer would mean another year of travel, plus however long the king's patronage took. Would Liv forgive me for taking so long to see Aron. Would she even let me see him at all in a year's time?

"Sorry, have to get to Chicago to meet my grandson."

Her shoulders slumped for the briefest of seconds before she regained her royal posture. "My father will be disappointed, as will I. Should you change your mind, my ship leaves tomorrow morning at 0900. Platform 7C." The princess and her guards marched out of the plaza leaving me alone to consider her offer.

I slept poorly that night, having checked the credchip the princess left. It was about half of what I needed for a shuttle, and I figured a decent meal and a night in a hotel might do wonders for any further busking.

The following morning, I found myself outside platform 7C with everything I owned. Could I pass up this opportunity, despite what it would do to Liv and Aron? It was sure to get me back on top, back on the biggest stages, back in the big money. No more dusty bars or clubs, no more busking.

The princess approached, now clad in a short dress that shimmered like a rainbow in the artificial light. "You changed your mind I see."

A lump formed in my throat. I swallowed it. "Yeah."

"My father will be pleased." She turned to one of her guards. "Mikhail, please see to Mr. Jaxon's baggage and find him a seat."

I started to hand my satchel to the man when the sun passed through one of the platform's small windows. More like a massive star than the brilliant light you'd see from Mars or Earth. It passed quickly through the limited view of the window, and it reminded me of the brightness of Aron's smile.

The dim light filled me with a warmth neither the moon nor Mars could provide. The thought of missing that warmth, or never feeling it again, pulled at me in a way I hadn't felt in a long time. I tugged my satchel back from the man. "Please tell the princess I'm sorry. There's another opportunity I can't miss." I hustled away from Platform 7C and located a nearby public terminal to send Liv a holo.

"Can't wait to see you. Be there soon."

Then I headed back to the rail station to earn what I needed for a shuttle to Earth. There was only one gig I cared about now—being a better grandfather than I was a father.

Siren Song at Midnight

David Farland

When I was a girl of ten, my father, Stefán Elegante, worked as a paleogeneticist for the Pacific Fisheries Commission, trying to restore extinct tuna and marlin, dolphins, and blue squid. He took me to his lab and showed me how he pulled bits of bone from fossils and dyed the DNA so his computers could read it and build living replicas of the cells.

"See, Josephina!" he said, pointing to remnants of a cell under his microscope, rainbow-hued ropes of DNA. "The fishes are still there, waiting for us to bring them back to life, and the DNA is a manual to tell us how." His eyes glowed as he spoke, and I did not understand half of what he said. "This is old DNA. I like the old stuff best. DNA that is a hundred years old is better than that taken from a living cell, for when a creature is living, so many chemical processes happen from moment to moment that sections of DNA often get torn loose and return into place reversed. But a cell that is a million years old is sometimes in better shape, because the cells heal themselves. In old dead cells, the chemical bonds between amino acids are so strong that reversed DNA returns to its proper place, you see!"

He watched me with his solemn brown eyes, saw my confusion, and he smiled softly. "Don't worry. Someday, you'll understand all of this, and more," he said, kissing my forehead. "You know, I sometimes wonder: if we destroy our world, do you think God could take this old DNA and rebuild us?" he asked, sincerely awed by this marvel.

I saw his fossils and understood only that, like God, he brought creatures to life from the dust of the Earth. On that day, I decided to become a paleogeneticist.

But somehow his hope died. Just as a wasp will lay its eggs in pear blossoms, corrupting their fruit, so despair corrupted him. Once he dared to dream of a restored world with vast rain forests, alive with the cries of macaws.

Wait. I am confused, exhausted to the bone. I'm not sure what to say. I must turn off the recorder for a moment.

[Two seconds of silence.]

I THINK I BEGAN TOO EARLY. I KNOW I'LL LIVE FOR ONLY ANOTHER FEW minutes, and I must record this while I can. Let me begin with the arrest of my father:

Last September, five plankton-harvesting ships exploded in a single evening. From childhood, I've seen these Chinese ships off the Chilean coast—floating ceramic cities whose brilliant halogen lights sputter like fallen stars in the evening out on the horizon. During the attack, I was working at El Instituto Paleobiologico in Cartagena, extracting DNA from fossilized dimetrodons. I heard a distant explosion, almost a popping noise, and ran out into the evening. One plankton-harvesting ship had exploded on the horizon, and where it had floated, a great violet curtain of spray was rising into the night, higher and higher, looking almost like a thunderhead. Beside me a small boy cried, "What is that?" and his mother, who perhaps wanted to protect him, said, "It is only angels, washing the curtains of heaven in the ocean."

I thought India must have attacked China, that the Plankton Wars had started again, that they might blow all of the ships. But if the Plankton Wars had begun again, they did so with a twist, for that night the Rio Negro dam blew in Brazil, and two million died as black torrents flooded down the Amazon.

A few hours later, the media revealed that the bombers were chimeras, genetically-engineered men that General Torres had modified to better adapt to life on other planets. They were an aquatic breed and had lived off the coast of Chile for years. By morning, the streets were ablaze with news of the attack by "Los Sirenos," the Sirens. The detonation of seven bombs was heralded as if it were a major war, and the Alliance of Nations began to hunt the Sirens. The news fascinated me, not because I longed for vengeance against the chimeras, but because the work of the genetic engineers who created these beings was similar to my own, yet a far greater art.

After the attack, the news showed Brazi mothers mourning for children who had washed out to sea as the Amazon flooded, twisted wreckage, and tiny orphans desperate for food. One commentator told how it could only have been a few Sirens who were gallantly bidding for control of Earth's waterways, trying to stop the plankton harvesters who continually stole food from their mouths. But his voice was drowned by others who decried the Siren's "crime against humanity." Experts paraded through the media, telling how destruction along the Rio Negro was only the beginning. They said millions in China and India would starve without the plankton harvesters, and they hinted hunger would strike in South America because of the loss of our fisheries.

My father had risen to become Director for the Pacific Fisheries Commission, so I called him on commlink to ask if these reports were accurate. He weighed each word, saying, "The Chinese pay so little for fishing rights, we won't miss it. In three months, they'll be harvesting like always." He sounded harried, tired, and I imagined he was under great pressure.

For a couple of days, my friend, Rosalinda, recorded news holos about the chimeras. We planned to watch the holos for entertainment, but as the holos displayed, I was horrified. Our Marines hooked electronic sniffers to stunners that looked like torpedoes; with these they hunted the Sirens by scent. When they scored a hit, they dragged the stunned Siren from the water, shrieking and flapping its tail. The sirens had pale blue scales covering their bodies, the color of the summer sky on the horizon, icy green eyes, and hair the silver of mountain water. Their women were delicate, with an unearthly beauty, and their cries as they were dragged from the waters sounded like the song of dolphins mingled with a human scream.

Most captured Sirens were women and children who could not swim fast enough to evade the stunners, and the powerful chemical jolt of the stunners was too much for them. Many women and children died. As we watched the children cling to dead mothers wrapped in seaweed, and as we listened to the wails of pain and grief, the horror struck in a way we would not have understood if we had seen the single broadcast of each capture as it happened. We lost our innocence, and Rosalinda ended up hugging me, offering me comfort late into the night. After that, I had no stomach for news. I avoided listening to it, did not think about it. I tried to put it out of mind.

Then, my world changed. Late in the evening on September 15, as I worked alone in my lab, a man crept in—a pale man with an effeminate face, dressed in putrid-smelling street clothes. His was carrying a metal bar, and his hand bled as if he'd cut it while prying the back door open. He stalked toward me nervously, sweat glistening on his brow, swinging the bar into his palm, watching side hallways for signs of others. My co-workers had gone home an hour before. We were alone. The way he looked, I thought I would be lucky if he only raped me.

"Josephina?" he asked quickly. "Josephina Elegante? Daughter to Stefán?" I nodded dumbly and backed away. He lurched toward me. "Here, get these to your father! It is mem-set!" He held out two small gelatin capsules the color of urine.

"What?" I asked, so frightened I did not know what to do.

He looked at me strangely, and smeared the blood from his hand across his shirt. "Mem-set—it is a mind-wiping drug. It keeps one's memories from being scanned. You must give it to your father, for he has secrets that he wants to keep concealed, even beyond the grave."

"What? Are you crazy?" I asked, backing away. And I worried, for it seemed obvious he was crazy.

His eyes suddenly widened. "You don't know?" he asked. "Your father has been arrested for giving explosives to the Sirens. It is on the news even as we speak! He has been charged with high treason and murder. He will surely be executed. As his only relative, you will be allowed to attend the execution. You must give these to him before he dies!" He held out the drugs, watching the halls as if he believed the secret police would burst into the room.

"Wait," I said. I thumbed the subdural presser switch behind my right ear and jacked into a simulcast news holo, keeping it on multitask so I could watch the stranger at the same time. My father, Stefán Elegante, was shown huddling among what must have been twenty Allied Marine troops, all of them in their space-blue armor. They rushed through the streets of Cartagena in a block, and peasants tossed bricks and burning sacks, shouting "Murderer!" The peasants looked confused. They did not know my father's crime and functioned only as a mob. The narrator said, "Now we see Stefán Elegante, alleged traitor to his species, rushing for cover." I stood in shock, as my father boarded a military transport. I jacked out of the newscast, thumbed my commlink again, and read in my father's code, but he did not answer the call. I jacked back into the news-cast: it showed my father on a small boat offshore from our beach home in Concepción, unloading boxes into the waiting arms of the Sirens. The reporter said the boxes held explosives.

I jacked out in shock, for I knew that this was all some magnificent lie, knew my father was innocent despite the holos. What was their evidence? Pictures of boxes?

"Please," the stranger said. "I'm a friend. I'm only one of dozens who helped give your father weapons for the Sirens. Many others like me still hope for a restored world, yet your father knows who we are. His memories will convict us. You see, the Alliance laws forbid the police from scanning the memories of criminals while they live, but once your father is executed, then his right to privacy dies with him, and Alliance surgeons will slice away his cerebral tissue so they can scan his memories at leisure. He knows this. He promised to take the mem-set. We all promised to take mem-set if we were caught. When you go to the execution, hold the capsules between your cheek and teeth until you get them to Stefán, then have him bite them. This is a powerful dose, enough for a dozen people, but you must get it to him at least two minutes before the execution. Once he breaks the capsules, the mem-set will form restriction enzymes. The membranes of his neural cells will harden, and the DNA in his brain will be chopped into pieces, destroying all his memories. Understand?"

The stranger wrapped my fingers around the capsules. "If any of us could hope to get past security to your father, we would gladly take this task upon ourselves. Please, save us! We are desperate!" he said, then he turned and ran.

I stood for a long time, holding the capsules, wondering what to do. I could not believe this stranger, and I wondered if it were some plot to discredit my father. That evening, I began trying to obtain permission to see my father . . .

[Two seconds of silence.]

I'M SORRY. I HAD TO TURN THE RECORDER OFF. I CAN'T THINK. THIS DAY has exhausted me. I am so angry that they call my father a "traitor to his species." He loved every species. Perhaps he loved them too much. As I record these words, I am sitting in my terrarium at El Instituto Paleobiologico de Colombia—the institute my father funded—feeding my pet euparkeria from a bag of eggs. The euparkeria are a small dinosaur from the early Mesozoic, the earliest age of dinosaurs, and they are a branch of thecodonts, the first true dinosaurs. They are the size of geese, with long graceful necks as delicate as a pianist's fingers, tiny front legs, and forest-green skin. On their backs are yellow-white speckles, the color that the primeval sun must have cast as it burned through fern jungles. One euparkeria licks at an egg with a long olive-green tongue, cleaning the egg yolk from inside a shell, looking for all the world like a small wingless dragon.

My father used to say that euparkeria are an important link in the chain of life. From them sprang many species: birds and pterosaurs, meat-eating carnosaurs, saurischian dinosaurs like the brontosaurus and supersaurus, and the ornithischians, such as the triceratops and anky- losaurus. If each higher animal species were a branch on a tree, the euparkeria would be close to the tree's root. They are one great main trunk from which higher animals evolved, while at the top of the tree would be an insignificant twig, a bud without fruit: mankind.

My father was not a traitor to our species. He only realized that we look on ourselves and think that instead of a twig, we are the whole tree, that we are the crown of creation instead of only another stem.

Anyway, my father was a military prisoner, and despite my pleas, I was forbidden to speak to him before the trial.

My friends disappeared, pretended not to know me. Even Rosalinda, a girl I've known since childhood, closed the door when I tried to speak to her. She shouted at me through the door, told me to go away, and she was crying, saying that the secret police had come to question her. At first I was angry and hurt, but her family had no political connections, and I knew it was better to keep my distance from her.

I accomplished nothing at work and did not eat. I could not ignore the instinct that drove me to believe in my father's innocence. I'd spoken to him at least three times a week for years—knew him better than anyone, and I knew he was incapable of murder. I searched his office, looking for proof of his innocence. His appointment books were gone, and only his computer logs were online. I sat late into the night, reading notes about the various genomes of extinct fishes, trying to extract some clue to prove his innocence.

I imagined that my father had been lured into this. Could it have been that he thought he was giving food to the Sirens? I wondered. That would be like him. He could have handed out boxes, unaware that weapons were stored in them, and now that he'd been caught, he would nobly protect the others with his life, even though they had betrayed him.

I so wanted this scenario to be true that I looked for evidence to support it. I read until my eyes burned from viewing every computer log, until perspiration trickled down my back. Late that night, an orderly came to the office, Mavro Hidalgo, an old man who had worked for my father since before I was born.

"Josephina, what are you doing here?" he asked.

"Looking for something," I said. "I don't know what—anything to prove my father's innocence."

Señor Hidalgo shook his head sadly. "I've already been through all those records," he said. "I've already thought about it. You want proof that don Stefán is innocent, but you won't find the proof in scraps of paper."

I looked at old Señor Hidalgo, my eyes became wet, and I blurted, "Are you saying he is guilty? You believe these lies?"

But Señor Hidalgo shook his head. "You don't need papers. The truth of his innocence is in your heart." He sat next to me, smelling of sweat and beans. He placed his leathery hand on my shoulder. "You know, your father has been sick for many years, suffering from depression." I nodded, for I'd known this. "When he was young, he was worse. For days at a time he would laugh and his eyes would glow, and he would come to work practically walking on the ceiling! Oh, he was so happy, he did not need wings to fly.

"But then, the smile would fade, and he'd come to work, and you would see him drag as if wrapped in chains, and he'd sit for days and do nothing. We were all afraid for him, thinking he might kill himself, so one day I asked, 'don Stefán, why do you put yourself through this? You could cure this malady with a pill! Then, why do you suffer?' and do you know what he said?"

"No," I answered.

"Your father told me that the time he spent flying through the air more than rewarded him for the time he spent in the abyss. He said, 'Mavro, I know you worry for me, and I know I could take the cure. But I love my illness. You people—how can you appreciate life as I do? How can you live even one moment with passion? It is all so grand, so beautiful. Even when I am lost in the blackest well of midnight, life tastes so sweet to me! Life is so sweet!"

Señor Hidalgo patted my shoulder, told me to go home, then began to straighten the office. I knew he was right. I didn't need more proof of my father's innocence than the life he'd led. My father could not have given explosives to the Sirens. I'd seen his innocence in the tender way he fed his fish by hand at the aquariums, in the way he kissed the pain away from my childhood injuries, in the way he relished to draw a breath. Life, all life, was too precious to be wasted.

That night, I drove to Concepción, to the sea house, and arrived at dawn. The police had scavenged the house until it was in ruins. My father's papers were strewn everywhere, and the furniture had been ripped apart. I cleaned the mess and walked the beaches in the mornings. I kept the mem-set hidden in my room, and twice the police came to question me, always asking names of my father's friends, of those I'd seen him with. I answered by declaring his innocence.

The details of my father's trial were never publicized. I learned through the news that my father was convicted of treason and accused of stealing a vast fortune through graft. He was found guilty of complicity in the murder of two million Brazis and was sentenced to die. I find it ironic that they convicted him in a secret trial, yet respected his right to privacy so much that they refused to pry his memories from him. Perhaps for them it was just a waiting game, and they believed they would get his accomplices in time.

After that, I learned that a news special would be broadcast by a famous reporter, a gringo cyborg named Todd Bennett who promised to have an "Interview with a Madman." The interview was advertised for days, and I could not sleep because I wanted so badly to see my father, to hear his voice. I watched the holo at home, enlarging the image so it filled the entire living room.

When the interview started, they showed Señor Bennett wearing a smooth white tungsten half-face with six glittering eyes that recorded all he saw in different spectra. The bottom half of his face was still human. He wore a glorious multicolored cape of light, which contrasted with my father's drab attire of prison blue, and it struck me that Señor Bennett knew the effect that his dress would have, for he looked as if he were a beautiful angel of light sent down to torture some damned soul in a tired hell.

"Can I begin by asking a few questions? " Señor Bennett said in flaw-less Spanish, using over-precise inflections common to those who speak with the aid of a translation chip.

My father wiped sweat from his face and pulled his long hair back over his shoulder, then looked out the window of a small cell. "You can ask," he said.

"Fine," Señor Bennett said. "Then let's establish your guilt. Records show that for months you fed the Sirens. In itself, that was admirable. But what caused you to commit the sin, this crime against humanity, of shipping them explosives?"

My father looked at the cyborg and said, "I am a fantasist, a dreamer. That is my only sin: to dream and hope."

The cyborg smiled placatingly. "Hope is no sin. It's one of the three great abiding virtues. When we die, we take it with us to heaven." I laughed, for I was correct in my assessment of the cyborg. He did want to disguise himself as an angel, and he was too stupid to be subtle about it.

"Hope has done me no good," my father said. "You want to establish my guilt. It has been established in court. I masterminded the War of the Sirens—if you can call it a war. I gave them explosives. It was not a sin."

"Surely," Bennett countered, "you do not expect us to believe that you acted alone in this act of terrorism? You have no expertise in explosives. You could not have trained the Sirens."

My father said calmly, "Believe what you will. If I had accomplices, I will die before I reveal their names." Then suddenly his mood changed, and he roared, "I will die!"

"You can't protect them forever," the cyborg affirmed.

My father only shrugged, as if his outburst of a moment before had never happened.

Bennett asked, "Tell us why you aided the murder of over two million people?"

"When I was appointed as Director of Pacific Fisheries, I hoped to save the world," my father said almost casually. "Ever since we first raped the Sea of Cortes and destroyed the world's richest oyster beds, we Latin Americans have sold the spoils of our oceans to the highest bidder. First the oysters, then the sailfish and tuna, dolphin and manta—'til we were left with nothing but algae and plankton."

"One moment," Señor Bennett asked. "These animals you mention, are they food animals that became extinct?"

"Yes," my father said, "temporarily extinct food animals."

Señor Bennett smiled. "I don't eat flesh, myself," he said.

My father roared, "You eat your own children!" Señor Bennett lurched back as if my father would strike him. My father stood and began pacing the cell. "When I was appointed director, I thought, 'Here I am at last: A man who can't be corrupted by graft! I can restore the ancient fisheries, rebuild seabeds laid waste by centuries of pollution. Today, because of continual algae harvests, our atmosphere has seventeen percent less oxygen than when I was born. You worry about the poor who have no food—what will you say to those poor in a generation, when the seas are dead and they have no air to breathe?

"When I took office, even the trash fish that used to eat our turds had become extinct." My father paced the floor, moving so fast, speaking so fast, he almost gibbered. "So I committed the sin of hope. As Director of Pacific Fisheries, I sought funds to resurrect extinct fishes and phytozoa, to give the oceans time to rebuild. But I received only promises of money. I tried to reduce the amount of plankton the Chinese could harvest, but Director Nestor de la Luz told me to keep silent. He said the Chinese paid too well and that we would have to let the harvests continue for another year. We were rebuilding after the war with the Socialistas, and he said we needed money for the reconstruction, so money never came to me. It took months and years before I realized I was only paid to be a figurehead—no one really wanted me to restore the fisheries. People had lost their taste for flesh. No one living today cares to eat the fishes our great grandfathers dined upon. So, I realized, I was just fooling myself."

"Is that why you betrayed your species?" Señor Bennett asked in a cutting voice. "Because you were frustrated in your efforts to reduce the harvest? Because you wanted to be more than a figurehead?" He was baiting my father, and I hated him for it.

"No!" my father said. "Emotions had nothing to do with it. For years I enforced the quotas as best I could, but when Nestor died and I took his place, I found that fisheries money hadn't been siphoned off for recon-struction; it had been going into Nestor's pockets all along! He'd stolen from us! And at the same time, I learned that for years Torres' old chimeras out in the ocean had begged us to halt the plankton harvests. These Sirens were starving. Nestor had kept their pleas hidden, fearing that if people knew the truth, they might protect the fisheries, and it would cut into the income he earned from graft.

"But I knew that no one would care. We wouldn't stop the harvests, so I took the bribes from the Chinese, just as all my predecessors had done, but instead of pocketing the money, I bought explosives!"

My father's eyes became wild. I wondered if he'd been drugged for benefit of the viewers. He sat down and then immediately stood up again and paced the room, back and forth, quicker than you would believe possible.

"Truly, I hoped to wake you all, but the explosions only dull your ears! You kill your own children. I pity the poor who will not be able to eat or breathe or escape this planet. Someday they will remember me as a hero for trying to stop this madness while we yet had something to save! We are a diseased branch on the tree of life, and because of us, the whole tree will fall into ruin. I commit the sin of hope no more!" My father began raving, and a curious light shone from his eyes. I don't think he saw the reporter any longer, saw nothing but his own death, for he cursed the world.

Despite his confession, I did not believe he was guilty. I was angry with his accomplices and wondered why the truly guilty party, the person who had trained the Sirens to use explosives, did not step forward.

All that night, I remembered my father's words: "I will die before I reveal their names. I will die!" Was that a plea? I wondered. Did he really want the mem-set so badly that he would almost announce it to the world? I sat in my room and replayed the interview. The man in the holo, the convict, did not look like my father. He did not look like some gentleman, nobly protecting men more wicked than himself. He looked like a killer, eaten by guilt and rage, unrepentant for his murders. As I watched him again and again, pacing his cell like a leopard, I began to consider: my father's illness had made him passionate, a man quickly moved by both joy and despair. He spent so much time walking in that dark abyss that I wondered, could some Siren's song at midnight, sung while my father was deep in despair and at his most vulnerable, have drawn him to his destruction? If, at just the right moment, the Sirens pleaded for weapons instead of food, would my father have succumbed?

As I record this, I've been remembering how when my father put me in charge of El Instituto Paleobiologico, he said, "Once you show people that we paleogeneticists can recreate life from the Mesozoic, they will see that there are no limits to what we can do. The concept of extinction will fall away, and we will be free to rebuild this world, turn it into a Garden of Eden."

Such was my father's hope. But six years ago I recreated the euparkeria and the world has regarded my work with meager curiosity and some fear. It was then that I first realized that my father's assessment of the world was wrong. He wanted to recreate rain forests, restore oceans to their pristine conditions, but once people saw my dinosaurs, they did not unite with our cause. In government hearings, bureaucrats decried the cost of such an effort. They said it would take generations to rebuild this world, that such an effort was impractical and would bankrupt nations. My father told them that an effort that took five generations would repay itself for a hundred thousand generations to come. Yet his talk was all for nothing. People eyed my father with the same curiosity and fear that they showed my dinosaurs.

Curiosity and fear. Here in Cartagena, we have a great zoo where they hope in the near future to exhibit some dinosaurs, especially the fierce flesh eaters of the Jurassic. Many peasants fear I will create such monsters, and that they will stalk the ghettos and eat their children.

Ah well, it is shortly past noon. My father has been dead for more than two hours. I feel tired, and my tongue and mouth are going numb, so I must hurry and record these words:

After the newscast, I sat in my bedroom and pressed the small yellow capsules of mem-set between my fingers, wondering how much pressure it would take to release the liquid inside. I worried that the poisons might escape if the capsules came in contact with my saliva, so I spat on them, then watched to make sure that the capsules did not disintegrate. I remembered a story of an old Socialista general who was captured in Argentina, and he'd poisoned himself with mem-set. I jacked into the computer network and called up the story, learned how he had taken the mem-set and lain paralyzed in his cell. Despite all his captors could do, he died within hours. The article noted that mem-set, because it is catalyzed by uric acid which is a natural byproduct of dying cells, is perhaps the only drug that is more effective in a deceased person than in a living being. Yet mem-set is also a deadly poison—for uric acid is present in small amounts in every human.

In the early morning, I walked the beach and looked out to sea, and among the ghost crabs that scuttled across the beach like something from a dream, I saw a dozen gulls flapping above a heap that looked like a corpse. I ran to it and found a child, a Siren of palest blue, wrapped in red kelp, drowning in the open air. She was gasping, and her eyes were rolled back. I dragged her back to the water and held her under the waves. I watched up and down the beach, afraid someone would see what I was doing, and a moment later a female Siren swam at my ankles in the foam and thrust her head out.

"Thank you," the Siren sang, and I looked into her deep-green eyes and saw gratitude burning there. For days I'd been depressed and frightened, but I looked in her eyes and felt only warmth and peace. The gentleness in that creature's eyes was so convincing, so alien, that I couldn't imagine the Sirens killing humans. I wondered, when the Sirens blew the dam on the Rio Negro, could they have been unaware that so many humans would die? Could creatures of the sea even begin to conceive how vulnerable we humans would be in their element?

Later that day I saw the Allied Marines out in the bay with their black gunships, dropping torpedoes into the water, hunting for the mother and her child.

After less than two months, the authorities declared the War of the Sirens to be over. The Marines imprisoned six hundred of them in secure holding tanks in Jamaica. I suppose the rest of them died. The Alliance slated my father's execution date, making him a single sacrificial lamb. I found nothing to prove either his innocence or guilt.

[Two seconds of silence.]

THE ALLIANCE DID NOT REVEAL MY FATHER'S LOCATION BEFORE HIS execution. All last night I paced my room, waiting for them to call to tell me where the execution would be held. At dawn, commlink tones sounded in my head. A woman told me to come to camp Bolívar, outside Cartagena. I rode to the Marine camp in a taxi, too nervous to drive, and I found a military shuttle armed with neutron cannons warming its engines just inside the gates. Two police scanned me for weapons and ushered me into the shuttle with a dozen guards. I knew even before we left the coast that we were heading for the desert—the soldiers in the shuttle were adjusting the color settings on their body armor so that it turned an ivory shade, the color of alkali soil. The sun shining through the shuttle windows reflected from their visors as if each helmet were a single white star opal.

We thundered south for fifteen minutes, then plummeted into a desert ghost town high in the Andes. The portals to the shuttle slid open, and my guards scurried like pill bugs from beneath the shadow of an overturned rock. They dropped to the ground and covered the old limestone buildings with their pulse rifles. The cold mountain air hit me, and a cloud of smoky-gray dust and chaff swirled up from the shuttle's landing skids. I stepped out and surveyed the town: the morning sun cast long blue shadows across each fold of the mountains, across each jutting stone. The light was so intense that my eyes could not focus on objects in the shadows. Everything was either black or white in this hard land; there was no room for grays.

From the door of one stone building, a dark little mestizo squinted at the bright sunlight. He wore the space-blue uniform of the Alliance Marines and smoked a thin cigar. He straightened his back, tossed his cigar to the dirt, and ground it under his heel as if it were a locust. "Senorita Elegante," he said, "I am Major Gutierez. The press will be here shortly, and you will not have much time to spend alone with your father before the . . . ceremony."

"Fine," I said, shaking. I held the capsules behind my teeth, hoping he would not search me. He ushered me to the tiny stone building, and my hope rose. The facility was a prison, hundreds of years old with anti-quated steel cages for the criminals, though all the cells were empty. I thought that if my father were kept in such a facility, it would be easy to pass the mem-set to him.

We walked down a long corridor to a darkened cell, and I saw my father huddled in a corner, sobbing. He was sweating profusely, as if he had labored in the hot sun, so that his hair hung to the side of his head like a damp black rag, and his jaw was set with fear. A soft orange glow in the air around his cell showed that a repulsion field had been hastily installed. Two armored guards and a priest stood outside the cell. My heart fell as I realized I would not be able to get the mem-set to him through the field.

"Can I go into the cell?" I asked Major Gutierez.

"I am sorry," the major answered, "but, no."

"Can I speak with him alone?"

"No," the major answered, but he ordered a guard to follow him as he left, affording a little more privacy. The priest would have left also, but my father beckoned, "No, stay! Please. I want you to hear my confession."

"Father," I said, "I'd have come sooner, but no one would tell me where you were."

"What does it matter?" he said, and he stood and looked out a small window. He placed his palms on the stone wall. His hands shook.

"It matters to me," I answered. "It matters very much. It matters to your friends." My father seemed so despondent that I wanted to see the hopeful fire that had once burned in his eyes, so I said, "I saw a Siren three days ago, a child. She washed up near the beach house. I noticed her only because a flock of gulls had gathered, waiting for her to die. Her skin was purpled, and her gills and fins were chafed. I pulled her to the shallows and held her underwater to breathe. After a moment, her mother swam up and took the child out to sea. The mother thanked me. If she were here, perhaps she would thank you, too."

I do not know why I told my father this in public. Perhaps I was angry with the Alliance and wanted the guards to arrest me—helping the Siren had been an act of treason. I felt that the government was corrupt, and I wanted the guards to prove to me how evil they had become.

"It was the pollution," my father said, as if he were lecturing one of his classes in paleogenetic engineering. "The acidic water makes their gills itch, so the Sirens come to the beach to let the sand wash through their gills and scratch them. Sometimes their gills fill with silt, and as they strangle they pass out and wash to shore." He fell silent a moment, his voice changed, filling with despair. "You should have let the gulls have that child! You should have let her die! She will starve if the pollution doesn't get her first. Better to let the child die!"

"How can you say that?" I asked. His dark eyes held no hope or solemnity, only crazed despair. He got up and paced across his cell, back and forth, full of frantic energy, and I wondered what had happened to him during the Alliance interrogations, wondered if he were sane. I wanted to ask if he were guilty of treason to his species. I wanted to ask if he had really given the Sirens weapons, just as I had wanted to ask for weeks, but at that moment I was suddenly too afraid to ask.

"Father," I said, "I love you."

He nodded, bobbing his chin with a lunatic grin. "Por supuesto. Of course, of course," he said, as if my love were a given. He was shaking, and he began to cry, then suddenly burst into a fit of laughter. "How is your work? How are the euparkeria?" he asked, not even looking at me, pacing.

"They're fine," I lied. I couldn't tell him that the government had seized our bank accounts. They claimed that, like his little private war, my father had funded my research with graft. I didn't have enough money to feed my dinosaurs for another week, so I'd made arrangements for the zoo to take them.

He continued pacing across the room, licking his lips, caught in the web of his thoughts. I spoke his name twice, but he did not answer. He swore softly. I'd never seen him like this.

I so wanted him to be happy. I tried to grab at his shirt through the soft orange glow of the repulsion field, and said, "Father, even now, doesn't your life taste sweet?"

My father gazed at me, as if trying to pierce my thoughts, then spat on the floor. I stumbled back a step, and in that moment I realized that he rejected life. Despite my childish faith, my father was guilty of murder.

Gutierez came to escort me from the room, back down the corridors of the old prison to a walled court. In the courtyard stood a dozen dignitaries, as many reporters, and six Alliance Marines with projectile rifles. My father walked into the bright sunlight in company of the priest. My father's hands and feet were shackled, so he took tiny clumsy steps, pulling at his chains.

A hawk was soaring on the thermal updrafts, and my father stopped to watch it sail over a ridge. "My God," my father said, "what does it find to eat here?" He looked across the desert toward the plains, and said to the priest, "Beyond those valleys, there were once rain forests. Great, endless forests."

One marine fidgeted with his rifle. Until that moment, I do not think I believed the execution would take place. I somehow hoped that others would recognize my father's innocence, that the great wise leaders of Earth would stoop to save him. I looked at the rifles, and a thin scream issued from my lips, and I bit it back, tried to control myself. The major escorted my father to a wall and stood with him a moment. Everything was so quiet.

The major said, "Señor, do you want a blindfold?"

My father looked at the ground and shook his head and sighed. Inside his cell he had been sweating, depressed, but the cool morning air dried his sweat, and I imagined that he was almost glad to finally finish it.

"It is traditional to offer a cigar," the major said. My father shook his head, still staring at the ground. "Any last words, Señor Elegante? Last requests?" My father only shook his head. One reporter coughed.

"I have a last request!" I shouted, and the major looked up at me. "Can I speak to my father alone, only for a moment, to say goodbye?"

"I am sorry," the major said, "but no."

"A kiss? Can I kiss my father goodbye?"

The major looked up at me, sighed. "If you wish."

I ran to my father. Everyone was watching, and there was no way to pass the mem-set to him. I was afraid he might swallow the capsules instead of break them, and I had no way to tell him how to use the drug, so I burst the capsules between my teeth, hard. The mem-set tasted bitter, slightly of anise, and I thought I might gag, but I held it on my tongue. And as we kissed, I spat the poison into his mouth, rubbed it onto his lips.

My father lurched backward a step and his eyes widened in horror. "Josephina!" he said, crying out as if begging to know what I had done.

"I don't want to live without you!" I said. "All our work is destroyed. I will always love you! God knows how to read the manuals of our lives. He will put everything back together. For a while—only for a while—the restoration will continue without us!"

My father threw his arms around me and wept. "No, Josephina," he cried. "I did not want this to touch you. I did not want to hurt you."

Major Gutierez pulled at my shoulders. "Do you think you could die, and I would not be hurt by it?" I asked my father. I grabbed him and held, and Gutierez let me hug him for a full minute, weeping, then the major spoke to me softly and escorted me back in line with the reporters. My father watched, his eyes riveted on me. He wept as Major Gutierez read the list of charges and called his troops to ready their arms.

My father shouted. "Someday, we will rebuild this world! The time will come when your children will play in rainforests, and canaries and hummingbirds will fill the skies! Every beast of the field will be reborn!"

The troops raised their rifles.

"Fishes will swim in your rivers!"

"Aim!" Gutierez ordered.

"Crickets will make music in your pastures, and whales will sing love songs in the seas!" my father cried. "You watch! It will happen!"

"Fire!" Gutierez shouted, and the rifles spat their bullets, filling the bright courtyard with smoke.

My father staggered back, red holes gaping in his shirt. He stared up in the air, beyond the heads of those in the firing squad, and his eyes filled with light, as if he saw salvation hurtling through the sky. The look on his face was so filled with awe, so compelling, that everyone suddenly turned and gazed into the sky also, and then I heard him cry "God," and he spun and staggered against the stone wall, smearing blood on the ash-gray stones.

I SIT HERE IN MY TERRARIUM AND LOOK AT MY LITTLE EUPARKERIA AND stroke his neck. I'm out of eggs to feed him, yet my wingless dragon stands on his back legs, tenderly searching the folds of my dress, expecting an egg to magically appear. It has been nearly three hours since

I broke the mem-set between my teeth. Opalescent clouds seem to be forming at the edge of my vision, and everything looks as if it is covered with gauze or silken threads. My feet and fingers are so numb I do not feel them, yet my mouth burns as if it is on fire. I believe the mem-set has begun attacking my DNA, chopping it in pieces so fine that in a million years, even God may not be able to put me back together. I cannot talk into this microphone much longer.

On my way home, I jacked into a news broadcast. The reporter says that the Alliance of Earth Nations is considering plans to exile the Sirens to Darius Four, a water planet without human occupants. So, the pollution will continue unabated. I could not help thinking that though the Sirens lost their brief battle, they have won themselves a world, while day by day we are losing ours.

Also on the news, I heard a reporter say that as my father died, he shouted "¡Vivan los Sirenos!" Long live the Sirens!

But that is not true. I was there. He shouted only one last word, crying with a thrill of hope in his voice: "¡Vivamos!" Let us live!

[Uninterrupted silence to end of tape.]

A Request

If you liked this anthology, please take the time to leave a review on the site where you purchased it and/or on one of the social media reading sites like Goodreads. Tell your friends that you enjoyed it. Suggest it as reading for your local book club. Request it at your local library (or more than one local library). This helps others learn more about the book and gets the word out. Please use the #troubadoursspaceprincesses and #hemeleinpubs tags.

Thank you for your time, and thank you for reading this book!

Find more exciting books to read at hemelein.com.

HEMELEIN PUBLICATIONS

Acknowledgments

As with all of these LTUE Benefit Anthologies, there are a lot of people to thank. All of our authors have donated their stories to help out the symposium: Jenny Perry Carr, Kate Dane, Cray Dimensional, Max Florschutz, Martin Greening, David Hankins, Henry Herz, Bill Housley, Wulf Moon, Elsa Nickle, Scott M. Sands, W. Jefferson Smith, Berin L. Stephens, Elise Stephens, DJ Tyrer, and Dave Wolverton (and his amazing family, especially Spencer, Forrest, and the lovely Mary). Nick Cole worked with us to select one of Dave's stories that worked well here, so we appreciate his help with that.

Thank you to Bradley Williams, our cover artist. He approached us a couple years ago, wondering if he could help out with cover art on one of our anthologies. When this one came up, I remembered this piece he had shown me when he first inquired. We asked for a few tweaks, and he delivered an excellent piece. We love this cover! It's simply beautiful.

Speaking of art, Kevin Wasden came through for us with the custom ornamental break he created. Here's a bigger version of it:

Kevin's turnaround on this decorative silhouette (even with the one change I requested) was phenomenal. It makes for a very unique ornamental break image. Thanks, Kevin!

On the production end, Heather Monson for copyediting and a variety of other things. Your help and insight is always appreciated.

As usual, we are grateful to all those who support the anthologies by spreading the word, sharing information via email, blog posts, reviews, and social media. We appreciate all those who buy them, too. You are awesome!

Thank you to all of the volunteers at LTUE over the years, both before we became involved and those who continue the legacy of volunteering today. The symposium wouldn't be able to happen without all of your hard work.

Finally, thanks to our families, who put up with us as we work on (and stress about) each volume. Thank you for letting us have this project that takes so much of our time.

—Jaleta Clegg and Joe Monson

About the Contributors

Jenny Perry Carr is group vice president of scientific services for a medical communications company by day, budding sci-fi/fantasy/horror writer at night, which sounds much like the beginnings of a superhero's bio. But alas, her only superpower is remembering random facts, like the human body contains trillions of microorganisms that outnumber our own cells by ten to one!

She has a PhD in molecular neurobiology from Yale University which influences much of her speculative writing. She's a Minnesota native living in North Texas with her husband. Her short stories have received silver honorable mention and honorable mentions from the L. Ron Hubbard Writers of the Future contest.

Her story, "Model Citizen: A Deadly Tale of Beauty", was published in the anthology *From the Yonder Volume 2: A Collection of Horror from Around the World.* She is currently working on a sci-fi trilogy.

❊

Jaleta Clegg was born some time ago and has filled the years since with plenty of make-believe. She writes science fiction adventure, fantasy of all flavors, and silly horror. When not writing, she enjoys playing with yarn, cooking weird vegetables, designing costumes and quilts, and generally messing around.

She has published eleven volumes in her Altairan Empire series, has written many short works, and had multiple collections collecting them, most recently *Waiting for Elephants.* Jaleta is co-editor of the LTUE Benefit Anthologies series.

❈

Kate Dane's motto is "Magic doesn't solve problems. People do." She has published *Sit.Stay.Kill,* a paranormal werewolf romance. Her stories have finaled in the Writers of the Future contest and taken second place in the Jim Baen Memorial Short Story Award 2020 (science fiction). She has taken several workshops from Dave Farland online and in person. She is a member of Romance Writers of America.

❈

As a child, Cray Dimensional loved reading fantasy books. In high school, she contributed to her high school literary magazine. She put aside writing while she pursued a career in software engineering. But that wasn't enough to keep her happy.

After her daughter introduced her to Wattpad, she wrote her first amateur book Psych Wars which she self-published in 2019. In 2020, she took workshops to improve her craft. Since then, she won two honorable mentions in the Writers of the Future contest and has a pending sale of a flash piece. She dreams to continue writing when she retires.

❈

David Farland (1957-2022) was a *New York Times* bestselling science fiction and fantasy writer with more than fifty novels to his credit. He worked as the lead judge for the *L. Ron Hubbard Presents Writers and Illustrators of the Future* contest, and has helped mentor dozens of writers who have gone on to become *New York Times* bestsellers, including Brandon Sanderson, Stephenie Meyer, and James Dashner. At the time of his passing, Dave lived in Saint George, Utah, with his wife and family. You can find out more about him at davidfarland.com.

❈

Max Florschutz was born in the wilderness of rural Alaska, and survived there for two decades before later moving. A long-time lover of sci-fi and fantasy, he published his first book in 2013, and since then has continued to thrill and delight audiences with unexpected adventures and delightful characters. He runs a weekly writing advice feature, "Being a Better Writer," at his website, maxonwriting.com.

❀

Martin Greening is an avid gamer, editor, writer, and creator of the *Ruma: Dawn of Empire* tabletop roleplaying game. His fiction can be found in the *Tales of Ruma* and *Cursed Collectibles* anthologies. He lives in sunny Sin City with his dog Arya.

❀

David Hankins writes from the thriving cornfields of Iowa. His writing journey began years ago in Germany as he made up stories to convince his daughter to go to sleep, which always backfired. Those midnight ramblings developed into a passion for creating new worlds while exploring the idiosyncrasies of this one. His first novel, *Death and the Taxman,* releases in April 2024.

❀

Henry Herz's speculative fiction short stories have been published in many different anthologies and magazines, including *A Hero of a Different Stripe, Daily Science Fiction, Coming of Age, Castle of Horror V, Metastellar, Strangely Funny VIII, Spirit Machine, Highlights for Children,* and *Ladybug Magazine.* He's written ten picture books, including the critically acclaimed *I Am Smoke* and edited three anthologies.

❀

Bill Housley looks into the stars at night, and they tell him their stories. You can find his other scribblings on his Amazon page.

❀

Joe Monson loves reading, books, and butter mochi. He has worked at a couple dozen different jobs during his life. In his current job, he valiantly battles worms, trojans, viruses, corruption, hardware, and updates to keep computer systems running while also expanding the accessible knowledge of the world.

He has co-edited multiple anthologies with Jaleta Clegg in the LTUE
Benefit Anthologies series, and he's the series editor of the Legacy of the
Corridor publication series from Hemelein Publications. His most recent
anthology, *The Horror at Pooh Corner*, was a successful Kickstarter and will
be released in bookstores worldwide in mid 2024.

Joe writes short stories, and is outlining a space opera adventure series.
He collects science fiction and fantasy art, but not as much as Paul (as if
that was even possible). He lives in the tops of the mountains with his
thoroughly amazing wife, three miracle children, and their pet library.

❈

Wulf Moon wrote his first science fiction story when he was fifteen. It
won the national Scholastic Art & Writing Awards, the same contest that
first discovered Stephen King, Peter S. Beagle, John Updike, Joyce Carol
Oates, and a host of iconic names in the arts.

Since then, Moon has won more than forty awards in writing, including
the *Star Trek* Strange New Worlds Contest, Critters Readers' Choice
Awards for Best Science Fiction and Fantasy Short Story of 2018, 2019,
and 2020 (for "Muzik Man"); Best Author of 2019, 2020, and 2021; and
the Writers of the Future, volume 35.

Moon's stories have appeared in numerous publications, including *Writers
of the Future, Deep Magic, Future Science Fiction Digest, Star Trek: Strange New
Worlds 2, Galaxy's Edge, Best of the Year* anthologies, and *Trace the Stars* and *A
Parliament of Wizards* through Hemelein Publications and LTUE Press.
His nonfiction writing guide, *How to Write a Howling Good Story*, was
released in 2023.

Moon is podcast director at Future Science Fiction Digest. Find him on
Facebook or visit his website and join the Wulf Pack at driftweave.com.

❈

Barely tethered to reality, Ruth Nickle spends her days weaving words
into colorful tapestries that become her stories. She began writing at
eleven years old after her wildly popular fan fiction of *The Hobbit* received
rave reviews from her mother.

She has a short story entitled "Rumpelstiltskin's Daughter" in the *Unspun* anthology, as well as a romance novel, *Come Home, Cowboy*, published under her pen name ELSA NICKLE. She received an honorable mention from the Writers of the Future contest, was the Conference Chair for the 2022 American Night Writers Association, and is a proud member of Wulf Moon's Wulf Pack.

❊

SCOTT M. SANDS is a speculative fiction writer, based in the Adelaide Hills in South Australia. When he isn't spending time with his beautiful wife and four kids, he's watching *Star Wars*, gaming, writing his next novel, and walking two golden retrievers.

❊

WILLIAM SMITH wrote his first book, *The Aliens Come to Earth*, in the second grade. Only a single copy was printed and bound, but he's been writing ever since. After high school, he worked in Alaska, earned flying hours toward his pilot's license, and traveled around Europe, all the while plotting story and character. Later, he decided he needed a formal creative writing education.

Will is a recent graduate from Utah Valley University. He strives to create flawed characters that readers will learn to love as they evolve. Will has written three novel-length unpublished manuscripts and one short story. This is his first time submitting to an anthology.

❊

BERIN L. STEPHENS is a professional saxophone performer and instructor from the thriving metropolis of Chugiak, Alaska. He lives in Utah and is the author of *Dragon War Relic, Time Gangsters, Delroy Versus the Yshtari, The Secrets of a Superhero's Assistant*, and *The Tales of Myrick the (Not So) Magnificent* (Volumes 1-4).

He has had short stories published in several anthologies and magazines, including *Parliament of Wizards, Warp and Weave, Wandering Weeds: Tales of Rabid Vegetation, Press Forward Saints*, and *A Mighty Fortress*. Learn more at berinstephens.com.

⚜

ELISE STEPHENS credits much of her storytelling influence to a lifelong love of theater and childhood globetrotting. Much of her work focuses on themes of family, memory, and finding hope after a devastating loss. Her fiction has appeared in *Analog, Galaxy's Edge, Escape Pod, Writers of the Future Vol 35,* and *FIYAH,* among others.

She is a Writers of the Future 1st place winner (2019). Elise lives with her family in Seattle in a house with huge windows to supply the vast quantities of light she requires to stay happy. Elise is currently seeking representation on her next science fiction novel. Learn more at EliseStephens.com.

⚜

DJ TYRER is the person behind Atlantean Publishing and has been widely published in anthologies and magazines around the world, such as *Winter's Grasp, Tales of the Black Arts, Pagan, Misunderstood, Sorcery & Sanctity: A Homage to Arthur Machen, Fantasia Divinity, Broadswords and Blasters, BFS Horizons,* and *Tales from the Magician's Skull.* He has a novella, "The Yellow House", available in paperback and in ebook.

⚜

KEVIN WASDEN is an artist, storyteller, poet, and educator. His artistic journey began in childhood, sketching comic book heroes and doodling for friends. Mr. Sylvester's 6th grade art class at Fillmore Middle School flipped a switch. There, he discovered the magic of light and shadow, forever altering how he saw the world.

He went on to study at Utah State University with mentors such as Glen Edwards and Gregory Schulte helped hone his drawing and painting skills. His quest for artistic excellence led him to study figure painting under Andy Reiss in Brooklyn, New York. As a professional illustrator and designer, Kevin created art for numerous book, periodical, and game publishers, including Avon Camelot, Baen, Fantasy Flight Games, Alderac Entertainment Group.

Kevin played a pivotal role as the creative director at Alinco Costumes, where he helped guide the creation of many famous mascot characters and costume designs for the Chicago Bulls, the Arizona Diamondbacks, the Oklahoma City Thunder, and others.

Throughout his career, Kevin has felt a deep desire to share his knowledge and skills with others. For many years, he served as a private art instructor and high school art teacher. In 2023, Kevin turned most of his creative energy toward making more personalized artwork for shows and galleries. He is currently an exhibiting artist at Urban Arts Gallery in Salt Lake City. He also participates in numerous local and state art shows. Learn more at kevinwasden.com.

❁

Bradley Williams was born in Ogden Utah. He pursued his artistic interests at Utah State University, where he gained knowledge in oil painting and composition principles and worked with Glen Edwards. He graduated with a bachelor's degree in illustration in 1993, continuing on to earn a masters of fine arts degree in 1995.

After finishing his work at the university, he moved his family to the New York metropolitan area where he worked as an illustrator for book publishers, magazines, and gaming art. Brad likes to paint what he experiences in life as he travels to find what inspires him. All of these trips have generated many wonderful images and strengthened his abilities as a painter.

His original works can be found in private collections across the USA, the UK, Hong Kong, Germany, France, Italy, Hungary, Israel, Japan, Australia, and Canada.

Additional Copyright Information